A DRAGON'S
PURPOSE

A Dragon's Purpose

Sedrick Bowser

This is a work of fiction.

All of the characters, organizations, and events portrayed in this novel are either products of the author's imagination or are used fictitiously.

Published by Author Academy Elite
PO Box 43, Powell, OH 43035
www.Autho rAcademyElite.com

Identifiers:

Library of Congress Control Number: 2020900583

Paperback: 978-1-64746-115-7
Hardback: 978-1-64746-116-4
Ebook: 978-1-64746-117-1

Available in paperback, hardback, e-book, and audiobook

Cover design by Ana Gyorgyiyoska.

". . . I know what you must be thinking. How could anyone attribute the common picture of love with a dragon? . . . But . . . it was not meant to be that way. Dragons were once the epitome of love . . ."

CHAPTER ONE

The smell of sweat. Adrenaline. A rush. Flames and then death. Another rises and another falls. *Arrows?* No. *More.* Firebrands.

Humorous.

I am fire. I am power. I am might.

I am death.

He remained still for a split second, taking in the dread and agony, the unspeakable truth of their end sinking deeper and deeper into his victims by the moment. The helpless thrashed, struggling toward life that now completely eluded them. He was enjoying the terror resounding everywhere in the screams of maidens and the wails of the young. A grin shattered his face and crept like a vine, growing into a malevolent glare of crazed ecstasy.

But now his stillness was done. Now he would act.

His eyes shot open after taking a moment to enjoy his carnage. He bolted out his long neck at the humans nearest to him and receded with his prize. Shrieks of pain and the taste of blood pooled on his tongue.

Frenzy.

Tensing his muscles, he sprang. His body twisted around with power, and his tail whipped towards those brave enough to stand against him. Debris of all sizes erupted from the surrounding architecture, showering the soldiers and fleeing citizens. Bodies erupted and launched from being impacted by the hurled stones.

"Fire!" A voice cried some distance away.

His ears perked towards the sound. Words that would be muted to other inferior creatures resonated loudly to him. His attention was torn away from the command, interrupted by the heavy clank of some kind of machinery and the rush of displaced air.

The world exploded.

His hindquarters screamed out. He lost his balance and met the ground in a heap—only his front claws held him up. His teeth gritted together as his mandibles formed a snarl.

Ire.

Smoke flared from his nostrils as he quickly scanned his surroundings from where the voice cried out. On the city's inner defenses, a small garrison of catapults and their operators shone forth.

Lucidity.

"Fire!" Again, a man roared, waving his arm as if he were a worthy leader, ushering his men to victory.

Trash.

He sprang into the air above the hurtling projectile. His magnificent wings unfurled and caught the rising plumes of scorching air that spiraled from the burning structures below. Higher and higher he flew, the clouds coming closer. With every stroke of the wings, he lined up with the sun to become a mere blot in the sky.

He closed his eyes again, and he enjoyed the freedom of the sky. No worries. No cares. No concerns when he was flying. He often thought it was strange that such a creature as he thought such things. Even more so during such time as a battle! Nonetheless, strange though he might be in his habits, he didn't change his scales.

He snapped his wings back to his side, throwing himself nose-first into a vicious dive.

Smoke began pouring from his nostrils in heavier and heavier torrents as he plummeted. Inhaling deeply, his mighty lungs released. His rage poured forth—his petrifying glory.

I am fire.

His chest beat like the battle drums of war. The catapult garrison swam in a high tide of his fury as he descended upon the fortifications with horrific speed.

Air rushed in through his snout, feeding the inferno that kept pouring upon his enemies from his maw. The trash fell, consumed by his insanity. His wings beat back quickly, launching him forward with all swiftness. His wall of flames parted around him as he embellished the city with more scars along every inch. *Victorious again.*

He shifted his wings and relented from his hail for a moment. He hovered above the wreck, taking in the full consequences of his power.

"No." His head began to turn desperately. "It isn't here, either," he muttered to himself. A look of longing shot through his large, scaled face, resting for a moment in the deep amber gems of his eyes as he searched vigorously what was left of the city. He flew over the burning wreck, his gaze casting about futilely. His once impervious grin waned and became solemn as a stone. His search stilled.

"It . . . isn't here." A whisper, loud enough for only his ears to hear. Finally accepting what he had declared to be the truth of the matter, he turned. His tail now hung limp. The joy of the attack was dead, depleted from his essence.

With a deep sigh, the dragon's dead stare found the horizon. In silence, Kast began the long trek home.

CHAPTER TWO

Aurah opened her eyes to the cold morning air. The fire had burned down to coals through the night. The hearth exhaled gentle puffs of smoke. She grimaced at the trial on hand, and her head turned to spot her slippers strewn across the room. Why did she feel the need to kick them off every night? Her bare toes clenched beneath the bedding at the thought of the floor. This was the worst part of any day for her.

Before her mind could object any longer, she grabbed the edge of her blankets and threw them to the side. She dashed from the bed in a stupor, grabbing each slipper as quickly as possible. She sighed in relief as her feet were wrested away from her greatest adversary: the cold. The stone around her was such a menace in the cool autumn mornings.

She turned to the dying hearth and stirred the ashes, enlivening the embers. She fed the coals a portion of tinder kept on the mantle and the fire crackled as it consumed the fuel. Her hands brushed each other off as she turned to her wardrobe to change into the day's dress. She had a special mission that day, a plan to say thank you to the one who had stood for her good since she was little and had given her so much. She smiled and ceased her monotonous task for a moment. Elizabeth, the Princess—her unofficial sister—had done so much to take care of her. Aurah had one of the best quarters for a servant in the palace and would never be found to have any attire stained or fraying. Her eyes drifted down to the clothing and her smile broadened. Elizabeth often tried to sell her on the idea of adopting a more lavish fashion sense, but Aurah had argued it wouldn't be proper for her, a mere servant, to traipse through the Kingdom in such a regal display. Elizabeth would then play the imp and scold Aurah, saying she would never attract a dashing man that way. Aurah chewed her lip. Every moment spent jesting with the Princess truly was a fond memory. She shook her head and finished dressing. Elizabeth may be entitled to marry, and a prince at that. However, Aurah was only a servant and had no real inclinations to any thought of that nature. Not yet at least. *Maybe.*

Shifting her thoughts back to the day ahead of her, Aurah grabbed her coat from the wardrobe and a basket from the corner of the room. It would be Elizabeth's birthday soon, and Aurah wanted to buy her a present from the city. The morning was the best time to visit the city and shop. It was early enough that she didn't have to worry about her chores right away, and customers really didn't start shopping until later. That was something that often left the few who did go shopping with special attention from the merchants. Aurah hoped they could help her find the perfect gift for the Princess. Elizabeth's birthday meant the world to Aurah this year.

Elizabeth was a strong leader with an extremely developed sense of justice, and she fought hard for her people. There had been many civil and law enforcement developments at the Princess's insistent pushing. That was why this particular birthday meant so much to Elizabeth— and Aurah—because she would, at last, be the age when the law allowed for an orphaned princess to ascend the throne if she had not first become married to an eligible suitor. Elizabeth would now finally be able to act as the people's ruler, addressing the dire situation on hand and answering the cry for much-needed justice, advances, and reforms. Aurah had the deepest hope for Elizabeth through this life-altering event, but she had no idea how the Princess would change, or how any part of their lives would change, for that matter. Aurah stopped and clutched the basket. She shouldn't doubt Elizabeth like that. The Princess had taken Aurah in like they were sisters. Despite the evident struggle ahead of her, Elizabeth would remain a source of life for the people. She would, as she always said, "bring about an unprecedented age of peace and prosperity."

The corridors of the palace seemed to disappear behind Aurah as she walked through them with her thoughts wandering. She found herself already at the front door to leave the palace vestibule. She reached for the door handle when it swung open, knocking her hand to the side.

"Ouch!" Aurah withdrew her arm quickly and tried to massage the pain away from her knuckles.

"Oh! I'm sorry—oh! Aurah! I didn't realize it was yo . . . I mean that anyone was there. I didn't think anyone would be up so early . . . ." Aurah looked up and saw one of the palace captains. *But not just any captain,* she thought, as her knees buckled slightly.

Dorian.

Aurah's cheeks flushed immediately. Out of all people, why did she have to run into him? She swallowed hard.

"Oh... I... Don't worry about it, Dorian!" Her hand suddenly throbbed a lot less. Did she speak too quickly? She forced a smile while her thoughts sought an escape. It was much too early in the morning. Her thoughts raged, deepening her blush. Why did Elizabeth always have to tease Aurah about the newest captain in the royal guard, leading the handmaiden to flounder so when reserve really mattered? Aurah gulped hard again. She hoped she hadn't let too long of a silence take place.

"It looks like you're about to head out. Are you going anywhere particular?"

Dorian smiled brightly at her, interrupting her musings. Dorian was a man who had a firm but gentle voice. Sometimes he was too quiet, but he really was a pleasant . . . *prospect?* Aurah gripped the basket in her hands. She needed to leave before her flailing emotions turned a molehill into a mountain. *Was it really only a molehill?* Her heart skipped a beat. *Point proven—it was time to leave.*

"Uh . . . yeah," Aurah stammered, ending with a broken laugh. "I was heading out to the city to find a gift for Eli . . . ." Her voice caught, and she coughed and spluttered. She hadn't exactly wanted her exploits to become known to others. She wanted to surprise Elizabeth. She looked up at Dorian, he beamed at her. *Great.* Her heart pounded in her chest.

"Well, it sounds like you're headed to the city. I have a . . . quick errand here, but I'm headed that way. Would you care for an escort to the square, at least?" Dorian stopped speaking for a second, then continued. "That is if you don't mind waiting here momentarily." His voice trailed off, and his face fell flat.

"Sure!" Aurah rocked forward, the word rushing from her lips. She chided herself for charging right into accepting his offer. *Yes, I mind! I can't go with you! I have to get away before I do something stupid!* She hadn't even sounded subtle!

A smile broke Dorian's face. "Wait right here, I just have to run to the kitchens for a moment."

He turned away without another word. Aurah stared as he disappeared around a corner on some odd task. *Great! Now she had to stand around and wait awkwardly.* She hoped she wouldn't be caught standing by herself.

Aurah leaned against the wall, counting the ticks as time passed by and thinking about Dorian. They had become mildly acquainted recently, often serving Elizabeth in their individual capacities at the same time. He was friendly, but took his duty very seriously and didn't always open up to conversation while he worked. There was one time, though, where his shift had ended and the Princess, occupied with her own business, called the captain over to have a *conversation* with him. Aurah rolled her eyes at how awkward everything had been. Elizabeth had barely introduced Aurah to the captain and started a conversation before she gracefully, but absolutely, made her exit to return to her business. *Thanks, Elizabeth.* The captain did deserve credit for maintaining the unexpected social call and exiting wonderfully with tact.

Aurah shook her head at the memory. Since then, encounters and conversations with Dorian had grown in frequency and length. It was natural to talk with the man, and they often found a lot of common ground. Maybe it wasn't Elizabeth's teasing that made Aurah so tense whenever she was around him? *Maybe.*

Aurah turned and stared at the corner where Dorian had disappeared. Was it minutes or seconds that she had been waiting for him? She pushed away from the wall and stood, practicing a pleasant pose with which to greet Dorian. *I don't want to discourage him, after all.* She began to turn absent-mindedly when her gaze met another's.

"Good mornin,' dearie! You're up early!"

Aurah jumped out of her skin, barely containing a cry. *Wonderful.*

"Good morning, Marrid. I hope all is well!" Aurah rubbed her forehead, chuckling quietly. The little old cook couldn't have appeared at a worst time. Why were there so many people about this early?

"It certainly is well," Marrid replied pleasantly. "What seems to have you out this early, Aurah?" The innocent cook didn't mince her words, jumping straight into the pleasantries. *Oh, nothing important, Marrid! Not anymore at least—I just like to stand around and have my emotions gutted and strewn about for all to see. Nothing like being humiliated!* Aurah bit her tongue.

"Well, I had an . . . ."

"Are you still there, Aurah?" A voice called out from around the corner. Aurah's blush returned. She turned away and stared out the front door. *Oh, look at that. We forgot to close the door. I guess in light of everything, that's a mildly reasonable thing to forget!* Aurah felt nauseated, and her stomach twisted. Mornings were supposed to be quiet and peaceful. Not . . . whatever this was.

"Yeah." Her voice broke again under the pressure. Seriously, this whole situation wouldn't have escalated out of hand if Elizabeth hadn't repeatedly teased her and pushed her towards a man that she hadn't even noticed previously. Now look at what Aurah had to deal with! Curse these emotions! *Was it really all Elizabeth's fault?* Aurah scowled at her thoughts.

"There you are. And the lovely, old cook herself!" Dorian didn't seem to be thrown off in the slightest at the surprise guest. *Lucky him.* Marrid turned and grinned at Aurah, a certain knowing in her eyes. *Yes, absolutely everything you think it is, you dear old lady.*

"Well, dearie, I'll leave you two be, lots of work to be done." Marrid turned away and disappeared around the same corner that Dorian had earlier. The old cook almost seemed to have a new vibrancy in her step. Aurah stood straight, not wishing for any more of this nonsense to go on. There was only so much embarrassment one could take before it transformed into tiny sprouts of annoyance, which then would grow into full-fledged displeasure. She looked at Dorian and realized he was carrying a large jug and a sack.

"Sorry it took so long. My sister works in the palace kitchens, and she often prepares my men and me some goods when we have guard duty." He held out the sack and the jug to prove his point.

Aurah forced a quick smile at him. *I wouldn't have minded just a little longer you know!* Being slightly annoyed at whoever was responsible for this madness was much easier to deal with than embarrassment. Aurah pushed past her feelings.

"Who is your sister? I work in the kitchens often. I didn't realize you had a connection."

"Her name is Sarah. Do you know her?" Dorian moved through the doorway. "By the way, I'm sorry to have put a kink in your plans by asking to escort you to the square. If you like, we can head there now, though." He smiled at her politely.

"Not a problem. I appreciate your offer." Her shoulders relaxed a little and she smiled back, more sincerely this time. It was amazing what an apology could do. "I do know Sarah, though most of my time is spent dealing with Elizabeth's food preparer—the older cook that was just here, Marrid." Aurah was glad for the change in conversation.

"Oh. We know Marrid fairly well. She's like a distant great, great, great, great, great aunt or something." Aurah laughed at Dorian's joke. The humor helped.

They turned and walked through the palace grounds, making their way to the front gate. The gate opened to the city square, which was usually occupied as a large marketplace, though it was also used for public addresses and announcements from the palace. The trip flew by as their conversation revealed more common connections between them and eased any tensions. Soon, Aurah lost track of all the tensions from earlier and even enjoyed the time with the captain. It was always interesting to note the amount of respect and approval Dorian commanded from his peers and even those older than himself. Aurah smiled to herself. After only a brief time with him, it wasn't difficult to see why.

"So, what has you out and about this morning?" Dorian finally inquired. Aurah considered her task, sighed, and then decided to confide in him.

"I'm looking for a gift for Elizabeth." She paused for a second as she tried to put into words what she was looking for. "I want to get her something for her birthday, something she will have to remember me by always." Her voice faded, not fully satisfied with that explanation. Aurah fidgeted in the silence that followed, wondering what Dorian thought of her now.

"Now, why would the Princess go and forget her best friend?" That was not exactly what Aurah had expected to hear in response. "I know how close you two are—most people do." Dorian seemed to have a talent for cutting to the point of things without much effort. Aurah slowed; her thoughts required more attention than could be spared on her steps.

"Well, you know. It's her birthday. Well, not just any birthday, but *the birthday*. The one when Elizabeth becomes overwhelmed with her monarchy ruling duties. When she eventually, if not immediately, marries and has no time for a lowly servant like me."

Aurah stopped walking altogether, almost embarrassed again that she would come off as silly. Why had she confided in Dorian? He was practically a stranger. A long sigh escaped her lips. She knew change was inevitable. She knew friendships were likely to be more difficult to maintain over time, and how much more so for the ruler of a kingdom and her servant?

"Well," Dorian began slowly, "you may be right in thinking things will change and that the Princess will have much less time for . . . *the help*." Aurah smiled slightly at the captain's considerate word choice. "Though, from a man's perspective, if she can refuse to marry as strongly as she has, and for as long, then I doubt she will be quick to change that facet of herself." He grinned at Aurah then carried on with his response. "That's normal in life, though. As for everything else, to the Princess, you are no mere help. I've seen sisters by blood act much less affectionately than the two of you. That Elizabeth, she cares for you fiercely and I wouldn't ever forget that, Aurah." Dorian smiled gently again.

Aurah let out an exaggerated huff, throwing herself into a walk again. She was glad to finally share her fear with someone and not be chided. She was beginning to appreciate Dorian's presence. His words sat well with her. *So thoughtful and kind, but... real.* She tossed another issue around in her mind, before deciding to confide in him again.

"How do you think Elizabeth will fare coming into power?" Aurah stopped moving again, turning to look at the captain, who had fallen in step behind her.

Dorian's face twisted slightly, and his hand rubbed his upper lip. Aurah hadn't noticed before, but he had a partial mustache. The hair was rather blonde, though, and seemed to struggle to fill his lip. She smiled towards the ground. Knowing something like that about Dorian made her very light-hearted. She looked back up and into his eyes. *His light green eyes . . . stop it, Aurah!* She hoped he hadn't noticed the slight diversion in her thoughts. He moved his attention to look in her eyes, as well. Aurah's heart fluttered again. *Guess he didn't see after all.*

"The Princess is bound very tightly to her justice. She is going to need all the help and love she can get to move through the trials that are laid before her." Dorian's response was well crafted. It was to the point, and supportive—not insubordinate of his loyalties—something important for a man of his office. He might be young, but they don't let just anyone become a captain. His rank said a lot about who he was. Aurah took a second, then nodded her agreement. Whatever was to come, Elizabeth would need the support of a loving and serving friend.

They completed the last leg of the walk to the square in silence. Aurah's thoughts fell to the changes looming only a short time in the future. Dorian walked quietly beside her, the sack and jug still carried in his hands. Their trip ended when they came to the gate blocking the path to the palace. The guards there took immediate note of their captain—*and who he was escorting.* Aurah immediately shrank behind Dorian, letting him take the lead. The growing mirth on the guards' faces was foretelling of an embarrassing situation.

One of the guards broke the silence first. "Hey, guys! Looks like the captain's back with the *goods!*"

"I certainly am, Davis." Aurah felt the sudden danger in Dorian's tone. "Aurah here agreed to help me assign the next member of our squad to latrine duty for the next three weeks." The man's face flattened instantly while the other guard's posture stiffened considerably. "Thanks to her, that task was much easier than I thought. I'm sure Matt will be happy with your work, though. He's fallen ill recently, and as often as he will be occupying the latrine, sanitary conditions will be critical."

The guard named Davis promptly seemed to lose the spirit he had initially displayed. The other guards barely held their posture under the gravity of what sorrow had just befallen their poor comrade. Aurah also had to bite her cheek at the man's unfortunate demise. She wanted to laugh, but she also wanted to blush at Dorian's defense of her.

"Open the gate, Bailey, Tuck." Dorian gave the command nonchalantly waving a hand lazily.

"Looks like the captain's got magic hands now." One of the two men sniggered to the other.

"I'm sure Davis would love an extra hand with those latrines, Tuck. All you have to do is let me know." Aurah grinned harder at the ground as Dorian threatened his men so casually. *He was ruthless!*

The two guards didn't dally, hustling to lift the beam that locked the gate in place. The doors swung open with a loud creak. Dorian turned his head to stare at the hinges.

"Davis, go fetch some oil for this thing. It's about time that squeal went away." The crestfallen guard jumped to attention and moved to obey quickly, heading up towards the palace. Aurah bit her cheek again. *Poor Davis!* Dorian led the way through the gate into the square, taking a second to hand off the sack and jug while *smirking* to the guard who had been smart enough not to mess with his captain. *Bailey?* He thanked

Dorian enthusiastically, but then bowed deeply and gave his captain a simple, but loud, farewell of "Your Majesty."

Laughter erupted from Aurah's lips, joining in with the rest of the guards as Dorian rolled his eyes and shook his head, chuckling lightly. The captain turned to look at Aurah and gestured slightly towards the square on the other side of the gates. Aurah's face stiffened considerably, startling Dorian, right before she curtsied and mimicked the rest of the guards exclaiming a loud "Your Majesty."

"Ugh! Not you, too!" Dorian grabbed his hair as he threw himself towards the square, leaving a wake of hearty laughter behind him. Aurah moved after Dorian, smiling at her joke and his reaction. She paused for just a moment on the other side of the gate to take in the world while Dorian was still shaking off the unexpected poke from Aurah.

Many of the merchants had risen and were slowly preparing for the day's profit. Swaths of cheap colored cloth hung as banners above their businesses to lure in customers. Aurah's lungs filled with air enriched by the smells of the city and the marketplace around her. The scent of fresh bread wafted from alleys, telling of an unseen bakery nearby. The smell of fire intertwined with the aroma of roasting meat. Her time around the kitchen told her it was a beef of sorts, and her eyes found a nearby spit to confirm the guess. Aurah's face crinkled slightly from smiling. She loved the city and all that it had to offer. Dorian had managed to collect himself and was walking away before he turned to see what kept Aurah. A small smile broke his features at seeing her relishing the waking world.

"I see you deeply enjoy the city." Dorian broached into conversation.

"Absolutely!" Aurah felt the most ridiculous grin cover her face as she turned towards Dorian. "I always get a sensation of peace and belonging when I see the people here. I think I even have memories from a long time ago about the city. They really are just thoughts and feelings, but they make me feel so good about the meandering streets and the busyness of everyone. The smells are my favorite. Each one is unique, just like the different people creating them." Aurah fawned over city life. She couldn't help but feel excited at the promise and potential the city held. She turned to look into Dorian's eyes. A slight blush filled her cheeks. She enjoyed staring into those springs of life more than she ever imagined that she would.

"I hope I didn't offend you by joking along with your men back there." Aurah offered her apologies. She often didn't see him in a setting where he could be lighthearted. She was afraid she might have pushed him too far.

"Those guys." Dorian shook his head fondly. "I'll only make Davis do latrine duty for a week." Dorian paused for a moment thoughtfully. "But he won't know that until the end of the week." Dorian grinned, and Aurah laughed. *Right. Ruthless.* "Well . . . I . . . uh, I guess I have to get back to guard. You take care, ok?" Dorian stumbled over his words. Aurah found that intriguing. She was about to respond when a guard came running up to Dorian, interrupting their farewell.

"Sir!" The man halted in a salute. A look of confusion crossed Dorian's face for a moment.

"You're from Damien's squad. Aren't you supposed to be stationed at the main gate?"

"Correct, sir. I was sent to relay a message to you, sir." *Strange,* Aurah thought. The man seemed deeply concerned about something.

"Ah, well what is it, squadling?" Dorian flashed a smile at Aurah. The nickname must be reserved for those under a captain or something. *Show-off.* She smiled back. The guard didn't seem to notice.

"Sir, Captain Damien sends word that a scouting patrol bearing Avante's crest is fast approaching the Capital. They will be here within half an hour." The guard finished, standing at attention. Dorian's face dampened. The earlier merriment was replaced by a furrowed brow.

"Avante? There hasn't been any word of this. Why would they break protocol?" *Strange.* Now Dorian seemed concerned. He turned to Aurah. "How long did you say you were going to be out this morning?" His eyes became distant and sat above a slight frown etched on his face.

"Not too long, I think. I have to be back slightly after the first bell to get back to my duties." Aurah looked at Dorian curiously. She didn't understand the implications of the news that the guard had brought.

"That's not bad. If you don't mind, would you be willing to check back in with me by the first bell? I don't think this oddity in regulation will mean that much, but I wouldn't let even my own sister out to the city if I thought it was even more dangerous than what it can be. I just want to make sure you're cared for." He offered her a vapid smile.

Aurah nodded while her hands fidgeted. Now she was confused, and she wasn't sure what to think about Dorian stepping in like he was. *He means the best.* She smiled back.

"Thanks, Aurah. I need to attend to this matter now, but I'll be looking for you at these gates around the first bell. I hope your endeavors go well!" Dorian turned to the guard. "Lead on."

The man nodded and turned, trotting steadily back the way he came with a piece of Aurah's heart following closely behind.

CHAPTER THREE

Aurah moved forward slowly, getting accustomed to being by herself again. She wandered aimlessly at first, enjoying the early hours and the vendors setting up their stalls in the large city square. One row after another was being slowly erected by the hazy-eyed merchants. Aurah turned and headed down a large avenue between the stalls into the streets beyond the square. The marketplace mostly offered fresh produce and other goods—nothing Aurah thought would meet her criteria for Elizabeth's gift. She wandered through the city, weaving over streets and across alleys until she came upon one of the bakeries she had smelled earlier. She knew it, and the owners, well. She had always managed to find her way here on her trips to the city.

Morris Baker, the owner of the bakery, strode out the front door carrying a few freshly baked barley loaves for the morning stragglers. Aurah closed the distance to the shop façade and the man.

"I see you have already soiled your clean apron, Mr. Baker." Aurah gripped her hands together behind her back. Morris Baker was the kind of person whose demeanor nearly demanded his acquaintances be witty and whimsical. One learned that it was better to try and take the upper hand as soon as possible.

"Ah, good mornin' to you, too, girl. I take it they couldn't stand yer howlin' and magnitude up in that fancy castle, so they cast you like a plague to us poor folk." He barely looked at her from the corner of his eye as he laid the loaves on a table. "I mean honestly, first it was taxes, now it's your sort. The oppression of the people will lead to revolt and rebellion, don't ya know." Morris paused his insult for a second, rearranging the loaves. His mouth hung slightly agape, then he looked up at Aurah, his mouth twisting into a wry smile. "You don't happen to have a sister, do you? I don't know if my poor heart could take the shock of the two of ya." He crossed his arms while his smile grew, squinting his eyes.

"Well, I don't know about a blood sister, but Princess Elizabeth is the closest thing I do have, I'm sure she would love to come to visit you and your glorious... *kingdom* here. She has a pleasant heart for company and *never forgets anyone*." Aurah put on the most precious smile she could muster. Morris froze pale, his eyes bulged slightly, and his crossed arms squeezed his chest tighter. He relaxed quickly, letting out a deep breath. "Ah, yer a demon, girl. Yer getting too good at this game of ours. You don't even let me..."

"Morris Baker!" A loud voice boomed out, cutting off any further talk. Morris's head snapped towards the loud voice. It was his wife, Elenor. She came stomping out of the bakery dangerously. Tiny clouds of flour puffed from her apron—a sign of who really was doing the work so far that morning. Aurah smirked.

"Quiet woman! You'll wake the neighbors!" Morris waved his hands frantically at Elenor, trying to shush her.

"How many times do I have to scold you about tormenting the lovely girl?" Her voice calmed, but the scolding remained. Aurah smiled widely, knowing Morris would never win their little game with Elenor around.

"But I swears she started it this time!" Morris threw his hands in Aurah's direction. "I was just defending myself!" His argument was pathetic and weak before his wife. It was no surprise that these two had married. It took a strong woman to deal with Morris's constant antics. Aurah had always admired Elenor.

"Don't you go blaming some young child for your miscreant ways, you heathen! Now go in the bakery and tend to the breads being fired. It's your turn to do some hard work for once. And wake your son. He's as lazy as you are!"

Elenor shooed Morris away into the shop as he feigned a pout. Aurah broke and laughed heartily, the bells of her beautiful voice piercing the quiet morning. "Oh, that man!" Elenor smiled widely. Her deep love for her husband was evident. "What has you out this early, Aurah?" Elenor wiped her hands on a towel, then began to prepare another display table.

Aurah reeled back her laughter while holding her side—she was in stitches. In reality, it may not have been the funniest thing ever, but she loved these people so much that it made her much more susceptible to a jovial spirit. She took a few more moments to collect herself. "My goodness, it's like you never laughed before." Elenor smiled at Aurah's disposition.

Aurah breathed out deeply and slowly. "Well, never like I do here. Your husband has a way with words."

"Yes, that he does—I hope you're not thinking of trying to steal him from me!" Elenor didn't even look up from her work. She could be just as bad as Morris.

"Okay! Okay. Ohhh-kay." Aurah found what little reserves she had left again and pulled herself away from her laughter. "I'm here to get Elizabeth a birthday gift. It's her birthday tomorrow and a lot of things are going to change. I want to get her something that will always remind her of me, no matter what." Her voice quickly sobered as she began to think and talk again of Elizabeth and the trials ahead. Silence filled the air, interrupted by the call of a bird and the baker's wife fumbling with setting up the stand.

"That's got to be pretty scary to face, all of that change." Elenor looked up from her work for a second, staring into Aurah's eyes. Emotion swirled for a second—it felt good to be understood.

"It is. I talked with . . . a friend of mine on the way down here from the palace." Aurah didn't want things growing out of control about Dorian, as there really wasn't anything substantial to base those thoughts on—not yet. *Maybe.* "My friend said something really good, that Elizabeth and I are even closer than some real sisters. He—they're right, and I'm trusting in every memory up to this point to hold Elizabeth and me through everything." Aurah's smile exuded her confidence in her words.

"Those are some wise words, they are." Elenor smiled back and turned to her work again.

Aurah hovered nearby, preoccupying herself with the buildings in the city. A man walked up to Elenor and bought half a loaf, then two soldiers came, each buying a loaf.

"It's so peaceful this time of the morning, I almost want to wake up this early every day." Aurah voiced her thoughts.

"If you did that, it wouldn't be so special anymore." Morris came back out of the shop carrying a fresh bundle of loaves. "The peace is sure to run dry, too. Soon the world will be awake and crawling and begging for every bit of bread we possess." His words made Aurah smile again. "I overheard you earlier, if you are looking for something special to give to her majesty, I would suggest the trinket shop over on River Street. It's known for curiosities and such. You might have some good luck searching there." Morris smiled back at her.

"I'll have to do that; I should probably get going soon. I don't want to keep Dor . . . Elizabeth waiting." Aurah nearly slipped. She bristled as Morris and Elenor both scrutinized her for a moment, probably noticing that she was hiding something. Morris was one of the last people Aurah wanted to know about any kind of interest in the opposite gender. Morris broke the tension.

"Here, girl. Take this." He ripped a chunk of bread off one of his freshly baked loaves. "This is my famous honey loaf. Best in all the Kingdom. It'll keep ya fed for a few hours, I don't suppose you've had your breakfast this mornin'." He handed it to her eager and waiting hands. It was still very warm and smelled delicious.

"Feel free to stop by whenever. It's good to see your face around here." Elenor waved goodbye to Aurah.

"Yeah! Especially since we poor commoners can't afford fancy mirrors and such to witness true beauty!" Morris rubbed his face in admiration. Before he could continue on, Elenor slapped him. "Yeowch! Woman, you've never been much an admirer of the arts!"

"Get your son, and fetch us some more water! And make it quick, or I'll turn your physique into what them people nowadays call 'abstract' art." Morris quickly scuttled off to carry on with the day's work. "Goodbye, Aurah, I hope you find a good gift."

"Goodbye. Thanks for the bread and the company!" She waved to Elenor and plunged into an alley in the direction Morris had pointed.

River Street was a bit of a distance away. It was nearly all the way across the city, in fact. Aurah was glad the city wasn't terribly complicated or impossibly vast. If dedicated, a runner could cross the city in about a quarter of an hour, dodging all the oddball alleys and misaligned streets, of course. She wasn't a dedicated runner, so the trip would take her a little longer. The bread from Morris kept her company for part of the trip, though. *Delicious.* It wasn't long before Aurah had made the last turn onto the winding street where the curiosity shop was supposed to be. On her right, the banks of the river, which cut through the city, flowed along the street edge for a short distance before swooping away. She followed the street farther down before it plunged into the larger Center Street, where the traffic increased as the morning moved onward.

Aurah's feet carried her mindlessly while she searched for the shop. Her brow furrowed when she arrived at Center Street. Did she miss it? Turning around and walking more intently, she realized two things when she arrived back where she started. The first was that there was no curiosity shop on River Street, and secondly, Morris Baker had to be terrible with directions, because Elenor would never have allowed him to send her on a wild goose chase throughout the city—*alone*. She also knew Morris had enough reserve to temper his pranks from that, so she was at loss. The shop had to be around here somewhere. Aurah bit the inside of her cheek and watched a man farther down walk away and turn onto Center Street. *Well, thanks, Morris. I guess you got the last laugh—and you're going to get away with it!* A small groan escaped her lips before she decided to ask for help.

Walking briskly, she approached the nearest shop and found an attendant just inside of the building.

"Excuse me, sir?" The attendant looked up from stitching a horse saddle. He smiled, and Aurah saw that he was missing a tooth or two.

"What can I help you with, miss? Are you looking to purchase one of the finest saddles in all of the Capital?" The man smiled at her genuinely.

"No, I'm sorry." The attendant's smile waned.

Aurah continued, "I've been given bad directions to a curiosity shop on this street, yet there isn't one near. Would you happen to know of one— in the past or nearby?"

"Well, there used to be a curiosity shop on this street, but it up and moved nigh a year ago. The name is Glovers and Kin. They did so well that they moved to a more established shop front over on Stoney Road." The man eyed Aurah hopefully, but she didn't notice. She was about to leave when a thought crossed her head.

"Are you sure it's there? I was just given some bad directions, and I want to make sure I'm not getting too far gone on this search."

"Oh, yeah. I pass by it every morning on my way here. My brother owns this leather shop, and I come every day to help work the business. You can certainly count on it being there." The man had barely finished speaking when Aurah turned and began to move quickly towards her new destination. Another thought crossed her mind. She stopped and faced the man again.

"Thanks a lot, sir! I'm sorry I'm not in the market for this fine leatherwork, but I will let Princess Elizabeth know of your hospitality and kindness. I'm sure she wouldn't mind giving you and your brother's business a look-over. The Capital is always in need of fine leather workmanship." Aurah turned for the last time and headed away, leaving the attendant staring wide-eyed in her wake.

The city was becoming more awake and alive the longer she spent pursuing Elizabeth's gift. The smells in the air had diminished somewhat since she had moved farther away from any source of food. Only the odd fire here and there tickled her nose. She eventually came to the spot the attendant had described to her.

Aurah stood still, ready to charge through a shop door at the moment she recognized the name Glovers and Kin. Her body began to tense when she failed to find the shop. She took a step forward, moving to look from another angle. *Nothing.* Aurah finally came to another conclusion—*she* was terrible with directions. Pessimistic thoughts lifted their heads at the opportunity to pierce the girl's joy. The shop was still nowhere to be found, and now her time was beginning to run thin. She didn't want to keep Dorian waiting, even in the slightest. *By The Face!* She cursed at the thought. What would he think of a woman who couldn't keep a time commitment? Her skirt rustled slightly as she began to hasten away to find the shop. When in doubt, just cover everywhere quickly. It was a faultless plan. *Probably.*

Her rapid pace carried her between buildings and through alleys. She found that weaving a path between other morning risers was steadily becoming more difficult. It didn't take much time before her search drew her into a slow run. Aurah darted around, sprinting through the throngs of people trying desperately to locate the shop. *Where had they all come from so suddenly?* She contemplated forgetting the shop and looking elsewhere, but she had already committed so much time trying to find it and there weren't any other places she knew to look. The bell chimed its half-hour mark. *Half an hour!* She had to find the shop—there was no way she could fail to get Elizabeth this gift. She could hardly focus on what she was doing. Her heartbeat quickened as she ran. If she couldn't get Elizabeth a gift now, there would be no more time in the future. She must succeed now. She absolutely couldn't fail.

She had no idea where she was going when a loose brick in the road gave way, and she fell, crashing into the ground. Elizabeth had often called her graceless. She preferred unlucky. Holding her leg, she took a moment to collect herself. Her knee had borne the brunt of her fall, and the impact of hitting the ground had stolen the breath from her lungs.

Ground. Stones. Pain.

Clenching her teeth, she stood up slowly. She grimaced from the pain, wiping a few chunks of the street off of her clothes. *Her clothes.* They were dirty and torn. There would disapproval. Her head fell into her scraped hand.

"Yes, Elizabeth, I know I am an adult." She whispered aloud—a response to the visions in her head. She took a moment to observe the odd side street she managed to find. This street was barely more than a glorified alley. Buildings rose on either side, crushing the street down so that no more than three men may walk abreast. The sun worked harder than usual to illuminate the dim ground, fighting against the cramped, tall buildings. The road was neglected and in shambles, the brick broken in pieces. Aurah promptly decided the shop wasn't down this way. In fact, she didn't remember seeing any kind of stores the past few streets—nor people or other signs of life, for that matter. *Foolish me!*

Aurah turned to leave when she heard voices drifting through the air. *Two...and... men...* Nothing unusual.

Except...

A single word cut out above the others, grabbing her attention.

The word moved forward through the dank alley and crested in her ears. The volume rose louder. *A beastly word.* She wouldn't have paid the voices any mind, but that word's very tendrils crawled forth, wrapping around her already frantic mind. Her imagination burned wildly at the magnitude of this word. It was a word unlike any other, and with such a weighty significance. A word not lightly tossed around in idle chatter. *By any.* A foreboding word. An omen of ill-fortune. Why in this filthy, lifeless and scum alley was this word used to converse? Then she heard the word again.

Dragon. Her breath caught in her throat.

Dragon. Her heart tumbled, forgetting its rhythm.

Dragon . . . oh, no.

Fear kicked her heart back into an unsteady thrum. She didn't like dragons. Not one bit. No one was particularly fond of even the idea of such a creature. Aurah despised the beasts just as much, and her heart squirmed at the thought of monsters. Though dragon sightings had been incredibly rare, rumors of attacks throughout the Kingdom were increasing. But there was no way they could be real.

Could they?

Dragon.

She turned to face the source of the conversation, trembling. Her palms felt moist. Nothing threatened to ruin the world more than one of those monsters. Everyone was so afraid of dragons. Why, then, would anyone find it pleasant to talk about these horrors? It wasn't worthy of the breath used in conversation. Even here, in this place.

Dragon.

She heard the voices continue, holding her rapt. Places, where dragons were a normal part of conversation, were not good places at all. Aurah glanced around, suddenly uncertain of her safety. The alley had many shadows and dark holes. *How did she ever miss what she was running straight into?* As much as she loved the city, she couldn't count how many times the soldiers had sternly warned her not to wander too far from the main roads. There were plenty of nests for rats to hide. The sounds, mere whispers in the shadows, tugged her again away from her thoughts. Who could be talking about dragons? Her skin crawled. She had a funny feeling that this was one of those rat's nests about which she was cautioned.

So why did she find her feet inching towards it?

Dragon.

Shadows in shadows. She saw monsters dance through the shade on the wall.

Dragon.

Drawing slowly to the opposite edge of the street, she closed in on an opening to an even darker alley a little farther down. Her heart pounded so loudly she was afraid it might be heard. She followed the low voices.

". . . boss says the *dragon* will certainly head here," a quiet, gruff, voice breathed in a spiteful tone.

"I don't believe it." Another, younger, voice retorted a little louder.

"You'll do well to keep your disbelief to yerself, runt. Never go against the boss. If ye did yo . . . ."

"I'll end up like all the other new kids." The younger voice dripped with contempt.

"You just don't get it, do you? You think this is a game? I've slit throats on those younger than you for fear of my own life. You should never have come looking for this curse. You'll . . . ."

The younger voice interrupted rudely again "Die one way or the other. Yes, I've heard repeatedly. That's our motto, the mantra we all live by. I've at least seen the destruction of what that beast can do. What do we have to start even opposing him? What plan can we come up with?"

"Yer just some dumb kid, so what do you know? I think it's 'bout time to keep yer trap shut."

"What do you think you're doing?" A voice screamed in Aurah's ear from behind.

Aurah's body jolted violently from the fright, and she let out a squeal of terror. Goosebumps raised along the lengths of her arms, and the hair on the nape of her neck raised as sweat beaded under her collar. Her fist balled up in pure animalistic reaction covering her face. What was that voice? It was the dragon! *No, it isn't, you foolish girl!* She chided herself harshly in her fear. Why did she never learn her place? She turned quickly, heart pounding. She stared the meanest looking man she'd ever seen straight in the face. Bald with scars etched the length of his head, the only noticeable hair was his brows. His eyes, a furious blue, raged against her.

"Answer me! What are you doing girl?" The two voices had cut off, though neither appeared from their shadowy crook. *Strange.*

"I . . . uh . . . I got lost! I was trying the find a curiosity shop when I tripped and fell in this alley. I'm terribly sorry! Please don't hurt me!" She clenched, deathly afraid of this blue-eyed man. A second of blissful silence passed in the air before the man spoke again.

"Glovers and Kin." The blunt statement rested in the air for another second before she realized it was poised as a question.

"Uh . . . what?" Her voice trembled, squeaking. The man's speech made no sense.

"Glovers and Kin. The curiosity shop." The man's harsh stare never relented.

"Yes!" Her voice squeaked in shock and trepidation. Her mind was overwhelmed, and she wanted nothing but to leave that place far behind. "Yes, I'm terrible with directions! I'm so sorry!" She shrunk away even further, her back against the wall of the nearest building.

"Back that way." The man spoke coarsely as he pointed to the road she came from, without taking his eyes off her. "Toward the river, two minutes down the road. It's your own fault if you miss it. Don't come back here ever again."

Aurah nodded feverishly and darted past the man, forgetting her pleasantries. *There isn't a thing pleasant about this whole farce!* She clutched her basket as she ran—the only other survivor of the day. She ran clumsily from the shadows of the alley into the light and through the surging tide of people. The roads blurred by, and she caught the glares of quite a few people as she shoved past them. Others stared curiously, but she didn't give a mere thought to what people would think—she ran.

Charlie stared as the strange girl took off in a dreadful fright. He must have overdone it again. He had a way with kids, after all. It was better anyway that she didn't snoop around, though. Things could get really bad. *Fast.* Shaking his head, he turned towards the two numskulls he left on guard and plunged into the shadows.

"Oh, it's only the boss!" Sarcasm dripped off the snot's voice.

Reaching out into the dim gloom, Charlie grabbed the front of a tunic and threw the unsuspecting body into a wall. With his other hand, he found the hair on the back of the kid's head and slammed his face into the wall.

"Ge' off!" The kid screamed.

What a weak struggle. Charlie threw the boy to the ground. Anger throbbed through his body.

"Listen here. Kid. You got yourself into this mess, nosing around where you shouldn't have. If you want to keep breathing, I suggest you keep that big mouth of yours shut and do as you're told."

It was dark in the slime hole where they stood. Charlie hated the dark, but they *needed* the shadows to hide. He could still see the pissant writhing on the ground—probably trying to come to grips the blood trailing down his face from his split brow. The snot opened its mouth to speak.

"I hate you people! I want to go home! I'm tired of being trapped in your stupid gang! I don't care how many times you threaten me with death and your stupid lies."

The kid spit after his little rant. Blood from his recent run-in with the wall flew and speckled Charlie's face. Moving slowly, Charlie wiped it off with the cuff of his sleeve. Then he dropped to the ground, tenderly selecting the few last words he would have with the kid. *For now, at least.*

"Keeping you alive is easy enough, snot, but if you tempt me, I'll start taking things from you." In a flash, Charlie's knife was trailing across the kid's face as he shoved his knee in the kid's belly, pinning him down onto the broken stone. Charlie touched the kid's nose with the blade. "Your nose—not going to look so good anymore, eh, runt?" Charlie's voice rasped out lowly. "Your ears." Charlie found the kid's ears with the blade and sliced. A small cut appeared, dripping a fresh rivulet of blood through the snot's hair. The kid's breathing changed, churning heavier and heavier. He tried to move, but Charlie held him firmly, pressing even harder. The kid moaned from the knee digging harder into his flesh. "Let's keep going, shall we? How about your tongue next? Oh, I can't wait till you keep your mouth shut!" The words spewed out of Charlie's mouth. He pressed the blade against the kid's lips, pushing harder with every moment passed.

Charlie found himself caught up in the lesson he was giving the kid. A wild look flashed through Charlie's eyes. *Please understand.* The kid let out a muffled scream, and fear welled up in his eyes and turned to the tears that poured down and mingled with the rivulet of blood from his ears. *This runt has no guts.* Releasing the blade, Charlie trailed it upward and leaned close, whispering into the kid's bloodied ear.

"Do you know how easy it is to remove an eye?" The flat of the blade moved and covered one of the kid's eyes as tears poured from beneath the metal. The kid was sobbing. No surprise. Charlie already smelled that the kid had wet himself. *Pathetic and weak.* He ground his teeth together. "If you ever . . . ." The kid's muffled sobs grew louder. "Ever!" Charlie was screaming over the young man. ". . . defy me again, I will take something."

He got up, leaving the kid on the ground to weep. Charlie spit next to the kid's head. Charlie stared for a moment. *Please understand.* There was one other thing he needed to tend to.

"Charlie . . . ."

A loud thud and grunt ripped through the tiny slime hole. Charlie landed his fist squarely in the other guard's face, felling him. Leaning over, Charlie spit on him. *Stupid Murdoc.* He stared down at the man, his fist clenched hard. This was a man he had no problem murdering. He never should have slacked at his post and let an innocent kid wander into a hole that he would never wander back from. In Charlie's eyes, that would justify Murdoc's death by any means.

"Murdoc." Charlie breathed the name out slowly. "If I ever catch you talking on guard duty again, I'll personally make you weep worse than that snot before I shut you up for good."

He turned aside, about to move on, but stopped. Instead, he pivoted back and lined himself up and planted a kick square in the other man's stomach. Charlie clenched his teeth again at the sound of the air rushing from Murdoc. It was all this idiot's fault. Charlie could hardly forgive anyone for ruining a kid's life like Murdoc's incompetence had done for the snot. If only he kept the kid away. *If only.*

Charlie began walking away when he noticed he was limping slightly on his recently used foot. He looked down, for a moment feeling out his step. *Scum must have broken my foot.* Charlie spit on the ground again before turning inside to their temporary abode in the Capital. It was the greasiest hovel he had ever seen. Charlie sighed, opening the door.

Good to be home. I guess.

CHAPTER FOUR

Aurah's lungs heaved as she eventually slowed her sprint into a forceful walk. She didn't stop moving for a while, then found a crate to lean against. She held herself, bending over as she tried to calm down and catch her breath. She had breathed harder from the encounter than from all of her running. The crate under her palms offered a reprieve that welcomed her to rest. She flopped enthusiastically onto the seat. The river flowed nonchalantly behind her, and birds chirped their morning song. She tried to focus on those soothing noises to calm her nerves. It hardly worked. Her hands failed her, trembling beyond control. She dropped her basked pathetically onto the ground and watched it roll slightly away. She rocked back and forth trying to alleviate the tension. *No, this morning has gone nothing as it should have.* She was frustrated and on the verge of tears at the failure of her endeavors.

She hated this—which was saying a lot coming from Aurah. She hated things not happening as planned, though she didn't know anyone who actually enjoyed a plan falling apart. She just hated to pick up the pieces and try to make them all work together again, all while feeling like her efforts spent were completely wasted. *No gift after all.* She hated how afraid she was. She hated how she never had anyone to show her how to be better at navigating the city, or finding gifts, or staying out of trouble. Aurah cringed. Longing for a parent overwhelmed her. She clenched the crate underneath her and didn't release for a moment. She had been under a large amount of stress recently, and this morning must have been the final straw before most of her reserves snapped, allowing emotion to flood over her like a raging river.

She exhaled deeply, relaxing her tension and letting go of her handhold on the crate. She looked up past the building tops towards the cloudy morning sky. No, she wouldn't blame her life on the apparent lack she wrestled with at times. She had never known her parents, but sometimes the void their absence left was enough to leave Aurah broken down and emotionally fatigued. She had hoped that with the giving of this gift she would find resolution in all of the change life was throwing at her. Elizabeth would have something to be reminded of Aurah always. Aurah could move on to things like marriage and raising a family. Life would just change as it does. Aurah had accepted that much about it, but life would also eventually move towards and stabilize in peace, away from the heartache life so readily poured like rain on the unsuspecting heads of the innocent.

Her tumbling thoughts halted for a moment, and she smiled brightly. *Dorian.* He was a stark contrast to the darkness of the world. She hadn't expected their time together this morning, but it really was enjoyable. Her mind moved through the rest of the morning and settled on the strange scene she had seen only minutes earlier. A shudder gripped her body. It was true that the Kingdom was suffering because of some sort of monster. Rumors were that a terrible dragon had appeared and was destroying every city in its path. That was the kind of thing to ruin the few bits of light she held. *And that man!* Aurah gripped the crate again. Not only was he associated with those who casually talked about dragons, but he bore the stench of evil. Aurah tried hard to push past the pessimism that was gripping her and took another deep breath.

It was easy to be grateful most of the time. It's just when her hope of the future became challenged—whether by Elizabeth's ascension, the destruction wreaked by a fabled dragon, or some scummy gang of criminals—that her fortitude began to break and issues like finding a gift escalated. Some sunlight streamed through the clouds, warming her. She leaned back to take in what bit of the rays she could. *Always a good sign.* She stretched her arms above her head. She would have to get moving soon if she was to find Elizabeth a gift before her time was up. The blue-eyed man had said two minutes down the road, but at her speed, it should have been more like half a minute. She gripped her hands together, hoping she hadn't missed it again. She picked up her basket and moved to the road. A line of shops littered the road in either direction.

"Barclay's General Goods, The Sleeping Cub Inn." She began to read aloud the various shop signs taking up her search again. "Raget's Parchments and Quills." The signs were ruinous to her hope. How much time did she really have left? Reading a few more, she ran down the list of options available to her. With a moment of thought, Aurah concluded there really weren't any. She moved down the street, beginning to falter again. *What could I have possibly gotten Elizabeth anyway? She is a princess, after all.* She tried to shake the frustration away as her mouth began to tremble.

"Glovers and Kin Curiosity Shop."

She stopped and stared, then read the sign again. *Glovers and Kin Curiosity Shop.* A smile cracked her downcast face. It was ethereal, it was magnificent, it was . . . what she was looking for. The store's window displays grew larger as she hurriedly approached and found the entrance. A bell rang, struck by the door.

Shelves lined the floors and covered the walls. The front of the shop opened to display some larger items, and room was made to traverse through the maze of curiosities. They were pleasing to look at, but not of interest to her. The musty smell of ancient papers and books pulled her from the rest of the world and brought her attention to some shelves holding a small expanse of aging tomes against the exterior wall.

"Hello, Miss. May I help you?" Caught off guard, she turned, to see an old greying man approach through one of the aisles. His footsteps were completely muted.

"Um, yes. I . . . uh . . . need a gift. It's for a special friend of mine. It's her birthday, and I want her to remember me always as she goes through . . . through a big change that is coming up." Aurah smiled as politely as she could muster. The old man's eyes glassed over as he stared at her, seeming to peer into her soul. She fidgeted. Someone his age should have had a tough time seeing past the cloud in his eyes, but this man gave Aurah the feeling his gaze missed nothing.

"It's quite the honor to serve the Princess and her loyal handmaiden." The old man's cheeks raised in a toothy smile. Well, what teeth he still had. "If you follow me, I have what you may be looking for."

Her mouth gaped open. *How does he know who I am?* He headed off to another part of the shop. *Weird.* At any rate, she finally was making real progress. She would have the perfect gift after all! As she followed the attendant, the rows of shelves passed. There were so many odds and ends for the hungering eye, and it was all so very captivating.

"Right here." The man's chest puffed with pride at the trinket, a necklace, which lay on a display with others. Aurah moved forward and looked closely. It was actually quite a fine piece of work. It was made of solid silver, edged in gold—she grimaced at the thought of the cost of such an object. The necklace took the shape of a small heart . . . held by a *dragon*. Her throat caught at the remembrance all things dragon that day and before. *No luck after all.* She sighed deeply and rubbed her forehead.

"I'm really sorry, but do you have anything else?" Her voice began to waver as she saw disappointment slowly fall across the man's face. "I mean it's a lovely piece and all, but . . . ."

"Dragons." The man offered. A small smile still lined his face.

"Well . . . yes."

"Young lady, do you know what this piece is?" The voice became matter-of-fact and proud. She prepared for what could be a long and unnecessary story.

"No?" Her resolve was beginning to break.

"I know what you must be thinking. How could anyone attribute the common picture of love with a dragon? Monsters! Demons! Beasts! Vile creatures of no moral integrity, but rather of pure and raw *hatred*."

Her foot stepped backward. She didn't like the way he had said hatred. The man continued slowly, and his features now bore a burden. He took a second to form his thought. Aurah doubted he could convince her, whatever he might say. "But . . . it was not meant to be that way. Dragons were once the epitome of love. Such magnificent creatures. Beautiful, really, what a dragon should be, not this horror story to frighten young whelps."

Aurah blatantly shook her head at such an outlandish claim.

The man's smile seemed to be fueled by her objections. "No? The legend us old folk tell is that dragons were given all of their power to give back out in volumes. To help and serve the world under their creed of love. It's just unfortunate that the tale depicts that even dragons can be—and were—swayed." Aurah wasn't sure with the man's eyes being hazy, but his vision seemed to grow distant for a moment. He looked back at Aurah with renewed vigor. "This pendant is a representation of the greatest love that exists or at least the idea of it, but I guess you are right young, Miss. Who knows anything real about those creatures, except what we witness and feel now?"

Controversy raged through her mind. It was a nice story. Nice if it were real, but she knew better than to believe something so outlandish and so fake. Doubtless. *Maybe.* Her lip became sore as she chewed it more, steeped in her contemplation. "I think it would be better if I didn—" Aurah cut off sharply as a loud ringing from outside interrupted her thoughts. *The morning bell.* "Oh, no!" She would be late to meet Dorian. There was no more time, so she made a hasty decision. "I'll take it! How much?"

The old man already had it wrapped in a fabric, and he placed it into Aurah's basket.

"Take it. Love must be shared freely. Take it and give it as a gift to her majesty." His eyes peered deeply into her own. Something felt right about the gift, despite her objections to anything dragon-related. Maybe it was the fact that her mind could hardly help but return to Dorian. She grabbed a handful of coins from her purse and planted them on a nearby counter—definitely not enough for this man's apparent treasure.

"Thank you so much! Let's just call it even now!" Grabbing the gift, she raced for the door.

The old man smiled. "I appreciate your business, Aurah. Come again!"

She flew out the door and to the street. It would be slightly harder to get places now with the flux of people moving to their morning destinations. She would manage, though. *Sorry, Dorian!*

CHAPTER FIVE

Aurah ran as fast as she could, the gift secured in her basket. If she hurried, Dorian wouldn't be kept waiting forever. She just hoped he didn't panic and come searching for her. *Would he do that?* It was a pleasant thought, though she would much rather not find out. She could only imagine the fear, worry, and anger on his features. She could hear it now: *"Aurah, you are terribly irresponsible, and I can't be associated with anyone who acts like you! My career is based on hard work, discipline, and punctuality—all of which are things you so blatantly lack. I bid you farewell, girl. May you find happiness elsewhere.* She gritted her teeth. *Shut up, Aurah.* She chided herself, trying to dislodge the silly thoughts. She did notice that she moved faster, though.

She slowed a little eventually, as the pace took its toll on her unconditioned body. It wasn't until she drew closer to the square where she departed from Dorian earlier, that she noticed something odd— the crowds of people were becoming harder to move through. *Strange.* The throngs of people should naturally be thinner near the center of the city. She pushed her way through as best as she could, any thoughts of running forward completely eliminated.

Something is wrong.

People stood together, facing towards the palace, their backs to Aurah. Yes, the city was a busy and crowded place as people went to and fro, but this was unusual. *No one moved.* The flow of people stemmed to a trickle until Aurah was completely stuck behind the masses. She could hear a cacophony of voices rising together farther up ahead in the square, but it was only mutterings and whispers to those back where Aurah stood. A spike of adrenaline shot through her stomach. This wasn't good—on so many levels. She wasn't accustomed to being out in the city. The simple life of the palace had caused in her a kind of life-atrophy, and no one would recognize her for the position as the handmaiden to their royalty. Would anyone help? What would she do if no one realized she was out of place here? Or worse, what if someone did realize that Aurah was who she was and harmed her as a means to hurt the Princess? Aurah found herself trembling for the second time that morning. Panic had begun to seep into her soul, and emotion caught in the back of her throat. *Patience, Aurah. Don't worry. You can make it far enough ahead, and then Dorian will get you. You'll be fine.* She clenched her teeth and exhaled. Her thoughts were good, she just needed to make it to the square up ahead. *Hopefully.*

Without waiting for another second, she pushed forward and found a space able to be traversed. Aurah began weaving her way through people, inciting a few comments of distaste and displeasure. She kept muttering her apologies, but moved forward, nonetheless. She had to get back to the palace. With every step, the square grew closer, and the buzz of voices resonated louder amid the crowd. Something definitely was not right. The closer she got to the center of the square, the more a lurking fear in her heart surfaced. As Aurah kept pushing, an alley on her right appeared clearly. She recognized it and its value immediately. *There is another alley that leads from there to the square!* And at the moment, the new direction didn't look so crowded. Aurah changed direction, heading for the alley. The voices in the crowd became more audible.

"Soldiers . . . ."

". . . Avante wiped out."

"So close . . . here now . . . ."

"Dragon."

That word again. Chills raced through her body, and the goosebumps came back. *Why dragons? Why now? What did it mean? What is happening?* Something moved, wrenching Aurah from her thoughts. Dark shadows swirled in the alley. *Not just shadows—cloaked men.* Aurah slowed as the realization of what she saw drew her mind back to her earlier confrontation with the bald man. Her stomach almost emptied itself. On second thought, she'd rather find another way back to the square. She turned to find a new route when a hand seized her shoulder.

"What do you think you're doing, you little whelp! Don't you think we all want to hear from the palace about what is going on the same? Do you think it's fair that some get to hear, while others don't? You don't just get to cut past everyone, you little tramp!" A gruff man with gnarled and crusty locks of hair crushed Aurah's shoulder in his hand, ripping her from her thoughts. He spun her about in one mighty turn to face himself. Aurah blanched at the reek of liquor on the man's breath. The people all around them were temporarily distracted by the man's tirade and shouting. Aurah thrashed hard to get herself free from his grip. Thoughts for the safety of her gift only briefly crossed her mind before the more pressing issues of her own security took their place.

"Please, sir, I have a good reason to get to the front. I'm sure you would be rewarded nicely for your help and my relea . . . ."

"Don't give me that crap, tramp! I know your kind would say whatever to get what you want!" The man's voice trailed off as his eyes glazed over in as much thought as was possible for someone in his state. He inspected Aurah as she squirmed under his leering gaze and crushing grip. *This is not good.* Aurah was just about to scream for help when a voice cried out.

"Hey! Let that girl go, you drunken brute!" Aurah turned her head as much as she could. It was Morris! He stood nearby on the edge of the ring around them. Aurah didn't know where he had come from, but he must have seen the commotion and recognized her. *Thank the heavens for Morris Baker!* She would completely forgive him for his directional mishap earlier. The brute responded to Morris by throwing Aurah to the ground and immediately landing a punch into Morris's gut. A loud grunt erupted from Morris who fought to remain standing. *Morris!* Aurah stared in horror as the brute wound up to land another blow on Morris.

The brute threw his meaty fist forward at Morris's face when a steel-plated gauntlet, clenched in a fist, was flung forward from the void near Morris's head and intercepted the brute's attack. A stoic hero deftly slid in between Morris and the brute, a look of magnificent fury radiating from his green eyes.

Dorian.

A sickening crunch trailed through the air above the crowd, followed shortly by a scream of agony. Guards filed in quickly, standing at the ready near Aurah and at other points in the circle. The drunken brute's hand—what was left of a hand—hung mangled and bloodied. The metal gauntlet did look vicious, but Dorian had to have thrown some serious power behind his attack to cause the damage that he did. The drunk narrowed his eyes, screaming at the captain, throwing his other fist forward.

"Dorian!" Aurah screamed from the ground.

In a flash, another thud silenced the brute as Dorian planted his fist into the brute's face. The drunk fell over, unconscious from the combination of Dorian's blow and alcohol. A tooth fell free of his mouth, and blood pooled slightly around his face. Dorian turned away from the fight towards Aurah and helped her up. Aurah caught the captain's eyes in

41

full force. While he didn't look flustered at all, she could only gawk at the tempest before her.

"Are you alright?" Dorian asked. Aurah stared, heart hammering in her chest. *Am I alright?* She couldn't think while staring into her savior's fiery green eyes. Her shoulder throbbed, but she wasn't seriously hurt. She opened her mouth to say something, but her knees became weak and gave out. Aurah dropped her basket, collapsing.

"Aurah!" Dorian lurched forward and caught the young woman. In a moment, the storm in the man was lashed and tamed. The very hands that violently destroyed her assailant gently held and cradled the enfeebled girl.

"Dorian, what's going on?" she murmured as she found her feet again, thankful for the man's help. A nearby guard—the one named Davis—reached down and picked up her basket for her. The gift was still wrapped and safe inside. She looked up and noticed another guard helping Morris Baker. "Oh! Morris!" She made to move forward but found she wasn't quite herself yet. The suddenness of the attack was unsettling. Dorian wrapped his arm around her waist and took her to Morris, Elenor was already there checking him. She looked up and smiled gently at Aurah. *They must have come to find out what was going on, as well.* Aurah looked and realized she was only a few streets away from the bakery she had visited earlier that morning. Aurah's mind thundered wildly. So much about the day was simply wrong.

"Aye, we nearly got the bastard, you and me, girl!" Morris smiled weakly at Aurah.

"You should have just fed him one of your loaves of bread, Morris. That would have taken him out faster than annoying him to death with your words." She couldn't help but poke fun at the baker. He smiled widely at Aurah.

"Getting' too good at this game of ours." He coughed and cringed.

42

"Are you alright, Morris?" Aurah asked. At that moment, she seemed a little weaker and felt Dorian's grip tighten around her waist.

"This roach wouldn't be done in so easily—he's too stubborn," Elenor spoke up for Morris. "Aye, his ribs are just a wee bit bruised, but he'll be ok." The man didn't mind not saying anything at the moment. He held himself in a way that favored the side where he took the punch.

"Dorian," Aurah spoke. "Could you make sure news is brought to these bakers so they don't have to wait out here in the crowds of people? I would like for them to rest at home if that is alright." Aurah looked over at Dorian, who nodded, a small, understanding half-smile formed on his lips.

"You two, go ahead and move on home. I'm going to send two guards to escort you there just to make sure this meat bag doesn't have any friends waiting about. Aurah, we need to be leaving now." Dorian nudged her gently forward. Morris and Elenor said their farewells to Aurah, who then turned away with Dorian.

"Make way!" A soldier's voice thundered, parting the crowds and making a path for Dorian and Aurah. Another sigh of relief escaped her lips. *This day just gets worse and worse*, she thought. Everything was supposed to go so much better than it had. Now everything was deteriorating. Aurah faced the square. The merchant's stalls were still erected, swamped with an unexpected tide of people. Unfortunately, they also took up a hefty portion of the room in the square, which made things cramped and more difficult to move about. She followed Dorian's lead as he and his men parted the noisy crowd and made their way towards the palace gate. She was thankful for his presence; the escapade with the brute earlier left her feeling drained. Slowly her mind recovered and the questions from before started to resonate again.

"Dorian, what's happening? Why is everyone in the city gathering in the square?" Dorian was silent for a moment but finally spoke.

"I was worried, Aurah, really worried. When I saw the crowd disperse and reveal you in the clutches of that scum, I... I don't lose my control like that. I'm sorry." Dorian spoke loudly enough to be heard over the crowds' chatter. He kept his face forward.

"I'm sorry I was late and made you worry. I had trouble finding a gift for Elizabeth."

"Did you find anything?" He was quick to ask, but he seemed different than before. His words were sharp, on edge. Something was wrong, bothering him, and he was doing his best to either hide it or tame the surging beast inside.

"Well, yes. I hope . . . Dorian, what happened? Something is wrong. There wasn't a city gathering scheduled, so why is everyon . . . ouch!" Aurah stumbled, and Dorian caught her shoulder to support her—the one the brute had torqued.

"Aurah!" Dorian's voice picked up some energy, and he released his grip as she flailed for a second. She caught her balance and breathed out slowly. She wasn't accustomed to pain, even minute pain like what was plaguing her now. She had lived in the palace her whole life. About the worst pain she had ever felt was accidentally kicking something that wouldn't move, or a burn on her skin—though there was a time when she had cut her hand on a broken piece of glass. She gritted her teeth and moved past the soreness.

"I'm sorry. I'll be fine. My shoulder is only a little bit sore." She breathed out slowly again as they kept walking. They had to get through the packed crowd and make it to the palace gate. "Dorian, why is everyone here? What is going on?"

Aurah turned to look at Dorian. Her eyes widened slowly as she took him in. The stoic man's face was pale and blanched. A ghost haunted his eyes as he navigated the flood of people. He tried so hard to be reserved.

44

"Dorian?" Aurah's voice trailed off. What was she seeing in the captain?

"I'm sorry, Aurah…" Dorian slowed his words, his thoughts seemed to escape him. "The guard this morning who came when we parted, he took me to some scouts from Avante, the nearest city to here—only a day and a half's march away. They . . . ." He trailed off, his blazing green eyes dampened, murky with something she couldn't quite place. "They brought news that Avante has been completely wiped out by the dragon. Not a soul is left to tell the tale of its destruction." Dorian's voice cut off as he stared forward, distracting himself by maneuvering through the square.

The dragon.

Here.

This close to the Capital.

Was there nothing safe anymore?

Terror gripped Aurah. She knew what was diminishing the spark in Dorian's eyes.

He's afraid.

She knew because she was terrified.

Everyone was.

Aurah's broken thoughts were interrupted by the looming metal of the gates. They had arrived. Dorian barked out a few commands to his men, and they opened the gate slightly to allow Aurah to slip through. The rest of his guards stood together, forming a wall and making a pocket of space to allow the gate to swing open slightly.

"I'm sorry, Aurah. I need to have one of my men escort you the rest of the way. I need to stay out here and manage this pandemonium. Will you be fine?"

He looked at her. Gentleness fell from the man's eyes. *Warmth.* Aurah felt wonderful next to this man. Nothing could get to her while he was beside her. She smiled at him and his struggling demeanor. Before she wasted another second thinking, she leaned in and kissed him on his clean-shaven cheek. *Warmth.* Love could dispel the dark shroud that fell on them all. She was excited about the prospect with Dorian, and she wanted to help him however she could. Maybe the kiss would empower him to face the oncoming despair.

Dorian stared at her, a look of shock ringing through his eyes. Then a smile broke his face, simple and small, but so deeply genuine. Maybe it was those beautiful green eyes, which sparkled brilliantly again, that conveyed the depth of the man's appreciation?

"Thank you, Aurah." Dorian was either at a loss for words, or he determined that he didn't need to say much. "Rest well. I will see you later." The smile broadened slightly on his face as he handed her off to another guard. She smiled back.

"Be safe, Dorian!" He gently motioned her to continue towards the palace, turning back to create a wedge between her and the raging calamity.

CHAPTER SIX

"We cannot allow this outrage to continue!" A voice roared. "The damage and destruction from this creature is absolutely unacceptable!" The argument was becoming heated again. These men had such a temper whenever they thought someone was insinuating they were wrong.

"I understand that, Phileaus. I merely was bringing up the point that we have no methods, strategies, or means to fend off an attack from this creature!" The original voice rebutted Phileaus's outburst. *More squabbling.*

"What about our siege designs? How is the progress on those weapons? They would certainly be able to damage and fell such a creature!" Yet another voice whined, begging to prove itself.

Elizabeth rubbed her temples. Even in the face of implacable danger, these men felt the need to be heard. She was tired of the constant bickering the counselors proffered. They were the reason for indecision and the failing nature of the Kingdom.

They are the reason justice is the weak, pathetic slop that it is! But I'll deal with all of that soon enough. . . .

"We are having trouble integrating our designs into practical applications." A slightly intimidated voice filtered into the argument. "In short, even with the developments we have come up with, our weapons would not be able to match the capabilities of a dragon. The dragon is too quick and agile, and these are just too slow and clumsy!"

The chief engineer, Arius, had disagreed with the modifications from the beginning, saying the weapons would never rise to their idealized usefulness. He was prone to launch into new lines of theorized weaponry. Elizabeth liked the man more than most of the Kingdom's other advisors, but he often failed to hold back on his tirades, berating everyone about the need to shoot the moon in the various realms of technology.

"Some engineer you are! Our kingdom is at stake and all you have done is complain about being tasked with a little hard work." Another voice rose up, attacking the engineer.

Outrage.

The voices began a new bout of shouting and insults.

Shoving her chair back, Elizabeth grabbed the nearest gavel she could find and smashed it into the table repeatedly until the head broke off and went flying. The rage rolled off of her shoulders in desperate heaves. The room quieted, as the red in her eyes glowed violently.

"If you men can't devise a solution peacefully, I will evacuate this great city, leaving your worthless carcasses to distract the beast. I want answers—now!—not your miserable excuses!" She was screaming. Every man sat down slowly. She may not be queen yet, but she would remember them when she did ascend the throne. "Now! Let's take an assessment! We don't have a plan. We don't have a weapon. We don't have any information about where or when this beast will attack. We don't have the means to transport what little we do have, and we don't have the resources to establish permanent standings for any of our pathetic solutions! Is this correct?" Let them feel her anger. This madness had gone on long enough. There would be no kingdom left by the time she ascended, and her next birthday was imminent.

The men took a second, a minute even—there was no perception of time in this room—before they began to nod vigorously. She breathed deeply and calmed her nerves.

"So, we know what we don't have. What do we have? Take a minute to assess your personal areas and present a summary—and make sure to leave your opinions where they belong." The men quickly glanced down to their scrolls and scripts. They all knew the information inside and out, but no one wanted to make the Princess believe they weren't taking her seriously. Temples throbbing, Elizabeth sat down and rubbed them again. It was like scolding children—and she had never scolded a child in her life.

Phileaus spoke first. *As usual.* "Your highness. The treasury is well-supplied. The wealth of these previous years has truly been bountiful. We are thirty-four percent above our usual funds."

Elizabeth ground her teeth together. *Two-faced, throne-kisser.*

"Our siege weapons have witnessed significant improvements to speed, accuracy reloading and all-around efficiency due to her highness's focus on improved implementations. However, while our technology may be able to damage a dragon, the likelihood of doing so is minimal and not cost-effective."

As we have heard. Repeatedly.

Elizabeth scowled to herself. Arius was reliable. In the brief time since the beginning of the dragon's attacks, the improvements the engineer had made to their technology were outstanding. If they ever got past this dragon crisis, they would certainly have the means to crush the rampant lawlessness found throughout the land. She was just frustrated at the impossibility of the situation.

"Milady, at your request, our guards have all undergone the specialized training. They will be instrumental in raising a standing army, should the need arise for such a force."

Joy.

Maximillian, the general of their forces. He was a terrific commander and of a reputable character. He had been the general since her father's reign and soon hers. He was a close friend to the royal family and the throne; that fact would never change, even after the tragedy that stole so much from Elizabeth. *And Aurah.* Elizabeth would not tolerate a weak justice as her parents had. She would make sure real justice was served to the criminal filth that would steal even life. No one would get a second chance to harm another. Elizabeth focused back on the report being given. Even in the midst of her other councilors squabbling, Max remained indifferent and untouched by their quarreling.

The rest of her advisors continued with their reports. Food storage was in good standing.

They had lost cities and an unforgivable amount of the population. Too many had died by the monster's attacks.

Their agriculture thrived again this year.

The situation wasn't bad, except for the dragon.

They had many resources, but to confront this enemy they would need more. They could only guess the most likely scenario and plan for it. She hated feeling helpless.

"Gentlemen, we have no options to confront this beast as we please. We have to prepare for it in the most likely scenario. It's a gamble, but it's all we have to be prepared defensively. Now that we have that cleared up, what can we do in anticipation of the beast?"

The councilors shuffled their documents in silent contemplation. Phileaus stood, pacing his thoughts out. Max, quiet as ever, folded his arms and dropped his head in meditation. No one liked to admit their weakness, but everyone knew she was right in her assessment. The silence lingered.

Elizabeth leaned forward, pulling the chair closer to the table. She placed her elbows down and held her head, beginning to breathe slowly. The stress was crushing. Would she lose her kingdom after all? Would justice be quelled and smothered? Even if it was weak and ineffective?

"Your Majesty." A hand gently touched her shoulder. It was an attendant.

"Yes, what is it?" She snapped a little before catching herself. She hoped they would understand the situation and not be hurt by the slight snarl in her voice.

"Aurah has returned from the city, Your Majesty. She is in the hall."

The attendant hurriedly moved out of the way as Elizabeth stomped towards the hall. That girl better have had a good reason for being out this morning. As Elizabeth approached the door, the attendant promptly jumped past her and opened it, standing to the side. Elizabeth could be quite fierce.

As the attendant closed the door behind Elizabeth, the light in the hall dimmed from the lack of a window. Elizabeth found Aurah standing alone against the opposite wall and barely contained herself from lurching across the floor to close the space between them. Aurah looked up to catch Elizabeth's expression, and her head dropped just as quickly in reaction. The monarch's steps stuttered for only a moment before she wrapped her arms around Aurah. Elizabeth felt a slight flinch in response before she felt Aurah fully lay into her arms.

The breath escaped Elizabeth's lips in torrents as her lungs heaved slightly. Her biggest fears were over. The stress was gone. *Well, mostly.*

"Aurah, are you alright?" Her lips breathed out into her sister's hair. Her grip squeezed tighter. Aurah moved to hug her back, she said nothing.

"Aurah, I know you speak the same language. Are you alright?" Aurah was playing her games again, Elizabeth needed her to be a little more serious right now, but she didn't want to totally drive her away. "If you don't answer, I promise to have the cooks cut out any sweets from your meals." Her mouth broke into a slight grin. She loved to tease Aurah and would have gone further, but Elizabeth needed to hear Aurah's voice. She needed to know that everything was alright.

"Mmmmmmm." A grunt. A mere grunt.

Alright, then. Elizabeth leaned forward to whisper in Aurah's ear. *"Forever."* That would break her.

"Uh! You're so cruel, Elizabeth!" Aurah's voice was muffled from speaking into the Princess's shoulder. Elizabeth's brow furrowed, not knowing how she felt about that reaction.

Frustrated?

Angry?

"I'm cruel? You didn't even let me know you were planning to go out to the city this morning! I mean, that's fine and all—you have my blessing, and you are a great worker—but what were you thinking? I could have sent an escort! Didn't you ever think that I would be *destroyed* if anything were to happen to you? The world isn't right yet, Aurah." Her mouth hung open slightly as if wanting to say more, but she couldn't.

Upset.

Scared.

"I'm sorry, Elizabeth. I hope you won't be mad at me for long." Aurah still didn't look up.

Elizabeth reminded herself that Aurah knew the truth of her love, so she squelched her anger. "I'm sorry, I was just so worried. It's never been a problem before but with these recent attacks—and then the news came in this morning, and the city's panic . . . ."

"And you think I'm graceless." An offhand comment Aurah thought necessary.

"And I know you're graceless." She could almost feel Aurah smile into her shoulder. By The Face, she was probably smiling herself. She pushed Aurah's face away so she could see it. Taking a step back, Elizabeth took a look. Aurah still avoided her gaze when she noticed dirt marks and a few scruffs in her dress. "Aurah, what did you do?"

"What do you mean?" Her gaze diverted even farther.

"Why is your dress dirty and destroyed?"

"Oh, that."

"Yes, that. Unless you tell me the truth right now, I really will starve your sweet tooth." Her eyes rolled at how ridiculous her comments were. No matter, the girl had had her chance to be a little more serious.

"It's nothing, I just tripped and had a little stumble . . . and maybe a slight . . . ." She ended her explanation with a long ummm.

Expression plain, Elizabeth grabbed Aurah's arm and pulled it up to view, twisting it. Aurah winced considerably. "That's a lot of scrapes and a really big bruise from a *little stumble* and a really big *ummm*."

"Ok. A little bit bigger of a stumble then."

"And the *ummm*?"

No response. Elizabeth had waited for an answer but received none.

She rolled her eyes again. "So be it. I'll have the dress patched and cleaned." She let Aurah's arm go. "It's fine if you want to keep some things to yourself, but just look me in the eye and tell me honestly you are alright and that there isn't anything pressing with which I need to deal."

Aurah finally looked up into Elizabeth's eyes. Knowing how purposely childish she was acting she broke into a big guilty smile. "Yes, I will be alright. The day went well . . . all things considering, that is. The Bakers send their love as always. You should really visit sometime. Morris would absolutely love to meet you, and their bread is fantastic! Oh, could you make sure Dorian has the support he needs to deal with the people outside? It's terrifying out there."

Elizabeth smiled at joy coming from Aurah about the city. The girl really loved it and the people there. There was, however, something interesting in the girl's words.

"Oh? Dorian is it? Why do you care what Dorian has to deal with? He is a mere captain doing his duty." *Take the bait, Aurah.* Elizabeth could hardly contain her smile.

"Well, we ran into each other on our way to the city this morning. He escorted me to the square and sent me off on my way..." Aurah's words faded. She had taken the bait *and realized it a little too late.* There would be no mercy for her when it came to her interests in men. This made Elizabeth feel *much* better.

"Go on, Aurah." Elizabeth did smile now.

"And . . . ."

"*And . . . .*" Elizabeth was ruthless. It wasn't her fault the girl was easy to tease.

"And . . . ummm." A fierce red fell across Aurah's cheeks. Elizabeth's eyes widened before she laughed with sudden understanding.

"Well, I'm glad the *ummm* had captain Dorian involved. I will make sure he is given a medal for his service to the Princess's loyal handmaiden. Though I doubt he will take anything, all the while saying, 'love is a reward in itself.' " Aurah turned with a loud groan, facing away from Elizabeth.

"You really are cruel, Elizabeth!" Aurah shouted. Still smiling, Elizabeth moved forward, wrapped her arms around Aurah, and lay her head on the girl's shoulder. Aurah immediately winced, flinching away. She turned slightly to catch Elizabeth's eye and raised an eyebrow.

"*Ummm?*" Elizabeth asked.

"*Ummm.*" Aurah nodded. Her eyes closed for a moment. "Elizabeth, is any of it true?" Her eyes opened back up innocently, looking straight into Elizabeth's soul—so ready to be attacked by the grievous burden of reality.

"I don't know what you heard, Aurah, but... Avante has been destroyed. By the dragon—*a* dragon. We haven't been able to confirm if there is only one or not. There is so much about the beasts that we just don't know." Terror filtered across Aurah's face as her hand raised to cover her mouth. Elizabeth knew Aurah was afraid of dragons—everyone was. "There are no survivors that we know of from the city itself." Elizabeth's throat seized as the reality of that statement hit her. "The soldiers you may have heard of that came to inform us were a scouting guard returning from their patrol to find their city destroyed and their families gone." Tears welled up in her eyes now.

"Elizabeth . . . ." Aurah grabbed her hands. "Will you be alright?"

Tears began to form as Elizabeth finally let loose a little of the emotion dammed up in her heart. Aurah moved close and hugged her, soothing the sorrow that was ripping at Elizabeth's soul. This was treacherous. There was no way to describe adequately the atrocity of the situation and the bleakness of the future. *The lack of justice!* Elizabeth's face set firm.

"Thank you, Aurah. I have to go now. I'll see you soon. Do me a favor—just respect my desire for your safety and stay at the castle until we can clear this situation up." Voice jittery with emotion, a few of the words cracked as she pulled herself back together.

Aurah nodded positively. "Just don't take away my desserts."

Elizabeth snorted at the unexpected humor. "Of course, dear. Now, I know you have work ahead of you. I will see you later." She kissed the top of Aurah's head and turned back towards the doors.

Those councilors better have used all the time she just gave them to devise a good plan. Their lives depended on it. Their future depended on it.

Aurah depended on it.

CHAPTER SEVEN

Timid footsteps skirted around in the shadows. What was it?

What was it?

Where did it come from? Instinct told them to run, and many of them already had. Their lives depended on silence. *Still and silent.* Only a few remained.

What was it?

The gentle gusts of wind fell into a steady cadence. The ground trembled slightly to match.

Stay away from the unknown.

It seemed to be warmer the closer they came to it.

What was it?

The wind reeked, and a putrid stench permeated the proximity.

Run.

What was it?! The closer they got, the more their fur raised. The world was changed.

Run.

Slowly it came into view, the shrubs and growth parting enough to give a glimpse.

Run.

It was *huge.*

Run.

Just a little more and they would know.

Run!

One more step.

A stick broke.

A sharp crack pierced the air.

RUN!

Heartbeats raised, every brave animal scattered and forsook their homes. Their instincts screamed against their curiosity.

The thing was alone again. The animals were gone. Gentle breaths escaped in a steady cadence. The ground shook from the beat of its lungs. Its heart hammered, pumping blood through the monster. Rolling over, it broke more of the forest in a crescendo of cracks and groans.

Kast lay on the ground, deep in his dreams. Peace was becoming of the curled and resting beast. Sleep was his only solace anymore. What had he become?

He rolled again in his sleep. As he sprawled out, his foot knocked out a tree. It fell precisely onto his hindquarters.

A screaming roar tore throughout the air.

Kast bellowed in pain, launching out of his sleep and onto his feet. The forest crunched underneath him. He kept weight off his rear leg and examined it. A big, murky spot had appeared, covered in dying scales. The humans managed to *hit* him. The wound had split open and bled slightly where a tree had fallen and crashed on it. It was painful, seizing and cramping. He had to work through the stiff muscle and make it loose. *The pain.* Kast gritted his teeth and winced.

Breathing out slowly, Kast began to drop his leg and stretched it towards the ground. He would work through it. The claws on his foot managed to reach dirt. A minor victory, but he had to keep going till the pads of his feet rested comfortably. As he pushed a little further, the muscles spasmed and Kast lost all ground that he just took. Pain ripped through him. He belted out a mighty roar and fell opposite his injury and lay on his side. His leg hung in the air away from the ground. It hurt. *A lot.*

"Scum." Hate seethed from his maw. He hated humans. He hated pain. He hated everything. *He hated every day he had to put up with this miserable reality.* Pangs shot through his body again, and Kast growled violently. He forced his breath to relinquish the desire to heave. He would not be humiliated like this. Rolling completely on his back, he used a fallen tree to prop his leg off the ground. It didn't feel broken, but it was deeply bruised to his bones and joints. It would take another day of healing before he could leave. Another sleep.

On his back, he managed to lay low, just below the tops of the trees of the forest. He was lucky. There was no way he could have made it home after so many assaults in a row. Now, this forest hid him for the moment. His head fell back, resting on the brush beneath him, to stare at the sky.

What was he thinking? There was no way any of this would help anything. There was no way this could find the answer and fulfillment he sought desperately.

But it was all he had left.

Right?

Who cared anymore?

He felt the grip of insanity just at the fringes of his mind. Darkness swirled, looming, waiting to dive in completely. Ready to consume. His actions of late seemed increasingly inspired by that insanity. Maybe he was already lost.

His breath caught and tears began to well up in the great dragon's eyes. He had done everything, hadn't he? He tried so hard, yet his greatest efforts amounted to the same as his dung! It was all so worthless. Chained to the meaningless cycle of day and night. Gripped by so pathetic an existence. There was no way out.

Well.

There was.

Kast shook his head. He shook his head hard as if trying to throw those thoughts out of his mind. So many other dragons gave up or gave in to their hatred. He knew the stories.

Once, he had come across a crater filled with the bones of a dragon who had impacted the ground with purpose. Kast flew and flew, fleeing the death that he found in that pit and the seductive desire towards release from all his pain. He hoped never to find that place again.

He shuddered violently.

How could such a proud and noble creature be broken to such a weak and enfeebled state? They were capable of such grand designs. But the world, he guessed, had a way of breaking down even the mighty.

No.

Light flared for a second, opposing the darkness in his mind. Glorious light.

Unknown light.

He wouldn't be overwhelmed!

Right?

No! He would persevere!

Can you?

He was going to achieve greatness! He would fulfill his purpose!

No, I won't.

"Go away!" He screamed as anger seized him. He let out a burst of flames straight into the sky.

He would never listen to the voice inside telling him he would fail. He . . . .

I will never overcome.

He fell, lifeless, on his back as his thoughts fought the same old war, on the same old grounds, in the same old way. He would never escape his fate. He would never fulfill his purpose before the insanity took him and led him to a place of hate and death. He could never conquer himself.

He had to fulfill his purpose before the darkness completely took him, no matter what.

Somehow.

No matter what.

His mind moved back to planning. What should he do? He had to fulfill his purpose no matter what. *How?*

Obviously, the chances of the human's cities producing the answer were slim. Five cities to that day—*six actually*—were razed in the name of his purpose. His attacks just kept getting wilder and wilder. Reason played into his plans less and less. Instinct guided him. He just needed to fulfill his purpose. He had to!

I have to . . . .

Yes, he knew that already! Why couldn't he focus? Blast this biting insanity! Nothing made sense anymore.

Failure . . . be angry.

The humans had what he needed. He would destroy every last one of them to find it! He liked the sound of that. He would *kill* them all, if necessary. They wouldn't keep him away from his purpose. They would never keep him away!

Now things became clearer. He had to murder that trash. He had to crush them all!

And the next attack would lay it all on the line.

What?

Where did he get that idea from? Why the next attack? Why everything?

Failure. Fear.

There was no point going on. This wretched life could burn. Good for those people who thought it worthwhile. Good for them. *Good for that . . . .*

"Trash!" His anger raged out into the world again. His hatred welled up, and his scaly chest pumped uncontrollably. The look of sheer malice coated his face, and he became resolved — resolved to murder humankind, to make it all or nothing. This was it. If it didn't happen next time, it wouldn't happen *ever*. All or nothing. If there was anywhere that held the solution, this would surely hold the answer—the key to his purpose.

Yesss.

Who cares? He sighed, resolved. He had his course set. There was only one place left.

He fell back into his slumber, *resolved*.

If only his insanity hadn't gripped him, then maybe his instincts would have warned him of the eyes weighing on him, watching his wild ramblings. He wasn't alone. Though, what would it matter if he knew who those eyes belonged to anyway? It wasn't going to affect his purpose.

Kast slept, resolved. He had his course set. There was only one place left to go.

One place, if any, which would hold his life's purpose.

One place—the human capital.

CHAPTER EIGHT

Charlie sat removed from a group of his men playing dice, just on the edge of their circle. He had a lot to think about.

It was impressive, the flow of a rumor. How quickly the ebb and tide of word of mouth carried the news. He had seen the soldiers come racing into the city, filled with fire and . . . *dread*. They had a look in their eyes that was indescribable. Charlie pitied them. Men were men, and being who he was, he cared about his men. He found that care extending even to others, not under his command.

He took a swig of his drink. The dirt helped to mellow out the rancid flavor. It was wet and . . . well, *wet*.

Where had that girl come from? That was all he needed to worry about. It was more than enough to keep the kid alive by passing him off as a new recruit. *Stupid Murdoc.* Worthless guard.

Anyone with a brain would know that Lizard Guts didn't have anything to guard. Instead, they needed to make sure to keep any poor soul from wandering into their doom. His chair held him as he leaned back and reflected on just how close that girl had come to death.

Good thing that. . . .monster had been gone.

Charlie had no name for his *boss*. He could only refer to him as the monster for lack of a better name and refusal to acknowledge his humanity. Charlie clenched his knuckles around the mug's handle before raising it to his lips. He had no idea how a human could commit the atrocities that monster did. Another swig and the bile burned his throat. *Good stuff.* They weren't allowed to have much of it anyway, so he might as well go as strong as he could. *Only The Face knows how badly we really need it . . . .*

His stomach knotted as his mind wandered to The Face. Many viewed that cliff as a god because of its incredible size and the stories told about it. Charlie knew better though; if it were a god, then it would have stopped that monster in his tracks long ago. He looked at the swirling liquid in his hand. The drink, or lack of it, hadn't been the cause of his unease. It was the band of mercenaries' profession—*hunting dragons.* The group was aptly named Lizard Guts by one of the numerous commanders before him.

Charlie let out a sardonic laugh. The dice stopped rolling as his men looked up and stared at him for a second. They turned back to their game quickly. It was a usual outburst, and they didn't dare bring it up. Didn't care either.

The group's name had managed to stick among the members. Charlie had been one of the rare men who had lasted this long. Lizard Guts had a peculiar chain of authority. Charlie was only the commander, and everyone thought him as the head of the whole troop. To them, there was nothing else. His position was the greatest point of advancement— but the truth was, Charlie was merely a puppet for the hidden master.

Charlie didn't know much about that monster—and he didn't want to, either. Charlie was not some yellow-bellied piece of work, but he was like a little child to that…*thing.* Charlie tensed, and his fingers thrummed on the tabletop lightly. Charlie was not the head of Lizard Guts, and he didn't like to think of the monster who was.

That monster went through commanders like fire in a hayfield. But not Charlie. There must have been something worth keeping him around for.

Charlie caught his thoughts from wandering any further, then shook his head. They were all prisoners to Lizard Guts once they joined. It was a life sentence, and no one, except Charlie, knew why.

Whatever. It didn't matter. It never did. He just was glad to keep order among his men. *And kill dragons.* He really didn't mind the work.

Pangs of regret rippled as he dove too deep. He downed another swig.

Empty.

He scoffed, examining the bottom of his mug.

The bottom always came so quickly, a sad reminder of how fast a man could fall in life. The bottom. First, you're full and then . . . you're dry and empty.

The wood table cracked loudly as Charlie slammed his empty mug into the smooth top. Charlie leaned back in his chair again.

The dragon.

The big bad dragon. This one seemed to carry a different air to him. They were weird creatures, always acting . . . *unusual.*

But that monster always seemed to figure them out. He was ten steps ahead of them! Lizard Guts would have burned to a crisp before it had started if it weren't for him. And there were . . . secrets. Things he did that made Lizard Guts work. The best part was that everyone thought it was Charlie who was running the show. They called him boss and listened to his opinion as law. Charlie scoffed again.

He didn't make any of the decisions. Charlie listened to that monster and obeyed. Perfectly. *Like a suckling babe.* Maybe that was why he was still in charge—because he realized how minuscule his being and position really was. He was nothing but a front to give that true beast a face. Charlie clenched his fist, then released it. That monster didn't seem to care if he was known or not, and Charlie wasn't inclined to talk about it. This led to a lot of uncertainty about how the commander achieved his position. There was always a challenger or two at the beginning of a new commander's leadership, but *they always went missing.* Some of the men understood there was something larger going on, something bigger than the commander, but that monster only ever talked with the commander in place. Even that was rare—thank The Face. A bead of sweat ran down Charlie's face. He had to be careful—even his thoughts didn't seem to be safe from that monster.

Charlie stared into the lodge's shadows for a moment before wiping the sweat away. He wouldn't be fooled. Lizard Guts was expendable. He and the rest of the men were fodder to help distract the dragons they did face. *We create openings.*

As if openings were needed.

He shivered at the remembrance of how every fight ended. The butchered beasts. Killed in . . . ways he just couldn't process. He wiped more sweat on the back of his sleeve. These thoughts made him uneasy. You didn't mess with that monster. Charlie tapped his fingers on the table nervously. He hated sitting around and waiting. He hated giving his mind berth to roam freely. He too often found himself reliving the worst of memories. Of past battles, of lost men, of . . . .

Whatever.

He leaned forward, reaching for his drink before remembering he had drained it already. *Blast it.*

Now they were ten steps ahead of this dragon, and as always, he had no idea how to deal with the mess. He could only keep the men disciplined and give them vision. Maybe that was his true purpose beyond providing a leader's face for Lizard Guts. A shepherd of sorts—someone to keep the flock together and out of danger.

He snorted. The men didn't even look up at his laugh this time. *Some shepherd.*

He caught his hand reaching for his mug again, then gritted his teeth.

"Ughhh! Skinner, make room for one more!" He had had enough of his thoughts. All they were doing was making him thirsty.

"Sure, boss," the one named Skinner answered. He grabbed a few of their makeshift tokens for the game and another set of dice while the others slid around to make room. He might as well distract himself in some fashion. Besides, it was good for a leader to be a presence among his men sometimes. He noticed the kid was among the group playing the game.

"Kid, you're doing well, learning when to speak." The kid had been silent all day, only breaking into a slight conversation during the game. *Good.* He needed to learn that there was a time and place to speak—and a way and reason, as well.

He saw the kid's jaw clench, biting back the all too familiar, snot-nosed remarks of his. So, Charlie had managed to get through to him. It didn't matter if the kid hated him, at least he had his life. It wasn't an easy lesson. *But this wasn't an easy place.*

"Tell you what, how 'bout I..."

"Not interested." The kid locked up again.

He had to be only just coming of age, not even a full man yet. This was hard for him. Charlie gave him his room, though. He didn't need to pile on any more difficulty.

Everyone had frozen in anticipation. They had all heard of their boss's little scuffle earlier. They were wondering if he really would follow up on cutting the kid to bits. In their eyes, Charlie was at times worse than the dragons. Well, those who hadn't realized something bigger was going on, that was.

"Whatever. Just don't forget our little chat." Charlie dropped the conversation and hid in the game. He was good at hiding his emotions. *He had to sometimes.*

The game progressed with little conversation. The presence of the men's boss brought a certain discomfort to the group, but it was mostly just the tension between Charlie and the kid. *Ungrateful brat.*

He looked at his roll, hidden from the other's eyes. Charlie would win the game right here and now.

Come. The deepest feeling of being beckoned ripped Charlie's attention from the game, racing through his veins.

"Whatcha got, Charlie?" the man named Skinner asked.

No answer.

"You there, Charl . . . sorry. Never mind." The man fell silent, looking away. The other men immediately caught on, and the kid's eyes widened.

Charlie was completely frozen. The game meant nothing now.

Come. The feeling of being beckoned intensified.

Sweat beaded on his arms and skin, his hands became clammy. *This . . .* this was never easy.

"Quit lounging around!" he yelled, pushing back his chair and standing. It took every ounce of effort not to scream. Was there nowhere safe?

The urges in his mind answered for him with the deepest impression of the void. *Nowhere.* Then . . . *mania.* Charlie blanched. Of course not. There was nowhere safe. *And this was that monster's game.* Turning violently, Charlie slammed into the chair he had been sitting on, knocking it over. His pulse quickened. The few beads of sweat from earlier were nothing compared to the torrent pouring down his skin. *Terror.* Charlie edged gingerly across the floor to the shadows, the hallway leading to his—that monster's—den. He could hear the men behind him watching. Their breathing screamed a testament to the fear they held. Fear from something they could never fathom. Something…that monster.

Charlie plunged from the light into the dark, a beacon of death calling him towards his doom.

His mind screamed. *Don't go! Don't go! Don't go!*

Come. Come. Come. The pressure on his mind responded. The evil joy conveyed to Charlie's mind was overwhelming. *Such despair! Such darkness!*

He lost his reserve and trembled. He fought for his composure. He had to be secure. *How?* He moved with more certitude, but the jitter never left his step. The hallway was short, but somehow it was infinite. The few candles lit on the walls seemed to be swallowed by the darkness, surrounded on every side by the *black*. Charlie shivered, and the battered wood creaked silently underneath his feet as if trying to muffle its own noise so as not to draw attention. *All of existence was cowering from this monster, and I'm heading right for it!* Charlie bit off most of a whimper. Such an unseemly noise. *Nothing was seemly here.* Was that a tear in his eye?

The hallway seemed never to end. Charlie's chest throbbed, heaving as he breathed in the stale air. Slowly, he counted his steps. One, two, was it fifty? A thousand? His heartbeat raced, and his tunic was drenched in sweat. He came to the end of his existence outside of the door that the pressure on his mind led him to. *How did this room contain the beast?*

How?

The pressure seared his mind and screamed the question back into Charlie's thoughts. The pressure changed its message—*the room.* Charlie became entangled with the deepest need to open the door. Every primal instinct raged against it, but who was he to deny that monster? There was no resistance.

The door.

His hand trembled as it reached for the door—the very gate to the netherworld—and he willingly pursued its secrets. *Please!*

Open. The pressure overwhelmed his pleading.

He counted to three and blasted through the opening.

Charlie fell onto the floor of the room. The fear in his mind fed his adrenaline and strength—but there was no need for it. There was no resistance to the door. It was just a door, after all. No, the door wasn't the problem—it would move. It was what swirled in the shadows beyond the door that would never move, no matter the adrenaline or force Charlie exerted. Charlie's eyes were fixated on that movement as he inched slowly past the mock security of a wall. His eyes widened at the sudden flash of the monster's mottled cloak into the fading light before it disappeared back into the shadows.

A crude, sick, laugh cackled out into the recesses of the dim room. The monster was laughing. He found Charlie's fear amusing, or maybe he found the terror that he inspired sublime.

Stand. The idea in Charlie's mind manifested irresistibly. That monster never spoke—never. He only dived into other's thoughts and planted his will there. Charlie obeyed that will. It was like drowning and thrashing around, doing whatever would bring air and life again.

Look.

Charlie tried to calm himself to observe, but the terror gripped him. His stomach was turning inside out every second he steeped in the blackness.

Displeasure. The pressure displayed displeasure. Charlie would have feared for his life right then, but the terror backed away, relieving Charlie of its weight.

Look.

Charlie could think clearly—or at least more clearly. The fear crushing him relented, though only slightly.

The first thing to cross his relieved senses was the putrid smell of death coating the room. *Blood.* Why did Charlie smell blood?

Then he saw.

It didn't matter if that monster had lifted the terror from the commander's being. Charlie felt sick, and his already destroyed stomach dissolved even further.

A large body lay on the floor. Its head was across the room. Charlie heaved out the drink from earlier. It was Kurtis. He

A DRAGON'S PURPOSE

could tell by the man's filthy hair. *Blasted drunk*. Charlie knew the man was heading straight to death with all his drinking. The last Charlie had known, the man was assigned to scouting and reconnaissance in the palace square earlier. Kurtis had never checked back in when his shift was over. Obviously, the monster had known where to find the man. There was no escape. Charlie had no idea what Kurtis had done, but it was obviously the wrong thing.

The pressure confirmed His thoughts. *Trash, rot, filth*. Charlie's knuckles clenched. He didn't know how he felt about the death of one of his men. Charlie had tried his hardest.

A muffled cry pierced the air, hooking Charlie's attention. What? *Where?*

More evil laughter belted outwards. The shadow paused its swirling for the moment, enjoying the scene before Him.

Charlie looked into the depths of the room trying to find the source of the noise. *There!* In the corner on the floor, three silhouettes lay huddled close together weeping. A man, a woman, and a child. Charlie couldn't see them, but the monster poured the repugnant information into his head.

Scum . . . the monster didn't like them. The pressure showed Charlie the people standing against that monster by confronting Kurtis. *Bakers . . .* a strange thought from him. Why did he care who these people were? Charlie tried so hard, but he couldn't save everyone. *Please, just put them out of their misery quickly.*

Immediately, in response, a purple orb glowed violently out of nowhere, lacerating the blackness. It launched to the corner and caught one of the people. A sickening thud popped through the air.

"Morris!" A woman's high-pitched scream pierced the air accompanied by the shrieking of a child. The noise warranted two more purple spheres to appear quickly from where the darkness swirled, flying straight for the corner. There was no pop this time, just an immediate quelling of the cries.

70

Specks of blood had appeared on the floor in front of Charlie. He clenched his teeth; thankful the darkness covered the horror before him. He had joined Lizard Guts in hopes of revenge. How aghast he was in finding out that the monster hidden under the surface here was just as bad as what he desired to exact vengeance upon. At least the family went to the afterlife together. Charlie envied them.

Worthless. The pressure painted the bakers into Charlie's mind. Then Kurtis. *Better.*

Charlie understood what he meant. He nodded, though the gesture was unnecessary. After all, the monster could see what was in Charlie's mind.

Another.

Charlie's brow furrowed. His terror had receded, allowing Charlie to think more clearly, but what did he mean?

"Charlie?" A small voice, frightened, chipped up from behind.

No! Charlie's mind screamed, toppled by the sheer force of understanding. *No!*

Yes!

Yes. The pressure in Charlie's mind conveyed pleasure. A tear fell from his eye. He wouldn't look—he couldn't. He had tried so hard to protect him. To protect the kid, but now Charlie had failed. *Completely.*

The pressure implanted Lizard Guts' orders in Charlie's mind. *Go.*

"Charlie . . . ." Astonishment fell from the boy's lips. He had no idea what was coming. *None.* The snot's voice alone nearly shattered Charlie's fragile facade. "Charlie, what's going on? I'm scar—"

The kid's voice cut off. He must have noticed the monster swirling over in the shadows. Charlie grimaced and turned, not paying attention to the kid. "Charlie!" the voice screamed desperately. Out of the corner of his eye, Charlie saw that the swirling darkness had pitched forward, entangling the kid in

71

that monster's horrible cloak as it dragged its prey back to the black. The noise of frantic scuffling and immediate sobs of horror rang out from the darkness. Charlie could barely hear the bones cracking over the kid's shrill screaming.

Charlie flung himself into the hallway, then back into the light—out of the darkness.

The kid's screaming never stopped.

He, that monster, was always—

"Form up outside, scum bags! We've got work to do!" Charlie belted the orders to the men.

He was always—

The group playing dice jolted violently. They had heard the screams. They were shocked to see Charlie come out, leaving the kid behind. The sounds of murder billowed forth from the clutches of darkness.

Charlie could read their faces plainly. They looked at him with trepidation. So, their boss had dealt with the kid after all. *Fine, let them think that!* He didn't need them to understand in order to protect them. In fact, maybe his men would obey him better if they feared him. They would listen to what he had to say, then he could protect them better. Charlie clenched his teeth. "Out, now!" He screamed. Every ounce of fear, anger, and pain exploded out in his voice. The men filed fast, leaving everything but their gear behind.

He was always—

Charlie waited for a second, as men had already begun to stream from the second floor, pouring forth from the many rooms of the abandoned lodge they had claimed sometime before. Tears poured out of his eyes. He would be the last man out. He would make sure everyone left in a timely manner. He would protect them.

Protect them from that monster.

Because he wasn't even human. *No way.*

He was always—

Charlie kept a keen count. The last man rushed by and out the door to the alley. Charlie followed hard after him and slammed the door shut on the fading screams. *Like the lid of a coffin.* Charlie sealed the kid in his tomb.

Then sudden silence.

A faint breeze moved through the alley, trailing across his skin. Charlie wiped the incessant tears from his eyes before turning outward towards his awaiting men.

Death.

He was always—

The alley was silent save the odd step from his troop. The place was dark enough in the day but had steadily grown pitch black with the coming night. This was the same alley where he had barely managed to save a girl's life earlier.

He yelled out to the men, barking his commands. No guards patrolled this abandoned section of the city. No one was around to hear the screams. *No one.* Charlie clenched his fists. His soul was rent in half. Another piece of himself torn to shreds and burned. He would never forgive Murdoc or any other man who failed to keep the innocent away. *Never.*

—insane.

Charlie moved with purpose. It wouldn't be long now before the world ignited into chaos. And they had work to do.

Always.

CHAPTER NINE

Aurah sat on the balustrade overlooking the city, her legs dangled to the terrace below. The wind whispered quietly, brushing her hair as if to tuck a stray blonde lock behind her ear. She was mildly fond of the color and the shape of her hair. It fell in waves to her shoulders with a slight curl. She reached up to twirl that stray lock in her fingers, as had been her habit since her little escapade into the city two days ago.

The evening sun had started its descent to the far horizon. Aurah couldn't help but wonder what lay on that horizon, now that it seemed the very seat of civilization was doomed to relocate there.

Aurah let go of the lock of hair to rub her jaw and chin. She had been clenching her teeth nonstop since that frightening day. She had nightmares of that alley, of those voices, of the crowds, of that drunk that attacked her. Her teeth clenched again, causing a spike of soreness. She massaged it gently before focusing on the city.

The completely vacant city.

Empty.

That was the best way to put it.

The city, or her life?

She didn't know. It was such an emotional time. First, fear of the worst reigned in her mind. Then, when the worst came, anger followed suit. Then there was sorrow, replaced with rage, followed by depression, hurt, confusion, rejection, and an impossibly infinite other awful reactions. Aurah tensed, suddenly consumed by the emotion, and slapped the railing.

"I hate you," she whispered out to the world. Her fist clenched suddenly. "I hate you!" She yelled outward to the sky before her voice cracked and fell to whimper in harmony with the wind, her arms wrapping around herself. Together they sang a song of the deepest sorrow for who knows how long.

Aurah stared, trying to take in the city as much as she could—the place that she loved so much. It would probably be one of the last times she would ever stare at her home; the streets that swam like veins through the turbulence of buildings, all rising above each other, vying for attention.

"Hey." A warm voice spoke out from behind her, hesitating. "How's it going?"

Aurah looked up, towards the voice. Tears had begun to stream down her face from the recently sung elegy. *Dorian.* Revealing her eyes to the man, the shift in his weight seemed to say he felt the weight of her grief.

"Oh! Dorian . . . I, I'm fine." Aurah could barely contain the surging emotion as she brought her arm up to wipe her eyes. She started when she found that the Dorian had come close and sat on the balustrade beside her, his hand resting gently on hers, those gleaming emerald eyes seeming to pour their light into her dreary world. Her breath caught and invisible tendrils constricted her chest.

Then tears, weeping, and sobs. Aurah fell into Dorian's arms. Somehow, that man-made his armor soft, the cold bits of metal and the hard leather comforting. Aurah cried harder at the thought that she was soaking him with her tears. There were no words. There was just the gentle pat of Dorian's hand on hers, while his other hand stroked her back. The smell of oil and sweat lightly cmanated from the uniform, covered by what smelled like scents of lavender. Aurah gripped Dorian in the tightest embrace she could muster. Soon her tears softened to gentle heaves and huffs. Dorian removed his arms and sat back slightly. The sudden end of the embrace was like a bitter shock for Aurah. She watched the captain remove his glove. She watched his gentle green eyes speak kindness, and his strong hand war valiantly by wiping the battalion of tears from her eyes. *Only the most courageous of men could have fought the war with those tears.* A deep sigh welled up from the pit of her belly and crawled its way out, ending with Aurah lurching back into the man's arms.

"There, there, Aurah. Everything will be alright." Silk and honey crested her ears. Aurah clenched his leather tunic hard. His gloveless hand continued stroking her blond hair, tucking that stray lock behind her ear. "Do you need someone to tell about everything?" Every syllable was a strike against her sorrow. Aurah sat up and wiped her eyes.

"It just hardly seems fair . . . you know?" Her voice rocked at first before gaining confidence. "I just . . . I just wanted everything to work out right and then the world blows up." Aurah clenched her fists together. "I'm sorry. I'm fine." She turned her head to avoid Dorian's gaze. She didn't know how to make sense and describe her emotions well, and she didn't want to wear his patience thin with her ramblings.

A hand caught her chin gently and tugged. Her eyes met his deep green ones. His hand didn't remove itself from her face, but instead, his thumb caressed her cheek before letting go and falling away. Aurah sniffled but held in the tears and reveled the feeling of wanting to just soak in this man's consolation.

"You don't have to be fine if you don't feel like it, Aurah." Dorian smiled gently, encouraging her forward. Aurah chortled slightly.

"A girl's got to ask how a man came to be so caring." Aurah smiled shyly. She didn't care anymore if she were revealed, though. The idea of being with someone like Dorian was more desirable than her safety. Dorian laughed back.

'Well, Sarah." Dorian shrugged casually. "Mom died when we were young, and Dad never came back from a scouting patrol . . . I took care of Sarah and was there for her just like she was always there for me." Dorian swung his feet around to hang them towards the terrace below, like Aurah. They both sat there for a moment in silence staring at the empty city.

"I'm sorry." Aurah looked over at Dorian, a new understanding in her eyes.

"For what?" Dorian smiled at her.

"Well, it shouldn't happen. Children growing up in a world without their parents. It just . . ." Aurah trailed off, turning back to stare at the city.

"I asked Elizabeth and she told me all about the both of you."

Aurah sighed.

Not a lot of people knew the truth about her and Elizabeth. She looked back at Dorian. Not a lot of people knew, and she was glad, but she was thankful that he knew. It was a piece of her history that she was ashamed of, even though Elizabeth had reinforced many, many, times that Aurah had had absolutely nothing to do with what happened.

"Yeah . . . ."

"I'm sorry. If that is overstepping the line, I didn't mean to . . . ." Dorian looked like he was about to make a tactical retreat immediately.

"Oh, no! It's not bad. I usually prefer to not burden others with the past, but for some reason, it's really comforting to know I don't have to hide that from you or try and find a way to tell you." Aurah bit her lip, and looked down, sneaking a glance back at Dorian. *Please don't have ruined this!*

"Aurah . . . ." Dorian spoke slowly. "If you can manage it, please don't worry. I really appreciate how strong you've been despite your circumstances." He let out a small sigh and then smiled at her. "Now, it makes a lot more sense to me why finding a gift for Elizabeth was so important to you."

Aurah looked up as the captain paused to collect his thoughts. "Elizabeth has been with you since the beginning, and for the longest time, she was all you had. The idea that something is going to rip her away must be dreadfully scary. I'm sorry you have to face that."

Aurah let her hand wander on the balustrade and draw imaginary patterns. They sat still for a time, the gentle breeze coating them and the sun beating away the autumn chill in the air. She looked up at Dorian, who turned to look into her eyes.

"Thanks, Dorian." Aurah gulped and turned to face the city. "I know it hasn't been easy. For either of us, for that matter. I'm at a loss for words. I don't know what to do. I haven't given Elizabeth her gift yet because I'm skeptical about it. Even if the gift were a wonderful way to solidify my bond with Elizabeth through the vicious changes ahead, what do I think now? The whole city is evacuated because of the high probability that the dragon is on his way here now to destroy the pinnacle of civilization itself. At least, that's what the advance guard signaled to us. So how do I stay strong through that? How do I fix things, Dorian? How do I make sure I don't live the rest of my life hurting? How do I keep Elizabeth and everything I know and love? Why does this have to all be so personal for me? I . . . I . . . I'm sorry. That's all so selfish of me, it's just—I can't figure out how to be okay right now. I feel like I'm losing everything all over again. I'm being herded like cattle. If only I was interested in eating grass, then maybe none of this would hurt as it does."

Aurah stilled for a moment, silent and thinking hard. "I just want everything to be the way it should be, and right now, I don't even know what that looks like." Aurah sighed.

It was like her very insides had been ripped outward, exposed before Dorian. She didn't care, though. As intimidating and daunting as it was to express her fears, it felt good. Dorian sat quietly, staring at the city. Aurah wiped her hands on the front of her skirt. *What is he thinking?*

"Aurah, I think you're one of the most fantastic, stalwart, brave, and wonderful people I have ever had the pleasure of getting to know. I've served alongside men who have crumbled under less pressure then you bear on your shoulders."

Dorian looked straight into her eyes. *Oh my.* If she thought his eyes were weighty by nature earlier, it was nothing compared to what felt like him using his eyes to convey truth. Maybe she wouldn't crumble from all the problems she faced, but she would crumble any day under his emerald gaze. She felt the weight of his soul through those eyes. His pressure was so profound. So, she giggled and blushed. Dorian's face broke into a grin. They stared at each other, smiling genuinely.

"Dorian?"

"Yes, Aurah?"

"Thanks." She turned back to look at the city but kept smiling.

"No problem." Dorian turned to look at the city as well. They sat for a moment before Dorian spoke up. "So, what is the gift that you got for Elizabeth?"

Aurah groaned. "Gosh, I don't know. I had finally found the curiosity shop after running into danger in what looked like an abandoned alley—"

"Wait. You did what?" Dorian interjected, startled. He looked at Aurah, his mouth agape.

"Um, well . . . I got lost. It turns out that maybe Elizabeth is somewhat right about me being . . . ." Dorian raised an eyebrow at Aurah. "Ummm . . . well, being a little bit careless sometimes." She smiled sheepishly at Dorian, who groaned, though his smile grew wider and somehow his eyes grew softer.

"Do I want to know?"

Aurah smiled bashfully again, though she couldn't help but feel mirth between them. "No, I don't think you do. It takes only the most fantastic, stalwart, brave, and wonderful kind of people to come through that kind of ordeal." She smiled without shame as Dorian reacted to her wit. Aurah's heart crumbled when he smiled back. *Wickedly.*

"I wonder then what kind of person it takes to deal with a drunken brute?" His eyes leveled with hers, his smile never ceasing. Aurah dropped her smile, assuming a look of horror.

"Dorian . . . ." Her hand moved towards the shoulder the brute had hurt.

Immediately the captain's face paled, turning ashen. "Aurah . . . I'm so sorry. I didn't mean to be insensit—" Aurah's sharp laughter interrupted him.

"You're cute, Dorian, but you make a battle of wits a little too easy." She smiled gleefully at him. He couldn't help but smile back, shaking his head.

"Anyway, Aurah!" He grinned at her playfully. "The gift?"

"Oh, yeah!" Aurah spun on the railing and slipped off, moving to a pile of her things. She grabbed a small bag and brought it back to Dorian. Aurah carefully pulled the necklace out of the bag and handed it over to Dorian. He examined the necklace, his face remained impassive until he spoke.

"Well, my gut tells me there is a certain meaning behind this jewelry." He spoke thoughtfully, considering his every word before speaking.

"Otherwise, you think I wouldn't have settled for something that would usually be considered an insult?" Aurah asked. She was hoping that somehow Dorian would pull together the meaning of the necklace for her and help make it a gift worth giving. Maybe he could help her feel okay with moving forward?

"That's probably the plainest, easiest, and best way to say it, I guess. Though, despite what you may call your ability to be lackadaisical, I think you're level-headed and unlikely to ignorantly sabotage yourself. I think that if you felt it was okay to get Elizabeth this gift, even if pressured—no—especially if pressured, I value gut instincts, then I think it's going to be a fantastic gift. I am curious, though, as to the meaning behind it, if I may ask you to share." He smiled at her and handed back the necklace.

"Well, the old man in the shop gave a story about dragons that is somewhat contrary to our view of dragons nowadays. He said that dragons are creatures capable of the most powerful love, but unfortunately, even they can be tainted and drawn away from their mandate to love. This necklace seems to be an embodiment and representation of the deepest love ever known. That's why when the bell was ringing, I couldn't help but hope it was true and decided it was good enough." Aurah shrugged, holding the side of her head and grimacing. Dorian opened his mouth to respond when another voice spoke up from behind.

"I think it's an excellent gift." Aurah and Dorian turned sharply.

It was Elizabeth.

Dorian leaped off the balustrade to stand at attention and saluted smartly.

"Oh, knock that off, Captain. I feel like there is hardly a need for those kinds of honorifics at the present moment." Elizabeth walked gently towards Aurah.

"That may be true, Your Majesty, but it is order that will carry us through these uncertain times. I intend to uphold that order and maintain justice." Elizabeth paused for a moment and looked at Dorian.

"Well said, Captain."

The Princess turned back to Aurah and smiled gently. "Come here, Aurah." Aurah moved more slowly than Dorian off the balustrade. The Princess laid her head on Aurah's shoulder and pulled her tightly against her. "I love you, Aurah. You have always been by my side. I don't care about politics, or formalities, or anything like that. You are my family and I love—." Elizabeth's voice cracked as a tear fell from her eye. "You will always be in my heart—no matter what." Aurah's tears began to fall afresh alongside her sister's. "Now, love, may I see the pendant?"

Elizabeth ran her hand over Aurah's hair as the maidservant lifted the necklace. "I heard your explanation to Dorian, and I know that maybe we all think terrible things of those monsters, but the very idea that you are giving me the greatest love possible will always rest by my heart." At that Elizabeth took the necklace and settled it around her throat. "See? It really is next to my heart, love." Aurah gripped her sister in a tight embrace again, tears silently flowing down her face. "It's alright, Aurah. I know it's scary and I know it's hard, but everything will work out one way or the other. Everything will be alright."

Elizabeth stood holding Aurah for what seemed like an eternity, stroking her hair. Dorian stood at attention the whole time.

"Now, Aurah." *What is this?* Aurah lifted her head curiously, confused by the sudden change in Elizabeth's tone. "I need you to listen closely, *very closely.*" Something screamed inside of Aurah's chest. Something that somehow knew what was coming. "I . . . I need you to leave the city with the rest of the citizens. Now, no questions. Move right to . . . it . . . ." Elizabeth dropped her hands to her side and became placid like a rock.

Aurah stared in horror at Elizabeth.

"What are you saying, Elizabeth?" *Hold it in. Don't lose it.*

"I'm saying I no longer need you in my service. There is no life for you here anymore. I want you—no, I command you to leave my side." Silence.

Awful silence.

"What are you saying, Elizabeth!" No longer a question. *Why? What?*

"Aurah, you are hereby formally dismissed from your duties as a personal handmaiden to the royal family. You are to evacuate the city with the rest of the civilians and move towards the relocation point. Captain Dorian here will be your personal escort." Elizabeth walked past Aurah to stand before the railing, staring at the city. "Now, go."

"Elizabeth!" Aurah screamed. Sense was senseless, direction was gone. There was just the pain of her heart ripping asunder.

"Captain, reports say that the dragon is nearly here. You must get her out of the city immediately!" Elizabeth shouted violently, never looking back at her sister.

Aurah swiveled her gaze to latch onto Dorian, who took a step in her direction. Betrayal coated her features. A look of pain shot through his.

"Now, Captain!" Elizabeth screamed, drawing Aurah's attention.

Dorian lurched and gripped Aurah's arm.

"Get off me!"

"I'm so sorry, Aurah! Please don't fight. Please come with me! Please!" She didn't submit. Dorian scooped a flailing Aurah off her feet and turned, moving quickly towards the way out. Aurah fought harder.

"Thank you, Captain. Please . . . take good care of her." The sounds of weeping rose from where Elizabeth stood, barely audible over Aurah's sobs.

Dorian moved fast, faster than Aurah thought he could while holding her. They were soon in the vestibule where they met two days before. Dorian moved to go through the door, but Aurah managed to grab the doorway, hanging on with everything she had.

"Aurah, please! You heard Elizabeth! The dragon is almost here! We need to go now!"

"No! How could you do this? I shared my heart, and you hate me! Why do you hate me, Dorian? Why?" Aurah let go of the doorway suddenly, causing Dorian to over-pull, toppling them both to the ground in a heap. Aurah lay on the ground, broken in a thousand pieces. Weeping. It was all really being ripped away. Elizabeth, her life, the city—

"Aurah, please! I know it doesn't make sense, but what Elizabeth did was because she loves you. I don't have more of an explanation than that. I can't convince you, but you have to trust me. Staying here to die won't be loving Elizabeth!"

"Why does she have to stay and die, Dorian? Why can't I do it, too?" Aurah shouted at the man, hate filling her heart.

"I don't know!" The captain shouted back. *Was that anger?* "I don't have the answers, and I wish I did. I wish I could have expected this, but I didn't." Aurah's mouth hung open at the realization that Dorian was in as much of a bind as she was. Her eyes suddenly dropped to his hand. *Gloveless.* He had left part of his armor behind. No good soldier would be so unprepared if they were expecting what was coming next. Dorian was caught off guard and in as much difficulty as she was.

Aurah's stifled her sobs. *Later. Or never again. Whatever.* She looked Dorian in the eyes. A different kind of passion radiated from them. *Was that fear?*

"You're right. I'm sorry. I won't fight you. Please get us out of the city." Aurah found the captain's bare hand and squeezed it, hoping to reassure him. He nodded his head and stood abruptly, pulling Aurah to her feet.

"We need to make it to the stables near the east gates. There are some horses left there. Aurah, I'm sorry for everything. I hope I can be a light of hope and comfort for you after this, but I don't expect you to forgive me or want me after this. All of that is secondary, though. We need to go now. The dragon is likely to be here any second." His voice carried a slight quiver at the thought of the dragon.

Aurah nodded slowly, but then looked into his green eyes. "Dorian, please don't ever leave me. I couldn't handle losing you, too." Tears welled in her eyes, hoping she hadn't ruined everything with him.

"I will always be there for you, Aurah." He smiled quickly at her, then looked at the skies as if the dragon were spying on them. "Let's go!"

Dorian turned, pulling Aurah forward.

Towards the future and away from everything she had ever known.

CHAPTER TEN

Kast hovered, hiding his large presence in the cover of the clouds. The sun bore down relentlessly onto their tops and his back. His eyes found breaks in the misty canvas and observed the city below. The Capital. The city of cities for the humans. It looked measly and pathetic. His body strained against itself. The sinews and tendons—every muscle—warred to barrel downwards and *murder* the humans. What an ache from the desire to see it all burn. *But control said not yet.* What was left of his control, at least. He needed to hurry if there were to be any chance at salvaging himself, a rescue from the sure insanity that loomed in his mind. He flew a distance, staying away from any holes in the cloud cover, to find a new vantage as he spied on his enemy. It didn't take long before he realized the city was emptied. No, not completely. The smell in the air was faint, but it was there. What were they were planning? The humans?

Failure. Be angry.

His body lurched again, ending in a vicious snarl. A glare seeped from Kast's features. His bones trembled at his impossible, undeniable *hate.* He fought himself back with a significant struggle. *Not yet!* He couldn't just charge in. Right? *Why?* Every inch of his teeth ground together as he combed through what glimpses of the city that he could.

Failure. Fear.

Maybe it was too late? Maybe all of the people had left? Maybe this last attempt had been completely stolen from him? Maybe it was too late? Maybe he would never fulfill his purpose? Maybe.

Failure.

"Wait," Kast spoke aloud, his eyes glazed over and lost himself in the realm of his insanity to be consumed by his singular goal.

Failure.

Something brilliant occurred to him. Inspired. Pure. Right. *Divine.* Why was he hiding again? They were humans! Not an enemy worth the thought!

Failure.

His mind plunged into visions of the coming devastation, entangling itself in the pleasures of the screaming and pain.

Failure.

His fire must burn.

Attack.

Kast blasted forward, plunging straight towards the city— *no, the ground*—he would stop short if he aimed short. The air whistled by his ears and the city presented itself, raging into his vision. He pulled sharply out of his dive twisting his whole frame into a spin along the length of his spine, alleviating the force of his descent. *Excellent dive.* He was barely above the tops of the...*buildings.* The gales he generated tore the structures directly underneath to pieces, razing many of those buildings to the ground. Nearby buildings and farther away down this *street,* roof tiles ripped free, flying off their perches, and shutters were easily persuaded from their windows. Kast dropped and landed in the street. It was terribly cramped for a creature of his size. The stone of the street cracked beneath his feet, his wings brushed the tops of the human structures, and his sides nearly spanned the whole distance between these buildings which opposed each other across the street. He let out a mighty roar to announce his arrival.

But no man stirred.

He growled as he waited for something—anything—to happen. Nothing did, though. Kast glared at the world around him. Something was wrong. The smell of fear wasn't tickling his snout if it was even there at all. He leaped back into the air, flying slightly above the rooftops. He circled, steadily ascending higher with every pass. His nerves were taut and his vision sharp.

The air felt wrong. His scales raised along the length of his spine in apprehension. He didn't like this. Where were the people? He didn't like being ignored. He, a mighty dragon! He would change their minds. Kast broke his ascent, and swam through the air, lining himself up with a stretch of buildings. Let them see his mark, maybe this will wake them up.

Kast sucked in the air around himself, his chest expanding outward, he launched his wings backward and shot forward.

Burn.

Kast breathed out his majesty. His fury would not be contained. The world below was bathed in a wealth of fire. Everything melted under his power. His grin broke out as the flames trickled to a stop. This pleased him. *So much.*

He must have more.

More!

Undeniable power—they all must know him!

Kast readied another bout of his heat, his wicked glare fueled by the destruction beneath him, and he rocketed forward through a particularly dense and susceptible section of the city *that would burn.*

His enjoyment lasted only a second more, the bloodlust clearing, as he suddenly came to a dreadful realization.

Everything had lined up. *Perfectly.* How had he been so blind to miss it?

He, a mighty dragon, had just fallen for such a simple trap, and it was now sprung. His force still carried him forward, while the corner of his eye told him a story.

Of pain.

Failure.

The humans launched their projectiles of rocks and sticks, their course lined perfectly with his own. The nearby structures erupted around the dragon, who spun his body to dodge the hailstorm. Jerking uncontrollably, Kast slammed into the surrounding structures. Adrenaline's beat bellowed in his ears.

The rain of missiles thrummed through the air and blasted the rest of the own buildings into insignificant pieces. Kast carried forward through the flurry, his body seeping the liquid of life from being impaled and pummeled.

He found his distance and landed gracelessly. His limbs refused to move. He threw back his head and neck and belted out a mighty roar, breaking what was left of the virgin silence. Windows shattered everywhere from the force of the scream.

Kast turned to look at his body, already tremendously sore and pained before this attack. Horror scrawled out on his features. His glorious armor bore signs of the sticks hitting. Swaths cut through his rows of deep brown scales. He grimaced; some of the projectiles had stayed attached. Bruises littered his hide and blood poured out everywhere.

Kast slowly started to quake. Puffs of smoke cascaded from his nostrils.

"They. Will. *Pay.*" Each word seethed from his maw. His glare blackened and decayed the world.

Failure.

Without a second thought, Kast grabbed the few bolts lodged in his hide and ripped them free, his shrill whines piercing the sky, but he didn't stop. Determination flared through his veins, trickling across his hide. *Or was it insanity?*

Failure.

He had to hurry.

He grabbed the next and pulled, and then the last, ignoring the tremors from his nerves.

His body screamed. The new holes were not welcome. He had to get a vantage point quickly. How had he missed them? *Mere men!* He had been looking. Right? He would fly above and check again, above their measly reach. He wouldn't let the trash mar him again. He would end them and their precious city.

Failure.

The ground gave way as the mighty beast threw his weight into a launch.

Wait.

Those weapons weren't maneuverable. He knew that from the past fights he had been in with the humans. They couldn't have made mobile a weapon that large. At least not with such a little amount of time to plan and prepare. Could they?

No.

Failure.

They were placed there and hidden in preparation. They knew he would observe before he fought. They set the trap. They knew his movements.

They knew his movements.

His instincts screeched at him, and light sparked in his eyes. They were waiting for him to gain his bearings. They were waiting for him to do what he was about to do. They knew how he would respond.

Failure.

Still launching upwards, he twisted himself and changed direction, heading straight for the previous siege weapons instead of the air. The movement now cost him much agony, but they wouldn't expect the counterattack so soon. *And their plan would be ruined.* He raced back the way he had just come. It hadn't even been a minute yet; the clumsy weapons would be unable to attack. Kast would catch them unaware.

He ripped through the stale air. His previous flames had surmounted to nothing. They would pay. He would find pleasure in their torment. He must kill them.

Failure.

The buildings passed as fast as they came.

And then he was upon them. A broken building collapsed nearby, and the earth trembled with his immediate presence.

He was right. His instinct was good.

Failure.

Adrenaline slowed time. He could see every face turning to stare. There it was. The smell of terror. Oh, the ecstasy.

Failure.

Shivers rippled through Kast's body at the sight of the rodents. They realized they had been bested. They could never have planned for his power.

Failure. Kill.

Kast swiped the nearest soldier into his claw and crushed the man, throwing what was left of his mashed carcass on the ground.

They would pay for their audacity.

Chest welling up, Kast incinerated them. The weaponry became cinders in but a moment, and their flesh boiled in the pots they called armor.

He breathed deep. Now the air was right. *There was fear.*

Let's try this again.

He angled his wings backward, pain a mere afterthought now. He leaped into the air and soared upwards, the plumes of his flames carrying him faster than any man would have been able to account for.

"Now, where are these rats hiding?" Kast broke into a wheezing laugh. Bloodlust had taken over again.

From his new vantage, he knew he was right. The humans had positioned many siege weapons around. How they hid them he had no idea, but most were aimed at his place of recovery, ready to catch him unawares.

Yeah, right.

An attack force coalesced in the nearby streets, set to finish the job when the dragon had been bested.

But it would not be so.

Kast's fire began to spread in a raging inferno, the heat warming his heart, igniting the passion in his eyes. He could fly now.

His wings snapped to his sides, throwing him into a descent straight at the rag-tag army hidden in the city's clutches. He laughed murderously, he lashed at the world, their misery his deepest fulfillment. Kast shuddered at the thought of his victory.

And then the fires stopped. Smothered completely. The charred remains were smoldering. The wind beneath his wings vanished, and the breath was wrenched from his lungs. The air changed.

What air?

Kast lost his advantage. He was confused. What had happened? Victory was his. It was within his claws. Slowly, at first, he felt it. Then more viciously he was surrounded by gales of air beating down on himself. His chest pumped as oxygen sluggishly inflated the cavities. He had to fix his flight. His body teetered from the torrents of air crashing down upon him. Could he even manage that? What had happened?

Turning his head slightly to the side, his eyes widened in awe and then desperate fear.

A cloaked man with hollowed and bleak eyes stared into his very soul. He stood on a rooftop, raising a clenched fist into the air as purple light surrounded his hand and arm. Power seemed to ripple from the man's core, and darkness seemed to swirl around, pouring forth—*from the very essence of his being.* Kast felt like the spirit of who he was being drawn in and consumed by this man. There was no way something else had caused this strange phenomenon to happen. It had to be this man.

He just stared as the dragon flailed through the air.

Kast smashed into the ground. The unexpected change in air pressure forced a crash landing. He tumbled, rolling continuously, tearing up every sign of humanity in his path. Debris and buildings were flung everywhere. His massive momentum never ceased to carry him forward, past side streets and the waiting army of men that had been his target. A shame he couldn't have done more damage to the humans if he were to land in such an uncouth manner.

Failure.

Kast's claws latched into the street, raking trenches through the ground as his momentum dragged him. His legs uncoiled, throwing him to his feet as he still slid backward across the ground, slowly coming to a stop.

Failure.

Numbed to his pain, Kast turned to face maybe the greatest foe he ever would. He had no idea how things would turn out. He didn't care.

I don't care anymore!

If he were to fail and die, this was as good and surefire of way to go. His insanity comforted him and led him to a place of takeover.

Takeover.

Nothing mattered.

Failure!

The haze on the brink of his mind flooded in and consumed him.

Rampage.

Kast lurched into a mighty gait, his powerful muscles tensioning in one second and recoiling with an impossible amount of force the next. Buildings whipped by again as he retraced his crash path. *Infuriated.*

Here was the cloaked man.

The Cloak! Kast rasped his fury, laughing at his opponent's new name.

Jaws open wide, his legs unleashed, Kast threw himself forward in pure velocity. He almost had this man in his maw.

A few more inches.

Almost.

Almost was not certain.

The man spread his cape and flew backward, rising higher towards the sky. Almost as if catching the air from Kast's brutal charge.

Bad mistake, human.

The sky was not a place for man.

Kast caught himself from his failed leap and landed all four of his feet together on the street. His eyes aimed towards the sky that The Cloak had invaded. Wasting no time, he thrust his tensed muscles and power into the ground, taking himself and his momentum upwards. This man wouldn't be able to get away so easily, no matter what manner of magic he used to evade his enemy.

The span between them vanished in a blink.

Kast was the sole fury in the sky.

Again, the cloaked hero was ready, though. He spread his cape to catch the gales of wind from Kast's pursuit.

Kast's maw broke in a smirk.

Stupid pest.

Ready with his fire. Kast followed up his charge with the inferno.

The Cloak might control air, but Kast was a dragon, and he knew fire more than any human would. *Ever. Know. Fire.*

Kast's flames caught the very gales he had generated, sending the jet of fire trailing through the burst of air at a magnified speed to completely surround the Cloak—ending the man's antics.

Fool. Kast laughed wildly.

No human could match a dragon. *No dragon could match Kast.*

The flames waned, and in a whirlwind were extinguished. Swallowed by some unknown magic. Purple streamed from the Cloak's body as he somehow floated through the air—completely unscathed.

"Die!" Kast screamed, and his wings lashed backward in impossible angles. "Who do you think you are, you bastard?" He clawed through the sky to slaughter the trash.

Proud dragons never talked with men, but as proud as Kast was, he threw everything away in the insanity that now completely gripped him. Charging headlong without thought Kast rapidly closed what was left of the distance between himself and the Cloak. Before Kast knew it, faster than he could see, The Cloak had gently landed on Kast's face, staring deep into his eyes with that same, never changing expression.

Astounded by the intrusion, tremors ripped through Kast. His defenses were overcome, completely exposed. He knew it must have shown in his eyes because The Cloak's expression broke.

Finally, he cracked a hideous smile.

Utter, heart-wrenching terror.

Failure.

Failure.

Failure.

In the man's hands, powerful magic began to swirl, the magic emboldening to the point of being visible. Lights danced in front of Kast's eyes, blinding him. *Purple lights.* A purple orb of some kind of magic. Purple would be the color that ended his life.

His life.

No. Not life—death.

This was it. Here was death.

At last.

Kast let go of it all, gently falling into his failure and into his sweet release. Breath streamed from his snout. His wings began to fade in their beat.

He had lost. Who cared? He was resigned, one way or the other.

Kast's body slouched under the weight of his failure. Pain crossed his face, welling up in his eyes. If only he had fulfilled his purpose.

If only.

Failure.

The Cloak's smile changed into a grimace, then raised the magic, a signal of the death to come. Kast followed it; his eyes fixated on the light. The fluid magic finally seemed to solidify, and the purple darkened more than before.

It was ready to kill.

Kast's eyes never closed. He would watch death before himself. He could see the movement of the spell. He watched every ripple in the man's cloak. The way the man's face twisted, visible but hiding his mysterious thoughts. Kast watched the arm begin to drop. Slowly, inch by inch. So slowly—was this what it was like to see one's own death happen? *So slowly.*

Failure. Die.

All he could see was the haze from the magic.

He watched it come closer and closer.

He watched The Cloak's face change.

He watched flames begin to encompass The Cloak.

He watched The Cloak slowly turn and, instead, throw the spell behind him at something he couldn't see.

He heard a piercing scream shred the air.

What?

Kast snapped out of his trance. Wrested from his demise, a horrible flash of purple light erupted beyond the flames. The fire faded leaving smokescreen behind.

Kast's heartbeat picked back up. He had no idea what had happened. His veins thundered, carrying blood and clarity. Whatever it was, it had consumed The Cloak's attention, who no longer faced towards Kast.

A gust of wind shredded the veil and the smoke filtered away. What was left was a *thrall of dragons.*

There had to be over twenty dragons swooping and diving, a slur of shades of brown and a mix of sizes. All were slowly making their way closer to The Cloak and Kast—surrounding them, flaunting their power with spurts of flame from their maws.

Where had they come from?

Kast's blood ceased its flow, and his heart failed to beat for a moment, stuttering at the sight before him.

It was impossible.

His jaw fell loose and his eyes glazed over at the visions before him. He was out of his league, and there was no way back in. He was finished, he was beyond his capabilities. Why were his wings even beating?

Mere habit.

The Cloak showed none of the same awe Kast did. The corners of his mouth pulled up; his joy complete. More than Kast ever could have pleased him. Wasting no more time, The Cloak's knees bent and unfurled, casting himself towards the monsters. Magic was already welling up around both of his hands.

He was the monster.

Time began to operate normally again for Kast. The sound of roars pierced through the air. The Cloak harvested every ounce of misery from his victims, who swarmed and attacked in a fury. The harmony of the thrall's attacks surrounded The Cloak.

Beautiful.

A sharp blast tore through Kast's back, every ounce of air once again evicted from his lungs.

He rested in a crater, still and stunned, as the dirt and dust began to settle around his bloody and mottled form. His mouth hung completely loose, gasping for air. His eyes were exposed to the world from the surprise, matching his mouth.

The ground. He had found the ground. Or the ground had found him. It wasn't good either way.

He was certain now that he was well beyond his limit. How had he completely missed being launched downwards? He must have tumbled through the air with wild acrobatics to wind up on his back. There was no way a mere human had enough strength to scorn him, a dragon, so.

But why did he care? He had lost. His life was meaningless, he had just thrown everything away. There was no recovery from every poor decision that he had made. The humiliation he just witnessed must have cleared his thoughts to some degree. They were clearer than they had been in some time.

Why couldn't his mind be muddled again? This confrontation was painful.

He lay in the wreckage, the feeling in his body hinting at immeasurable pain to come.

Maybe come, that is. He knew his fate. He was resigned, after all.

He stared at the Cloak in the sky doing the impossible. Bouncing from dragon to dragon, dropping one after the other into the city below. The duels and fighting were drawn out. The combatants clashed, filling the air with a dull throb from containing their full capacity.

But still, the dragons dropped. All dead. Slowly but surely. Losing to a single man.

Kast's eyes followed a much larger and deadly looking dragon in the group take a couple passes at The Cloak, narrowly escaping his grasp but always managing to come away unscathed. From the corner of his eye, at the edge of the thrall, he noticed a much slimmer and sleek dragon hovering beyond the assailant's assault. Something in Kast—maybe his intuition—didn't completely abandon him in his insanity, and said this one commanded the thrall of dragons, even that much larger and powerful beast that darted in and out.

A dragon dropped right next to Kast's head, covering him in dust and debris.

What am I doing? his mind screeched.

Kast rolled over, cringing from the cries of his screaming body. He somehow knew he still had a chance. Maybe his intuition really was still there. Kast lifted his head, not caring to be cautious. Not knowing what he was looking for.

Somehow, though, the crash had cleared his head. Maybe it was the pain. Maybe it was the unexpected chance. Maybe he was faced with the reality that he would never fulfill his purpose.

Failure.

Stop it!

Without direction, Kast began to move as quickly as he could, his head on a broken swivel but searching, nonetheless.

He walked and walked, moving at barely more than a crawl. Much of the city nearby had been demolished, leaving him space to stumble forward. *Thankfully.*

What was driving him? It was all over anyway. The Cloak would be finished with the impressive thrall of dragons soon enough and then Kast was back on the list of those to kill.

Kast's thoughts clenched suddenly, and his body tensed desperately.

He froze as if caught in some spell by The Cloak.

But The Cloak is busy with the dragons above.

Could this really be happening?

Kast's chest began to heave unsteadily. The pain from before wasn't even able to do this to him. His legs nearly gave way. Tears rolled down his enormous face—the deepest reserves unstopped. His head had almost carried his attention past it—he had almost missed everything this *whole* farce was all about.

He retched at the thought.

It.

The fabled it.

No.

Not it.

Her.

She was beautiful. What had caught his eye? What was it about her? Why was this the answer? Why was she what his essence cried and longed for?

He didn't know.

He didn't care.

All that mattered was that he would have *her*.

CHAPTER ELEVEN

So empty.

Aurah hated the city now. Empty. Lonely. *Silent.*

She ran hard after Dorian, hoping to make something of all the recent hurt. They reached the street, and the world passed by quickly from the pace that Dorian set. She tried to console herself that everything would be fine.

Lies.

Aurah clenched her free fist at the thought. *Were they?* What was true? What was the good of the world that she desired so desperately? The city was destroyed. The man she had fallen for was stealing her away from her place of joy, and her closest friend had betrayed her.

Did Elizabeth really betray her?

She knew the answer. She just couldn't come to grips with the pain.

A large shadow and a loud whooshing noise stole her attention. Billows of gust threw her skirt around her in torrents. She threw her head around to see what the source of the sudden disruption was, and then she looked upwards.

Utter *horror.*

The dragon.

"Dorian!" Aurah screamed as the man pulled harder on her arm. It hadn't been long at all since they left the square when the dragon plummeted menacingly from the sky.

The dragon.

It had shown up after all. *The thing looked like the end of everything, prancing and parading through the air.*

"Keep going, Aurah!" Dorian screamed back again, barely looking at the girl or the sky.

The dragon had seemingly appeared out of nowhere wielding a mighty wrath. The world erupted into a mass of chaos and confusion upon its arrival. They ran through the streets now and cut across alleys. Aurah's dress hindered her somewhat. Dorian didn't seem to notice as he dragged her frantically. She grabbed the dress with her free hand, hiking it up as best as she could, while her other arm felt like it was being torn free as she tried to keep up. The dragon hadn't been here long at all, yet it already had changed her world. *It didn't even need to show up to destroy her peace, though.* Everything had been going so perfectly, then Elizabeth betrayed her, and Dorian, and the dragon. *The dragon.* Aurah clenched her teeth as she ran. Her feelings of fear seemed to be replaced now more with feelings of anger and even hate. *Whatever.* Now Dorian was saving her, and the dragon was continuing its vicious attack, with nothing standing in its way. Where was the retaliation Aurah had heard rumors of? All of this just couldn't be happening. It was terrible. *A nightmare.*

Dorian led her, making their way towards the eastern gates. Thankfully, the east gates were some of the closest to the palace. It wouldn't be long before they reached the wooden doors and were hurriedly on their way to catch up with the rest of the fleeing city. She squeezed Dorian's hand and felt more secure. Maybe they could escape to make something of life and rebuild. *Maybe.*

Aurah snuck a glance behind her. The dragon was back in the air again after setting foot in the city. The sheer destruction the beast carried was impossible to comprehend—like the size of The Face. The dragon dived, flying right at them and releasing its legendary flames. Aurah winced in reaction to the fire but, it seemed to be out of range. Debris scattered, launched by the magnitude of the wind force from its wings.

"Aurah! Look out!" Dorian stopped suddenly, turning to slam into Aurah, throwing her into an alley that was nearby. She lost all her thoughts in the confusion.

Slowly.

Aurah saw the debris now. *Where had it come from?*

The gleaming green beacons of Dorian's eyes turned and stared at her. She saw everything at that moment. A small smile broke his face. Those beautiful emeralds sparkled with a joyful gleam, speaking an undeniable truth.

She would live.

Immediately, a splintered wooden beam, like a hound, found Dorian and impaled him, crushing him against the wall above Aurah. Gusts of wind whipped by carrying other bits of debris, *and threw around the color red.*

Aurah screamed.

Gasping, she covered her mouth or tried desperately to move her hands to cover her mouth. They flailed uncontrollably at the sight before her.

Real?

She screamed more, shudders growing into the shrieks that pieced above even the wind.

Dorian's mangled corpse fell from the wall. Aurah tried not to look, but she couldn't shut her eyes. She lost control of her whole body. It refused to move. Her fingers raked the broken wall she leaned against, and the stone street beneath her. Her mind trying to find some bit of reality to grasp. *Something. Anything. Please!*

Dorian.

It happened so quickly. There was nothing. *Nothing*
Nothing.
Nothing.
Nothing.
Nothing.

Nothing.
Nothing.
Nothing.
Nothing.
"Nothing!" Aurah screamed the only word she knew. Her eyes were wide, taking in everything, yet seeing nothing. One hand tried desperately to scrape the pain from her face—the other clawed across her scalp. The girl collapsed completely and lay in the alley gasping. Her body couldn't breathe right. She couldn't understand what she was seeing.

Where was she?

What was she looking at?

Dorian—his eyes! Before her. Muted and blackened by his death.

Aurah lay heaving. She retched all over herself and passed out.

Elizabeth stood, enraptured by the destruction before her. Her tear-stained eyes were welded to the scene.

It was impossible.

Impossible!

But reality continued before her, challenging her every denial. Who was the man in the cloak? Where had he come from and how could he fight on even ground—*no*, higher ground than the beasts that ruled the sky above and the earth beneath?

Her mouth gaped, tasting the bitter wind of dust and ash. The foul reek of death wafted on the billowing currents of air. She clutched Aurah's gift around her neck. A new habit was formed for when the Princess was overwhelmed.

There was no way this was possible.

Her steps thudded on the stone terrace as she ran along the balustrade. She turned to see the first dragon laying in the wreckage of his fall. *Dead?* She could only hope. The problem was that now there was a whole thrall of dragons raging above the Capital. So much pandemonium.

And that man...

Had fate had compassion on them, after all? That would be the only explanation for the sudden appearance of an adversary to the dragons. No human had ever trumped one of those beasts, yet that man was in the dragon's territory of the sky, fighting what looked like an army of the monsters—*and winning*. Elizabeth was amazed. She couldn't remember the last time she had been utterly astounded, but *this*. This was *awesome*. She stared at the sky, trying to follow the fight. The raging collisions resounded through the air and beat in her chest. She lowered her head and massaged her neck from looking up so much.

Aurah.

Elizabeth's mind moved frantically to the girl. She made a fist and slammed it into the stone railing. The pain in her hand was nothing compared to that in her heart and the confusion that welled up, challenging her decision to have her sister removed. It hadn't been that long since Aurah had been hauled away, screaming. It was even less time since Elizabeth had heard the end of those screams. Pangs of guilt ripped through the Princess and she shook her head. *Betrayal.*

No.

It was the right decision. There was no way Aurah would have survived here with the dragon's attack. Elizabeth didn't completely understand her own actions herself, why she felt the need to stay behind with the city. She couldn't explain the feeling, but she knew she needed to be with the city when it was burnt to the ground. The city was a part of the ruler. A deep part. If she lost her city, there was no point to continue forward. She would only be a hindrance as a ruler of a broken and burnt kingdom.

Aurah, though, had to go on and live. The Princess's sister was innocent in all of this. A humble servant. The girl deserved a chance to live a peaceful life with which she was enamored. Elizabeth was grateful for the chance to employ Dorian to be the one to lead Aurah away. She would grow attached to the man and find peace beside him. Elizabeth shook her head, trying to alleviate the guilt. Aurah had to survive and make something of the poor life that fate had handed them.

Something caught her eye.

Elizabeth had nearly missed it. The movement was so . . . *subtle.* She leaned forward, gripping the balcony's handrail, and stared into the shadows of the city. *Shadows. No, men.*

The city should be empty except for the few reserves of soldiers selected for the fight—and they were elsewhere in the city out of sight.

Why then are there men running through my streets?

Without thinking, her glance shifted to other parts of the city, searching vigorously until . . . .

There!

More men.

And there!

The more she looked, the more she saw.

There is an unknown troop operating in the Capital. My city! Elizabeth stood, dumbfounded by their appearance on top of everything else happening.

What do they want, and why are they here? Her mind raged at an answer on the brink of her thoughts.

Of course! Realization pieced her mind.

Her eyes shot to their cloaked savior.

They're his.

Her hand covered her brow, dampening the glare of the sun that decided to peek through the cover of clouds above.

Impossible.

Her reserve broke as she watched the cloaked man. She let out soft gasps, her breathing clutched in her lungs. Then the battle above changed.

The beasts are desperate. They are all diving at once! Impossible! She stumbled backward, trying to take in the whole scene before her.

Could she trust their unknown savior to prevail? In unison, the dragons swung down on the man. The whole kingdom's finest offensive plan fell in shambles faster than anyone could follow. Those beasts were mighty foes, and now they stood at the mercy of a cloaked man and his mysterious soldiers.

After some amount of time, her hand moved down to her chin as her mind raced to conclusions.

What should they do?

What can we do? She scoffed at their weakness—her weakness.

Her neck cramped from staring up high for so long. She dropped her head and relieved the knots in her neck again. She looked up, ready to process the battle.

And her heart caught in her throat.

CHAPTER TWELVE

Aurah woke with a start shortly after passing out. She rolled immediately and faced the far street, quenching her vision. *There was nothing there. Nothing to see. Nothing.*

Nothing.

Nothing.

Nothing!

She clenched her fist and immediately sprang from the alley floor. She ran to the street, away from her soul, which still lay heaped on the ground, *broken by evil incarnate.*

She looked up in the overcast and cloudy sky. Barely astounded at what she saw anymore, yet her heartbeat still spiked and called out the lie of her temporary asylum. A speck in the sky that looked a lot like a swirling cloak was flying and bouncing through a horde of massive bodies. Not just bodies, but—*dragons!*

Aurah's mouth gaped. There had only been reports of *one* dragon. Now there was an army of the beasts, and they were attacking that one speck in the air. Her eyes widened.

"Is that a man?" Her thoughts brazenly escaped her lips, betraying her facade.

She ran back towards the center of the city, where she had just come from. *What was she doing?* The battle beckoned to her, maybe there would be a sense of justice for . . . .

She didn't know and didn't care, either. She had lost her soul and a chasm lay in her heart.

She filled it with muck. *Just get over it.*

The only thing she had left anymore was . . . *Elizabeth.* Who's Elizabeth? She couldn't place the person in her memories.

Oh. *Remembrance.* Elizabeth. She had thrown Aurah away though, *hadn't she?*

No! Never!

Not Elizabeth, Elizabeth loved her. Elizabeth was her sister, the only family Aurah had left. The only thing worth striving for.

Aurah ran, changing her direction towards the palace instead of the city center.

Curse this blasted dress! Aurah grunted in frustration. She stopped running through the destroyed street—the world had erupted in such a brief time. She reached down, grabbed the fabric at the hem, and tore as hard she could. It wasn't as easy as she had imagined, but she pulled harder and eventually the dress let go of itself. It tore unevenly, but it would suffice and allow her to run. She did the same to the other side. She would have to apologize to Elizabeth for tearing another dress—her sister would be angry at her again. That wouldn't make much sense though since the dress had already been covered in . . . blood.

Blood . . . .

"Nothing!" Aurah screamed suddenly, clutching her head violently as she tried to catch the breath that infinitely eluded her lungs.

Nothing . . . .

Aurah jerked forward in a desperate sprint. Elizabeth was in danger, and Aurah had to save her! Maybe tomorrow everything would go back to normal. Aurah didn't ponder much, as she had to get to Elizabeth's side. Free from the inhibitions of the dress, the world flew by even faster than before. The battle above erupted with violent forces blasting outward.

Each time one hit Aurah, it felt like her heart stopped in her chest. She was heaving after a short time running, but she had to save Elizabeth.

From what, you stupid girl? She cut to a sudden stop and chided herself. It was good not to run. She breathed, trying to recover what the sprint had stolen. The city was in shambles with many buildings decimated. It was amazing the palace had remained so intact and largely unscathed.

The palace.

Aurah faced the building and for the first time processed the scene that lay before her. A dragon was crawling forward from a massive crater, limping towards the palace. Elizabeth stared into the sky, completely oblivious to the danger that was *hunting her.* At least, it looked like it was hunting her.

What do I care about Elizabeth? She betrayed me! A single tear crawled down Aurah's cheek.

She didn't believe that. *Did she?* No. She loved Elizabeth. She would save her, after all, though she was absolutely helpless to warn Elizabeth in what seemed like a timely manner.

What am I doing? Aurah screamed at herself, her mind a rampage of fleeting and failing thoughts. Nothing made sense anymore. She just needed to get to Elizabeth and save her. She needed to—

Aurah charged forward relentlessly. Her stamina and purpose were refreshed and they empowered her. It was only a few days ago that she complained she wasn't in good enough shape to cover the span of the city in one dash, but now she could have done that very task many times over in half the usual time. The world blurred by her. She was back in the square. The square where . . . .

She shook her head, running. She just couldn't bring herself to confront that gaping wound. There was nothing that could heal that rift. She poured her feelings into every step, propelling herself forward. The dragon was nearly to Elizabeth. Aurah wouldn't be too much longer, either.

Past the gate that . . . *nothing* . . . had left open behind them.

Past the stairs that . . . *nothing* . . . had led her down.

Past the doors that . . . *nothing* . . . had fought her through and convinced her to not fight anymore.

Past the halls and stairs and winding corridors. Aurah raced up flights of steps and through the palace. She sped towards Elizabeth, praying that she could make it in time to warn the Princess of the imminent danger. As low as the dragon was creeping on the ground, and as preoccupied with the battle in the sky Elizabeth would be, Aurah knew the Princess would never notice the dragon in time. Aurah nearly cursed at how engrossed Elizabeth was prone to become at times.

Aurah looked out the nearby windows as she sped by. She lost track of the dragon. All the more reason to get to Elizabeth faster. *How long had she been running?* Her lungs screamed their torture, but the whine was pitifully quiet compared to the dirge in her heart.

She was almost there. It would be only a few more seconds before she could shout to warn Elizabeth, and then they would escape back through the palace to make something of life, to rebuild. It would work out. *Maybe.*

Ahead light streamed into the hallway from the library's doorway. The balcony would be right after—she would make it!

Aurah rounded the last corner into the corridor leading out to the balcony and jumped to the last doorway between her and Elizabeth, taking in the scene that lay before her.

Aurah nearly screamed.

She wouldn't make it. She would never make it in time.

The dragon slowly extended its claw towards the now frozen Elizabeth, who stared right at the impending doom. Aurah couldn't understand what had possessed the dragon to kill Elizabeth, out of everyone in the city—especially in this manner.

Aurah's eyes dulled with sudden understanding. The faithful handmaiden realized the terrible truth and shot out the door towards the Princess.

The smoke of the smoldering city timbers rose and wafted over the balcony and through the air above. The dust of shattered stones billowed higher and higher, encroaching on the buildings left intact. Blood laid heavy on the air, the smell of death nauseating to even the most experienced. The screams of dragons and the resounding explosions from far above clawed their ways into the ears of all who would hear.

But Aurah had eyes for only one thing. The only thing she had left. The person she cared for more than any other in the world.

Slowly, but in a dead sprint, one step after the other. One heartbeat, contending with the noise from the cry of war, and then another. Not breathing, but chest heaving. *She ran.*

Then a new bout of debris and dust erupted from the palace, filling the air. The body of a dragon protruded from the walls and roof of the now collapsed corridor where Aurah just came from, a corpse was thrown by the unknown defender above to distract the approaching dragon below. The man was trying to impede the dragon's progress towards the Princess. There was now a glimmer of hope for Aurah.

The dragon that had been reaching for Elizabeth was temporarily blinded.

Closing the distance, Aurah's hands found the tender embrace of the only family she had ever had. Time stood still as her eyes conveyed her love for her sister. A look of horror scrawled out upon Elizabeth's face as the Princess understood the faithfulness of her most loving and loyal servant—no—her best friend, *her sister.*

Barreling straight into Elizabeth, Aurah threw her away from the dragon's claw. She felt the appalling grasp of death latch around her instead and immediately was ripped away as the dragon retreated with an impossible veracity and vigor.

This was the end.

Aurah stared at Elizabeth for a second, and then blacked out, overwhelmed. Maybe she would die. Maybe she would live. Maybe she would figure things out later.

Maybe.

CHAPTER THIRTEEN

The wind streaked across Kast's face and down his body. The flight home had been one of his worst *ever*. Not only did he need to be gentle carrying his passenger, but his body was mangled and broken. The trip carried him over the large expanse of forest which covered most of the human kingdom. Kast grimaced at the challenge he had in climbing high enough into the air to hide behind the clouds. He was lucky there were some clouds to hide behind in the first place. Then there was the challenge of ascending before the massive cliff that rose *above* the clouds themselves. The humans' land was split in half by the obstinate earth, and Kast beat his wings against damnation to overcome that sheer face.

Kast lowered his head in defiance, though, and his worry receded, replaced by a smile. He had retreated from the city with his prize. *He did it!* He felt his chest grow even hotter than when he made his flame. His passion lived again—no, it burned for the first time. The thrill, this throbbing in his chest. His dead heart beat again. *Not just beat, it was a battle march!* Kast lifted his head, beaming at the clouds surrounding him. The air suddenly felt a lot less oppressive and chilling. His wings beat with renewed vigor.

His heart . . . his heart!

Would it continue to drum? Did he really just beat all odds of finding his purpose? His joy? Did he really conquer the insanity and looming darkness that had grown in strength, plaguing him? Kast thought about all the ground he covered in the past two days of flying, especially with that cliff in the way. The humans were completely out of the picture, even that . . . cloaked freak. Those dragons . . . well, he left while they were still dealing with The Cloak. They hadn't followed—he hoped. He smiled even wider at that thought.

I'm hoping. This is what hope feels like!

Kast's body convulsed without warning, locking his wings, and he plummeted with absolute conviction. Tremors pulsed through his sinews. Panic latched to his rasping breaths warring with his pain. His body was seized and frozen, but his heart defied those restrictions, hammering ceaselessly. He felt the scales along the back of his neck and spine raise on end, each piquing with the piercing needles of pain and the fear of the fall.

The clouds broke as Kast hurtled towards the ground, dragged by the force of gravity. His eyes were peeled open by the raging winds and the sight of the rocky spires climbing from the broken world below.

Kast immediately flipped his right wing up, or what little of it he could control, and caught the wind, throwing him down in a spiral.

It was enough to avoid plowing into the side of the tower suddenly before him, but now he had an army more of the things to navigate, and farther ahead the spires grew larger and larger to full-grown island plateaus.

Let go! He screamed at his body, rocking his frame to dodge another spire. His wing barely clipped the side, veering him right at another. His left wing was utterly useless, crippled by his petrified body.

Come on! Not now, not now! Panic had already set in, and now it was desperation that drove Kast. There was no time to think, just react.

Gritting his great maw, he tucked his right wing, throwing himself into a roll to the side, as his claws clutched the prize fervently, but he hoped also gently. The spire zoomed by him.

Another near miss.

Kast was heaving, his eyes roaming for some kind of safety. The plateaus were already much closer—the spires were thicker and cluttered now. He rocked his mass back and forth, weaving between the stone columns. He had to slow down, but if he slowed too much, he would lose his glide and drop like a stone.

Wretched body! Don't fail me now!

Kast hated himself. Stretching every limb, he didn't even register the agony he was putting himself into. He had to survive. He had to make it back home. He couldn't fail. He wasn't going to be this close and lose it all to one of his body's tantrums. He must make it home.

Come on! His mighty heart hammered in his ears.

Then release.

Glorious release.

Kast unfurled his wings with a resounding snap and moved with purpose now.

One spire flew by, then another.

The spires weren't even spires anymore but large mounds of rock, those plateaus he had seen from a distance earlier. Either the earth grew odd or something had broken it once, shattering it into the many, many pieces that were the spires and plateaus.

Whatever the case, now Kast had his work cut out for himself. *Again.*

Cutting through the air, Kast sliced the wind with his wings, diving back and forth—*charging*—through the obstacles before him. He had his hope. *He would not fail.*

His eyes darted around almost as fast as he darted through the snare he had fallen in.

There!

Kast rolled again, realigning himself with his—*their*—salvation.

A large stretch of air. Open enough that Kast spread his wings as much as he could. With a powerful thrust down, they rose above the plateau tops and with another rose above the broken forest that sat on the tops of those island plateaus. Kast recognized immediately where he was at.

Almost home!

It looked a lot different from the *scenic* route, but Kast knew where he was. The plateaus had all grown enormous, much larger than him now. His maw stopped its clenching, widening back into a ferocious smile. He began to slow himself down steadily.

He had done it. He had finally won!

His body seized again.

Kast's heart stopped and failure gripped the lizard as he dropped back down into the narrow lanes between the plateaus.

This time there were no deft maneuvers left to him. None. His eyes widened. *Except maybe…*

Kast found his home, up ahead, and he saw that with a little maneuver, he could be lined up perfectly.

With every ounce of concentration that the magnificent dragon possessed, Kast pointed his nose towards an opening in the side of an enormous plateau. The entrance to his home. His body mostly unresponsive again, Kast dropped as much of his wings as he could to break against the wind and slow down. The space to fly between the rocky mounds had decreased drastically. Kast had chosen it as his home for its very ability to prevent another dragon from doing what he was at that very moment trying to do. *Except by choice of course.*

The entrance raced towards them. If they were slowing down, it didn't look like it. Kast clenched his teeth again. *I have to.*

Kast filled with resolve and he shifted his weight, throwing his side into the jagged stone wall of the plateau next to himself. It was excruciating, fighting his wings to maintain a pathetic glide while slamming his body into stone. Without control, all he could do was hope his body would slow down.

It worked.

The entrance approached a little slower. *It will have to do!*

Kast faced the next part of his landing with complete determination. He ran the layout of his den through his mind until he knew just how he wanted to crash. The plan with the best chances of surviving intact.

The entrance arrived, and Kast's wings wrenched against the opening.

Goodbye, plans.

Stones blasted everywhere from the impact and Kast was thrown face-first into the rocky floor. Bouncing up, he slammed into what looked like the wall and ripped out a large chunk of the rock scattering dirt everywhere.

Kast felt numb. Blackness was edging closer, taking over his vision. He had just enough left, though, to see that that last hit sent him spinning.

Right into what looked like the other stone wall

Headfirst.

Blackness descended.

CHAPTER FOURTEEN

Aurah fought to free herself from the dragon's grip. She didn't care if the beast felt her stirring or moving. Like a frightened beast, Aurah fought. It felt like she had been struggling for hours—she probably had been. She was trapped in the monster's claws and she had no way out. Thankfully, the monster seemed to be nearly dead from their crash landing.

It was horrible. Being crushed in that monster's grip and being hauled through the air. Aurah had run out of tears and a voice early in her captivity. She didn't have to worry for long, though; she had fallen unconscious quite often during their flight. It felt like she couldn't breathe most of the trip. Her chest ached the whole way. When they landed, *crashed*, she lay curled up in the dark clutches of that monster. She recovered as best as she could.

Aurah beat against the dragon's scaly fingers, trying to pry herself free. She had been at her escape attempts for quite some time to no avail. She was exhausted and her body ached. She had never felt this kind of pain before. She was so frail and new to the horrors of the world. Ignoring the pain, she leaned against the wall of the dragon's hold, as tears fell over her face.

"Elizabeth . . . please help me." Aurah wept and hit the dragon over and over with a weak fist. "Elizabeth . . . please.

Don't leave me. I don't want to be here anymore. Please, Elizabeth."

A flicker of light broke through the dragon's clutches, causing a spike in Aurah's chest. *Hope.* With feral savagery, Aurah threw herself at the dim shimmer of light only to hit headfirst into the dragon's claw. Again.

Aurah fell back down and wept. There was no way out. Why didn't she let Elizabeth be the one to be taken? Elizabeth would be able to handle this. Aurah had already lost so much. She lost her home, her life, her sister, she lost . . . .

"Nothing!" Aurah shrieked, ripping her already shredded throat. Shaking, she beat her fists into the dragon's scaly fingers. "Nothing . . . nothing . . . nothing . . . nothing."

The girl, once handmaiden to the Princess, fell down sobbing.

Aurah had lost everything.

Her efforts to keep it all intact failed.

She had nothing anymore.

Realization filtered across her eyes, piercing even the darkness.

She had that. She could do that.

Her hands moved to her own throat.

Aurah took a deep breath and squeezed.

Harder.

She pushed her fingers deeper into the skin, cutting off her air.

Harder.

She felt her pipe. She was ready to crush it.

Harder.

Her fingers dug down.

Harder!

She screamed at herself, shoving her nails down as hard as possible.

They wouldn't go any farther.

Aurah tried again and failed. She just couldn't do it.

Not that way.

Her eyes brightened again. All she needed to do was find something sharp. *Rocks!* The dragon's hand had released enough that pebbles and a slew of other rocks had fallen into her scaly cell. Her hands fumbled in the dark. Loathing the feel of the beast, she brushed past many rocks not suitable to the task. Most were round, or too smooth. She kept searching until she found a piece with a jagged enough edge to give her hope.

Aurah gripped the larger stone in her hand and poised her other wrist, ready to cut. She wouldn't give the dragon any pleasure. He would wake—if he woke—to a pile of blood and a lifeless corpse. For some reason, that thought brought Aurah great comfort. She grinned wildly into the darkness and lowered the rock to her wrist.

Elizabeth.

She pushed down hard.

Morris and Elenor.

The rock fumbled in her hands and she had to rearrange it between her fingers.

The city.

She pushed it against her vein again. Yes, the dragon would suffer.

Then *nothing* filled her mind—before he . . . left her.

Understanding flooded Aurah. She couldn't kill herself. She wanted to live too much. But how could she live here? How could she fix everything? She tried so hard to make sure nothing broke, but she had failed horribly.

The rock fell from her hand and Aurah dropped, unable to hold herself up. What was life now? She couldn't move forward, could she? She couldn't even cry anymore, broken by the conundrum in which life immersed her.

A loud huff of air gusted from outside of the dragon's claw and in a moment later Aurah found herself dumped from her prison. The rock beneath offered a hard greeting, stunning her. It took a moment to realize what happened.

The dragon had released her!

Aurah stood as fast as her body would allow. She was in a massive cavern crusted with years upon years of rock formations. As pretty as it may have looked, nothing was more beautiful than the light billowing into the place from outside. Aurah had an out, and it didn't require her to bring her days to an end.

She moved with determination towards her escape. She could make it home, and she could fix everything. She and Elizabeth would always be together. The city would welcome her back and . . . .

Nothing.

Aurah gripped the side of her head and clenched her teeth. She had to get home first. *Focus on that.* The cave floor was mildly smooth, though she could tell it had been inhabited by the dragon for a while by the many score marks on the stone and dead scales coating everything. There was a stench to the place, though it was neither foul nor rotten. Aurah pushed to the opening, weaving between large chunks of rocks and boulders that littered the floor and stared aghast at what lay before her.

She had never heard of anything like what she saw. Massive land plateaus stood, surrounding her. She couldn't see much above them because they rose far above her view, though the distance between each plateau allowed her to see a fair distance before her view was blocked by another plateau. Directly in front of her, a large gash cut through the side of one of the other plateaus. It looked fresh and must have been where she felt the dragon's first impact before crashing into the cave. How far did this world extend? Aurah hadn't been able to see anything while trapped in the dragon's claw.

As daunting as the unknown formations were, it wasn't as scary as what she had to do. Aurah looked downwards toward the distant ground. There were many rocks, and pieces of the plateau jutting outward to use as handholds and the larger boulders offered frequent platforms for her to land on. There was even an occasional tree latched into the side of the plateau. In some sense, the way down looked like a vastly disproportioned stairway with the steps ranging from a single step to ten. The distance she had to descend was much larger than anything she could compare to; the ground was a small thread weaving between the bases of the rocky towers.

Aurah clenched her fists and tried to quell her fluttering heart. She turned and looked back towards the dragon and pursed her lips into a tight line. She had to move forward. She had to fix everything. She would rather die by falling than by the hand of the scaly monster. Aurah hated every second thinking about what lay ahead, but she turned around and began to lower herself down the side of the rocky formation.

Elizabeth stood at one of the windows in the throne room. She dared not think of the events that had recently occurred. *She could not.* Nor could she consider how long it was taking her servants to get her results. Elizabeth clenched her jaw in *fury.* She slammed her fist into the windowsill, while her other hand dragged its nails across the smooth stone. She watched as torrents of her people flooded back into the city. It had been two days. Two long miserable days. Two days without justice. *That creature will pay.*

"Your Majesty!"

"Did you finally do as I commanded?" Elizabeth snapped, shouting at the soldier who stood at attention, waiting to speak."

"Yes, Your Majesty! The unknown troop of men you mentioned has come forward and are waiting to spea—"

"Well, send them in already!" Elizabeth screamed at the man.

"Yes, Majesty!" The soldier turned towards two others at the entrance and motioned for the doors to be opened before he turned back to Elizabeth and spoke again. "Your Majesty, the man that leads this group has asked to be introduced as Charlie, of Lizard Guts."

Aurah lay on the large rock, huffing. She could hardly feel her arms or legs, let alone her hands. She stared up. All the way back towards where she had descended from. She dropped her head back towards a resting position and closed her eyes. Her lungs just didn't seem to refill to their capacity. Her chest continued to pulse in cadence with her lungs as she lay trying to rebuild not only her strength but her will.

It was terribly difficult.

All the moving forward required of her. All the trying to find hope when hope seemed to be crushed as staunchly as . . . *nothing*. Aurah tensed. She was getting better already at burying her hurt, and she wasn't going to risk exposing it now. Her hands found the stone beneath her and she pushed herself quickly over the side to grab hold of a rock. She didn't care if her body screamed against herself. She didn't care if her fear told her she might fall and die. She had already died a thousand deaths. What was one more?

Aurah looked down, a rare occurrence as she scaled the wall. The farther down she got, the easier the climbing became, and what she saw told her why. There were bigger landings and more distinct handholds below her. The ground, surprisingly, was no longer far away. It looked like she wasn't much higher than one of the buildings back home in the city.

She was almost to the ground!

A surge of hope spiked through her limbs. Unexpected excitement at her accomplishment coursed through her veins. She could do this!

Aurah swung down towards the next handhold—and missed.

In a mere second, her enthusiasm was replaced with horror as the feeling of falling stabbed its blade through her chest. Arms flailing, Aurah dropped a short distance and slammed into a large boulder before rolling off and crashing into the ground another short distance below.

Aurah lay stunned as tears began to well up in her eyes. The air burst from her chest again, though for another reason. Pain laced up her right side, especially her back where she had hit the boulder above her landing spot. She had never been so thankful for dirt, though. It was soft and spongy beneath her. Aurah patted the ground with the hand that she hadn't landed on and crushed. She couldn't connect with reality. She was dazed from the impact, so she stopped moving, waiting for the adrenaline to retreat and her heartbeat to stop pounding in her ears.

Sound came back eventually. The only thing she heard at first was her own whimpering and tears mingled with the coarse sound of her chest beating trying to find more air. *Why wasn't there enough air?*

Aurah lifted her hurt arm, trying to find the feeling in it again.

Blood.

Her arm was scraped along its length and rivulets of blood trailed down the skin.

"Ow. Come on, come on." Aurah laid back, muttering and crying to herself and didn't try to move. Her body ached and she just wanted to give up. Now that she had gotten her wish her body had calmed down. Now that the adrenaline ebbed, she wished it hadn't gone away. All up and down her right side, her body ached.

Soon the throbbing dulled a little, and she noticed more about the world where she had just crashed. She heard trickling water nearby and noticed the moist smell of earth around her. The sun managed to shine down this far, but it didn't look like it had a continual influence. There were many mushrooms and other fungi. Everything seemed wet. The alleys between the plateaus were very wide, though Aurah couldn't figure out how the dragon managed to fly at all, considering his size. Maybe she would get lucky and the monster wouldn't be able to get her after all?

She looked back down at her body. The bleeding had stopped quickly on her arm. She pushed herself back up, favoring her wounds, and managed to stumble to her feet. Her breathing was ragged, and her chest hurt with every inhalation. Her side pained her terribly. She wasn't familiar enough with the sting of injury to know if anything was broken. Aurah began to stumble across the moss-covered ground and over the spider web of streams flowing around the plateaus.

Aurah walked slowly towards the base of the plateau where the score marks from the dragon rested above. She was proud of the deduction and decision she had just come to, though it held much less weight for her now. She would head back the way they had come. *Clever.*

Aurah made it to the plateau and looked up. The score marks were still there, though she could barely seem them from down here. Fresh stones from the dragon's impact lay all around this hidden world at the bottom of this strange place. *Whatever.*

She turned to continue on when she heard splashing behind her.

Lots of splashing, and the sound of many padded footsteps.

And ragged breathing.

A wretched stench filled her nostrils.

And a shrieking howl that raised goosebumps on her skin.

And another, and another, and another.

All around her. So many.

Snarls and growls.

Aurah closed her eyes, resigned to the fear and the failure that crippled her.

CHAPTER FIFTEEN

Kast wandered the dark corridors with apprehension. He had been wandering for hours with no sign of progress except a strange tiredness that seemed to lace its way through his . . . *body?*

He had no idea what he was. He didn't like it, and he wanted it to stop.

He ran again. A frivolous attempt. Running got him nowhere. The dark musty corridor flew by again, but he only had the blur of the walls and the tiredness again to show for his efforts. Kast sat, or something that felt like what he recognized as sitting. Nothing he did felt like what it should be, like what he knew as normal.

His chest gasped for air.

He looked around the corridor again.

He spoke.

"What!" He screamed. He knew it was no use. His voice had done nothing to change his circumstances when he used it before. So, he sat, the abnormal feeling coursing through the simple action.

Was this punishment? Was this his reward for all those acts of murder he had committed? Kast leaned back against the wall. His chest still worked from his running.

Tears fell down the mighty dragon's face. Sobs erupted and wailing began. He hadn't been broken to point of weeping before, but now that he had, it felt exactly as it should. Even in this strange place.

Kast wept. All he had wanted was to avoid the looming insanity, as was natural for every dragon. How did any lizard figure out their purpose and fulfill it? He had been trying for quite some time now. First, he fought against what he felt was the answer. Then he succumbed and began attacking groups of humans, working his way on up to cities, then the human capital. And all he had to show for it was nothing but misery and now this place.

Well, there was . . . something. It felt like a light. It felt like his fire had filled his veins. There was a word for this feeling.

Life.

Kast smiled.

How had he forgotten?

He had found life!

Or something that feels like life. A voice spoke in Kast's mind.

Wide-eyed at the sudden presence of another, Kast watched the corridor suddenly begin to whirl by, moving faster than his quickest flight—much faster. Kast saw something black appear on the far horizon, racing towards himself. *Horizon?* Yes, the corridor stretched for eternity. Kast saw now what he had missed before.

And in a mere moment, Kast realized he hadn't seen enough, though, as the black slammed into his weird being, throwing him through into an infinite void.

Trembling, Kast stood, surrounded by black nothingness.

You have been quite a troublesome dragon.

Quite troublesome indeed.

The voice possessed a slight rasp, but a definite growl. It wasn't friendly. Kast looked around desperately, trying to find the source of the voice.

Hey, I'm behind you.

Kast twisted violently, whimpering.

A large purple orb illuminated the world around Kast. Human bones and corpses covered the ground at his feet, and blood seeped, pooling into oceans beside him. *And a cloak flew, holding the orb.*

Kast screamed out, trying to deny the man holding the purple magic.

Scream, filth! The voice laughed at Kast, and sinister cruelty coursed out through every chortle. The Cloak threw the orb into Kast's chest. The world was erased suddenly, leaving Kast heaving out his nonexistent gut. The bones and blood were erased, and The Cloak transformed into a horrid swirling darkness.

Now, come dragon. Do you really think I'm the bad guy here? I supported you through every attack. I lent you power and . . . clarity.

"What do you want?" Kast screamed.

Me? I just want you, Kast. And I would prefer if you weren't so intent on abandoning me for some petty purpose. That hurts, you know—a lot. And I'm not very keen on being pained. Do not test me . . . . I am always your worst fear.

A chunk of the darkness separated from the rest and formed The Cloak again, which lurched at Kast before erupting into smoky tendrils of darkness.

Kast cowered low, and quiet sobs rocked his ethereal frame. "Please, stop . . . please. I don't want anymore . . . ."

But I am the way towards what you genuinely want . . . .

"What I truly want?" Kast's head darted around, trying to locate the speaker. He had to be here around her somewhere. *Right?*

Yes, what you want . . . .

Rage. The void zoomed away, replaced with light that seared Kast's eyes. All around the different memories held their own territory, occupying the void where Kast knew he was. Somehow, they all meshed at the seams to make a glaring cascade of his life. They were moments of Kast erupting out in his insanity. Anger coursed through the dragon's livid and scaled body. His rampages always started with an insatiable rage.

Hate. The voice growled, and the visions changed to Kast pummeling human after human. A trail of blood and decay left in his wake. The cries and weeping of the innocent before and after. The essence of his being stirred at the remembrance. Tantalized by the memory of hate that relieved the hurt he felt—the condemnation with which he was stricken.

Destruction.

They floated above every ruined city Kast had destroyed. Pillars of black smoke rose from the fiery infernos below, consuming the cities. Kast floated in horror. He knew what he had done, but it all seemed so . . . minuscule in light of . . . .

Me? The voice offered the conclusion to Kast's thought. *It feels good . . . Kast.*

"No!" Kast shook his head and closed his eyes, trying to block out the painful reality.

Kast.

The dragon was filled with a new dread. He hadn't meant to kill. It had all just seemed so natural, it seemed like what he should do.

Kast... You know you wanted to do those things. Do not lie to yourself, Kast.

Kast gripped his head and tears fell as he wept. "I don't know what I want! I just want this to stop!" The voice laughed more.

Kast, do not think you can escape me. None may escape me. You are mine. You are mine, dragon.

"Leave me alone! Kast bellowed, wide-eyed and frantic.

Kast, give in to your wrath. You are a mighty dragon! All must cower before you.

"I . . . I don't want . . . ." Kast stumbled over a nothingness as he receded, trying to retreat from the awful confrontation. He knew for certain he hadn't wanted to do those things. But . . . .

Yes. Yes, you really did want to do those things.

Kast dropped to his knees and raked his claws over his body. Or what felt like raking his claws over his body.

He looked up and suddenly saw his memories twist and churn together in a maelstrom, losing their light and becoming a black, undefinable monster.

Terror.

Kast quivered, trying to escape as the monster charged at him, ramming head-first into the mighty dragon.

CHAPTER SIXTEEN

Kast jolted awake, convulsing from the strange nightmare that he had just had. His claw roamed desperately and felt his body, making sure he was indeed a dragon still.

He was. *Or . . . .*

"No!" Kast rolled off of his side onto his feet and cowered for the inevitable attack. An attack that never came. His pulse raced, filling his veins with hot blood. Veins that burst from his wide petrified eyes.

There! Kast twisted fast, spinning to face the shadows and his powerful tail ripped through the pile of rubble that had encased him. *There?* The dragon's heart continued its vibrant thrum, filling the dull lifelessness of the cavern with his heat. Light poured into the cave from the wide opening, making shadows dance all around. Kast searched the shadows, his long neck sore from its tense craning.

The shadows moved again. Kast jerked violently, crushing the stone between his strong claws. He would have just closed his eyes if he weren't afraid of what he would find when he did.

"Please . . . ," he whimpered. "Please, leave me alone." A whine. "I just want to be okay!" A silent scream.

The dragon collapsed onto the stone floor again and held his massive head. His wings folded, tucked sharply against his body. His tail lay wherever again. It was bad manners for a dragon to leave his tail wherever it may lie. For the fleeting time that he had been raised by his thrall, it had been instilled that a tail must not be left in the way of others. The pain from said others *accidentally* stepping on his tail was enough to drive that point home. He hadn't stuck around for long.

But now, *who cares?* Kast wept, holding his head. Why was his mind filled with these visions of horror and pain? Why was he doomed to insanity? Why—

Insanity!

"Insanity!" Kast jumped to his feet, every feeling of horror and glum replaced with one single, all-consuming, brilliant thought. "My purpose!" Kast nearly screamed from his jubilance. This time his head swung around energetically, searching for his purpose.

He had finally found her!

"Hello?" Kast could hardly contain his excitement. With this, he could now finally rise above the pain of his being and become what he was meant to be! He was finally free!

"Hello? Where are you?" Kast called out, waiting through the echoes of his own voice to hear the one new voice he had craved for longer than he could remember. Why was it a she? He had no idea. It had only fully made sense when he had seen her standing atop of that human creation, watching his glorious splendor as he raged his battle. She most certainly would be impressed with his ferocity. Most certainly.

The dragon stood among the quieting of the cavern. Evening would come shortly, and then dusk into night. Still, the dragon waited for the warm voice to call out to him and pull him from the quagmire of his insanity. He cocked his ear towards a direction from where he thought he had heard something. Now, he was hearing the shadows. A few more seconds slid by.

Nothing.

She wasn't there. The sullen realization crept through the dragon's frame, scale by scale.

She isn't there.

"Hello?" A hoarse whisper ended in a loud thud as the dragon hit the floor again, his tail laying even farther out of place than before. The dragon lay lifeless on the stone. He hoped and wished that the embrace of the rock would surely suck the soul from his bones. He hated this.

Silent tears gushed from the mighty beast's eyes, pooling on the rock. Maybe the stone would eat those since the dragon's soul wasn't good enough.

Kast wept. He lay sprawled out, weeping. He had nothing. There was no way it would ever amount to any good.

The sounds of a pack of Savages cut lightly through the air. They sounded far away. Probably right below Kast, all the way on the ground, for all he knew. Their cries came out again. Kast knew those sounds. The sounds of those vicious monsters hunting, circling their prey.

Poor creature.

Then the worlds aligned.

"No!" Kast screamed throwing himself off of the ground in one heartbeat. In the next—

He was already out the entrance of his home.

CHAPTER SEVENTEEN

The now-familiar pull of fear gripped Aurah from her core. The monsters surrounding her snarled, rage streaking across their features. Long bristly strands of dark hair erupted in spotty patches on the creatures as if trying to escape their horrid masters. A stench poured from the abominations and shriveled the girl's nose. They had deep yellow eyes, the same yellow that coated their rotten tooth stumps. One took a step forward, slowly, and hunger dripped off its tongue. Aurah had already cut the air with her scream. She backed up a step towards the towering wall of the plateau, matching the pace of the beast's approach. With her body the way it was—broken from the fall—she wouldn't be able to dodge or move away from the thing if it decided to pounce.

It snarled. The others slowly approached, closing in on Aurah and sealing her against the wall with a very wide circle. Sweat beaded down her neck onto her back. Her throat clumped at the terror before herself. *It's coming!*

One of the beasts lunged.

Screaming, Aurah dropped to the ground against the objections of her body. Her hands reacted, thrown upwards as the only means she had to save herself. A worthless gesture—her hands would never have stopped the thing.

She was dead!

But the monster never impacted her.

Instead, she heard a loud whistling through the air, followed by a furious roar and an earth-shattering impact that left her slightly dazed. Something hot and wet coated her abruptly, startling her back to reality. The sudden silence following the eruption was broken only by a large, panting, huff. She uncurled her back tenderly and looked up from the ground to see why her enemy hadn't killed her yet.

Her eyes gaped, struggling to understand the scene before her.

The wolf-like creature that had attacked lay in a mashed heap on the ground, crushed by a massive, deep brown, and scaled tail. Aurah's mouth dropped opened, frightened and in awe of the dragon who appeared out of nowhere. The monsters had scattered, breaking their trap to dodge the weight of the dragon. She was sicklily enamored by the vitality and resourcefulness of her captor. *The dragon*. Her mind wandered out of its wonder and realized that what she had felt coat her when the dragon had landed was the blood of the predator that had sought to devour her. She retched out only what an empty stomach could provide. Her body quaked, irritating her tender bones. The adrenaline coursing through her veins conversed with her fear and instructed her survival instincts, numbing her pain in return for the impossible demand.

Aurah slowly rose from the ground, pushing through the tension in the air from the standoff between the dragon and the beasts. A feeling of nausea gripped and tilted the world, swirling it around violently. Her hand of its own accord shot out to a nearby boulder to steady herself.

The wolf-like monsters snarled at the movement and the standoff ended.

A single monster charged the still dragon, leaping and latching its vicious jaw into the dragon's neck.

It fell in a shower of blood and whining. Aurah saw the life of the creature dripping from its mouth. The dragon's defense was impenetrable. The dragon crushed the beast with a staunch fist and challenging defiance.

The rest of the monsters shot forward in a crazy mass, racing towards, away, and past the dragon. It was madness. The dragon dug its claws into the ground while throwing its body forward to catch one of the beasts who was lurching through the air towards it. The wolf creature impacted the dragon's shoulder and flew to crash into the other plateau.

A howl pierced the air.

Aurah backed up slowly, trying to put as many of the large boulders as she could between herself and the fight.

Smoke rippled from the dragon's snout and then flames shot out, coating the sides of the plateaus and the moist ground. The beasts lunged out of the fire's path, charging towards the dragon in unison contradicting their madness. Steam rose from the earth and streams. The dragon roared its fury and swung its whole body.

The mighty dragon's tail whipped over Aurah's head with a gale that rustled her tattered dress and found its mark.

Blood erupted from the beast that caught the full force of the dragon's might.

Up high above, the sun fell behind a cloud, and Aurah caught what looked like a horrific smile cross the lizard's face as the dimming enveloped the bottom of the plateaus in darkness.

Flames pieced the void, lighting up the world.

A shrieking scream cut Aurah's hearing, throwing her down in pain again, sending her hands to cover her crying ears.

The dragon roared, fully proud of himself.

The embers from the ground gave off a steady red glow that mingled with the sunlight that slowly climbed down the plateaus as the clouds began to move. Aurah watched the dragon dance skillfully between the tight plateaus, pouncing on and crushing beast after beast.

The dragon let out a terrifying sound and suddenly crumpled onto the ground.

One of the beasts had slipped around behind the dragon and latched itself onto the scaly hide. Blood trickled down the dragon's flank. *The dragon's defense was penetrable?*

The dragon spun its whole body around, casting the beast from its hold right into the plateau wall. It didn't get up.

The dragon roared again and crushed the last of the beasts in the middle of its charge. By now, the sun had reappeared from behind its cover and the whole scene from before was replaced by pools of blood and mashed or burning corpses. The stench that filled the air fought an endless war with Aurah's already struggling lungs.

The dragon's head swiveled back and forth looking for any more signs of the beasts as it turned slowly. *Towards her direction.* Terror laced through her veins, sending her scrambling haphazardly backward over the rocks and boulders.

Without hesitation, the dragon faced her directly and closed the distance between them. Aurah was stunned and couldn't form coherent thoughts. The beast stared for just a moment before reaching out one of its front claws—the front looked more like a pair of hands and the rear looked more like feet. *What did she care what he looked like?* The dragon grabbed her around her middle, lifting her from the ground. *She hated that.* It was the picture of doom, the claw of a dragon reaching for her. She moved her arms just in time to keep them free from its clasp, ensuring that she wouldn't get trapped within its enormous palm again. Horrendous *pain* swelled through her bones. Aurah cried out involuntarily, trying to stifle any sign of weakness before the beast. She had still been in pain from her fall, now the dragon's *tender* grasp wrought its destruction once again.

I hate him.

Gripped by her compelling loathing, she berated the dragon's hold on her with what power she had. Pain drove her mad. She hated him so much! She didn't care what happened. The heartless wretch would know its turpitude. She wailed unceasingly, not caring how the dragon leaped into the air and flew back towards the top of the plateaus. The pain stole her breath away. She didn't stop her struggle.

They rose above the dragon's cavern, all the way to the top of the plateau. She beat the claw surrounding herself without end. *The claw.* What a picture to depict its heinous prison. They broke above the tops of the plateaus and over the forest on top, causing Aurah to fight harder. The dragon stopped pumping the air with his wings; holding them still, he began to glide. The dragon dropped to the plateau with his home somewhere below and landed in an abnormal and small meadow in the middle of the forest on top.

The dragon set her down in the dirt, allowing Aurah to collapse to the ground—her body only served to inform her of the pain in her bones. She couldn't stand immediately, so she tried rolling pathetically across the ground. She stopped moving after a dramatic lack of success. She felt the dragon's gaze and instead of fooling around any longer, Aurah made the slow climb back onto her feet.

A steely gaze met the dragon's apprehensive stare. The beast twitched, and Aurah dropped her eyes to see the beast's claws. Instruments of destruction.

She hated him.

The scaly foot-claw appendage suddenly moved to the side slowly, then stopped. She watched it with rapt attention, tensed and ready to react to whatever it threw at her. It moved again, back the other way. Her head swiveled, following it. She wouldn't let the claw swallow her again. She wouldn't. *Never.* It moved, this time upwards, so slowly. She followed it upwards until her eyes met the monster's. She gasped from the pain of her head moving and from sudden realization.

It's toying with me!

Its mouth twisted upward, and its eyes projected mirth.

It's pleased!

Aurah dropped to the ground suddenly and let out a wail of pain. *What now?* She could almost hear her thoughts aloud—the angst of the situation fueled her anxiety. How bad was her condition?

The dragon dropped its claw, the evil game ended, and suddenly it seemed concerned. It moved its head closer to the ground, inspecting Aurah. *Trash.* Aurah gripped a small rock and flung it carelessly towards the direction of the monster's face. *It missed.* The girl cried out her pain and sorrow. She was finished. She just couldn't move on any longer. She couldn't fight. There was no way out of this.

The dragon moved its head even closer, then lay it on the ground. A loud thud and the cry of stone being crushed lashed out into the air above.

It stared intently at her.

Monster! Her thoughts raged. She lay mostly prostrate on the ground now, her body a convoluted shape trying to alleviate the immense pain. She couldn't move anymore. In fact, she wanted to die right then and there.

A white light streamed from the dragon.

Aurah's eyes flew wide open in surprise—not only at the light that had begun to drift across the air towards herself but also at the fact that the dragon's eyes matched her own. Surprise, as only she imagined a dragon could show surprise, filtered across the beast's gigantic face.

Then the light surrounded her.

Relief!

Aurah's body unfurled, releasing the tension, pain, *and even . . . hunger.* She gasped desperately as her body seemingly began to heal itself. The pain in her back, and the rest of her body, dulled to a dim numb and then vanished entirely. Cuts and other simple wounds were gone. A gust of wind hit her. She looked up at the dragon who was breathing heavily—its eyes were wide, too.

Aurah felt a fear unlike any other she had ever felt.

What had just happened was completely impossible—even more than the ridiculous situation she found herself in, even more than a dragon destroying the known human world.

The beast before her stumbled to its feet and nearly collapsed for a second. Aurah started and stared, incredulous at the monster's sudden weakness. It shook its head and its step began to firm. A small growl resonated from the deep chambers of its throat. The dragon stood listening to the world and taking everything in with wide eyes. It seemed . . . *uncertain* before it relaxed only slightly. Aurah came to grips with her healed body and tilted her head towards the dragon, her face scrunched into a leer.

How. Dare. That. Monster.

The dragon seemed to notice her raucous displeasure. Reactively, it moved backward, its ears flat against its skull. Something broke deep inside of Aurah, and every ounce of goodness was incinerated at the appalling creature. Aurah screamed, tearing her voice in moments.

How dare it heal her?

How long did she hold her howl? She didn't care. If she could do anything with the last bit of life that she had, it would be to let this atrocity know her loathing for its very being.

The beast seemed to notice that message, too, as a scowl broke out onto its face. Victory was hers. The beast lumbered to face away from the girl. Discontent coated every inch of its body. She didn't care. This was a mighty battle won! The dragon retreated to the sky, not looking back once.

Aurah's insane howling turned into a burst of harsh laughter, cackling at her deed. She cackled and threw herself back onto the ground. She stared into the expanse of the sky above the treetops. *The sky. The sun . . . life?* Her demeanor broke. Her laughter turned to sobbing as reminiscent memories flooded her mind. The embrace of her sister, Elizabeth, consistently comforting her through the most painful of them, always assuring and promising the most outlandish things. She snorted in her weeping—*Elizabeth*.

Then she remembered.

Nothing.

Aurah clenched her fist and slammed it into the ground, screaming her hoarse voice raw with pain.

It was all gone. Forever. She was now the prized trophy of some warped creature *forever*. Was there any hope? She didn't know.

Aurah lay, falling asleep, tense and restless, as nature gave the hard earth for a cradle and a soft breeze for a lullaby.

Would the dragon be a problem? Why did it heal her? Would it kill her?

What could she do even if it wanted to?

Hot tears ran down across her cheeks in the deepest of lamentations.

There was always hope. Or should be. *Had to be, right?*

Maybe.

CHAPTER EIGHTEEN

Fallen limbs and sticks broke and the earth was disturbed by a frantic running. Aurah sprinted through the trees, diving into a large bush on the edge of the clearing—a clearing that Aurah knew the dragon had created, judging from the old broken limbs and gouges in the trees. Aurah held deathly still, trying to quiet her heartbeat, and hoping that her newfound stench wouldn't give her away.

The dragon swooped again—Aurah felt the monster's leering eyes raking across the forest trying to find something. *Her.*

Hold it. Stay still. Aurah let the words resonate through her mind; she dare not mutter her thoughts aloud. Her heartbeat hammered, not only from the sprint the dragon's sudden appearance wrought forth from herself but from how much she *longed* for a chance to murder the beast.

Two weeks.

Two *horrid* weeks.

That's how long she had endured this hell. It was worse than hell the first week. Now… well, she didn't wake up nearly as often hoping the heart in her chest didn't explode. It simply felt like that all the time now—a tightness ripping her chest wide open. She wanted to scream. She *did* scream. She lost her breath, and often in the night she would pass out from every episode and lay still in her broken sleep.

There was no way off the massive plateau the dragon had left her on. It was this life or death, and she wasn't ready just yet to say goodbye—to Elizabeth, and the rest of the life she had known. Aurah gritted her teeth. She wasn't allowed to think of the past anymore. It detracted from the present.

Aurah always stayed out of sight, which meant she often walked *or ran* through the forest thicket encroaching the center of the plateau where the meadow was. She hadn't taken one step into the meadow since the dragon had dropped her there two weeks ago. In that one moment, on that day, Aurah's life had been instantly transformed into a vile game of hide and seek. It was treacherous. She would never live another moment of peace again, never rest without imagining the eyes of that monster caressing her broken frame and enjoying its treasured trophy.

A whoosh of air blasted across the treetops and the dragon stopped its passes to hover over its own created meadow. She felt its gaze again and shuddered. She would never give in to the monster. She would never appease it.

It seemed always to leave its home on a somewhat regular schedule, often returning a brief time later. Each time he returned, the beast flew low over the top of the forest trying to find his prize. It seemed routine—

—except, this time something shocked Aurah.

The scaled monster dropped something into the meadow and flew away, diving over the edge of the forest without a second glance. Aurah watched with glazed eyes until she was certain the beast was gone.

What had it dropped? Aurah saw the lump lying partly in the meadow. Thankfully, it was close by. She found herself succumbing to curiosity.

No.

She shook her head trying to dissipate the craving to know. She looked apprehensively towards the sky. *Maybe if she was quick?* She looked between the unidentified object and the looming sky, then sprinted, bursting free from her cover.

Aurah covered the distance rapidly despite her blistered feet and shredded dress. The mass quickly filled out, revealing... *steam?* Aurah stopped beside the curious object. Her mouth watered immediately.

Some kind of animal—meat—lay charred and steaming. The dragon had given her... food? Aurah threw up in her mouth and spit to the side removing the bile from her mouth. *Food?* Her fists and toes clenched in anger. She threw herself back towards the way she came only to realize that motion was just a thought.

It couldn't hurt . . . to have a little bite, right?

Aurah crouched, hunched over the meat. Her fingers shook on her hand. The war between her hate and her hunger raging in her appendages.

Aurah jumped back and growled aloud. She didn't have time for this! Her eyes raked the empty sky desperately before looking back at the steaming meat. The smell wafted upwards, filling her nose. She had almost forgotten the smell of meat.

No.

Yes!

A shadow moved in the corner of her eye, and Aurah attacked the dragon's gift. Digging with her broken nails and burning her fingers, Aurah severed a large hunk from the carcass and ran back to the shadows.

A path of tears followed in her wake at how miserable and desperate she had become. How could she have ever accepted *anything* from that creature? She betrayed herself. For a mere morsel of meat? Aurah wept with every bite. Her belly yearned for more, yet disgust tightened her gut, nearly causing the girl to spew out the brightest spot she has had in two weeks.

Under the cover of trees, Aurah wept at how weak and shallow she had become to accept the very death of herself.

Kast lay on his belly, his head slumped in front of him. It had been two weeks, and the girl still hadn't shown herself. It was ridiculous. Kast didn't understand it. For whatever reason, she didn't accept anything about him. He didn't know what the problem was with her. Why did she hate him so much? *Why?* It wasn't fair. The dragon's chest bellowed as his lungs filled then released with a gust of air.

Why?

She should have become used to the new life by now.

She's just being selfish, Kast. . . .

The world went black at the words of some unknown voice, and Kast felt himself disconnect from the stone underneath him.

Kast spun around in the void that had surrounded himself. Terror laced through his scales and sinews. He was here again. *Again!* Ever since that dream, Kast had had flashes of darkness seize his mind.

"Where am I?" Kast screamed. It was pathetic, a mighty dragon like himself throwing his might into a roar and having it only come out weak. *Powerless.* It never mattered what he said. The voice never said much. This place where he wound up, it was terrifying and it was empty.

Are you ready yet?

A shiver rippled through the dragon's scales.

"Re . . . ready? What do you mean ready? Answer!"

No answer.

Be ready, scum. The time for change is here. The time for darkness burns.

Consume.

Kast's eyes flicked open. Anger seethed through his scales. *Why?* He hated the episodes with that infernal darkness. The darkness he thought he had conquered was back. *And strong.*

The dragon gripped the stone with his claws, raking them through the grooves he developed in the rock over time. *Why?*

It's the girl, Kast. She's the problem, not me. I wish you—

"Go away!" Kast screamed, and then his voice fell into a whine and whimper. The dragon dropped his head again. *Why?*

Why? What was his purpose if it wasn't this girl? What went wrong? What had he missed? The signs, they were a convoluted puzzle pointing generally, but surely, towards her. So why did Kast still feel incomplete? Why was he still wrestling with his insanity like before—no—worse?

It's time, Kast . . .

A tremor rippled through the dragon. The beast felt a consuming heat in his belly and bones. He wasn't supposed to be this weak and there was only one explanation for the way he felt.

It was all the girl's fault. She was supposed to be the answer. She was supposed to fix everything.

Kast threw his tail and slammed it into the side of his cavern. Anger gripped him stronger and stronger. His jaw clenched, grinding his teeth. Why did he ever try to win this pathetic woman's affections? Kast beat the wall again with his tail, his face crumpling into a mighty furrow. Why did he ever believe she could fix the rifts in his life? Kast beat the wall for the third time, sending a shower of rocks cascading down around himself. *Why won't she just submit and respect me and make everything right? Why is she making everything worse?* Lifting his tail, he wound up to hit the wall again.

A loud crack and rumble ricocheted through the cave and in the next second Kast lay crushed into the floor by a gigantic section of the ceiling.

Kast blasted upwards with all his strength and threw the rock to the side. Quickly on his feet, he turned and thundered out his fire, burning the rock that dare touch him. He was breathless by the end. There was pain, but he would deal with that later. He was heaving. He was absolutely infuriated.

The dragon turned towards the opening to his cavern. He couldn't tell the difference anymore between the real world and the weird black world where the voice culled the dragon forth. Dregs of darkness seeped from every orifice surrounding the beast. The dragon almost heard the manic laughing ring through the eternity of his mind.

He had had enough of this. He would confront the girl and settle the score right now. It was time she respected him—*a dragon*. That would take care of her *and* that blasted voice and those visions. Kast had had enough!

He stomped towards the opening, stopping short of the edge. The sky was cloudy up above, but the sun shone down through the shadows of the massive ravines between the plateaus and through the large opening in his cave. It was afternoon and soon would be evening.

That girl—

Kast paused and breathed in deeply, fueling his life, which burned the darkness now.

—would answer for everything.

CHAPTER NINETEEN

urah hunkered lower at the dragon's sudden explosive landing. The world seemed to shake and crack far more than was necessary. With only a glance of her eye, she saw the red glow of fire behind the smoke in its nostrils. *Its scales . . . are they darker than before?* The hide on the monster was nearly *black*.

The monster snarled expectantly. Two weeks give or take, and the beast finally snapped. She tried hard to cover her rasping breaths while fighting the urge to run to the farthest edge of the plateau, away from the dragon.

The beast's long neck glided through the air, carrying its gigantic head. The tremor in her hands told her it was looking for *her*. Then—

"Human! Come out and face me!" The dragon roared brutally, severing her from her thoughts.

Aurah's nails immediately clawed the rocky earth beneath her, trying to find an anchor to stabilize herself. The air stopped its escape from behind her lips, hiding in her lungs.

It can talk? Aurah's thoughts screamed, a tempest in her mind.

She had no idea the things could speak.

It can talk?

No one ever had the faintest idea that dragons could talk.

The broken handmaiden quaked. Something was deeply wrong about such a creature having a voice. That creature didn't *deserve* to be able to speak. It just . . . it disrupted the understanding of life that humankind possessed.

Aurah fell backward the short distance to the ground and leaned against a tree, trying to find support in the midst of her life collapsing. She was beaten and worn from all this fear. She had thought she was getting better at handling it, but now—now she was faced with a new and disturbing facet about dragons. The last solace she had—her mind—was breached by the few syllables this dragon had spoken.

The beast stood expectantly in the clearing, its voice thick with menace and hate. Aurah was surprised the trees hadn't melted from the deep, vibrant growls of its voice.

"Come out!" The dragon screamed at Aurah's hesitation and spit out the flames lurking deep within its nostrils. The trees really did fall, succumbing to the torrent of the dragon's hate. A fire now coated the trees, burning brightly with smoke rising ceaselessly towards the sky. The heat herded Aurah through the vegetation, away from the fire. She ran over fallen logs and through the undergrowth.

From the corner of her eye, Aurah saw the beast's head snap towards her direction, immediately locked on her position. Her heart stopped its pounding, whether to hide from the dragon or in fear of what was to come next, she wasn't sure.

The dragon poured out its inferno right at Aurah.

She screamed, falling to the ground as the trees cowered and died beneath the flame, Aurah crawled at first, then ran back between the two fires devouring the forest on either side of her.

"I said, come out!" The dragon's voice screamed hoarsely, as impossible as it all sounded. Aurah felt her chest constrict. Her body ached and breathing was hard, and it didn't feel like it was just because of the smoke racing around her. The heat coated her from both sides. In a few minutes, the fires would clash together and consume her spirit.

Or.

Aurah turned, plunging from the cover of the trees—

—to face the dragon.

"What do you want, you infernal savage?" If she was to die, she would wound the monster. She would accept her death, but she would also make sure the beast knew she hated it with all her passion. "You've done nothing but be a carbuncle on the backside of this blasted world! Your putrid existence is menial and *pathetic*."

The last word hissed from between her teeth, somehow louder than the crackling and sizzling of the wildfire behind herself. There was no hope left. She lasted two weeks, but the darkness got to her. The monster had gotten to her. Nothing reassured her as it did before. There was no way out, no more hope to fix the world that she had desperately wished would remain the way it was. Now, she didn't care if she faced a creature infinitely more powerful than herself. She was broken and would charge head on to death. She *hated* the dragon.

"I would hold my tongue if I were you, human. I am in no companionable mood." The dragon turned its head towards the girl, its words enforced by the evil gaze seeping disgust for her. Its fury and hate for her rolled off its every fiber.

"Good! I wasn't needing a companion." Her retort was bitter. "In fact, I don't need a worthless mongrel like you! You're a waste, worthless, and your best will never amount to anything! You can't even . . . ."

"I said, shut it, human!" It didn't look like it would take much more of the verbal abuse. It was weak. *It was shaking.* The dragon turned its head off to the side of the young woman and let loose more of its flames. The heat was *unbearable.* Aurah dropped to her knees, searching for any relief. The monster had definitely heard her. She could see veins pulse in its eyes,

SEDRICK BOWSER

and its body heaved under the weight of her words. She didn't care. She hated it. *She was ready.*

"Is this what you do to every human girl you come across? You just kidnap them, make their lives miserable, then murder them out of your stupid anger?

"I said . . . shut it!" It turned violent, beating its wings, throwing Aurah backward from the ground, towards the tree. She hit hard and clutched her side in pain. Her eyes went wide suddenly. *What had she done?* The dragon trudged closer, and every step flamed her fear. She thought she was fearless, but *she wasn't ready to die.* Sweat ran down her neck, and she turned to crawl away.

"I noticed your efforts are enfeebled, *trash.*" It seemed to enjoy berating her with insults. "This is all your fault. I was supposed to be revived by your presence. Now, what do I have but another burden—another scar! You're trash! You are!" It wouldn't stop screaming out its hate.

Aurah found her feet and pushed off the ground, rushing away towards anywhere. She didn't want to die like this. *She didn't want to die.*

"You!" The beast faltered in its speech, fury taking over its mind. It wasn't going to let her go so easily. "Done! You're done!"

The dragon lurched outward, grabbed his prisoner and with a toss, threw the girl across the meadow in the direction from where he had come. The air erupted from her lungs. The pain was excruciating.

"No, please, stop! I don't want to die!" Aurah screamed, sobbing all down the front of her tattered dress.

The dragon glared and smiled maliciously. It took its time stepping towards her, then the beast leaped again. Aurah turned, trying to run to no avail.

The dragon gripped her and tossed her again. Much higher and much harder. Her breath caught, as she nearly passed out from the stress of the dragon's throw. This time the forest sped by under Aurah and then *nothing*.

Aurah dropped fast. Down past the top of the plateau, alongside the rocky tower. She couldn't see from the wind whipping by. She closed her eyes.

This was it.

She was dead.

She would hit the ground, far, far below.

She would be a mere snack for those monsters or whatever other forsaken creatures dominated this place.

She didn't want to die, but maybe this was for the best?

Aurah fell, resigned to her death. It was oddly comforting to accept her fate. The stress of trying to fix everything rolled off of her shoulders. She breathed out, the air in her lungs joining the air zipping by her. It wasn't going to be much longer until she hit. It was a surprise that she hadn't hit the side of the plateau yet either as it widened to its base. Probably the dragon threw her intentionally to the middle of the chasm. *Whatever.*

Aurah forced her eyes open, submitting them to the protective tears that gushed out. She had only fallen halfway down the side of the plateau. Time must have stood still. It was taking forever to hit the ground.

Aurah turned her head to the side slightly.

Her heart failed her again, and the stress landed back onto her shoulders. The claw wrapped around her. Her bones had to be broken now for sure from the pain. The dragon, with a desperate look on its face, beat its wings and rolled onto its back.

Then darkness.

They slammed into something hard. The impact recoiled through the dragon and into her bones as she and the beast slid across the world beneath themselves. Her eyes quit their watering and adjusted quickly. It was dark and it was dim.

The dragon's cave.

It had saved her again. For what? For its own desire? It had wanted to kill her just a moment ago. What was happening in this monster's mind?

The dust began to settle. Cracks and groans in the cavern echoed violently through the cavern. That was worrisome. The dragon released its grip, and Aurah fell a short distance to the ground and collapsed. She was in a lot of pain again, though it felt a lot less than when she first had come to this place. She managed a half-crawl, half-crouch and scuttled away from the beast.

Was there no end to this torture?

The monster remained still and its large chest filled out right before collapsing under a large exhale. A gash in its skin had appeared since it landed. It must have hit really hard to damage itself.

"What a hypocrite!" She screamed. Mere feet away.

The dragon rolled suddenly and caught Aurah again. Its grip around her tightened, shoving the air from her chest.

"No." The dragon collected itself. It seemed stiff from the hit, too. "I wanted the pleasure myself."

Aurah gasped as the dragon finally looked up. Its amber eyes radiated ire. Its snake-like tongue flickered out, licking its lips.

Its grip grew tighter, and the blood began to rush to Aurah's head. This was the worst way to go. The monster was torturing her. The tongue shot out again, this time trailing across her face. She threw up, but whether it was from the revolting sensation of the dragon's tongue or her innards beginning to be crushed, she didn't know. *She didn't know.* She was going to die! In a moment she began to remember the biggest memories of life. Most of them consisted of Elizabeth. Then there were a few of . . . *nothing.*

Elizabeth. Her mind wandered back to thoughts of her only family. Her sister. To the Princess's disposition now that Aurah was gone. Elizabeth.

Elizabeth.

Aurah's mouth shot open with sudden realization, and a plan came into place.

"Wait!" The little air left wrestled its way from her lungs. Would it work? She didn't know, but it was her only chance.

To her surprise, the squeezing stopped. Stopped progressing, at least. She would have to manage with that.

"I . . . know why . . . I don't ful . . . ful . . . fill you!" She wheezed horribly, the words forming roughly. She wasn't even able to say some things.

But to her joy, the crush relented enough. Air came surging back into her lungs. Her chest inflated, heart pumping from the new life gained, though it hurt. Her chest didn't have much room to operate; she was still very much constricted.

Aurah tried to focus on her captor's expression, but her body refused. What must be going through its mind right now? When she began to take too long to speak a growl and slight nudge indicated that she had better continue.

"I . . . I am not the human you saw! The one that you wanted, or whatever you were doing!" She looked up now, an act of force and sheer will. Shock and anguish blazed like fire from one point to another across the dragon's features. Its eyes were glued to her. "When you were reaching for the other woman that you saw back at the Capital, debris erupted clouding your vision. I took the opportunity to shove her out of your way. I'm not the one you want. She is!" Aurah stumbled in her speech.

Aurah had reservations about condemning Elizabeth so, but it was her only chance. This beast seemed to be completely lost in its mind. Maybe she could trick it? Maybe they would have developed a better means of fighting off dragons by the time she got back home. Maybe that man, that speck in the sky, would be there to disrupt this atrocity again.

She began to shake violently, not of her own accord, but by the dragon's hand. It was bathed in a shroud of rage. She could feel the tremors of its violence seizing it from the inside out. She had ruined everything for it. Before she could process the next steps of her plan, it spoke.

"I guess I don't need you, after all." Barely more than a whisper but being this close to its gigantic maw, the words drowned her.

Stupid, Aurah screamed at herself. She hadn't foreseen this possibility—the dragon going off on its own, not needing her. She needed it to need her. She reacted before it could finish crushing the life from her. It would have no sympathy, no attachments this time.

"But you do! You do!" She screamed as the grip resumed its position of crushing her. No luck, he didn't listen this time around. She had only one more idea before giving in completely. "You'll never . . . find her . . . without me!" Her wheezing resumed and short, shoddy breaths filled her lungs. The grip released again.

"I can crush you with one, little, gesture, so tell me what I need to know!" It blasted her with its anger.

Her ears rang sharply, sore from being so close to such a loud noise. Her arms and feet kept trying to find spots to prop herself up to find relief from being constricted.

"Do you want to die or not!" It finished its roar.

Aurah shook as much as her body would let her in its position. How she was still alive, she would never know. The very possibility that she could walk away from this with only bruises, tenderness, and a sore side, confounded her. If the dragon believed her, then the next two days of flight would be miserable. The dragon would not be merciful towards her.

Before Aurah could give a response, shock took them both.

Five colossal forms appeared at the opening of the cavern, landing with echoing thuds. The rock all around them shuddered as if cringing from the unexpected weight. The large chamber was filled immediately by the unexpected visitors, blocking the few rays of light that already struggled to crawl inwards.

Dragons.

Her captor startled and spun to face the threat. Aurah lost her sight for second, dizzy from the sudden force in its hand. Where had they come from?

"Oh, sorry. Lover's quarrel?" The smallest among them spoke. A high pitched and raspy voice called out, but it was not as loud as her captor's. The small, deep brown dragon smirked.

Silence fell. Her captor said nothing, taking in their forms.

"Come now, that's no way to treat your guests." The small dragon opened its mouth again, offering a challenge. A smirk again.

"One . . . two . . ." Aurah, in the midst of certain death, scowled at her captor counting. Its grip tightened around her, causing more discomfort. She had missed her chance to get her arms free and keep her whole body from being crushed. "Three . . ." She could feel him moving slightly as he counted and then his count was interrupted by snarling laughter.

"Four! Five!" The small dragon screeched again, cackling madly. It seemed to have found her captor's response amusing. "I have an idea, dragon. Let's keeping counting!" It pivoted slightly to face the entrance and screeched loudly. Silence. Then thunder rang out loudly—no, *not thunder.*

The air outside was abruptly disrupted by the sound of war drums pounding feverishly. Soon crash after crash traveled through the plateau from far above. Rocks broke free from the walls and ceiling everywhere, causing the stones to crack and even groan somehow. A slew of other crashes barely reached their ears from outside the cavern entrance.

The little dragon turned back towards Aurah and her captor and screamed. "Six! Eighteen! One million! You're surrounded by an outstanding force that you *cannot* defeat, scale slime." It emphasized its last words slowly, driving home the point.

Aurah felt the pulse of her captor increase drastically. Its heartbeat steadily pulsated her very core through its grip on her.

"Wha . . . what do you want?" Her captor stammered, trembling from this unexpected turn of events. It was horrifying to hear a dragon's voice, let alone hear a dragon's voice carry so much fear and intimidation.

"We have been watching you for quite a time since before the attack on the human capital, scale slime. And now that we have finally found you, we require your loyal service to the mighty Vasiss, sole ruler of all lands, all nations, all peoples, and all beasts!" Pride welled in the tiny dragon at the mention of its sovereign's name. "Kill the girl and come with us. That is your only option, and this is your last chance." The feigned mirth vanished from its voice.

Somehow, the small talking dragon managed to stare down its snout at Aurah's captor. Sweat streamed down her neck from the rising fear and the dragon's rising heat. Her brilliant plan had failed. These dragons would be the death of her. *All of them!* From the looks of things, that death wouldn't wait much longer.

"No." Her captor's voice rang true and clear. Aurah stared intensely as she felt the dragon's heartbeat skip.

Defiance? Why? Regardless, it was most likely a lose-lose situation for her, but her only hope now was to bet on her captor. She hated that she was dependent on that creature.

Rage flushed through the small dragon's face. The other beasts in the room broke out in their devilish grins. "Kill him." The tiny dragon gave the order casually, seasons of practice sheltered in his voice.

The claw around her pulled her inwards, protecting her, as a look of surprise shot across the unwelcome dragons' faces. Her captor had taken the initiative. Barreling forward on three legs, he plowed into the oppressors, trying to break free from their containment. *He failed.*

A large dragon slammed her captor into the rock wall to the side. It roared and the others fell back. This dragon was a little lighter brown in color compared to the small leader. It looked intently, taking pleasure in its task.

"Let me go!" her captor roared. Desperation poured from its words. Aurah panicked with the dragon holding her. Her captor was working not to crush its captive. She looked up at her captor as best as she could—*were his scales . . . lighter?* Something strange was happening, and Aurah could only remain helpless in the dragon's claw.

"Do it again!" The little dragon took a step back, allowing the attacking dragon room enough to thrash her captor. Aurah stared petrified at the oncoming monster. This was all so impossible.

The large dragon, quick on its feet, slammed into her captor again and beat him into the wall. Her captor took a pummeling trying to protect its captive. She felt the dragon's clammy palms and saw blood trickling down its side. Her captor's blood coated the wall that it was being beaten against. If walls could bleed too, then the chips and cracks littering the stone would be the equivalent of blood. The wall was probably longing for relief, as much as her captor.

The attacking dragon backed away as the little leader cackled madly at the violence.

"Kill him! Kill him!" It cried.

Encouraged by its leader, the large dragon began approaching her captor again, slowly, leaving a large gap between the two. *Well, large for Aurah.* Her body ached in the dragon's claw. The beating had shocked her body tremendously. The pain burned deep down. She wouldn't be surprised if somehow, they made their way out of this tragedy and her whole body turned blue-purple from a wealth of bruises.

The attacking dragon lowered its head, locking in its claws to the stone, ripping Aurah from her thoughts. She felt her captor tense. *Even more pressure on her body!*

Then her captor did something strange.

It slammed its tail into the wall. Aurah ached from the vibrations she felt through the dragon. A human wasn't meant to withstand the same kind of things a dragon was. Her breathing was ragged. Her captor slammed its tail again into the wall and loud crack ripped from the rock.

Then the large dragon charged ferociously. Her captor managed one last slam of its tail before dodging out of the way, letting the charging dragon slam into the wall.

Then the world began to shake with an angry chorus of cracks and the coarse noise of stone being ripped from itself.

Something big broke from the dragon's impact. A flurry of stones exploded free from the wall as a tremendous rift split up the face of the stone wall, wrenching rock from rock with a terrible grinding noise that would not stop. As the pieces fell, Aurah tried to move her head out of the path of a burst of sunlight. *Light?* Then more pieces fell from the wall and more light poured into the chamber.

Her captor ran desperately for the entrance of the cave past a slew of stunned and confused dragons. They stared at the attacking dragon, whose leg now lay pinned under the weight of a large section of the wall, screeching terribly for help.

Her captor was faster than the understanding spreading across the other dragons' faces. More chips and waves of stone pelted the occupants in the cave. Dust filled the air and dirt fell everywhere.

The little dragon turned slowly towards the two escapees as understanding finally filled its features. Fear wrestled understanding for a place to rest on its face.

Aurah stared forward, gawking at the awesome destruction and how it raced outward through the stone, leaving a trail of cracks and falling stone in the ceiling and walls. She couldn't tell whose heartbeat she felt anymore.

She knew in an instant what was happening as the stone world around them began to crumble and teeter wildly.

Aurah's breath caught not from being crushed, but because she secretly hoped that her captor would somehow escape its cave.

The plateau was collapsing.

CHAPTER TWENTY

Kast ran.

His head hung down as he hurtled past the intruders in his home.

His claws gripped the stone, launching him forward. It wasn't even a few seconds before he was over the edge of his cave, slicing through the air, straight for the distant ground.

Kast kept his body sleek, plummeting quickly. There were exactly thirty-five—*thirty, now*—dragons waiting to murder him and the trash lying in his clutch. He shot a look over his shoulder towards his former home.

Kast threw a wing up reactively, barely dodging a massive hunk of the plateau, and his stomach caught in his throat. He threw his weight immediately to side, rolling away from another section of falling death.

Time slowed for the dragon as his focus shifted completely towards his next moves. Not even a minute had gone by since that filth broke the wall of his cave, felling the whole rock formation. Kast's den had been filled by the weight of all the rock above it crashing down, almost instantaneously. Kast had known the place was extremely unstable; maybe that's why he chose to make his home there. He had hoped it would have crushed him unexpectedly, never allowing him to escape to the cruel world again. He had hoped it would become his grave. Instead, it had saved him. *How ironic.*

Kast judged the plateau in front of him, gauging the amount of space he would have to fly through the channels between the other plateaus. He had to fly through the cramped space; the moment he rose above the top of the plateaus and their forests, he and his captive were as good as dead. They may not even make it as far as the air above the tops. *They probably wouldn't even make it out alive flying down below.*

Kast darted forward, nearly rounding the next plateau now, maneuvering through the hordes of the falling stone, even trees now—some still had the scent of fire to them. The dragon gulped hard and then locked his eyes on his route forward. He dared not look back for fear of losing speed. He must be swift and careful.

A loud explosion ripped through the air from above, sending a violent shockwave through the plateau to the dragon's side, Kast couldn't help but look.

The sight was incredible.

His plateau had tipped forward, crashing right into the plateau he had just managed to reach.

More chunks of stone erupted from the plateau far above, and now down at Kast's level rocks launched outward, spraying the air and catching Kast off guard. There was so much pressure behind those painful projectiles.

Darkness invaded the deep channels, blocked by the destroyed titans of earth warring with each other. It was nearing two minutes since the collapse of his home, and he needed to move faster.

Kast felt the blood racing through his long neck. Sweat dripped heavily from his scales only to be caught by the raging wind and carried away. Tension coursed freely through his tendons. It was all he could do to not crush the key in his hand. The key to his purpose fulfilled. *Truly this time.*

Kast clenched his maw tightly. *How dare she?* He let his claw grip that much tighter. He poured the rest of his fury into rolling to the side and diving beneath a shower of boulders.

By now, the dragon had shot past the plateaus and began veering away from the colossal destruction. His body ached from the beating he received earlier. *All because of this stupid girl in his hand.*

Kast . . . .

Oh, no. The dragon's heart gripped.

Just kill the girl, Kast. Why must you hurt us like this?

The plateau behind filled the air with deafening roars, but Kast could barely hear the sound of the breaking stone.

Kill her? Kast's heart assumed a convoluted rhythm. His wild eyes darted around and panic seized control. He should kill her, shouldn't he? After all she had done to him?

Stop fighting, Kast. If only you had listened to me earlier and hadn't fought me, then you wouldn't be in this situation.

Kill her?

Kill her, Kast. You are the most powerful. You are—

A giant rock slammed into Kast's hindquarter, ripping him from his trance. The dragon bellowed out a roar of anger and turned to decimate the rock that dared to touch him.

Kast gasped, an awful sound from a dragon.

Not a rock! A—

"It's time to die, nest scum!" A horrid voice boomed, following up with a jet of flames.

Kast tucked the girl deeper towards his belly and wrapped his body around her as a shield. A dragon's hide could stand quite a bit, but the heat was quickly unbearable.

Kast dived without a second thought and reverted his direction back towards the torrent of thundering earth. There was only one way he could even possibly hope to make it out alive.

The dragon pursuing him turned out to be multiple dragons, all heaving their flame on him. Kast didn't care. He flew hard, and fast, and retraced the distance he had already covered. The storm of rocks and boulders picked up again as the sun struggled to send a ray of light or two down to their tomb.

Kast dived, ducked, rolled, spun, and used every ounce of his flying experience to dodge the dragons on his tail. By his count, there were only eight of them, but he didn't focus on their numbers. He focused on the number of rocks filling the air.

Kast stopped darting between the rocks and slammed the air with his wings, blasting forward. There was thankfully a wide enough avenue through the pieces of the plateaus that were falling. He heard yelps and screams as the dragons behind tried to keep up *and failed.*

Kast smiled to himself. This felt good, destroying again. He flew straight to one of the last massive sections of rock, landed and pushed off, quickly changing direction to weave into a clearer opening of air.

The two falling plateaus had begun to fill the ravine from the bottom up and now a third plateau, which had been hit by the second, had begun to lose its standing. Kast climbed towards the sky, leaving what he once thought was the safety of the tight corridors behind. The dragons were able to fly well and were smaller. He would never get away from them safely down below, but Kast knew that with his larger wings and more powerful beats he could keep ahead of the brutes in the open sky.

Kast nearly smiled at his cleverness, cleaving the air with his powerful wings; which was freed now from all chunks of rock except the wispy dust.

Then he broke above the tops of the plateaus to greet the emboldening sun,

His heart dropped.

Aurah had no words. The flying was a horrible experience. The dragon had squeezed much too hard, and the heat of the other dragon's flame scorched her, even within the dragon's

protection. Her captor flew through the crazy mess of the falling rocks, and she watched their pursuers falter beneath the hail and turn away.

It happened so quickly.

Now Aurah was squinting from the bright sun and the whirling air—and was staring at the most horrendous sight ever.

Aurah gaped at an army of dragons, all surrounding the point where she and her captor emerged from the depths below. Some were sitting on the tops of the nearby plateaus or floating idly in the air waiting for them.

And these weren't small dragons. They all were much larger than the dragons below, except one that was enormous—nearly the size of her captor, if not larger. Aurah felt a familiar sense of dread—maybe she had been seeing too much of these beast's scales. She was sick of dragons.

Her captor seemed to billow upward, frozen.

Then the dragons all inhaled, filling their lungs. The air gusted around Aurah and tossed her hair wildly. As the air grew very thin, the dragons all seemed to stand perfectly still except for their slowly inflating chests.

Then they deflated.

Fire clawed its way from every last one of the scaly beast's throats.

She suddenly heard her captor's heart start again, pounding violently. Then its wings snapped outward and whipped the air.

Aurah hunched her head, sealing her eyes shut, trying to protect herself. She thought she had felt an impossible force before, but now, the dragon's speed was incomparable and so was the pressure exerted on her body.

Aurah heard the dragons behind them. Their roars were loud. Her body was covered in sweat from fear and heat.

Aurah forced her eyes open to look towards the disappearing ground, the beginnings of the evening sun illuminating the expanse before her. The swath of the plateaus' destruction was already completely out of the young woman's sight.

What insanity.

She finally began to process the events that had happened so quickly, shutting her eyes again. Fear peaked as she thought about the situation she was in now. Her body must be reacting slowly to the danger around her, hardened by the terrible time spent as the dragon's prisoner. Her heart and mind both landed on the same driving question.

Will I make it?

She didn't know. The whole experience was surreal. Being kidnapped by a dragon, living in a foreign place, in a foreign way. Her captor trying to kill her, other dragons trying to kill her captor—and everyone was racing back to the capital. Aurah was in hope of salvation. Her captor hoped to make a body switch. And the other dragons hoped they would catch their prey.

Aurah had no doubt they would.

She scoffed at her plan. There was no way her stupid ideas would ever work. What hope was she clinging to? Why couldn't she just accept death? She was weak.

A loud screech and a ball of flame caught her attention, warming her skin against the rush of air. Aurah didn't open her eyes yet, letting them recover from the racing wind, but she knew the dragons had to be close behind, gaining even.

Her captor flew low, somewhat close to the tops of the thinning rock formations. She hoped it wasn't because it was afraid of crashing.

Aurah felt her lips press hard together in a scowl. The only feasible creature to put her trust in was the very monster poised to harm another soul and kill.

The air raged around her, whipping her hair and trying to keep her eyes shut, but Aurah wrestled them back open against the cutting blades of wind. A forest loomed on the horizon and grew close. Fast. *How fast were they flying?* She didn't know if the forest was a good thing or bad. Locked facing forward, she hoped the beast had a plan to do something about these other monsters on their tail or they were both dead. *That might be for the best...* Aurah drew her lips together even tighter, her brow furrowed.

The rock formations below had already turned in to spires and were shrinking in size the closer that they got to the forest. Trees laced more frequently between the rocks, growing into the forest. Aurah had no idea where they were. The trees thickened and the rocks were laced infrequently throughout, barely visible beneath the treetops anymore. The earth beneath the forest still looked choppy, like a giant fist had beat it into a mess of rolling hills and a great many valleys.

Aurah finally gained perspective at their speed before the wind forced her eyes shut again. In a single second, ten to twenty trees had flown by. She hadn't traveled this quickly with the dragon before. Even the thought of the world speeding by made her nauseous. She peeled her eyes open again, hoping her body didn't recede into a fit of dry heaves. The treetops kept flowing by, only a slight distance beneath themselves. The dragon descended as close as it could to the trees, rising only to dodge the odd ones sticking above the others. Her captor's heart raced at a rate to match their pace. Its wings were a flurry of beats, tearing through the air.

Flames shot by them from behind, dissipating into the air—a sharp reminder not to get comfortable. Her captor's claws dipped slightly to the side, enough to show Aurah the dragons on their tail.

Their lead was completely lost.

The dragon's arm dipped back under, then slightly outward again. Turning her head to watch, a scream escaped from her lips as a dragon dived upon their back. The pursuing beast swung forward hoping to disable her captor with its claws reared.

To the dragons,' and Aurah's, surprise, her captor barrel-rolled, bringing up its free front claw and dragged it down the length of the attacker. Blood exploded, pressurized, from the dragon's belly. It screeched, dropping to the trees below and disrupting the growth.

It had to be dead.

Aurah searched the pursuing dragons whenever her view allowed. She had recognized that little dragon back in her captor's cave as the one from the attack on the Capital, but she hadn't yet seen that uniquely giant one. *Maybe it was gone?*

Her thoughts were interrupted by the descent of her captor. They also slowed down tremendously, causing Aurah's insides to lurch forward uncomfortably.

What is it doing?

Another dragon swooped, taking its turn at an attack, when her captor grabbed one of the nearby tall trees, bending it sharply, then releasing. The sudden tension and relief rebounded the tree back at their assailant, utterly thwarting its maneuvers—and probably its consciousness, if not its life, based on its sudden descent beneath the canopy.

Her captor rocketed away again, stroking the wind aggressively. Could the monster keep this up? There were still so many dragons following them, she couldn't count them all in the short glimpses she was given. They all followed at various distances.

Another dragon lurched forward in an attack. Her captor swerved to the side, dodging the attack as the dragon carried forward, turning around for another pass, but it would never make it.

A flash of light clashed with the rising twilight. The dragon rolled through the air, dropping dead into the trees below.

More flashes burst by Aurah, picking off the dragons. All but her captor. The bolts of light seemed to be intentionally passing by them.

Then she felt her captor seize. A terrible shiver was wrought through its body. Aurah looked up as fear flooded its face, and its skin became cool and clammy. It was facing some terror that haunted its mind. Aurah mimicked the beast before smiling to herself.

Good. Be afraid, you beast.

She didn't have time to guess what had gotten into its head. As she faced forward again, she turned just in time to see a vicious purple and pink ball zero in on her captor and catch him square in the chest, a slight distance from the girl herself.

Aurah stared shocked.

What was that?

She didn't have any clue how she should feel at the moment. Was her captor dead? That meant her own life would shortly be forfeit. The resistance in her bones rose again. She didn't want to die.

Then she felt and heard the dragon's wings beat again. *Not dead.* Then what?

Something rained into her hair, showering her and catching in her raging hair. Aurah stared at the beast's claw around herself to find some of the unknown material piling before being swept away.

Scales? She stared at the flakey mess, her brow furrowed.

The dragon's flight stuttered, interrupting her thoughts. She looked around at the world before turning back to her examination. *What?*

Her mouth fell open and her body stiffened as she abruptly understood. She watched as the wind ripped at the dragon's armor, peeling it off and throwing it to the world. The claw that held her was shedding. The scales had to belong to it. That wasn't the end of the oddness though—the beast's flesh was changing, too. The hard defense of scales and skin softened, beginning to resemble the color and feel of her own arm. She could feel the strength of its grip lessening and incredibly enough, it seemed to be growing smaller.

What's going on?

She looked again at the world and balked.

If she thought that they had dropped closer to the ground and trees before, it was nothing like actually crashing into them.

CHAPTER TWENTY-ONE

The world spun out of control, and the sound of crashing and breaking flooded Aurah's ears.

Direction lost all meaning as she held on and was violently tossed.

Tree after tree pelted them. *Ten to twenty in a second.*

The dragon kept her mostly sheltered, but an occasional branch whipped around its guard, catching her now exposed legs and arms. Even her face took a beating.

Adrenaline kicked in, unlike anything she ever felt before, giving her superior clarity and understanding. The pain from the branches was nothing but a minor inconvenience. The wind was disrupted by the growth and it was easier to see below, save the dimming light and the obstacles of trees.

Her captor faced it all, too, though it somehow hung onto her despite its weird transformations and the crash.

The changes became increasingly more rapid on the beast. It didn't even look like a dragon anymore. From what she could tell, it was more akin to a large clump of flesh, shrinking with every second.

She was spun upwards to lay on top of the dragon. It had rolled over to aim what had been its back towards the ground.

Then they hit the ground.

The impact was bone-jarring.

The crater was absurd, and the ditch that trailed after it from their crash had to be just as ludicrous.

Her chest unexpectedly began to rock in a mad guffaw. *Now I'm insane or dead!* Her laughter was maniacal. She wasn't shocked at her madness. Was she broken? Or was this a result of the situation at hand? Aurah had no idea, but she couldn't help but laugh. This close to death, who wouldn't? *Right?*

The beast beneath her jerked to a stop, ripping her from its clutches and sending her rolling forward, free at last. The monster must have lost its grip completely as it shrunk to oblivion. *Good.*

Her rolling away came to a jolting halt as Aurah caught a tree with her body. A groan tore from her lips, filling the darkness that surrounded her in the depths of the forest. Adrenaline wouldn't help her much longer. She needed to move while she could.

Aurah shoved off the forest floor and charged forward. She used the tree and its branches to steady herself in a haze that oddly brought her sobriety. She wanted to see what had become of the monster. She stumbled and fell. *Run!* Her brain screamed. *Run! Run! Run! Go! Go! Go!*

Aurah let out a scream, pleasing her rush of adrenaline.

Wild and untamed, the forest was thick with undergrowth. Vines fell everywhere, laced into the treetops and their many limbs. Layers of dead leaves and other plants coated the forest floor, muting the sound of any walking, *or running,* except for the sound of snapping sticks being trampled underfoot. The aroma of pines mingled with the earthy smell of decay and dampness. The trees hoarded most of the light from the already dim twilight.

One foot after another. Her right side possessed a voice that steadily screamed louder and louder, but now was only one of many pains vying for attention. She heaved out her empty gut. She was certain from the pain that everything was bruised now. Adrenaline was only an empty negotiator with her body. It offered empty promises of hope and relief. *Such a scoundrel!* Aurah laughed again, ending in a sharp gasp. She couldn't think straight, though she knew exactly what she was doing. *Right?*

Who cares!

She grabbed the trees with as much strength as possible, pulling herself back towards the final resting place of the wretched beast. She would spit on its grave. Manic laughter laced her groans of pain.

The crater where the beast lay felt far away, but she knew it was just her inability to move well and process uninhibited that made this excursion take longer and seem far more stretched out than it should have. It's funny how one is acutely aware of every second when each moment is drenched in pain. All she cared about right now was spitting on the beast.

The vegetation gave way to reveal the monster's impact crater. It destroyed a wide swath of trees where they had hit and even more where they continued sliding forward, disrupting the forest. The path seemed to steadily grow thinner the closer she got.

Aurah stumbled back towards the end of the impact. She had rolled something akin to twenty trees away before actually catching one. That was lucky in such a populated forest. The long roll dissipated enough of her momentum to make the stop less destructive. The vines in the way probably helped quite a bit, as well, though Aurah had her doubts based on what her body was trying to say.

This was all its fault. Anger flowed through the channels of her mind.

It was all for naught. Her pain, her sorrow, her certain death—for Aurah would most certainly keel over and accept death as soon as she spit on the wretch's grave. Maybe she would live? All alone in the forest with no idea how to survive, all by her…

She jerked out of her skin.

A low moan escaped the crash site.

She trembled, hesitant to move forward. Her mania dissipated in an instant.

What is going on?

She heard another moan and some rustling.

Her foot hesitated at first, then she inched forward as carefully as she could. She was prepared to run at any moment. *If she could.* She knew that she would force herself to. Maybe she would die? *Hopefully.*

The edge of the crater was right before her when she saw it.

A fleshy arm and hand protruded from the dirt at an odd angle. Her eyes darted back and forth taking in the whole scene. The dirt pulsed in cadence, shifting slightly. The arm moved. Then a foot appeared. Her hand covered her mouth.

"Help." The moan was a word, a single word. "Please." Another whimper, ending in a hiss.

The dirt shifted, falling away in a cascade to reveal a face.

It was bruised, the only hair on the mutilated face was eyebrows. Brown, short-cropped hair fell haphazardly from what should have been its scalp. An average nose, though twisted and bleeding, hung over a mouth with broken teeth. One eye was swollen shut. The other was wide open—

—A deep amber gem.

Aurah nearly screamed.

"Help, please." The broken mouth barely moved. The eye never left her face, pleading for relief.

This man . . . .

This man . . . .

He was her captor—*the dragon.*

Somehow.

She stumbled backward, falling to the ground painfully, aghast and completely caught off guard. Never would she have imagined that this was the heinous creature's fate. Her gaze fell to the ground, at a loss for action until a rock caught her eye.

Before she could process, her body revolted against the storm of pain. Her muscles tensed and became animalistic, coerced by the primal wave of wrath balling up in her gut.

Baring her teeth, her legs exploded.

She lunged for the rock and it fit her hand perfectly as she tore it from the dirt. She threw herself over the crater wall and on top of the man buried beneath the earth.

Teeth parting, a vicious roar tore free, screaming out her pent-up rage and loathing for this horrendous creature. Her glare shot death as the one amber eye turned dark in hopeless realization, *begging for mercy.*

It would find none.

The rock fell hard, backed by the pain and misery of the young woman.

One strike, it cut the face.

Two strikes.

Three.

By the fourth strike, the face was screaming. The monster must not know how to control its new form just yet.

Good.

Five strikes.

Six.

Aurah screamed, her rage drowning out the meager pain of the trash beneath her. Every blow with the rock unlocked another tier of passion bottled up inside. The deepest pits of her heart released their murder.

Seven strikes.

Eight strikes.

Nine strikes.

By the time she reached ten, she stopped counting and just embraced fury. She would be the monster now. She didn't care. She hated it. She hated it!

"I hate you!" She screeched, venom glazing her eyes. She fell into a glorious rhythm. The face stopped screaming after a while; Aurah didn't, though. She kept her lungs billowing out their load. She kept her arm warm, throwing the rock again, and again.

A minute passed before she finally collapsed sobbing over top of the mutilated face, blood pooling everywhere. Her heart broke. This wasn't her. What had driven her to such extremes?

I hate it.

She repeated those words in her mind, but her heart failed to chime in its response. Her heart was numb. She was broken in so many pieces.

Who cares?

She slowly crawled away from the scene. Numb.

She needed to leave. Somehow. If something were around, it would certainly have heard that episode.

Where to?

Anywhere but here was good.

As much as her body would allow, she rose from the ground, one burden gone, and a new one in its place. She moved forward slowly, as fast as she could. She hobbled, gripping the trees for support. This time her adrenaline abandoned her to her own devices. *The scoundrel.*

She would never survive. Her thoughts were delirious. The world spun with every step. Was this darkness? Was this instability in her heart?

She stifled it. There was no answer. She crushed her rising thoughts and tuned her senses into the world around her.

Her steps carried her far away. Time was irrelevant, or was it? She didn't know. She stopped to breathe for a second, slowing down her movements.

Slow.

Focus on reality, her thoughts admonished her.

Slowly.

She laid an arm across her chest and leaned against a nearby tree. Her lungs quieted as she breathed deep. In a few moments, her composure was restored—for the time being, at least. She had no tears. Not yet. Her reserves of tears were depleted. Maybe later.

Maybe.

She had lifted her head from its rest and turned to keep moving when she heard it.

Wildly.

Unexpectedly.

Wonderfully? She didn't know.

A high-pitched shriek shattered the world. Loud and close.

Then another.

And another.

A whole pack.

Those monsters. It was more of those beasts.

Aurah gripped the tree. There would be no end, no relief in sight for her. There was only death in store. She would never make it home. She was cursed to death. Some god, some destiny, whatever there was, had condemned her to the worst.

Who cares?

She wrapped her arms around the tree, finding solace in the only support she knew at that moment. Maybe there were some tears left after all. Maybe she could still claim to be human.

Maybe.

Growling shredded the quiet ambiance. Vicious snarls from the horse-sized beasts berated her broken frame.

Oh, well.

A high-pitched whine from one of the monsters overturned its pack mate's growls.

"Yah! Get tha' beasts, men! Save the bounty!" A voice screamed over the noise. The whistling of arrows flashed by Aurah's head. She dropped to the ground, weeping and gripping the tree.

What cruel plan did fate have laid out for her now?

The sound of men's footsteps raced past her towards the wolf-like monsters. Battle cries erupted all around.

Then it stopped. So quickly.

Silence rested in the air, interrupted by footsteps. Lots of footsteps. They ended nearby.

"She's a purty one, she is. She'll fetch a fair price once the ouchies be gone." An iron grip wormed its way into her hair, yanking her to her feet.

Aurah's fist flailed out towards the voice and connected with a satisfying thud. The hand released its grip with a cry of pain. She had never thrown a punch before in her life, and her fist was letting her know that fact explicitly.

"You filth!" A knee connected with her stomach, dropping her to ground, followed by a kick in her gut, expelling the air from her lungs. What did she need air for?

Aurah let out a breathless sigh. There would be no end to the pain.

None.

"Knock it off, you rock skull! She's no good damaged or dead. Corvis, carry 'er to your horse. We need to leave before more Savages show up."

A strong grasp found her arm and dragged her to her feet. She wasn't ready to stand yet. She wasn't ready for anything. She was completely lost.

She turned her head to see her new captors when a bag brought darkness and ropes brought restraint. Her body cried out against the pain and her voice moaned slightly.

Where to now? she wondered gently as her mind faded to blessed unconsciousness, carried on the shoulder of an unknown enemy.

CHAPTER TWENTY-TWO

Aurah first woke to a dreadfully cold world. She heard voices over the ringing and pounding in her head, though barely.

"She don't look like she'll make it. Boss says to let her struggle to live, we ain't wastin' no nothing on 'er."

"Good. Then I'll be the one to kill the whore for good."

Aurah fell back to the dark embrace of sleep.

A sneeze woke her the next time. Her body shook from a hot chill, and she groaned in pain from the sudden stress. She glanced around the dimly lit room, moving as little as possible. A row of vertical lines interrupted the fading light that stood against the gloom, coming from a single dying candle on a table. *Outside her cage.* She was in a cell.

Sleep took the girl again.

A sharp pain ripped her awake. Blood poured down her arm.

Something black moved in the shadows on her arm. Aurah grunted and weakly threw her arm over to get rid of the shadow. *She hit something furry.*

A high-pitched squeak retorted back, biting her arm again. Aurah thrashed, throwing off the rat. It scurried away. *For the time being.*

Aurah gripped her arm as the wound trickled down and slowed. There were no tears.

The world around her was dark and damp. The stone floor broke through what appeared to be her bedding—straw which she had guessed had caused the sneeze earlier. She really only remembered the idea of a sneeze. The pain was receding, leaving Aurah again with a clouded mind that wished for release unto death.

The rock beneath herself was moist and freezing. Her tattered dress could hardly be called that anymore. It barely even covered her in places. *Who cares?*

Aurah lay holding her arm near the bite

"Oh, the purty gurl is awake now, is she?" A shadowed face appeared from a doorway she just now noticed.

She tried to sit up, but her body wouldn't let her. Instead, her muscles tightened in insubordination and her throat seized, making it hard to swallow. She was going nowhere anytime soon. She fell back onto the straw, relieving what tension she could. At least it was softer than stone.

She stared, drunk on pain and exhaustion, tired of being powerless and taken places against her will. She now hated every second of life—now that it had betrayed her and thrown as many horrible things at her as it pleased, things no person should ever have to experience. *So why did she?* Her face scrunched and emotion welled up in her eyes and chest. Her throat tightened regardless of her efforts to relax it. She sniffled back what she could and turned her eyes onto the man in front of her. He was looking down at her arm, and she thought she saw a smile appear on his twisted face.

"Hah, tramp. Hope you get sumthin' nasty from that little bite." His voice cut through the darkness. "Well, don't start with yer blatherin' and sobbin' again. We've only just got used to ya not screamin' in yer sleep." The owner of the voice walked forward into the light. He was a grimy man, and a nasty sneer was plastered on his face, revealing rotted stumps of teeth. He wore a basic amount of armor, chain mail over a leather tunic, and a sword was strapped to his side. A scar traveled from above his left eye across his skull, interrupting the hair that grew there.

Aurah had shifted enough to see the man. The most prominent feature she saw was a dark violet bruise surrounding his eye.

"What happened to your face, sir?" She could barely sputter, but she said it anyhow. She didn't know if she should be thankful or regretful to Morris for her smart mouth.

"Tramp!" The man snatched a mug of some liquid from the table and dumped it on her.

It had to have been some kind of alcohol. It reeked and seeped into her already destroyed clothing and hair. Worse yet, it was cold and stole the little bit of warmth she had. "Keep yer mouth shut if ya know what's good fer ya!" He spit on her face then turned around flustered. He exited the room quickly.

Aurah gingerly wiped off the spit. She wouldn't weep. She refused to shed a tear. Yet another lock fell on her already desperately isolated heart. She scoffed instead.

She still hated that monster, that dragon.

But now, these monsters she faced were her own skin and bone, and she hated them, too. She wouldn't give in. She reveled in the payback she had dealt that beast. She dreamed of the payback she would give to these cretins now.

She fell back, covered in bile, cold and wet. A stench covered her. She didn't care. Exhaustion took her and she slept.

Yelling. Sounds of war. Iron clashed against iron. The dragon flew above the city carrying an enormous sword in its claw. It breathed its fire, burning everything. Catapults and ballistae fired repeatedly at the sky to no avail. Elizabeth stood beside her as she watched the madness unfold, a panorama of destruction.

Then, more dragons came. They all flew with synchronicity, like a swirling wave of the sea. Air whipped by, disturbed by the mighty wings of the creatures in the sky. She heard the screams of men. Pain resonated in her ears.

All of them fell to the power of the mighty dragon.

Then the cloaked man appeared.

Who was he?

A strange warmth crept through her belly.

This man! He had come to save her! He must love her! She giggled amidst the warring, the fire, and the death.

The cloaked man leaped into the air, and magic surrounded his blessed hands. He charged straight at the enemy. He was about to kill the dragon with the sword—*her captor and enemy!*

The cloaked man was abou . . . .

A scream of agony echoed loudly, pouring in from the doorway.

Aurah shot upright, wrenched from the most pleasant dream she had had in quite some time. Pain seared through her body from the movement, though it didn't restrain her as badly as before. Every bone ached. The haze in her mind had not left, and she only felt slightly less like she was dying.

Aurah slowly pushed to her feet and moved to grab the bars of her cell. She found a smile breaking over her face.

It was the cloaked man! The dream was a sign!

Aurah gripped the bars heartily and smiled deliriously at the darkness on the other side of the doorway. The cloaked man was the only one who had confronted and beat the evil that her captor was. Obviously, that was because he had loved her. *Aurah.*

And now, Aurah was sure he would stride up to her, a path of destruction and these dead men laying behind him. The thought brought her a fountain of happiness. Her savior would find her behind these rust encrusted bars and would shatter them by force alone, without need for keys. He already had the one key he needed, and that was the key to her heart.

Her stomach fluttered and her heart beat for the first time in forever. She couldn't remember the last time she had been this excited. In fact, she couldn't remember far back at all, so she just smiled at how nicely life was treating her.

The screams and the cries grew louder.

Aurah fawned over the visions of grandeur of her savior.

Then the screaming grew to a climax, accented by a few slight glimpses of shadows on the other side of the door.

The man she had seen from earlier suddenly darted into the room with terror etched across his distorted features. He had his sword drawn and looked poised and ready to strike.

"Hey! There's another one in here! Get them! Kill them all! Then come for me! I'm in here! I'm in here!" Aurah yelled as loudly as her voice would allow.

"Shut yer mouth, you brat!" The man turned his back to the doorway and pounced, stabbing his sword at her through the bars.

The arm and the sword stopped immediately.

Aurah slowly noticed the large figure standing behind the man. *How had she missed the shadow slipping up behind him?*

A swirling cloak had caught her attention. Her heartbeat raced again, forgetting reality.

Her dream really was a sign!

It was her savior!

The cloaked man.

The brute's face turned ashen as he realized what her smile meant and why his sword and arm refused to obey. He tried to twist around to fight, only to expose himself to the intruder.

A shadowed fist flew forward in the dim light and caught the man in the chest. Blood expelled from his mouth. Aurah tried to focus on the scene before her but her head throbbed.

Her savior grabbed the man and spun lightning-fast, crushing the man into the stone wall. Aurah couldn't be sure, but it looked like the stone had been fractured, impacted by the man and her savior's power. The man fell over, completely lifeless, blood pooling beneath his body.

Aurah smiled happily.

It's over now for sure.

"I'm so glad to see you!" Aurah screamed loudly at the man. She was so excited. This was the start of a new beginning. So much hope had filled her spirit again. Now she could fix everything and the world return to normal. Even a wonderful savior had been given to fill her life. She couldn't exactly remember why, but there had seemed to be a huge, painful, hole where a savior had once fit before. Now that hole was filled again. Aurah smiled, dazed but happy.

The cloaked man turned its head and every happy feeling burned to a crisp in an instant. She remembered why there was a hole in her life.

Dori—nothing!

Nothing stood in front of her.

"D, d, Dorian!" Aurah screamed, horrified. The mangled and bloody face of the captain stared back at her. It remained expressionless.

This wasn't happening! Aurah trembled before the walking carcass of the man she had cared so much about. It wasn't even a man anymore. This wasn't the Dorian she knew. She didn't want to see him. She didn't want to remember, but she couldn't lie to herself with him standing right in front of her.

Her teeth gritted. Life was evil. Life hated her. Life was worthless, and it was pointless playing these cheap games. Aurah leaned over and dry heaved.

Dorian looked around and moved. He seemed to walk clumsily; his body must not have healed. In his rush, he knocked over the candle, and darkness overtook them both. Aurah barely heard his movements as her palms moistened and she stepped backward. She didn't want this. She wanted to be left alone to die in this cell.

A loud boom resounded around her, splitting her head and worsening her headache. Then a hand reached out and grabbed her arm, hefting her up and supporting her. "Stop," Aurah muttered weakly. She was getting tired of being grabbed by her arm and lifted. It now felt like her arm was being torn from her shoulder.

Dorian ignored her and dragged her through the darkness. He was moving quickly, picking up pace. They exited the cell room and turned corner after corner, rushing through the darkness. It was strange. Sometimes he stopped moving altogether and waited, then proceeded. Aurah thought she heard fighting and screams in the distance. The look on Dorian's face seemed to confirm that something was amiss, but if Dorian was here, then who was doing all of the fighting? What was happening?

Eventually, they broke free from the depths of the foreign construct. It was dark here, too, though it smelled fresher and made Aurah feel somewhat better. There was an uneasy snorting nearby. She looked.

It was one of those wolf-like creatures, come to finish her off!

Dorian moved towards it, though. Fear gripped Aurah's already unsteady heart. What was he doing moving towards that certain death? Her pulse thumped wildly. What if the beast tried to kill her? Dorian would never be able to stand against the beast!

His gentle hands supported her, taking her to the beast. She tried to refuse his intentions but was powerless in mind and body. Dorian laid her arms over the beast. It felt weird, different than how it looked. She turned her head slowly. The beast had at some point changed into a horse. Now she had some idea what was going on. Dorian was trying to escape with her.

She stopped resisting and let her savior help.

Supporting her waist, he lifted her in a way that helped her mount the animal. Strength and warmth coursed through her legs. Her eyes unleashed newfound tears. The animal brought so much comfort, a stark contrast against the darkness that enshrouded her for longer than she cared to remember.

Maybe Dorian really was alive, and she had just missed something. She felt her heart aching to be in his arms. Maybe she should stop doubting and stop making life more difficult. Maybe she was the problem all along? Dorian moved and fumbled with the horse's reins tied around a post. Suddenly he ripped the reigns free from the post, breaking the leather before he jumped onto the horse behind her. He wasn't smooth at the motion, but he was strong and steady.

Aurah slumped forward, too tired to process Dorian's strange actions. The warmth from the beast crept into her skin. It was the softest thing she had felt in quite a long time. Dorian flailed oddly, shaking the reigns. It took a moment, but he finally motioned the horse forward. They moved quickly, and the world blurred around them as they left behind the strange walls of stone and the fading cries of fighting.

The world of darkness encircled the two on the horse as sleep culled Aurah into its depths of rest and security.

CHAPTER TWENTY-THREE

Aurah woke, and a pain thundered in her skull, rattling her brain. She squinted hard, her eyes taking their time to accustom to the bright light next to her. A campfire crackled an arm's length away. The warmth was wonderful, but the sharp illumination did nothing to alleviate her headache. She turned her head away to stare at darker things.

She screamed.

Whoever had saved her filled her vision, sitting only slightly away from her feet, wrapped in the shadows wearing a loose cloak, a length of leather was tied about his waist to hold it in place. A hood covered his face as he stared at the fire. The memories came flooding back at the sight of his cloak, ending with the sweet salvation that he had brought to her. She regained enough of her composure to remember the good he had done for her. Her heartbeat slowed down, but her mind raced towards unanswered questions.

Who was he? There was no way he could be . . . *Dorian,* as she had deliriously thought earlier. That was a ridiculous presumption. Aurah's throat knotted, so she moved on quickly.

Where did he come from? Maybe most importantly—*can I trust him?*

She reflected on the memory of being in that cell. Her head hurt, but she could remember a lot of what happened, though not clearly. It all seemed surreal. She thought through what she could process of their escape and remembered the impossible strength this cloaked figure possessed. Maybe she shouldn't trust him after all? Was it the cloaked man who appeared at the Capital so long ago? It would make sense, his strength.

The memories of crashing with the dragon were *very* obscure, though she remembered the justice she had dealt to the dragon. She smiled, knowing she had killed that beast. The dragon's den seemed like forever away, yet it couldn't have been too long, *right?* Her stomach churned at the recollection. The conditioning of the recent past began to cry for her to flee. She moved to her feet tenderly, pushing herself to leave the haven of warmth by the fire. It was time to go.

"Wait."

So, it has a voice. A very coarse and unpracticed voice. It carried a strange accent.

"Why? Why should I wait?" Her tone carried no patience. There was no mercy or tolerance when it came to defending what was at stake. *She would never be taken captive again.*

"We . . . you . . . I . . . ." He stumbled in his speech, seemingly unable to decide what exactly he wanted to say.

"Listen, it was nice to be rescued, but you didn't need to do it. I don't have the time, strength, or energy to put up with a senseless meat-bag. Find some other damsel to rescue. I need to get somewhere, fast." She turned to leave, her hand cradling the side of her head.

"That's just it. Where are you going?" The voice commanded the air and left a void in its wake. He stayed silent, almost expectantly. He seemed to realize how he came off and changed his statement. "At least until morning, when it's light. I'll give you the horse and point you in the right direction . . . if you like, that is." His husky voice cracked at the end of his offer.

Aurah had no response. She stopped on the fringes of the safety of the fire, staring off into the dark forest. It was a good question and a tempting offer. Maybe if her head wasn't knifing her every second, she could work out her situation and the best course of action, but as it stood, she knew she wouldn't make it far by herself. Or maybe she could make it out there after all. Did she dare trust a stranger?

Her hand moved from the pain in her head to cover the pain in her heart. The world hated her. It was her fault for opening herself up to that pain. If only she never trusted anyone she wouldn't be in this mess. Her heart longed for the safety of nothing. Not even Elizabeth seemed to offer enough comfort for the chasm rent in her heart now. It would just be pain and sacrifice again with Elizabeth. The Princess would just use the handmaiden while convenient and then throw her away. There was no depth there. *Was she ever sincere? Or did Elizabeth just feel sorry for the orphaned child of her parents' personal servants?*

What about her own heart? Aurah moved her hand again to stifle the sobs pressing at the back of her throat. Her shoulders rocked. She hurt. Physically, her body took a beating that would break most men. She hoped it was luck that kept her in one piece up to this point. She feared that her body was hiding an internal wound, waiting to dump the consequences on her at the worst time conceivable. Maybe it wouldn't be long until she would just drop dead. *Who cares?* She didn't. She found if she cared too much, then disappointment was certain. *Whatever!* She was shredded. Torn into tiny pieces that no one was ever capable of putting back together. The dark of the night that lay in front of her eyes resonated the bleakness of her now cursed path. She was doomed in life—what little bit of life she had left that is. She inhaled, trying to pull back her tears.

"Why should I trust you? Don't toy with me. I am stripped of my endurance." Her voice cut the air harshly. Quiet gently filled the space her words once occupied.

"I . . . ," the hoarse voice stumbled again.

Aurah turned to look at what would be the unknown man's face. It was hidden in the shroud of the cloak's hood. He stood, and his body rocked unsteadily from the motion, though he seemed to straighten up and fill with resolve.

"I'm choosing right now to make my goal helping you if you would have it!" The voice filled with emotion, becoming louder. "But I can't . . . I can't begin to reconcile that end with the thing that I am now!" He was nearly shouting. He moved forward suddenly, falling onto his hands and knees before her. "Please! I . . . I have nothing left! Help me! I can't understand myself. All I have is helping you! Please." The hoarse voice broke into a cacophony of sobs. His emotions were wide open for Aurah to see.

She stared wide-eyed at the man and fear gripped her heart. *Why?* Was this all a lie? Was this peace and security a façade? Something churned inside her and something was putting together pieces faster then she could cognitively process.

Would she never be rid of her nightmares?

Was there nowhere she was free?

"Ta . . . take off your hood," she stuttered. Her stomach seized at the realization of what was before her, sobbing on the ground. *Please, no.*

The man wrested his tears into submission, wiping his hidden face with the back of his hand. He leaned back, resting completely on his knees. He grabbed his hood and pulled back.

Aurah screamed. Insanity gripped her in wrenching pangs. She looked all around desperately until she found it. A rock. It had worked before; it would work now. As many times as she needed! She leaped to the rock, ripping it free from its home. It was bigger than the last rock she used. This one took two hands and all her strength. Turning to face her greatest adversary, she charged.

The dragon . . . the man . . . *the thing* flinched, but then he dropped his arms. He stared back at Aurah, straight into her eyes. Her footsteps closed the space between them. Two hands wielded the rock above her head. Ready to strike. The closer she got, though, the more difficult it was. It was like trudging through muck. His amber eyes—there was a weird spark in them. Both were open now, surrounded by a scabbed and swollen face. Bruises discolored his skin completely. Bits of dried blood littered his lineaments. His mouth was shut. She was glad. It would have been grotesque seeing the disheveled shape she imagined that part of him was in.

She stood right next to him, the look of a wild woman in her eyes, the rock poised in the air, yearning to attack something.

Move. She commanded her arms. *Crush!* She screamed at herself. *Kill him! Kill him!* Her body trembled with rage at the sight of the monstrosity only a few steps away. No longer a dragon, but never a real man. A horror, with no place in the world. *Put it out of its misery!*

But those eyes. He dropped his head, breaking gaze with her—resigned.

The rock thudded into the ground.

"I hate you!" Her hands balled into a tight fist and were thrown backward as her face flung closer to the beast. It would hear her for sure. "I hate you so much! You ruined everything. This is all your fault!" There was no silence in the forest now. "You murdered so many people for yourself! You destroyed the world for yourself, and you expect us all to just appreciate you! Well, I hate you!" The rock drew her eyes again.

The world became silent again for a moment.

"Say something, you wretch!" Aurah screamed again at the beast. There would be no peace for this trash before her. It was lucky it wasn't eating the rock right now.

More silence. She was getting tired of yelling at it. It didn't care. She was about to scream again when it cut her off, pure sorrow lacing every syllable. *Like it had a reason to feel sorrow.*

"I . . . ." His first word was cut off by a deep whimper resounding from his core. "I can't begin . . . ." His body shuddered out more sobs. "Begin to reconcile that end with the thing I am now." His strength shattered. An unending torrent of sobs erupted from his already hideous face. "I have n- nothing left! I can't make sense of myself anymore. I can't do this, I can't! I . . . I . . . let me take you back. It's all I have. It's the only thing that makes sense in my confusion! I don't know myself, bu . . . but . . . but I . . . I know . . . I know this one thing. Let . . . let me take you back!" He broke. He was done. He strained to put out those last words, his body shaking violently. His hands fluttered uncontrollably by his side as the grief of his situation overtook him and his control. He fell and wept at her feet.

Aurah stared. She couldn't make sense of what played out before her. *What did it want?* She didn't understand it. She didn't trust it certainly. Was she even in a position to trust it? It. *Him?* Let it weep there. As far as she was concerned, the only payment it could offer that would be acceptable would be its head, but death never amended the wrongs, never took away the scars. It just stopped more from happening.

But . . . .

As a man, they could end him at the Capital. He would be vulnerable.

Stop. She couldn't believe she was seriously considering his proposal. She would never accept its help—even if the plan had the light of revenge at the end of the tunnel. She hated it. The rock again caught her attention. It was bulky, but maybe a heavier rock would finish the job this time. She wouldn't stop until he was dead for sure. There were plenty of ways to make sure someone—something was dead. Her hand gravitated towards the rock but stopped. Her eyes wandered back towards the weeping mess of a thing on the ground before her. Her hand dropped back towards her side.

"Whatever." The words were lackluster and compassion-less. She turned around, bending slowly to grab the rock. She moved towards the shadows and found a tree outside of the rim of light the fire produced. The rock hit the ground with a dull thud and she gingerly lowered herself to the ground, grasping the tree every inch on the way down. Every muscle screamed against her use. Laying down, she laid her arm over the rock and rested her head against it. It would suffice.

Her eyes hazed over and closed, and a peaceless sleep took her.

Kast lay on the ground, his body was compressed and small. Tears felt different on the face of a man. Maybe that was because his face was still swollen and disfigured from the girl's effective use of a rock? He didn't know. He was balled up; somehow, he lay on his side. The side of a man and not a dragon. Everything he had, his pride, his power, his flight, it was all gone now. He was now so weak even a young woman could severely injure him. *A young woman did severely injured him.* His mind wandered to times when the humans could barely phase him. His breathing fell short and sighing. Memories of days as a dragon. Now they were hazy. The eyes of a man constrained and enfeebled him.

It was a miracle that he had managed to control as much of his body that he did now. The pain was searing as the rock fell over, and over again. At some point, he lost consciousness and faded to the blackness. The look of the girl though. That look rivaled a dragon in its rage. His arms clenched himself tighter, his eyes warily moved to see what the girl was doing.

She was asleep, but not soundly. He hoped she didn't start screaming again. He clenched at the thought. At first, she had screamed regularly from the top of the plateau. Kast heard it every night before the girl managed to control her dreams. It was disturbing, and he didn't know why or understand it. In fact, the more he looked back at that time, there was a lot that he just couldn't grasp or understand. He scoffed, or something like a scoff escaped his untrained lips. He didn't understand then and definitely didn't understand now.

He sat up, stretching his fresh body from its sorrow and warmed his hands on the diminishing fire. The soft glow retracting from the surrounding world, drawing back into its source.

He did know one thing though. They couldn't stay still for long. They needed to move quickly.

As fast as possible.

There was a demon on their trail, and neither of them would be able to survive his fury. He rested his elbows on his knees and held his head, the situation weighing him down.

Why is that... *thing*—here? It became hard to swallow.

Kast never met a human or anything, like The Cloak before.

From one hell into another. Or maybe hell was a lot worse than he thought, and it had all of the worst enemies he could imagine. Kast rubbed his eyes, trying to wipe away the reality that lay before him.

Dragons behind, The Cloak in front.

Now all his worst enemies were chasing him, but he had no reason to run anymore. The only thing that made any sort of sense was to carry out the last goal that he had had—to return the girl home. But that was the extent of his feelings.

It made no sense. The recent tragedies left him with absolutely nothing, yet this seemingly random path called his attention when everything else remained silent. "Don't quit!" it cried, looming just on the fringes of his sanity. He tried to grasp it, but it just slipped away. He didn't know why it still remained when all else had left him. It had been a deceptively shallow end, but it was all that he had now.

His thoughts had always plagued him, always driving him towards some enigmatic goal, just like now. Nothing about that would ever change—even after something like the cataclysmic transformation he just experienced. There would always be something new and intangible about whatever goal possessed him. His goal would always disappear, leaving him directionless in whatever mess he was found.

Kast practiced gripping his human hand. It felt right as if all the anger his thoughts merited coalesced into his fist. He hated thinking about his purpose and direction and the anxiety it caused. The mysterious but driving nature of his purpose impelled him forward, yet he could only understand a few vague obscurities. Never once did a newly discovered fact of his purpose line up with a previously known fact. Occasionally, an old facet would once again be made clear, but whatever he had on his mind faded back into the void.

He had faltered and stumbled in his pursuit for his purpose. His rage was pent up and it cleaved his heart. It was all their fault, the filthy humans! *He would kill them all!*

Kast was startled by the sudden spike of intensity and broke his gaze from the dying embers in the fire. He looked over at the girl again for a moment, before turning his gaze back.

No. He couldn't grasp that end anymore either.

What had once brought an ecstasy of relief now brought the tumultuous tides of apathy and pain. Thankfully, the urges to maim and murder the human race seemed to disappear along with his previous goals.

Kast didn't know if he could sleep. He was actually quite scared to experience sleep as a human. Especially with The Cloak hunting them.

He had woken in the dirt that was to become his tomb to a smell that plunged him into despair. He fought his unresponsive limbs, reveling in every twitch and fidget, all of it a wealth of minor successes which moved him towards a greater victory—or semi-victory. It was extremely difficult to move as fast as he had needed while only capable of small motor functions. *But that smell.* He shouldn't have been able to smell it as a human unless humans could smell pungent, soul shredding terror. Kast was fairly confident that they couldn't.

He had run, though, or what he thought was running for a human. Every second cured his steps, solidifying them slowly into a prolonged and practiced stride.

Somewhere in the middle of all of that, he had caught a new scent. Men, Savages, horses and . . . *the girl.*

The fire nearby cracked loudly startling Kast from his reminiscence, and pleasantly devoured the last bits of wood.

Kast had no idea what possessed himself to chase the girl. Probably the same thing that shoved his head into the dirt at her feet. He was pathetic. He had been tactless in his approach of the group of men that had captured the girl, blinding confronting them and even stealing their clothes on a whim that he might stand out otherwise. He didn't have the time then to process his decisions; The Cloak's presence was growing larger after all.

Now, this is where he was—in the middle of the night after life had blown up, leaving him without a sense of direction or purpose. *So be it.* He resigned to what he couldn't control. He would just push through to the one thing that he knew he had.

A soft moan broke the silence and drew his eyes away from the fire to look at the girl. Her dreams were disturbing her. He hoped she didn't scream. They didn't need to make their impossible situation any more difficult.

He turned back to the fire. He would keep watch. Then he would wake her. Then he would take her back to the Capital.

CHAPTER TWENTY-FOUR

A stiff breeze blustered over the ground, or rather, the tops of the plateaus. A broken forest swayed gently in the breeze and stretched into the distance, split by an unimaginable array of rifts and crevices isolating the plateaus.

Snide stood atop of a large plateau near the recent battle with the hermit dragon.

Snide was a dragon of dragons, one of the largest that he knew of—*save one*. He was so large that he was either on equal terms or a little larger than the hermit dragon they had been tracking and trying to *recruit*. He was most certainly a bit bulkier than that stray lizard.

Smoke wafted towards the sky, carried away by the breeze. They had managed to scorch a large bit of the forest into ash during their attack. The ravenous fire devoured the forest on the tops of the plateaus. It was probably a good thing there were many splits to guard the fire against spreading too far.

Snide stood atop the large plateau and shook his head in a slight, almost, denial. He, a dragon, just couldn't wrap his head around the magnitude of damage caused by felling that first plateau. The large dragon stared down into a crater that could easily be filled with thousands upon thousands of dragons. And all of it came about quickly. It had started with the collapse of the first plateau, then the next and the next and the next, and so on. The giants of stone toppled into each other like they lacked the ability to stand up by themselves anymore and were looking to their eons-old comrades for help, only to drag them down too. Snide still wasn't completely sure if the destruction was finished or not. A twinge of cracking and thundering drifted through the air. Miles away, something was still breaking.

Snide stared down to where his twin brother lay under the wreckage, caught in the collapse of the hermit dragon's lair. Twin dragons, from one egg, were strange and rare occurrences. They weren't similar twins either. Snide had earned his name for his size and undisputed ability to overpower any other dragon—*save one*. They called him Snide because he often seemed emotionless from the lack of expression, which was actually accounted for by his affinity for the physical rather than the mind. He was by no means stupid, though. He was just built for one job, and his strength accomplished that job well.

His twin, on the other hand, was the complete opposite. Slick had earned his name for his brains, and only for his brains. The fact that he had little to no capacity for the physical was no dilemma to Slick, though. He quickly gained a moniker for his tactics of manipulation and deception, pitting his enemies against each other. While Snide understood the fight and the meaning of war, the Silver Serpent was leagues beyond himself in devising strategies and plans. It was strange that in the few times that they fought each other, neither overcame the other. There was a skirmish between the two of them once, and it was a painful memory for Snide because he had lost his temper, and there were multiple deaths as a result. Slick had managed, somehow, to convince a few other dragons to help him with a head to head match against his larger, more brutish, twin. Snide felt the emotion then, and he saw out of the corner of his eyes the fear that he wrought in both participants and onlookers. It was like a . . . darkness had seized him, and then he had stood over his tiny brother who trembled beneath Snide's hulking frame. Then the darkness had receded, and Snide acquiesced to a draw.

Snide absolutely would not glory in the deaths of his fellow lizards.

Snide stood atop the large plateau with only seven of his thirty-five strong thrall remaining, including himself. There had been a total of eight dragons left alive, but he had sent one lizard back home with the news of Slick's death. These were all good lizards—solemn, obedient, and disciplined. And they were all that was left. How shocked had he been when he sent the remains of the thrall to pursue the hermit dragon and only seven had come back. Snide turned back towards his lizards. One had come back with a broken leg. Snide grimaced when he had seen that.

It took forever for a dragon to heal . . . save one.

The very same one who just now appeared as a speck on the distant sky. A slight vibration flowed through Snide's large veins. His scales *always* raised slightly in *his* presence. Like spilled blood, the blotch of black seeped across the clouds, covering the ground below in the most despairing of shadows. They were closing in, fast.

Only a few seconds until their arrival.

Snide moved to stand in front of the remains of his thrall. He had them line up at attention with their backs towards the edge of the plateau. It would allow for the most room. There would certainly be a need for room in a moment. Snide stood, enjoying the hiding place of his thoughts for a few last seconds.

Snide and his twin had struggled the first couple years of their life. Most of the time, they had spent their life in insanity, trying to kill everyone—though, for some reason, never each other. It was highly unusual for dragons like themselves to be kept alive under such circumstances, but it was mostly due to their being hidden. Back then, any dragon who had shown insanity was ended quickly; there was no mercy for something so *evil*. There had been a lot of steps in place to

201

help a dragon accomplish their purpose and avoid the danger of insanity that would seize control otherwise. For Slick and Snide, though, there was no chance. They were born doomed.

Then, despite what seemed unchangeable, the impossible happened.

Their insanity disappeared nearly instantaneously.

The air gusted violently above Snide and his roaming thoughts.

The twin dragons had realized later that they shared the same purpose, and that their purpose had been broken from the start. Snide and his twin had possessed an unknown occurrence for dragons— their purpose had been specifically tied to something that didn't exist at the time of their birth.

A streak of black descended like lightning to the smoldering remains of the forest on the plateau.

Specifically tied to a *dragon* who hadn't existed yet.

The world went dark as the sun was blotted out from the sky, and thunder roared all around.

But not just any dragon.

The dust cleared slowly, trailing upwards across a hulking, pitch black, frame that was unquestionably much, much, larger than Snide.

That dragon was this approaching thrall's Brave.

Not just any thrall—not just any Brave.

The Majesty and his Royal Court.

The plateau shook violently from the dragon's explosive landing. The ensuing Royal Court split apart, leaving most in the air with the thunder of their wings and a few more to land alongside their black Brave, *The Majesty.* Dust mingled with the dying plumes of smoke from the burnt forest, carried off by the wind.

"Greetings, Snide. *Brother.*" A deep-throated voice filled Snide's ears.

Vasiss.

"Hail Vasiss!" Snide's lungs billowed out their greeting.

"Hail Vasiss!" The dragons behind billowed out their responding call.

"Yes, yes, all very good." The black dragon paced in front of Snide, waving his tail to emphasize his words. "You know, Snide, I had begun to worry about my most trusted Braves." The Majesty strode freely towards the edge of the plateau, tucking his wings back and letting the air run over their scaly fringes. "Being taken off guard and thwarted on a simple recruiting expedition. The wings of my heart flailed in their flight at the thought of my brother's difficulty."

The Majesty stared out at the crater, then exclaimed suddenly, as if realizing what he was looking at for the first time.

"Whoa! Snide! Did you do this? I must have underestimated your prowess! Would you just look at all of that . . . ." The Majesty's wings stretched outward. "Space! Would you just look at all of that space!" The Majesty turned towards his brother, tucking in a wing as he stretched the other out gesturing towards the open expanse, a look of excitement covered his face. "How'd you do it? No, no, don't answer that. I know exactly what happened! Quite efficient that messenger that you sent me. I hope you don't mind, but I offed him." The Majesty dragged the tip of his wing across his throat to accent the statement. "It was the middle of the week, ya' know. Terrible time for terrible news. Or maybe it was the end of the week?" The wing stretched and scratched the top of its owner's head. "Oops. Oh, well." The Majesty's wings flared out in a shrug before he turned with a hop, prancing to the side.

The plateau beneath groaned from the movement. A shudder rippled through the standing pillar. It had taken a hit earlier from another falling plateau, but it had managed to resist falling. This stone giant had been sturdy but was failing.

"Oh, dear. These things certainly aren't that strong." The Majesty jumped again, this time back towards the edge of the plateau. "Why do you think that is, Snide?" Snide kept his mouth shut and his thoughts empty, just like every other dragon in the presence of The Majesty. "Well looky down here!" The Majesty was gripping the edge of the plateau, digging his claws into the rock, and letting his head hang to stare down the length of the plateau. The rock under the weight snapped and crumbled, toppling the dragon and a large section of the plateau's edge. "Help! Snide, I'm falling!" The voice roared, accompanied by the clatter of rocks against the edge of the plateau.

Snide stood still, keeping his mouth shut and his mind empty.

"Oh, right!" Snide heard The Majesty's voice yell out from below the plateau as if in a sudden realization. "I'm a dragon!" The thunder of those mighty wings beat the air, muting the noise of his Mighty Court's flying. The Majesty bounded over the now broken edge of the plateau and landed with a quaking thud in front of the still Snide. The plateau groaned more violently and began to rock. "I see! Well, Snide—" The Majesty's tail moved forward and draped over Snide's shoulders. "I'm really thankful for this family reunion. You, me, and, your tiny scab of a brother, Slick. Been a long time since we had a family get together." A long forked tongue lashed outwards from The Majesty's mouth, licking his lips. A dark smile pulled at the corners of his great maw. "Tell me, brother, where is Slick, that Silver Serpent?"

Snide was suddenly gripped, the Majesty's front claws piercing his scales, and was thrown towards the edge of the plateau. Snide hit the ground and sent another large chunk flying off. The plateau began cracking, the stone on top slowly separating as the whole pillar slowly tipped, initiating its descent.

"See! Look Snide! Isn't it beautiful? Don't you just love the world and nature and a hulking pile of rocks that will just lay and rot—though I guess not, since rocks don't rot. Oh, well. Listen, Snide, we don't have much time until this thing falls, and we all die." Vasiss stomped over to Snide, and the world tipped and broke more. "The rocks below may not rot but the body of my most beloved brother lays underneath this infernal grave. If only he alone had been born, then you wouldn't have stolen the body and missed the brains." Vasiss faced the open expanse. "Well, Slick! I hope you rot well. You won't be missed either!"

Vasiss turned, walking back towards the middle of the plateau, leaving Snide to hang on as the plateau tipped.

"Snide…" The world grew quiet at The Majesty's voice. Tension suddenly filled the air.

"Dead!" Vasiss shot back towards Snide, screeching that single word. "Dead! Dead! Dead, dead-dy, dead, dead!" The Majesty stood over top Snide, screaming at him. "Tell me who is responsible for this insult against my name! Who is to blame for the death of my brother? Who!" Teeth rearing, his face carried a fierce glare. "Who? Tell me now!"

He grabbed Snide's head with his claws and stood on his rear legs and stared viciously into the smaller dragon's eyes. Vasiss threw Snide's head against the ground and raced towards one of the remaining dragons lined up behind Snide. "Was it you?" He breathed out his rotten breath, his face inches away from the dragon. "No! Was it you? He jumped to another dragon. "It was you! I know it was!" His forked tongue lashed from his mouth and traveled over the dragon's snout, along his cheek to his ear. Vasiss stared expectantly. "No, it wasn't you, either! You don't taste guilty!" The Majesty stared intensely for a moment longer, breathing heavily into the face of the dragon, the spit glistening on the side of his face. "I know who did this crime, this villainy!" His head turned slowly towards Snide's exposed belly. "It was you!" He launched suddenly into the air, aiming straight at Snide.

Snide closed his eyes. So, it was death after all.

Vasiss passed over top Snide and crushed one of the Mighty Court, floating above. The unsuspecting dragon wailed out its surprise, trying to remove itself from the bite of its Majesty.

Vasiss grabbed the dragon's jaw and ripped it free from its face. The lizard whined pathetically as death tore the mighty from its proud position.

No one moved.

"It was you! You did it! You, you, you, you!" Vasiss screamed at the corpse as it fell still. "That's what you get for sneezing! Sneezing, you blasted wretch! Not with me, you don't!" Vasiss laughed his wheezing laugh, berating the now lifeless dragon, hanging in his clutches.

"Wait! You didn't sneeze!" He beat his wings meagerly as he held the corpse out in his claws and stared at it. "Oh, well!" The Majesty dropped the body, sending it spiraling down the hundreds of feet to its rocky grave. He turned back to Snide and dropped right beside him. "Where is the filth that somehow eluded your grasp? Answer!"

Snide quickly unclogged his throat of the welling terror.

"We lost him over the forest, Majesty. We were ambushed by a powerful enemy . . . ."

"You were, were you?" Vasiss quickly cut off his brother's statement. "Well, now, that doesn't sound good!" Vasiss shot out his tail and caught the back of Snide's neck. With a jerk of the tail, Snide was ripped from the ground and his brow was slammed straight into Vasiss'. Their eyes were mere inches apart, the fire in the Majesty's blazing into Snide's. "Tell me, oh, tell me, Snide, why I should care?" Vasiss' bloody brown eyes raged at the emeralds of Snide's.

"The cloaked man, sir." Four, rasping, words. Snide knew he wouldn't be able to say much so he made his words count.

Immediately Vasiss' tail relinquished its hold.

"Well, why didn't you say so sooner?" Vasiss turned and walked away nonchalantly, treading skillfully as the tipping plateau was near to releasing its hold, the pieces nearly separated. He stared towards the east. A moment passed as he processed the meaning of Snide's four words. "That changes everything."

Vasiss tensed quickly. "We hunt the scum that defied my reign and killed my brother!" Unfurling his wings, he coiled his body, tensioning to launch towards the east, but stopped mid-takeoff. "Snide." His voice was calm and collected—driven. "You know there is no place in my army for the lame. Kill the beast with the broken leg. Your soldiers are to fall in behind the Royal Court, and you are to take the place of the new . . . *opening,* in my guard. For your failure, you are no longer a Brave in my army." Vasiss launched away with the Royal Guard following suit. Dust and ash blasted everywhere. The plateau let loose a final groan and gave way, plummeting straight towards the bottom of the pit.

"Hail Vasiss!" Snide found his lips forming the words as he leapt into the air.

"Hail Vasiss!" The dragon's behind him echoed. All but one, who refused to pledge his allegiance for fear of death and the weeping that now rocked his frame.

Snide turned to what was left of his thrall, all floating in the air. *All except one.* Snide's hardened heart was well versed in numbing its pain. He stared dutifully at the lame dragon who stood alone on the shattering rock.

All that is necessary. He reminded himself.

Snide began again to fulfill his purpose by obeying his little brother.

CHAPTER TWENTY-FIVE

Kast woke with a nasty start. He shot to his feet. His head was wavering, trying clear the haze. It took moments before his mind fully awakened. *What happened?* He looked around as rays of light had begun to filter down through the trees. He must have fallen asleep. It still looked like it was early morning. The sun had barely begun to rise. He scorned himself. They needed to move, and fast. The girl was still asleep, curled up and trying to stay warm. Autumn had been coming for some time now. It would become cooler and cooler. Bending over, he grabbed a bag that had been tied to the horse. He hadn't really noticed it before, he was captivated with the task of getting away from danger, and fast. Thankfully, it held some things to start a fire; information he had gleaned from his time observing the humans. Humans really were fascinating, though he had scoffed at their inability to produce fire at will without the help of something like striking metal against rock. Kast sighed. *Just look at me now.*

He knew he should be concerned with food and water, but he wasn't hungry. Or rather what he thought hungry felt like as a human. He didn't even want to expose himself to the world of the human tongue. *So primitive.* He clutched the bag between his hands. Inexpressible emotion filled his now shaking hands. *I will pay you back, you cloaked trash.* His face released slightly from its scowl and looked at the girl. In a quick toss, the bag flew through the air, landing beside her head. Her eyes ripped open and she was on her feet almost as quick as he was from waking up.

"We need to leave immediately." The words came out matter-of-fact.

She stood, wild and ready to strike. Her eyes jumped frantically around, absorbing her surroundings. It was a painful business trying to rush through the waking up process, particularly with so much at stake.

"It looks like there is some food in the bag, though not much, so make it last. I remember seeing a brook on the way back to the road, we'll stop there for water before moving on. I don't know this world from the ground so I don't know when we will find more food that we can eat..." Kast faded to his thoughts for a split second, then continued, waking back to reality. "Nor if we'll make it to the end of this day." Kast breathed in deeply then cut away crisply, leaving the girl to sort through the morning daze.

He didn't know if he wanted any conversation with her. Even if he did, *how?* He approached the horse instead. The animal picked at a prickly patch of weeds. It looked doubtful at the weed's value as food. Kast clenched his now human hands. He had never really interacted with these creatures before, except for slaughtering them alongside the humans, of course. He had little idea of how to provide for an animal's needs. *Let alone my own . . . or the girl's!* Nothing like not even knowing how to take care of oneself or others to show how unprepared for the world one was.

The horse snorted, passing on the unacceptable vegetation. Instead, it just kept nudging him in the arm with its nose. He stared at it curiously, backing away slightly. "What?" Kast muttered apprehensively. Had the beast gone mad? Why was it nudging him? The chances were slim, but maybe dragons weren't the only creatures with a purpose to fulfill. Maybe this thing was displaying its own insanity from its own kind of failure? He had never pondered a horse's life. He was never really involved with the things of the human world before. Things were much easier when you were bigger and unchallenged—there was no need to learn their world. Kast's throat caught and he dared glance down to look at his hands. They were responding better and better now, but they just felt so . . . .

He suddenly reached out to place his hand on the horse's face only to retract his fingers quickly. *Wretched thing tried to bite me!* He had half a mind to slaughter the monster and take the meat with them. It would serve them much better than as a transport. He might be condemned to a human form, but his instincts and thoughts would always be dragon. His gaze started wandering for a weapon, something lethal enough to finish the horse. Maybe they had one of the human's sharp metal cutting devices, *a knife,* in the bag. They could chop the beast up then. His search was interrupted suddenly by a scraping noise. Kast's search for the source of the noise drew his attention back to the horse.

"What are you doing?" He jumped, his voice grew louder, and his eyes bulged wildly at the sight before him. The horse had released its teeth and was now dragging them through the nearest tree. "Stop that immediately!" He grabbed the lead rope and pulled to pry the horse away from the poor plant. The horse turned and snapped its teeth at him again before returning to the scraping. "Blasted beast!" Kast held the rope tightly, backing away as much as he could.

"It's hungry." The girl pushed her way past Kast and held up a small bag over the horse's mouth. Her tone was coarse and unkind. She didn't look at him. "Idiot dragon. You don't know anything about horses, or humans." Her words were cold and to the point. She didn't look at him at all.

The horse continued to consume the contents of the bag greedily.

"So what way are we going, beast?" She spat out the words. Her eyes never once met his. The old familiar burn of hot, hot, anger seared Kast's belly.

"My way! And that's all you're going to know, as well!" How dare she? The miserable filth. To rival a dragon. Even confined in this pathetic form, he would still be more than capable to rip the life from her. He thought of all the mockery she had committed against him. Never again. I'll burn her alive if she ever . . . . A strange pounding filled Kast's ears and his vision blurred.

The girl looked up into his eyes and gasped suddenly, tearing Kast from his thoughts to see the color draining from the girl's face.

What was it? What did she see—in his eyes, nonetheless? Kast stared back as she dropped her head, his gaze a force blowing her away.

Maybe she had seen something that would make her stop her pathetic pettiness. One way or the other, he would make her acknowledged him. She would fear him. His teeth clenched at all the unpleasant names he yearned to call her.

Whatever. Be afraid, you little whelp.

The horse had stopped eating and stamped its feet expectantly. The girl stared at the ground. Something had unsettled her. *So what?* She removed the feed bag from the creature and put it back in larger bag Kast had thrown at her earlier. Impatient, he moved towards the horse. It was time to go. They had already begun to lose too much time to nonsense. He had one foot on the step-thing, or whatever humans called it, and was about to pull himself up onto the creature when he noticed the girl shrinking back away, confusion and dismay written across her face. Kast's shoulders slouched as the situation suddenly hit him.

For the love of! He couldn't believe her gall. "Fine! You ride the horse!" He put his leg down and turned to stomp away.

What was he thinking, needing her? Curse his own mind! He was insane, after all.

"What is your problem, beast?" The girl's voice was loud, stopping him cold in his tracks. He did not need this pathetic human making things even more difficult. Kast spun, closing the distance between the two of them. He cornered her against the tree the horse had been chewing on. He threw his fist out, striking the tree above her head, splintering it. It wavered dangerously from the hit.

Kast's body quivered, looming right above the girl. His fist clenched hard enough that his human claws drew blood from his palms; the knuckles were already ripped open from the strike. "You get on the horse." He breathed heavily and glared so hard into her eyes that it hurt his own somehow. "And keep up . . . ." Another exhale. ". . . or you're Savage dung." The last words crawled up from his blackened heart. She would learn respect. He turned away violently. He was leaving with or without her. He gritted his teeth and fought the anger that welled up at the image of her hand covering her mouth while tears from her widened eyes poured down her cheeks.

This had to be the worst of all his *brilliant* plans.

His hopes.

He shook his head and trudged forward.

They had long since found the main road again and passed the stream he had told the girl about. Kast had stopped and drunk his fill before she arrived on the back of the horse. So, she had decided not to run away. He didn't give her much time to drink. He would make sure she knew not to disrespect him again. Kast took off after a brief time. The inconsistencies of his character were a sharp pain in his soul. Last night, he had needed, desperately, to confront the girl. She . . . needed to know what she was dealing with. For some strange reason, it was important that he be honest with her. Kast was at a loss to understand the feeling, particularly in light of the amount of anger he still felt for her.

The woods passed, tree by tree. The sun rose higher and pierced the leafy veil above. He could hear the rhythmic plodding of the horse behind. Kast timed his pace by the number of trees passed in a regular span of time. They were moving with a very quick step, about half the pace of a full-on charge. The girl managed to trail only slightly behind. The blood on his hands from his claws digging in earlier had stopped its trickle quickly, but the human sweat coating them kept them moist. They absolutely must keep moving. He could barely come to grips with the fact that the cloaked monster was hunting them, but there was also the presence of the dragons he was deeply worried about. They were proud creatures, dragons. They would not allow themselves to be humiliated as Kast had done. They would come looking. *They would not fail.*

Kast moved even quicker, his step matching his racing thoughts. Maybe if he was lucky, the dragons and the Cloak would clash while hunting him and the girl.

One was allowed at least one impossible dream, *right?*

Kast glanced behind himself and felt a horrid grimace form. He swallowed hard, trying to rid his face of the emotion his heart had smeared all over it. A single tear dropped before the dragon managed to renew his mind with focus.

They had moved for the span of a few hundred trees by Kast's count before he finally felt a sharp pang in his gut. Hunger for humans was the same as dragons after all. He stopped and waited for the sound of the steps of the animal to catch up before he turned to speak.

"What's wrong?" The girl's voice hummed with fear, but also excitement.

What is going through her mind?

"I . . . feel hunger. I must eat something." He scowled at the admittance of words from his lips. He turned to face her. *What is going through her mind?*

The girl stared at him, and a look of *wonder* crossed her face.

A furrow creased Kast's brow. He didn't like any of this— needing *permission* or needing to talk about his need to eat. Before, he could have done whatever he wanted, and there was none to challenge him. He stared back at her incredulously, at a loss for words himself. At a loss for emotions.

The girl finally moved to open the bag and rummaged around inside of it before pulling out a fist full of something. Reaching out her hand, the girl held the substance to the dragon's hand. Just as he was to take it, she threw it to the ground and pulled the horse away hard to continue down the road.

Kast stared. He didn't feel right then. Maybe that was because he didn't know what to feel? Or, rather, what he was feeling? Visions of rampage and murder were his primary desire. He shook his head, remembering the goal on hand— aside from surviving this lunatic, human girl.

Kast slowly collected the scattered substance. It had the smell and feel of meat, though hardened and dry. Blood wouldn't drip from this meat. Kast stared at the food in his hand. The feeling of hunger in his belly had dissipated completely, and a knot was left in his throat instead. Kast sighed and pocketed the meat into the cloak he had taken from one of those men. Its putrid stench and hard texture were some of the only real things to him anymore.

Looking up, he moved to catch up with the girl and begin again to set a pleading pace.

Never before had Kast run so hard away from death.

CHAPTER TWENTY-SIX

The forest passed by more acutely. The sun moved directly above them, and Kast was thankful for the cool autumn weather. He didn't know how humans handled the heat and wasn't looking forward to the burden of dealing with it. It wasn't until the sun had passed its noon position that they were confronted with another episode.

Kast stopped abruptly, ahead of the girl. The footsteps of the beast resounded behind slightly before stopping. There was no question to follow this time. He stared forward intently, doing the best he could with his human body to perceive what lay before them. Doing his best to not let his emotions destroy the girl.

"There are humans up ahead, girl. I suppose our journey is over faster than I thought. I guess I can finally get rid of your stinking carcass!" He tried to sound joyful, but his gut twisted uncomfortably at the revelation of losing her. He needed her.

He needed her to need him.

What would happen now? Would he really succumb to his insanity? He had lost everything. Now the one and only thing he did possess would be taken away, as well. Maybe he really would just lie down in the dirt and die. That thought grew more pleasant.

"Indeed, dragon. I can see them from here, it looks like a merchant's caravan." Her voice sounded dull and uncaring.

He imagined the apathy painted on her features—except her eyes. Her eyes had to have hate swimming in their depths. *And pain.* Kast cringed and his body tightened. He hated how he sometimes saw things from *her* reality.

Kast ground his teeth together, his brow changing into a hard crease. At the last, it still turned out to be a terrible plan. He would be rid of her stinking corpse and would once again try to fulfill his purpose, though, now as a man, he didn't even know if he had a purpose anymore.

The caravan had quickly spotted the two travelers and had taken up a defensive position. A small troupe of guards created a line in between their cargo and the travelers.

Kast approached without care.

A voice rang out from the line of men. "Hold your spot and don't come any closer bandit!"

Kast stopped within shouting distance of the caravan. He didn't care about some ragtag human guards, but he did stop. He needed to do everything that he could to get them to take his burden away. He already had begun to regret begging to take the girl home. *He was certain to kill her.* Such a foolish, reactive decision.

"We're not bandits, and we won't approach. I just ask that you take the girl to the next city. She'll be the ward of the nation at that point and no further hindrance to yourselves." He hoped he sounded like he knew what he was talking about.

"Fhurner is located a ways away. You're asking a lot, stranger who claims he is not a bandit." Kast had never negotiated before, but the voice seemed to be a skilled opponent. The negotiations in question at that point were mostly a strong "leave now." Kast didn't think he had much of a chance to convince them, but he would try until the end anyway. *Pity.*

He may end up having to take the girl all the way back, after all. His fist clenched again. *There was no way this would ever work.*

"You're free to the horse as payment. If she follows me, she isn't likely to survive. You see . . . ."

The voice cut him off. "Keep your mouth shut, bandit, before we shut it for you!"

So, he was to be stuck with the girl. Kast was already in a terrible mood due to the pestilence of the girl. How did he come to be so desperately confused? An odd mix of hating her and needing her? All within the span of half a day? He spit on the ground. *Disgusting human habit.* He reprimanded himself for the brief action.

"Bandit, you have a minute to move your hide away from this caravan before we gut you, the girl, and the horse. Move off the road!"

What a demand, threatening him, a magnificent dragon, of all creatures. These miserable human whelps would realize their insignificance. Kast raised his voice loudly, challenging the threat. "Come and meet your demise, worthless creatures!"

"Stop! We're not bandits! Dragon, they'll kill us! You're a human now, somehow. Stop being stupi—"

"Shut up, wench," Kast growled, and the shrill voice of the girl cut off from behind him. His body vibrated violently. *How dare she try to control him?*

"Dragon! Please!"

"Shut your mouth. I have no care for a single breath that escapes your lips." He tried to sound as heartless as he could. The mercenaries in front closed the distance quickly. Kast guessed that many people out here didn't take chances. These soldiers really did show experience. They left a few men behind still to guard their cargo, while the rest charged the looming threat.

Looming threat? What was he doing? Kast had no power as a human. His pride would be the death of them both. *Whatever.* Maybe this was for best. Kast wouldn't be responsible for the girl, after all. In thought, this was an excellent plan. No more worry. No more running. No more need. No more girl harassing him. No more stupid purpose and insanity.

Kast smiled.

It was a suitable time to die.

The mercenaries stayed quiet as they covered the distance. Another aspect of experience. A lesser soldier might expose their position to other unwanted enemies by yelling. Kast had never faced a challenge like this before. He looked at his hands. He had never faced a wise opponent on somewhat equal terms. He glanced up at the number of attackers approaching. *Unequal terms.* If he were still a dragon, these mongrels would be nothing, falling to a heap of flames that washed over their bodies.

What if I kill them all? What if they die, too? Maybe it was good that he wasn't a dragon anymore? Maybe it was good that he would die here. But did the girl deserve it? Kast looked around wildly.

What am I doing?

They were nearly overtaken. He could hardly hear the voice of the girl behind him, begging for their lives—her life. Even if the soldiers relented, would he? A smile broke his face, a familiar, delicious smile. *Killing humans.* He hadn't found pleasure in this for a little while, but something in his mind seemed to push him forward to this edge. *But the girl.* The rage dissipated again.

The men were nearly surrounding Kast and the girl when a loud cry broke over the racing footsteps.

Bandits, in droves, flooded the road from the surrounding forest and closed in on the largely unprotected wagons.

The mercenaries stopped and turned, horror inscribed on their faces as they realized their terrible blunder.

"Go! Protect the wagons!" The voice cried out its orders. The men turned and ran, almost faster now that their fight was visible before them. They weren't worried about being quiet anymore.

Kast stood, trying to process his place in the fight. Should he just murder them all? *And the girl!* His mind screamed at him. He wasn't responsible for this mess, so he wouldn't dredge himself in their lousy affairs. He would just move on with the girl in tow. His flash of bloodlust had been stifled again. In its place, the feelings of dependency welled up again. He needed her. *Blast it, confounded mind!*

"Dragon!" The girl's voice cried out.

"What now, human?" He flung himself around to confront her. He was not happy with the way the situation had stirred up his scabbing emotions. He just wanted to harden into a callous and move on.

"Please! Help them! They don't deserve to die. Please, help the caravan!" Tears ran down her face as she begged him to help.

Why? Why did this girl change her position as fast as he did? Was there something in the water that they drank? First, she hates him with a passion, now she is begging him for help. It was just like himself; how he couldn't make up his mind whether to take her help or kill her. It made him angry, the swirling emotions. He tried to find the solace killing them all had brought, but he couldn't find it anymore. It was tucked away again in the deepest pit of his heart.

"No chance. We're moving on before we get set back any further." There was the aspect of The Cloak to remember. Yes, they needed to move. The bandits outnumbered the caravan guards greatly. If Kast hadn't lured those men away from the wagons, they would have had a much more suitable fighting chance. Maybe that was what the bandits were waiting for. An opening.

But wait! Why did he care? He was a fierce and mighty dragon! The petty squabbles of men phased him not. He looked down at his hands. His thoughts stabbed him tenderly a thousand times. *A mighty dragon. Huh.*

A sour, dissatisfied look of disgust formed on the girl's face. She was angry again. This time she didn't say anything, she just surprised Kast. In a quick motion, she riled the horse up into a charge and ran past, straight for the fray. She was racing towards the battle before he had realized what she was doing. The bandits were already swarming the unprotected wagons, and the guards were nearly back, joining into the fight. It would be a blood bath, and the stupid girl was headed straight for it.

"Curse you, girl!" He roared, throwing himself into a headlong charge. Before he knew it, he overtook the horse and the girl. A look of surprise shot across her face. He didn't stop though. He carried on, covering the distance the guards had in a fraction of their time.

The guards were engaged in combat in front of him, and they were being slaughtered.

Kast searched the trembling battle line. He needed to fight without the worry of hurting the innocent. *Why?*

Who cares?

The distance disappeared as Kast approached rapidly. *Now.* His mind seemed to command on its own. Before he took another step, he brought his feet together and leaped. His power expelled the ground far away as he flew above the heads of those clashing against each other. *What was he doing?*

His eyes welled up with shock. He had never seen a human display this kind of strength before. He flew over the tops of the soldiers and the bandit's heads and well over the tops of the wagons. Something was definitely off. Now that he thought about it, he couldn't imagine a human punching as hard or healing as fast as he did. He couldn't fathom the full extent of his new paradigm of living.

He landed amidst the bandits, surrounded by the wagons, and he brought both fists balled together with him. He felt the spine of one bandit give way under the sudden impact of his landing feet and watched the neck of another twist into a fatal position as his fists collided with the man's head. *Two down.* He jumped to the side, dodging the swing of a sword.

A clumsy swing. He couldn't help but scrutinize how pathetic these bandits were. They survived only by preying on the weak.

He threw a punch at the bandit, now exposed from his swing. The punch connected, breaking the man's jaw free from its hinge sending him flying away. Kast stared, and the adrenaline coursing through his veins slowed time. He had certainly never seen a human punch that hard before, either. His contemplations were interrupted by another sword stabbing at him. *Let's try something.* He caught the Bandit's sword hand, narrowly dodging the blade's thrust itself. He smiled as he crushed the man's hand around the sword, and more shock fell over his face as he also crushed the hilt of the sword. He might not be a dragon, but he was somehow still enormously powerful. This might not be so bad. He had managed after all to grow accustomed to using the new body. He could make something of his life. *Stop.* His thoughts trailed in their insanity again.

A blinding pain pierced his arm. He had spent too much time contemplating things. He reacted quickly enough that the deep cut only flayed the skin on his forearm.

Air tore through his throat in a vicious roar. He was done playing with these nest maggots. He threw out the cut arm, his frenzy carrying him through the pain. His hand found its target and he ripped out the bandit's throat. A fair trade, though one he wouldn't make again. He found himself favoring his right arm to do most of the work. He was always surrounded by bodies in the battle—alive or dead.

Wave after wave of bandits charged him. It seemed like forever, but he knew the cowards wouldn't have committed so many lives to an enemy they couldn't easily best. *How did he know that?* Time must have gone by fast, and he must have killed quickly. In a moment, the bandits cried out their retreat. They were bested. Kast felt so alive. This time his killing had felt much different than before. He couldn't quite place the feeling.

He looked and horror seized him. The bandits were running— right through the girl's path. The horse bucked as a bandit's undisciplined blade cut the beast, sending it stampeding away. The girl fell through the air, tumbling gracelessly as the horse jolted away. The bandits were swarming all around.

They're going to kill her!

Kast felt his gut become hot. Hotter than he ever knew a human could feel. The heat like a dragon's flame swirled in his belly.

Kast watched his arms shake with an indigent fury, then they stopped, controlled, focused, *decided.* The wound on his arm had disappeared, new discolored flesh had taken its place. His eyes settled on the girl again as she fell through the air and the bandits were about to stampede across her frail body.

Kast blinked.

He held his eyes closed for a second and when he opened them, he was holding the girl. He would have been surprised but the fire in his inner being held his mind steady. He looked at the bandits, terror etched into every one of their features as their bodies fell to pieces.

He turned back to where he had been standing. A swath that cut across the earth told the tale of his sudden attack. The speed and power of his movement disfigured the world. Bodies lay in piles alongside the trench, filling it with their blood. He looked down at himself. He was covered in blood. Their blood.

The bandits, what was left of them, raced away, disappearing back into the trees from where they came. *Good.* The world quieted down.

The girl stirred and pushed her way out of his protection. He moved forward, setting her down on her feet. He didn't say anything. There was nothing for him to say. Her face blanched at the death all around, and the blood covering him—covering her a little. She threw up, emptying herself of what little food it looked like she had eaten. Her expression turned to anger again as she faced Kast.

"I hope you're happy. Those bandits sent our horse running and ruined our supplies. Not only that, but you let them kill the innocent and who knows who else! If you hadn't been so selfish to taunt the guards as you did, everything would have been fine!" She glared violently at him. This girl was out of her mind.

But Kast wasn't. He still felt the clarity and resolve from the fire within. He just looked at her. He already recognized their pack of supplies, and how it was destroyed, soaked in blood. Oddly enough, none of that mattered right now. "You give me too much credit, girl." His response was short and to the point. He couldn't remember the last time he felt this clear. He couldn't remember the last time power surged through him like this—*if ever.* He looked up. What remained of the caravan stood hesitantly, anxiously waiting to react. He knew what he had to say to them now. He took a step towards their direction.

"We . . . ." Kast couldn't finish even one syllable.

The fire in his gut went out and he crashed to the ground.

CHAPTER TWENTY-SEVEN

Charlie sat on the back of his horse. He knew how hard the pace they carried was on the animals, but that monster running Charlie and the rest of the men wouldn't relent. Sometime in the early morning, the strange connection in his mind that the monster used began to rampage through Charlie's thoughts. *He was not happy.* Charlie winced at the idea of something angering him.

Charlie led the way on the main road, and now that they were finally out of the woods, their pace soared again. The monster became especially ecstatic. He overwhelmed Charlie's mind with feelings of urgency and visions of murdering them all if he caught up to them. Charlie had a few crisp words with the men about moving quickly and proceeded to set a steady speed on the verge of racing. The men would just have to keep up.

That monster always rode or moved behind the bulk of Lizard Guts, which was another reason most had no idea about him. What was driving him so hard in the first place had completely eluded Charlie. It was extremely rare for that monster to get so worked up over anything. It was so tempting for Charlie to lose composure when he did. What was his goal? Maybe what had happened two weeks ago held the answer?

The uneventful road and the horse's rocking gait lulled Charlie's thoughts away—to think back nearly two weeks ago on the attack of the Capital.

Charlie waited on the shadows of a rooftop near their place of lodging. The skies were clouded, but not so much to block out the sun. The city had emptied, but Lizard Guts had stayed hidden. Waiting. That monster had wanted to make the best presentation to the Kingdom as possible. That was why he had given Charlie the orders to impersonate the soldiers of the Capital and send a warning signal the previous day. The Capital's lookout scouts were a nice idea, but they would never be able to provide a timely warning to evacuate the citizens from danger.

That was all anyone could do anyway—run, or try to. No one had a chance to match the strength of a single dragon. This meant Lizard Guts didn't, either. It was all that monster. They were just pawns in a greater ploy, whatever that might be. Charlie ran his hand over his face as if trying to wipe the stress from his brow. He found himself doing that increasingly these days. It was a tough spot to be in, the middleman between a flock of sheep and the big bad wolf—if a wolf could even remotely be likened to that monster. No, there was something much worse about his very being.

Charlie's idle musings were interrupted by the fury of a dragon breaking from the cover of the clouds. It was a big one, maybe even the biggest one that they had hunted, and it was diving straight for the city. His hand fell to his weapon. Whatever it was, it came from that monster's provision and was the main strength of Lizard Guts, not including the monster himself. It was some sort of bolt slinger, but they never loaded bolts onto the things, they just pulled the trigger and magic released from some unknown depths. If it weren't for

Charlie's hate for the dragons, he would have never picked up one. Regardless, it was necessary.

He lost the dragon's position in the sky for a moment, only to gain it again as the thing rocketed away from the death trap the Kingdom had laid. *Clever, very clever.* The only weapons these people had were large, bulky and inefficient. But somehow, they had forecasted the dragon's whereabouts and hid the siege weapons. It truly was a display of the brilliance of some of the best minds in the Kingdom—*but also the frailty of the human condition.* The dragon ripped away, untouched as far as the Kingdom would be concerned. They had lost their chance, and the rest of their plan would rot with them.

Time to work. Charlie dropped to the street below; it would be dangerous exposing himself on tops of the buildings. He set a steady jog. Every man had their orders. *Don't interfere.* They were just supposed to stand by at the ready. Everyone thought this was so Charlie could take the credit. No one minded staying out of the fight, letting Charlie have the glory. It was all another elaborate lie to blind the men to what was really happening.

When it came to fighting dragons, as unnecessary as it seemed, the monster took no chances. *None.* There was zero chance of him failing. He always stood on his enemy's carcass. *Always.* Yet, he still had Lizard Guts stand by, at the ready with the mysterious magic bolt throwers. *Like there was something out there to be prepared for.*

By now, everyone in Lizard Guts would be convening near the chosen location, where that monster would show the city's leaders and the monarch just who was capable of answering the dragon's threat.

Allowing the beast to attack the Capital was really just a show. Lizard Guts could have hunted the beast ages ago, but for some reason, that monster hadn't commanded it. Instead, Charlie found himself now racing around to serve as back up, alongside the rest of his men, waiting for The Face knows what to happen. The men would certainly have more questions.

A tremendous roar disrupted the air. *Well, the thinned air.* Charlie hated it when the monster used his magic and removed the air from an area like this. The strain on their lungs was a nasty feeling. Loud crashing began to crescendo in the distance. *More destruction.* Charlie ran his free hand over his face again. *Just end it already!* But no. He knew that monster would have his fun by toying with the dragon and by tricking the people here to gain their trust. The street he was traveling crossed one of the main roads and he had a clear view of the fight though it was some distance away.

A swath of destruction lay behind the charging dragon. Charlie's boss stood in the line of the dragon's might about to be crushed. Charlie looked on, his curiosity demanding despite his better judgment. The dragon closed the space. His boss was within a dangerous distance of the beast. To the dragon's surprise, the monster caught the gales and flew to the sky. *The dragon is dead.* Charlie dropped his head and ran to fall in position. What a fierce clash between monsters. Charlie's gut always turned at the thought of how much of a monster the true head of Lizard Guts was.

Well . . . this is what he signed up for. The death of those scaly mongrels.

By the time he had come near to where he should wait, the monster was already near finishing off the dragon, high above the city.

Movement in the corner of his eye caught his attention. Charlie's body froze mid-stride, his jaw slackened losing tension like the rest of his body.

Impossible!

Sweat beaded on his neck, his hands shook on their own volition as he wrenched his bolt thrower from his side. In the sky was an entire thrall of dragons! Lizard Guts had never faced so many at once. They weren't prepared for this. How did the monster even miss this?

Did he miss this?

That monster seemed well pleased. The pressure on Charlie's mind conveyed a misplaced euphoria. He was happy, happier than Charlie had ever known him to be. Charlie watched the sky as he leaped towards the thrall. Charlie couldn't believe his eyes. The dragon in his vise-like grip was thrown to the ground under the force of his leap. It crashed causing the earth to quake violently. A feeling coated Charlie's mind telling him to stay back.

That monster didn't want anyone to interfere.

The horse snorted and whined, whipping Charlie back to reality from his recollections. He looked up to observe the road ahead. It was still clear, winding through the woods, and the trees stood tall on either side looming high above. The canopy spread densely over the road. They wouldn't be bothered. Out of all the bandits and other trash that gallivanted through this forest, there was none who would mess with Lizard Guts. Everyone knew who they were. Charlie glanced behind to check on his troupe. They looked ashen but placid. Ever since the Capital, that monster had revealed himself more, casually dropping his presence into all of their thoughts. Charlie dropped his head again to let his mind wander, remembering why they were all the way out here in the first place.

It was the day after the dragon attack. For the first time, Charlie saw that there were entities powerful enough to challenge Lizard Guts.

Charlie was discomfited. He couldn't tell if the confrontation with the larger mass of dragons was part of the plan or not. And that wasn't even the worst part. The worst part was what the first beast had done, setting their goal farther away. At least that's what that monster had conveyed at times through the strangling thoughts.

That monster had been happy, but now . . . Lizard Guts had failed to demonstrate their capability.

There would be questions about whether they could accomplish what the Kingdom would want—because that was important for some forsaken reason. They had let the monster capture and steal a young woman. Word was that the girl had saved the Princess from that fate. Charlie's stomach churned. *Poor girl.*

Charlie wasn't too surprised when that monster had decided to move forward with the plan. But as it stood, the dragon attack was traumatic for the Capital and any unknown being, dragon or not, would surely be counted as an enemy. Charlie didn't imagine the Capital contained massive stores of mercy now. They were to give the people of the Capital some time to collect themselves before Lizard Guts would approach with a coalition proposition. While the men had waited for Charlie, and Charlie for that monster's direction before proceeding, the Capital had, to their surprise, immediately sent for Lizard Guts.

That monster had projected an overwhelming feeling of approval and excitement at the new turn of events. Lizard Guts fell in step, knowing full well anything less than perfection in their display was grounds for dismissal—*permanently.* Charlie frowned. It was at this point, for some reason, that the monster had begun to be more involved with the men, more than just Charlie. Lizard Guts, which once had little to no idea of that monster's existence, now began to put the pieces together from increasing interactions with him.

He still kept to the shadows, but he was freely speaking to the minds of Lizard Guts. The smart ones realized something dangerous was responsible for the pressures on their minds, and only a few made any sort of ties to the cloaked figure that had fought in the sky.

Those soldiers whom the Capital had sent to approach Lizard Guts, in turn, led them back through the ravaged city towards the palace. They made their way through the palace gates and over a convoluted path. Charlie noted the tactical defense embedded in the layout of the various towers and other structures. Before they knew it, they had moved into a massive corridor inside the palace and now stood waiting before two huge and ornate wooden doors.

The soldiers that led them had split, standing on either side of Lizard Guts, while their captain moved inside the throne room to announce their arrival. They didn't wait long before the doors began to open, and a voice cried out the formalities of both parties. Charlie marched forward, the rest of his men strictly on his on heels.

The room was longer than it was wide and was well-dressed in the Kingdom's standard. The floor was a smooth marble with marble pillars rising from the floor on each side of the room at periodic intervals. There were arches with windows high up on the walls letting in dim light—it was overcast outside. A royal-looking carpet stretched from the doors to the end of the room where two thrones sat. Only one had an occupant. A young, black-haired woman sat; her posture unreserved as she leaned forward with her forearms resting on her knees. Her head hung over her clasped hands, staring at the floor. Charlie couldn't help but feel something was off. Something was wrong. He stopped his march a short distance away from Her Majesty and the rest of his men followed suit. He stood solemn, waiting for a response and standing ready.

"Your Maje . . . ."

"Did I say you could speak?" Her head turned towards the steward who must have been in charge of the procession. "I'll talk when I'm good and ready." Her voice cut through the air, leaving a chasm in its wake. She turned her head back towards the floor.

Charlie fought the urge to fidget. Something about this woman unsettled him.

"Why?" Her voice crawled out from under her hanging head.

She was answered by silence. Charlie had no idea how to process this.

"Why?" The voice was firmer this time.

"Why did we help?" Charlie found his voice and the words to say. He shifted his weight.

"Why didn't you stop those blasted beasts, you sorry, good for nothings!" Elizabeth screamed, rebuking Charlie and Lizard Guts.

She lifted her head, unnerving him with what he saw. She should have been a beautiful young woman but was instead a human bearing the deepest grief. Black sleeplessness had begun to fight the swollen, red-rimmed, and tear-filled eyes. Already her face seemed to have shrunk, following the contours of her skull. At second glance, her hair was unkempt and neglected. *Such despair.* Charlie reflected on his own pain. He clenched his teeth, moving past the memory. Whatever the case was, He needed to tread well with his responses.

"There were many surprises yesterday, Your Majesty, many of which would have been more than enough to the end the existence of this city."

"So, you expect to be rewarded for your actions then, I take it?" Elizabeth snapped out her response.

"Might I remind Your Majesty that it was you who had summoned us here? I should make it known that this troupe of soldiers has by far made more of a difference with these dragons than the Kingdom ever has."

"Such gall! And before the presence of your Queen, nonetheless!" Elizabeth refused to let Charlie walk away with the last word.

"Prin . . . Queen. If you have a point, I suggest you make it quick." So much for peaceful negotiations.

"This *troupe* of soldiers is not the ones who have made a difference with the dragons, my good sir." She let that statement settle. "Where is that cloaked man?" Her eyes, bleak and dead, stared straight into Charlie's soul.

So, she had managed to discern the operating nature of Lizard Guts, but she had no idea what she was asking by mentioning that cloaked monster.

"Leave." She looked to her servants and attendants, soldiers, and any other under her command. They were being ordered to leave.

"Your Maj…"

"Leave!" She screamed at the man in charge of the procession again. "Leave!" Her rage was only getting louder. Soon her people all shuffled out of the room. It was just her and Lizard Guts. "Where is that man who fought the dragons on equal—no—greater ground?" She stared resolutely at Charlie then, her hardened eyes piercing him.

What was he going to say to this now? To explain the mysterious nature of someone so . . . *evil.* Before he could open his mouth to answer, what light brightened the room was quenched, plunging it into pitch black. Darkness surrounded them and then it was gone.

Charlie nearly screamed from the sight in front of him. He felt his men shudder in awe, confused at what was happening.

That monster had appeared.

He stood hunched slightly, wrapped in a tattered and dirty cloak. His hood covered his eyes. His height was slightly above average, but the way he stood made him seem less than he was. The pure sense of ire and evil radiating from him made up for the slack in his posture. His breathing seemed heavy, and his whole body fell into rhythm with his breaths.

What frightened Charlie most, though, was the girl's reaction to his sudden appearance. She didn't even flinch.

The monster cracked a broken smile at her audacity, and maybe even the fury that welled inside of her.

"You are a twisted wretch, aren't you?" The Queen just stared at him.

Wheezing laughter escaped his lips, off-beat and shattered.

"Can you find them? Can you save her?" Hope welled up on her lips. Her tough demeanor seemed stressed.

The laughter stopped, and he just stared at her.

"If you do this and murder that reeking filth of a lizard, your reward is your choosing."

The monster stared longer at her in response.

Charlie felt a large thought push itself onto his mind. "Your Majesty, one has to be willing to accept the reality of the situation." He felt his words fall numbly from his lips. The worst position to be in. One where hope is mutilated by reality. Light by darkness. He grimaced.

She stared straight into the pits of that monster's eyes. "Go anyway. Slaughter the beast and bring her back to me. Your reward is your choosing."

"Ho, Charlie!" A voice pulled the commander back to the forest road again. The call came from their forward scout, a man the others called Lard.

"Quit the yelling, Lard. I hear you. What is it?" Charlie's sudden recall to reality was a hard transition. He felt like he almost had understood something about that monster's reasons for all of the extra madness they were enduring recently. Though, why Charlie would put himself to reliving those memories of him, he had no idea.

"Approaching caravan, two minutes up the road."

"Great." He had been enjoying their time alone. It would cause a hold up trying to pass any merchant peacefully in this part of the world. "Men, line up on one side of the road!" He called out. He hoped they could just pass without conflict. That monster would be especially drawn to conflict. Charlie frowned again before relenting his worry. There was only so much he could do. He would only worry about his own men.

The caravan rounded the last corner and faced Lizard Guts. Before Charlie could negotiate a word, the guard's swords were drawn, and they had a line formed. *Fast. These men were well trained.* Charlie admired the soldier's fortitude when something began to nag at him. The men standing opposite of them were bandaged and the wagons seemed to be less than pristine. Their reaction was *instant.* Something was wrong. This caravan had recently seen battle, and these men were strung tight, expecting danger at every turn.

"Bandit scum!" A man stepped forward from the line, opposing Lizard Guts.

Charlie was about to reason with the caravan when an urgent question pressed upon his mind. That monster was curious. "Why do you look like you have come from battle?" Charlie asked the man. He hated when that monster put questions in his mind.

No response.

"What happened to your caravan?" Charlie asked again.

"Move along, trash!" The man cried out again.

Charlie was about to retort and tell the man just exactly what he would do when the pressure on his mind shifted. He would move along after all. Charlie gritted his teeth.

"Keep to yourselves then, caravan." He answered their call, frowning, and led Lizard Guts past on the far side of the road, leaving the caravan to keep traveling—straight to their death.

For some reason, That monster had become interested and involved.

CHAPTER TWENTY-EIGHT

The highway through the forest passed by. Aurah sat on the back of a horse, guiding another that was carrying the dragon... or whatever it—he—was now. Her new cloak, the food and the horses for the dragon and herself seemed more like appeasement from the caravan—gifts that were intended to buy peace and seemed to say, "Please, spare us!" She hated taking things wrongly because of fear, but they wouldn't have been able to survive without the gifts. Aurah looked down at the cloak she was wearing. Her clothes from the Capital had been mere rags and she was thankful now to be wearing something more suitable to weather the trip. *And something more private.* Privacy seemed to be a rare commodity in this part of the world.

She noticed the trees passed by more quickly when she let her mind wander. The only problem with that was confronting the pain lurking in the depths of her heart. She clenched the reigns, frustrated and angry at where she found herself. Her body seized, gripped by her own ridiculousness. *Maybe.* Every one of her actions masqueraded as mistakes, failures that cried she was at fault. She couldn't bear to think of the audacity of her actions towards... him. She was tired of the emotional turmoil, and she was beginning to lose count at how many times he had saved her.

Her heart had been crushed, and her life had been completely changed in the worst way possible. Now she spent every moment coping with the helpless girl she was. Now she was not only traveling with the nightmare, but . . . she was helping him. *Disgusting.* Why couldn't they just die? Him first, though. *Maybe.*

That was another thing she couldn't understand. How in one second her heart would race at the thought of torturing him, and in the next, it would relent—punishing itself, instead, for being so twisted in such a manner. That probably made her angrier than anything else. Her emotions were a rebellious whip. Flying one direction, then another of their own accord and destroying everything. It was a whip that controlled her, invoking unspeakable agony. How could one put into words the depths of her feelings? Her hurt? Her pain? She was just a victim of a terrible tragedy.

No. She refused.

She would never allow herself to accept such a complacent stance. *But . . . I can't do it.* Aurah ran her hand through her greasy hair at the oppressive thoughts, only to catch her fingers on a snarl. Jerked out of her mind, she rubbed the sore spot for a moment, shaking her head.

There was no answer. There was no solution, no fix, no way would she ever be okay again. She would never be able to overcome the festering seeds of hate, planted where grace and love once flourished. Her demeanor would never brighten another room. It would never warm another spirit. She was ragged and spiteful—and it was all because of the unconscious beast riding behind her. *Maybe.*

A heavy sigh broke the silence behind her. Angling herself, she watched him come back to consciousness. His eyes slowly fluttered open, the haze of sleep seeping away as he became accustomed to the light again. His lips moved.

"Where are we?" His voice was scratchy from his sleep. He turned his head looking side to side as if trying to determine their whereabouts.

Yeah, right, dragon. You think you can just ask questions however you please!

Despite her burst of annoyance and hate at the beast, she had no idea where they were. Aurah had just kept following the path as the caravan told her. She didn't want to play her previous games with him. She didn't feel much of anything right at the moment. "I don't know. The caravan said to keep following the path until it splits, the nearest city is to the southeast."

"How much longer till the path splits?" He was sitting up now, stretching as best as possible on the horse.

"The path split hours ago." Her replies remained blunt as she stared forward. If she had to be right next to the creature physically, she wouldn't be anywhere near him emotionally or in her thoughts either. A low sigh rasped outward, past her lips. *What was she thinking about right now, then?* There was no freedom or peace from this cruel, cruel, creature. He invaded every solace she possessed.

"Hours? How long was I out for?"

Aurah clenched her teeth. She couldn't stand having any sort of conversation with the monster. Silence hung on the air between themselves.

"Well?" His voice had become even more demanding. *How was that even possible?*

This was just what she needed. To have him wake up and speak only to hear his own voice. Aurah thought forward of how they would approach the Capital, and how he would be surrounded, and *killed*. She gripped the reigns again. The caravan and the bandit fight told a completely different story of what would happen, though. *Would he never cease to be a menace?*

"Girl! I asked you a question!" He interrupted her thoughts abruptly. She couldn't answer him right now. Her reserve had reached its limit. If she talked, her tongue would unleash and
. . . .

"Well, answer it yourself then!" Her tongue was unleashed. Aurah's volume increased drastically. So did her hate for the creature.

"We don't have time for your little games, girl! If you want to get home safely, I suggest you listen closely to what I say!" He was angry now. "How long have I been out? Let me remind you I fell unconscious as a result of saving your sorry hide!" He pulled up alongside her on his horse, cutting her off. Aurah nearly smirked at how graceless the dragon was at the action. Of course, he didn't know how to ride a horse. "Answer me!" he shouted at her.

White blanched on the back of her knuckles, and her arms quivered dangerously. She wanted nothing but to end this heartless villain. "A day. You've been sleeping for a whole, stinking day." It was pointless to be angry, but Aurah was aghast at how proud and self-righteous this beast was. She looked him in the eye, directly defiant. "The battle with the bandits happened about this time yesterday." Her breathing was ragged. She needed to regain control despite how much she hated the beast. She would quell her own emotions, lock them away, and hide from the pain. Emotions were pain. That was a satisfactory answer. If she didn't feel, she wouldn't be hurt—whether from her own condemnation, or others' brutality. She wouldn't be tempted by the monster's incredible stupidity.

"A day . . . huh." He seemed taken aback now, all hints of hostility swallowed. His face was healed completely of any bruising or any signs of the rock, Aurah's fingers itched. His amber eyes looked towards the sky, over the treetops, clouded in thought. "What happened?" He turned his gaze back to her. "Did you see what had happened? All I remember is

needing to be somewhere very quickly . . . and then I was."
His voice faded.

A knot caught in Aurah's throat. What had happened the
previous day had terrified her. Immense and unknown power.
She could hardly believe what little she saw. It was no question
that the Capital would have difficulty killing the dragon, even
as a man. The knot in her throat released slightly.

"Faster than I could follow . . . ," she forced herself to
say. Maybe her words would make him realize just how much
of a monster he was. "You *moved* towards me, through the
bandits escaping right over me. Then they weren't trying to
escape, they just . . . *died*." Aurah gagged at the memory of
those corpses falling to pieces. "And then you were there. I
don't know how." Her voice wavered and the emotion spilled
out. She would have to get better at suppressing her feelings.

He turned his head away and looked up the road. "How
long did the caravan say we needed to travel before we reached
the next settlement?"

"Well, um, I don't know." This was the part she wasn't
looking forward to. She felt so small and weak. Her appetite
to expound upon his failings was completely eradicated by
her own recent blunders.

"What do you mean, you don't know?" His voice picked
up its stern disapproval again. "It's not a question you have
to figure out. How long did they say it would be before we
reached the settlement?"

Aurah dropped her head and hid behind her filthy locks
of hair. She remained silent for a different reason this time.

"Girl!"

"Ten hours!" She forced herself to answer. "Or so . . . ."
She mumbled that last part. It wasn't her fault. *Yes, it is.*

He stared wide-eyed at her. "Ten hours?" His voice dripped
incredulity, slowly pronouncing every word.

She nodded her head uncomfortably.

"What in the name of all creation were you doing for the last fourteen hours then, girl?" His voice hiked in volume and he threw his hand out at her in an unconscious gesture from the overwhelming anger radiating from him.

She hunched lower on the horse, ready to take off and run away. She didn't need him after all, *right?* She couldn't bear his anger, not when it was right, not when she was responsible for one of the biggest screw-ups ever. She had tried so hard to be faultless in front of the dragon, but then she had messed up their directions. Now the dragon had a reason to be angry at her, but she couldn't have done better. She had only lived in one place her whole life! It wasn't her fault she wasn't good with directions and maps and traveling, and whatever else. Right? *Maybe.* "I thought I had taken the correct path at the fork. When we didn't get anywhere, I thought that if we kept going, we . . . ."

"You thought! You thought! You thought wrong, girl! And now we are who knows where hunted by those dragons that crashed in on us— I hope you haven't forgotten how we managed to get so many of them killed! You should have thought of that when you decided not knowing how to travel was okay! You have no idea what kind of situation we are in! The dragons aren't the only ones chasing us, there's also— he cut off his rage.

"What?" Aurah asked, confused by the sudden stop to the beast's madness. *Was this what caused him to be so afraid before he was changed into a man?*

"Nothing." The dragon turned and jumped off his horse, storming off into the trees and disappearing.

Aurah clenched both hands over her mouth. She couldn't restrain her emotions. Tears poured down her face as stifled wailing erupted from her hands. Survive. Don't survive. Hate. Don't hate. Feel. Don't feel. All of this was pointless beyond measure. This monster, this struggle. Survival and existence. Somehow all of this was her fault! She was cleaved from home, she was exposed to the dragon's torture, she was assaulted time and again by rotten men, and she was expected not to make mistakes. Her shoulders rocked from her weeping. Leaning forward, she wrapped her arms around the animal's neck, finding comfort in its soft mane. This was all too much. She would never make it through this mentally, even if she made it physically.

In a flash, the dragon was back from the trees with a look of fear on his face.

"Get off the horse, girl! Quickly!" He raced to his horse. "Quick undo this lashing! We need to get under cover immediately!

"What?" Her tear-filled eyes could hardly comprehend his motions, and her mind could barely register the words he said.

"Now! Off! We haven't a moment to spare!" He grabbed her, to her disgust, and put her on the ground. Sore from sitting so long, Aurah undid the lead on his horse and handed it to the dragon as she pulled on her own and followed him towards the trees. *What was happening?* She was so confused, and she didn't know what to feel. *Kill your emotion.* She murmured her mantra in her mind.

"Come quick, girl! We need to hide from the skies!" On the edge of the trees, the dragon disappeared through the growth. It wasn't horribly dense, but it wasn't clear either. It would be difficult to lead a horse through the thicket.

Holding the reigns even tighter, she pulled the horse through the growth. Her ears twitched. *What was that?* A quiet thrum began to vibrate through the air.

She moved her feet quicker, fright beginning to take hold at the unknown sound. Into the forest, she plunged on the path the dragon had made. Step by step, she threaded her way after him through the dense trees and vines. The vibration in the air grew louder, and distinct beats billowed across the air.

"Here, girl!" He called from a nearby rock outcropping. A small ledge stretched a short distance over the small valley they were in, reaching out to hang over the forest floor below. A perfect hiding place. *But for what?*

She clambered through the forest, one step after the other.

"Now, girl! They're here!" His voice cried out with urgency.

With one last pull, she managed to get the horse and herself underneath the cover of the rocks. What were they hiding from? What was that beat in the air?

Then she saw it.

Looking up to the sky, waves of dragons drew near. It was a horrible sight. The mass of dragons from before reigned supreme in her nightmares and this group made that one look childish—pathetic, actually.

The horses snorted uncomfortably. The dragon worked to calm his and she followed suit, holding the animal close, comforting it.

Then she saw a thing of *nightmares*. As if any dragon weren't such by itself.

This was one was pitch black. As dark as a moonless night where not a tongue of fire was found anywhere within leagues.

The dragon leading this thrall filled her vision through the treetops. The closer it got, the less of anything else she saw. Even the dragon standing next to her, when he was a dragon, was dwarfed by this new monster's size.

Aurah's mouth hung gaping at the atrocity.

If death ever had a harbinger, that dragon would be it.

The trees rippled and swayed from the force of the gusts created by the dragons' wings. Leaves, loosened from the season, tore from the trees and wafted all around. She hoped the leaves would only provide more cover to hide them. *Maybe.*

Both she and the dragon man stood frozen in place. Even the horses seemed to cease to move—refusing to budge an inch under the sharp eyes of so many dragons. Time seemed to be still while the scaly beasts passed overhead. Aurah could nearly count her heartbeats. Her lungs held their air.

The beasts were moving so fast the whole ordeal lasted less than a minute. They seemed not to have noticed the two hiding below. *Maybe.*

When it was nearly another minute since the last dragon passed, Aurah freed her lungs to breathe again. "What was that?" She nearly screamed, fear jerking on every nerve.

"That," he shuddered. "was the most dangerous creature in the world." Staring at the ground, his chest heaved.

"What does that mean for us?" She asked, petrified at the turn of events.

"It means . . . ." He stumbled through his words, and a look of confusion rested on his face for a moment.

"It means hell." He looked at her, she could almost see the reaper in his eyes. He paused for a moment, never taking his eyes off her before he spoke. "Come on. I think I know where we need to head." He grabbed his horse and began to tread farther away from the road.

"How do you know where you're going?" She couldn't help but ask, as she had no clue what to do to get anywhere.

"Those dragons, that black beast, they're looking for something." He swallowed hard. "Until they find it, they won't bother themselves with other things."

"How do you know that? What are they looking for?" She found her voice rising, the answers already lying inside of her mind.

"It's simple, girl—they're looking for us." He coughed violently, covering his mouth with a fist and turning away from her. He seemed to fight some deep and terrible urge. His chest pumped, consuming air like it wouldn't have any for much longer.

"You can't know that!" She found the hair on her neck rising in horror. They were running from *that* now? There was no way they could make it back. Their chances of succeeding just plummeted to beyond nothing. Even if she returned home, they were now that monster's prey. There would be nowhere safe anymore.

"You can rest assured they are after us. But for some unknown reason, they only know the general area to look, and not specifics. We need to move before they figure it out." He picked up his head and kept moving.

"Well, why this direction then?" She couldn't help but ask. Her hate for him, drowning in the fear that the dragons had brought to them.

"The dragons are looking for us. They won't be sidetracked from their vengeance, so they are probably avoiding human settlements . . . probably." He kept moving.

"So, we just head in the opposite direction and hope for the best?" She couldn't wrap her head around it. Things just get worse and worse. They were doomed to failure. They should just end it all here.

"It's better than heading in the same direction and hoping for the best." He replied curtly. "Let's go."

The dragon released a loud sigh as he draped himself over the horses back.

They had made it. Aurah found hope in the new discovery. Where they were wasn't important. What was important was that the newly found road was different, and it offered hope.

"Come on, we have to keep moving." The monster mounted the horse and began to follow the road.

Hours had passed as they slowly, painstakingly, moved through the woods. Aurah pulled her horse completely onto the road. The underbrush had given her some trouble and she wanted to make sure the horse wouldn't be hurt. The dragon was already starting to pull away before she mounted. She sighed heavily as well. Nudging the horse forward, she began to follow the dragon. How much more of this nightmare would they have to endure? She caught up to him and rode in silence behind, letting him lead the way. She wouldn't ever take charge of their heading again.

The road aimed upwards, making the already weary horses move even slower. The sun had begun to set an hour ago, and dusk was filling out. The dragon finally crested the hill shortly after they had begun to travel on the road.

"Girl, look at this." The beast called her forward. What had he found? Aurah pulled the horse up alongside the dragon to look down at the world.

The road rounded over the top of the hill to slant back down towards the bottom. At the very bottom of the hill, the road ran straight into the brightest spot she had seen in this dark, dark night.

A city—nestled at the bottom of a valley. The woods encroached on one side and a large meadow lay on the other. The forest continued around the meadow, surrounding it while a river cut through and ran near the city. The city was nearly two thirds the size of the Capital, and all along its walls, fires had been lit to provide light during the night hours.

"Good! The gates are still open! We need to hurry, girl." The dragon looked down at the horse, unsure of how to command the creature.

"Like this, beast." Aurah kicked her heels, pushing the horse into a quick trot. She turned her head, smiling to herself as the dragon struggled to control the horse. The slant downward was relieving to the horses. Only a little bit farther and they would be in the safety of the city. Maybe she could sleep somewhere warm for once. *Maybe.*

It was a short distance and didn't take long before they reached the city's main gate.

"Stop!" There were a handful of guards standing at attention at the gate, and the one that seemed set apart from the others spoke up. He must have been the captain. Aurah clenched her reigns in response. A captain and his soldiers. It brought back horrendous memories. Aurah's gut hurt at the reminder. She eyed the dragon beside her from the corner of her eye.

The captain called out again warily. "Keep your distance strangers and state your business. Oh, and maybe you would care to explain why it is that you are rushing towards us?"

Aurah pulled on her reigns immediately, stopping the horse a slight distance away from the guards. The dragon followed suit and they both faced the onlooking soldiers. "Yes, sir. Please let us have stay for the night within the safety of the walls. It is cold and dangerous out here." Aurah spoke up before the dragon could attempt to ruin things. Aurah remembered how his attempts to talk to the caravan had gone. She would prevent that if at all possible. "We were afraid to miss passage into the city. That is what accounts for our racing at these late hours, captain."

Something suddenly occurred to Aurah. An idea. Inspired by the draw of the warmth of a bed. A bath, comfort. Humans. *Why was she traveling with this beast again?* She thought of the beast's strength, even as a man. But surely, the soldiers could take care of him themselves, here and now?

"In good order, ma'am, you've barely managed to make it but if you pay the tax, we'll let you in."

"Tax. How much is the tax?" Aurah inquired.

"Two littles." The captain replied.

Aurah looked down at the new knapsack the caravan had given them. She knew there was a money pouch in there somewhere. Reaching for her bag, she began to rummage through until she found the coin purse. She closed the knapsack and dismounted the horse. She would be the one to pay. A girl was less of a threat to the men, and the dragon had no idea what he was doing. And besides, there was something she needed to do.

As she approached the captain, the guards stood at the ready, no doubt a result of dealing with a thriving culture of bandits and other scoundrels that roamed these woods. She pulled out the two coins and held them out to his hand. He reacted, reaching to collect the tax when she dropped the coins. The captain and Aurah bent at the same time to grab the coins off the ground.

"Help me," she whispered through her teeth. The captain seemed not to hear her. "Help me!" The words were hissed between her teeth. Who knew if the dragon had an abnormally good sense of sound or not? The captain looked up at her. He had heard her mutter and he caught the look in her eye. Something flashed through his eyes. *Understanding?* She was doing her best to motion towards the monster on the horse with her eyes. The captain blinked in response. Did he understand after all?

"Thank you, miss. I hope you enjoy your stay. Harrington is a good place and will treat you fine. I do hope not to cause an inconvenience, but horseback is prohibited in the late hours, as the noise tends to disturb the residents." The guards all shifted at the statement. What metal they wore clanked in unison.

Aurah moved back towards her horse gingerly. *What had she just done?* She grabbed the reins of her horse and led it forward. The dragon just stared, but in a second slipped down from his mount and began to lead the horse forward. Unaware. Oblivious.

Aurah moved past the guards first, pulling the horse along. There seemed to be a tension that built a wall between them, but they let her pass. The captain didn't seem to be concerned with her. Aurah floundered completely in disbelief that she had turned in the dragon. Her emotions stretched even thinner and anxiety weighed on her shoulders. She turned and looked at the dragon. He looked up and into her eyes.

Something seemed to register.

In a flash, the captain knocked him to the ground. The horse, startled, reared and fled down the dark path. The rest of the guards seized the dragon's arms and legs, arresting him in place.

They didn't hold him for long.

The dragon's powerful core twisted, and he threw off the guards hanging on his arms. A guard planted the butt of his spear in the dragon's ribs. A yell chortled from the beast's lips as he turned to grab the spear from the soldier. He missed. The guards who were thrown were back in the fray, trying to find an opening to latch onto the beast and bring him down. A horn blew behind Aurah. A yell from above on the wall cried out. A short distance away, more crying called out from the blackness of the city.

Aurah backed away from the commotion, afraid of the highly likely possibility that the guards would fail. A guard blasted through a doorway with stairs on the inside of the gate. He must have been a sentry on top of the wall. The guard barreled forward, charging the group and knocking them all over. Loud yells erupting from the pile of men, as more reinforcements arrived to surround the dragon.

Aurah stared in fear. Her back was now against the city's wall. She could retreat no farther. What would the monster do to her now? He would kill all of the soldiers and then her. She had revealed herself too soon. It was all a mistake. She would certainly die now and every attempt to fix any facet in life would show for what it really was—a meaningless effort.

In a powerful eruption, the pile of soldiers was picked up and thrown off the dragon. The beast stood, chest heaving, having just expended a roar from his exertion. An odd glow seemed to encompass his body, dimming with every second but radiating, nonetheless. A stream of blood flowed from above his brow.

His gaze though fell right onto Aurah. His fierce amber eyes sat below his brown tufts of hair. Piercing right through her.

Her skin tingled as she met his stare. *Oh, no.* She had thought about this and had been sure of her decision. But not anymore.

No, no, no! This dragon *was* responsible for the torture, hardships, and danger imposed upon her life. He wanted to take her back for his own sake, more than hers. If he even really wanted to take her back! She had no obligation to the creature. This was the right action! The beast deserved a just recompense!

So why did she feel wrong?

Every action led to more doubt. Every decision created more conflict. She was brought trouble in heaps, and she would not be held responsible for removing herself from that trouble. Aurah shook her head and returned the monster's gaze. She was tremendously bold to defy her enemy in such a manner.

He dropped his eyes. His body's tension released. Guards that he had thrown off charged him again. The rest that showed up after surrounded the group, just waiting to help, but the dragon no longer resisted. He held out his arms, palms up, waiting to be taken. The guards arrested his movement completely again, this time with no resistance. They held him staunchly until a soldier shackled him, thick chains laced from his wrists to his ankles. The guards led him away, spears at the ready. Poised next to his body.

The captain approached Aurah, minor scuffs and bruises littered his face. *An angry face.* She turned slightly avert his gaze.

"You have some serious explaining to do if you don't want to join your buddy, *ma'am.*" Aurah scratched the back of her hand and fought to regain her breathing. What could she say? She was a loss because of the situation herself.

"Sir, have you heard of the attack on the Capital, near two weeks ago?" Her voice was stiff and emotionless. She didn't dare look the man in his eyes. Was it because of the fear of confronting him or something more . . . *personal? Stop.*

Nothing. Aurah blocked her thoughts. She was getting better at hiding her feelings.

"Everyone has heard of the attack on the Capital, ma'am. I fail to see what that has to do with anything." His response was matter-of-fact and crisp. There was little room for idle chatter.

"Has there been a bounty or some kind of search for a young woman put in place by the Prin . . . ." She caught herself. Elizabeth would already have had her birthday and ascended the throne. "The Queen?" She turned and looked the captain in the eye.

The man took a second, taking her in before his eyes widened.

"No way! Are you kidding me? Then who in the world was that? Never mind. Marks, take command of the gate. Girl, you need to come with me immediately!"

The captain placed his hand on her lower back and towed Aurah away towards the most majestic looking building in the city of Harrington.

Exactly where the procession of guards leading the dragon was also headed.

CHAPTER TWENTY-NINE

Aurah stood at a window overlooking the city. She was staying in a room until the Capital could respond and give direction on how to proceed. Aurah clutched tightly to the hope that she would be brought back to Elizabeth's waiting arms. That's what Aurah would want, at least.

Aurah stared at an empty tray of food. The meals back home were definitely more comforting and familiar. But then again, that was home, and after everything she had been through, anything was the work of miracle hands. She stared at the cloak the caravan had given her, next to a pile of soiled and shredded linens—her dress from before. The last two weeks in the world had not been kind to anything in Aurah's life. Harrington had provided her new clothing, and, at her request, it was hardier and more travel-capable clothing. Fine leather had replaced soft cloth and fabric. Her time in the dragon's world had taught her not to trust in anything except her own ability. She would make sure she was prepared now. Shame on her if she were ever unprepared again.

Aurah reached up and tied her hair with a strip of leather. She had asked to shave off all her hair, but Harrington wouldn't let her for fear of her not being recognized by the Capital. A ponytail was easy and would be something she wouldn't have to waste time with.

She moved her hands into the air from the knotted leather tie as she stretched her arms above her head, hoping to help a sore spot in her back release. She sat down on the bed, biding her time. Her body was torn between the most restful sleep she has had in quite some time and the nightmares lurking beneath the surface of her mind. It didn't matter how nice life became for her now. Nothing would ever remove the scars she had gained.

After the captain had collected her, he had put her through interrogation in front of a few other heads of the city. They had all asked her questions. Details about her time after the dragon had stolen her away. It was not a few times that she broke out in sobs from the remembrance of those terrible memories. Sometimes she wasn't even able to speak words to describe things. The captain and the others stood in awe at her story of survival in the worst of hells.

They had asked specifically about the other dragons who had assaulted her captor and her. They were shocked to hear about the transformation and the bandit attack. *Who wouldn't have been?* She could see the blood draining from their faces at the mention of an even bigger thrall, and their black leader, and how the dragon she was with said they were searching for himself and Aurah. They had given her quarters, and at her request, food and a bath, though not without much debate over whether it would be safe for the city to harbor the dragon and herself. Thankfully most had voted in favor of not evicting her nor the dragon in order that they may be the city responsible for returning the girl and bringing justice onto the beast. They considered the chance that Aurah may not be who she said she was small. Unfortunately, they also considered the chance that that black dragon would find them to be small as well.

It would take some time before the Capital returned their response to Harrington. Even by bird, a response from the Capital was nearly two days away. Upon its return, they would lend a guard and make the journey to the Lowlands, and then the Capital. The inquiry with the Capital concerning Aurah was merely a formality, they would have sent her immediately to the Capital to be judged. Rather, the real hesitation came from what to do with the dragon, now turned human. The risk was too much for the city alone to decide.

Aurah laid out on the bed now. The soft pillows were comforting, and the air was warm. She was safe now.

A tremble shook the room, pulling Aurah back to reality. She shot up from the bed. Her door was hanging open. *Strange.* She stood. Who had come into the room? She was told a guard had been posted outside her door, something she found much relief in. She went to the opening and poked her head out into the hall.

"Hello?" Her voice reverberated off the stone walls.

The world trembled again, shaking her to the core. A strange sound carried through the halls, calling her from her room. She stood in the doorway looking down the passageway.

"Hello?" Her voice called again.

Nothing.

She took a step. And then another. She found her feet had begun to carry her towards some unknown destination.

The world rocked, throwing various wall pictures off and toppling what other decorations littered the hallway. She had to clutch the wall to hold herself steady. Her feet didn't help her one bit. They kept walking of their own accord, *dragging her against her will.*

Soon the world changed, subtly at first, but then in more dramatic measures. The stones changed and an undeniable stench filled the air.

She was back in that monster's cave.

Aurah knew she had to have been dreaming now. Another nightmare. She must have fallen asleep, but . . . this dream was completely unlike anything she had ever experienced. *It was so real.* So real, in fact, that she had no idea if it was a dream or not.

Despite her resistance, Aurah's feet never stopped moving for one second, and she plunged into the depths of a looming blackness.

The rocking grew more violent and frequent. Through every miserable moment, her feet carried her, reminding her of the tragedy she had endured. Sweat ran down her neck, her heartbeat thundered in her chest, and she was fighting the world's now constant trembling. A light appeared in front of her. Dim and distant at first, it quickly grew, and the dragon's den morphed into what looked to be a circular room in a dungeon. Her feet had stopped moving, and the world had quieted. There was only a single door in this room. She turned her head, looking behind. There was nothing but solid wall behind her. *Where . . . ?*

Her feet finally responded to her insistence. She searched the lengths of the curved walls for a way out, but nothing interrupted the stone except the periodic torch. The wall continued around and connected with itself. There was no other entrance, nor exit. Just that one door.

She moved closer. Curiosity had gripped her. The door had bars over the window. She moved gingerly, ready to spring at the first sign of trouble. Her feet shuffled slowly over the smooth floor until the door stood inches away. She pushed herself up on her toes to look through the bars.

It looked . . . normal. There was a passageway, with stairs leading to somewhere else.

She reached for the handle to open the door when she realized it had no handle. She looked around. There was no way out.

"Um, hello!" Her voice called out through the bars as she knocked on the door.

"What!" A deep and gravelly voice screamed at her. A large head covered in a cloak appeared on the other side of the bars.

"I think there has been a mistake. You see, I don't belong here, locked away. Please let me out."

"Oh! So, she says she doesn't belong here! She says to let her out! She says, she says, she says!" The voice, a man's, rose with every syllable, roaring at her at the end. "Let me tell you something, you little puke! You're here because of yourself. You'll never be free. You've locked yourself away, and there's no hope for a miserable puke like you!" He kept screaming, senseless words and noises emanating from the dark hood.

Aurah backed away, horrified at the voice.

"Please! There must have been some kind of mistake! I don't know anything about this!" She pleaded desperately with the man.

"Please! She says!" His voice cackled strangely at such a deep tone. "Tell that to him!" A hand pointed behind her.

She turned hurriedly. What could possibly be behind her?

The world had changed in an instant and she was on top of the plateau. The sky swirled with the light of an army of purple clouds, a singular massive front that crawled slowly forward. On the other side of Aurah's vison, an equal front of inky black clouds crawled forward, somehow warring against the purple. Something *nasty* was swimming in their depths. Something *evil.* The world tremored again, and this time Aurah saw that it came from the colliding clouds.

Aurah stared in awe at the thundering and warring sky. It made no sense but left her sick to her stomach. What was happening in the sky should not be.

Aurah dropped her head to find a way out of this dream, though she was certain now that it couldn't even be called that. It was something more. It didn't matter. She needed to leave.

It didn't take her long to see that there was nothing around except the ash of the burnt forest and . . . .

"Me." A horrid voice scraped outward from behind her. Aurah screamed and jumped away from the voice, falling to the ground. *It was the beast!* He was back to a dragon, and his scales were pitch black, rivaling the black in the sky.

The grass had changed into a mass of crawling critters that trespassed all over her body. Her screaming rang out loudly, accompanied by a wild thrashing as she was swarmed by the nightmare. The world began to tremble again as the dragon laughed viciously at Aurah's misery.

"This is all of your doing, you miserable filth! You should never have betrayed me! I will have vengeance! You—" The dragon faltered in its speech as light poured from its body. "No!" The beast screamed louder as more light burst forth. The critters torturing Aurah left chased away by the light. Even the pain she felt dissipated in its warmth. The dragon turned into black smoke, circling above the light. Beneath . . . .

It was her captor? But as a man. On his knees. His amber eyes stared straight into hers.

What?

What was he doing? What was going on? Was this real?

Who cares?

Aurah screamed at the dragon, the man on his knees. How dare he? This was all his fault. She would *never* forgive the beast. How dare he interrupt her dreams and save her. How dare he permeate her mind and intrude on everything that she was?

"I hate you!" she screamed at the beast.

His eyes never wavered, and as quickly as it rose away, the darkness plummeted like a meteor, crashing down on the dragon turned man, smothering the light. The blackness swirled and formed back into the dragon it once was, laughing. It stopped suddenly, filling its chest. It pointed its black snout straight at her.

Then released its flame.

Aurah never stopped screaming under the flame.

The fire continued to overwhelm her as she thrashed in the flames consuming her.

Thrashing.

Screaming.

Screa—

"Girl! Wake up!" A loud voice yelled at her, shaking her desperately.

Aurah's eyes ripped open, her voice hoarse. Tears coated her face. That dream was terrifying. It was worse than a nightmare. Her body convulsed from the terror.

The voice belonged to the captain that had rescued her at the gate. He was such a welcome sight. Maybe he had come to check on her? *Who cares?* He was here now. She wept and clung to the man. She wept and didn't stop. There was so much that she had been holding in. It felt good to let it all out. The captain held her, soothing her sorrow.

Minutes raced by. Would she ever be free from these scars? Could she ever recover? She rested her hand on the man's arm, and with a gentle push indicated she was fine or would be at least.

"Are . . . are you alright, ma'am?" His voice was soothing and filled with honey.

She wiped her eyes, her hands rubbing as if to erase the sorrow. She nodded. She would be fine. She looked up, and her eyes bulged, her bones tearing from her skin.

"Not for long, you little whore!" The man screamed at her, but it wasn't the captain anymore. *It was Dorian.* "This is all your fault, Aurah! You will never be okay! You don't deserve it! You've ruined everything! How dare you use me and leave me like this?" Dorian, right before Aurah's eyes, morphed into his mottled carcass and death crested his eyes. "How dare you ever consider forgiving that monster?" He raised a dragon-like, clawed fist and swung at her.

Aurah jolted upright, torn from her sleep. She threw a hand to cover her mouth as sobs ripped through her body. One hand wouldn't be enough, she brought the other up quickly, stifling her weeping. She hit herself after a moment, desperately hoping she was awake for real. Like hitting herself would do anything.

She would never be alright.

Her body ached from its tears. Her reserves were exhausted again. She let herself calm down, only an occasional shudder rippled through her chest.

Then the world quaked again.

Aurah's eyes open wide, fear gripping her. There was no way she was still in that nightmare. Was she? She flung her legs off the bed and stood, distrusting the very fabric of reality around her.

Another quake trembled. Her arms shot to the side to help her disturbed balance. She felt it through her legs. There was no way this wasn't real.

The window! She looked up and raced over hoping to find the source of the shaking. Her hands landed on the sill. The city lay sprawled out before her. The keep was on a small hill, raising it above the rest of the city, and it had a few different floors. Aurah was on one of the uppermost. Between the keep and the city was a large square. Looking at the square she realized what she was seeing.

Dragons.

The whole horde of them that had passed overhead in the forest. They were here now. Her fingers gripped the sill. *They're looking for us.* Her heart hammered in her chest, and the world seemed to spin and distance itself from her. She clung tighter to the sill. She needed air. The soldiers and the guards had managed to arrive and confront the dragons. No fighting had happened yet. There was a balcony just down her hall. She grabbed the latch on her door. *Unlocked.* It was unnecessary, after all; she had matched their descriptions perfectly. The door swung open. The hallway was empty.

She stuck her head out of the door. "Hello?" No one responded; the guard was gone. *Probably called away by the dragons outside.* She stepped out, taking stock of her situation. A shiver ran up her spine. This was too much like the nightmare. She shook her head. There were more important things to do. She needed to move forward.

She raced down the hall towards the balcony she had seen earlier on her way to the room. Maybe she could figure out what was going on. Her thoughts skirted around the truth that the dragons would probably find her and the one who had stolen her. It didn't dawn on her to be petrified. Maybe her heart had hardened completely. *Good, let trouble come.* She pulled the door open and stepped out on the balcony. She hid behind the door opening. Her eyes bounced around from dragon to dragon. She looked up to see even more dragons circling in the sky. There wasn't even enough room for all the dragons to land in the city.

Something in the sky caught her eye and she followed it, aghast. It was the massive black dragon that had led the thrall in the woods. The sight made her afraid at last. She doubted that a single soul could look at that creature and feel anything but fear. In a quick maneuver, the monster angled its flight and shot towards the ground.

The ground and city erupted underneath its fury.

"Pathetic human slugs! Listen closely to the ruler of all things!" The dragon roared out its declaration.

She could hear the dragon's talk fine. Despite all that she had endured, it would always unsettle her to hear a dragon speak, especially this one now.

"I am your god! I am your king! I am your death! Your life, your breath, your fear!" The guards in the square stepped back from the weight of the monster's words. His very voice crushed stalwart men like children. "My name is Vasiss! And

I am a merciful and benevolent king!" His tail whipped out and lashed the ground in front of one of the soldiers' formations. Chunks of rock and debris pelted the men, causing them to take a more defensive position and to back up even more. The beast threw his head back and cackled at the frailty of the humans. "I have but one goal, and I will let you live. Give me the man and woman who killed my brother! I know that they are here!"

Dragons sat perched across the city on buildings and open ground, staring at the spectacle their king was making with the humans. Creaking and groans echoed out from the buildings whenever the dragons shifted their weight. They might seem like they were lazing around, but Aurah could see even from a distance that they were tense and prepared to spring.

But what for? What could possibly challenge this vicious monster? She found that she had begun to clench her fists in anticipation. There was no way not to be affected by the monster's presence. She couldn't imagine the soldiers below, standing face to face with the beasts. They didn't have any fortitude to deal with the dragons. She gulped hard from sympathy as her own memories flooded back for a moment.

Just then a man stepped forward. Aurah gripped the sill even harder. *He was going to turn them in.*

The man looked up at Vasiss.

Faster than she could follow, the black beast swung his body, whipping his mighty tail forward and crushed the man where he stood. Blood erupted across the ground underneath the dragon's massive tail and the surrounding area. Aurah stared, shocked, as horror filtered across her face. That man hadn't even said a word! Her heart feared now. Her reserve cracked. Her mouth hung open. She could almost taste the death in the air.

"You're dead!" The dragon roared. Then laughter. *Laughter?*

Evil laughter and despicable words poured from the monster's mouth. The beast picked its tail up to see part of the mottled corpse clinging to it. "Filthy maggots." He shook his tail clean, wiping it the rest of the way off on a nearby building, causing a whole side of it to collapse. Vasiss stared, shocked. "Sorry 'bout that. Oh, well." The dragon did the equivalent of a shrug with his wings before speaking again. "Where are they?" He screamed the words, roaring out his insanity. His fury lavished terror across every soul in the city.

"Make way! Move! I said, move!" A commotion caught her eye as a much quieter voice than the black dragon's, screamed out. Another man, one of the few who had argued to get rid of Aurah and the dragon, had begun shoving men aside, racing towards the keep.

For me.

He was going to hand them over after all. He was going to save himself, his city. Could she blame him? *Yes.* She could. She would blame him very much so.

Aurah raced away, towards the door. She had only one hope now. Her movements seized at that thought, her mind processing the situation at hand. *Curse that wretched creature!* She found herself gripped again. Wrapped in its clutches, she would never escape. By some sick imagining of fate, she found herself dependent on the very scum she tried to scrape off of her soul. *It will never end.* Her thoughts despaired. Aurah's head twisted hard back towards the dragons.

A vicious, ear-splitting scream rocked the world.

Aurah had to cover her ears it was so loud. She fell against the wall confused and frightened.

Then it stopped, just as suddenly as it had started. She stood still, recovering from the sharp pain in her head. The vision that greeted her eyes stunned her.

Multiple dragons lay dead or twitching on the ground, their blood pooling in rivers around them.

The bolts of light that had led up to Aurah's captor's transformation had returned. In a fury, the projectiles pelted the horde of dragons, sending them scattering into the sky.

Vasiss roared his fury. "You will die a thousand deaths for your transgression!" Jumping into the air, his wings beat, carrying him away. It was like kicking a hive of bees. The dragons on the ground launched into the air after their master, and the ones already in the air fell in line behind him. The projectiles became fewer and fewer as the targets decreased in number.

Vasiss, distinguished amongst his thrall, let out a commanding roar. A dragon lurched free from the pack immediately, dashing to the ground. The bolts of light picked up, a hail of death towards the descending dragon.

But not one touched the beast.

Dashing back and forth, the dragon swam through the projectiles, dodging with uttermost precision. The dragon snapped its head down, plunging into a dive while spinning its body around in a perpetual roll. Close to the ground, obscured by some of the taller buildings, Aurah couldn't make out what it was doing until it receded with its prize. *It looked like a man.* Using both claws the beast twisted the man, ripping him in half, and then threw the remains towards the city.

It screamed its victory.

The entirety of the thrall above echoed its cry of glory with a shrieking roar of their own—all but their King.

The assailing dragon held no ounce of strength back and beat the air until it climbed out of the bolts of death erupting from beneath itself, to fall back into the circling death that was the thrall.

Aurah was terrified at the complete involvement of every dragon in the thrall. She even spotted the giant dragon that had confronted her and her captor before.

Vasiss finally released his roar after moments of nothing but circling. The dragons responded to the new battle command. They dispersed in every direction, aiming straight for the city. Anger reverberated from their hides as they began to decimate the city.

There would be nothing left of what was once human.

Streams of fire coursed through the streets and alleys. Dragons barreled through buildings. Aurah covered her mouth at the horror of innocent death. No one would remain. *None.*

And then the bolts of light picked up again, firing with pinpoint accuracy. The unlucky or unskilled fell from the sky like rain in a storm. That was exactly what this was—the most furious storm ever, and it rained dragons and their fire.

Her eyes blazed open, barely taking in what she saw.

Then, the fire died. The air thinned, Aurah gasped again for breath as the dragons above stumbled in their flight, dropping low.

Every. Single. One.

Vasiss beat his wings back hard and pounded the air more than before to stay afloat. He spun around in the air, searching. Searching ceaselessly.

Then he roared out once more, his wings beating the thinned air.

He found something.

The most impossible something ever.

A cloaked figure stood encompassed in torrents of purple light.

He stood, defying the armies of the black dragon.

Holding two dangerous purple orbs of light, the cloaked man lifted his arms and threw the orbs into the ground. *Into each other.*

The man blasted faster than a dragon into the sky. The air distorted around him, Aurah watched something like a splash in a pond expand outward, ripping through the air. Before she knew what was happening, the wave caught her in the chest and threw her off her feet into the wall behind her. The air had been thinned, but now her lungs had been completely emptied. An explosion tore her ears to pieces, and her head throbbed as she watched the blur of the man shoot straight through a dragon and out the other side of its body. He didn't seem to lose a single ounce of speed. The noise of his actions came to Aurah moments after she watched him commit them. He erupted through one dragon after another before finally stopping to land on the back of a beast. The unfortunate dragon's body broke, blood erupted as it was launched from the impact. The man jumped between beasts felling them in one hit if even a full hit connected.

The sight was mad, yet it was glorious in some sick and magnificent way.

But then trouble always happens.

The brutal king of a dragon ripped through the air with equal force and connected a shattering blow with the cloaked figure, sending him raging straight towards the ground.

A crater erupted in a mere second, leveling streets and buildings.

Vasiss stayed in the sky, hovering above the man that he had attacked. That wasn't enough to keep him down though, he was back in the sky by some unknown force, with the same rage. Aurah struggled to follow the fight.

In a flash, Vasiss was reeling backward through the air, completely caught off guard. The man had returned the strike, with extra in return.

If Aurah had thought that the first wave of sound that connected with her was massive, it was nothing compared to the fury of these two striking each other. Aurah covered her ears.

How could any human match that black beast? What empowered that cloaked man and put him on equal terms? Vasiss displayed just how nimble of a creature he was despite his mighty size. A kick followed instantly by a swinging tail. Every hit connected, but nothing seemed to phase the man in the cloak.

Likewise, he displayed his prowess, blocking every attack. The dragon was too quick for him to dodge but by some miracle, he deflected the might of the blow and always returned. It was beyond her understanding of reality to know how a human managed to stay in the air. Maybe his attacks were such that they propelled him higher? It would be hard to find the high ground in the air against a dragon.

Or maybe...

A bright light flashed in front of her. A dragon crashed in the square in front of her. It was a warzone everywhere. Flashes of bolts, and dragons mutilating any human unfortunate enough to not already be crushed or burned.

Her eyes were sucked back towards the sky by a purple flash. And another.

The cloaked man had lost his cloak, but now he was surrounded in a deep purple, almost as if it were a replacement. Missiles projected from his hand, keeping his opponent at bay. His magic had given him the upper hand, but now without a platform to launch against, he slowly drifted towards to ground. Too slowly to be normal. His magic cloak must be helping him.

Just then, against all odds, a dragon lurched straight up from the rubble beneath and distracted the cloaked man. He killed the assailing beast with minimal struggle. But it was enough of an opening.

Vasiss plummeted, lashing his tail forward and catching the exposed man with the full force of his being. The cloaked man blasted away, out of the city and into the forest, Aurah watched an awesome impact appear in the trees as dirt flew into the air, as far away as her eye could see from this vantage.

The cloaked man was surely dead.

Vasiss released a torrent of flames straight above himself to celebrate his power.

There was no more time. There was no hope, not without *him*.

She turned to race to find her captor, but she turned face-first into the man who had raced to find her. He had been watching the battle, too. He knew Vasiss still raged. A crazy look reigned in the man's eye, his long brown hair draped over his face causing shadows across his crooked nose.

"Please. Please, no, don't do this!" She begged for mercy as she backed away. The other side of the balcony had another door, but she would never have it opened in time.

The man approached cautiously, and then lunged, grabbing her wrists. In one fluid movement, she grabbed the man's chain mail with her free hand and threw her knee into his groin. Aurah didn't relish her lucky shot, but she knew she wouldn't allow herself to be taken captive ever again. His grip released instantly as he let out a grunt of misery. She shoved off of him, throwing herself through the open door behind the man. He wouldn't be deterred for long.

She raced down the corridor.

With every beat of her heart.

She hoped fiercely that somehow, she could find the dragon who had ruined her life.

CHAPTER THIRTY

Kast leaned forward, held in place by the shackles around his body that chained him to the cell's wall and floor. Even the ceiling. The guards took no chances to his confinement. He sighed painfully. The metal clasp around his chest restricted a lot of movement, and consequentially his breathing.

The air managed to squeeze past until he found a more comfortable position to rest—if comfort was a word that could be used at all here.

He couldn't stand it. Something was happening. Something big. The explosions. The roaring of dragons. His worst fear was happening. They were found by *that* nightmare of a dragon. Kast sighed again. He tested the strength of the metal around himself, his wrists shot apart, but the metal still held. The noise wasn't the worst part of the situation. It was a strange... feeling. So familiar, but so incomprehensible. Two forces that seemed indomitable repeatedly surged towards each other. He had never felt anything like it before, and it made the hair on his neck stand on end.

The guards had quickly departed from their post, called towards some unseen task. That was when Kast realized quickly how stuck he was. *These chains!* He wrenched his wrists against the holds again. And again. He stopped, it was hurting himself, yet doing no good. He sighed deeply.

He couldn't blame her. Not in the slightest. He had already resolved since he first came to this cage that he wouldn't blame her. It was good that she was going home. It was even better that she realized he was just leeching off her for his own gain. He couldn't blame her, but he really wished things had happened differently.

He was angry a lot of times. Or rather his anger was a cover for his fear. That girl seemed to trample straight into his fear over and over again. He had been exposed way too much to some helpless human girl. He was a proud and mighty dragon! He looked at himself for the millionth time. He was still having trouble adapting. It was like losing a limb or becoming paralyzed, and there wasn't anything he could do about it. He sighed and then gasped in pain. He had inhaled too hard and his chest crushed against the metal. He didn't even know the girl's name. They had never gotten around to that part. In fact, they hadn't gotten around to much talking at all. He couldn't blame her after what he did. *Right?* Was it wrong? His actions? He lay against the restraints, nothing but silence for his mind to wander through and confront the pain dwelling just beneath the surface of his being.

An explosion vibrated through the stone, reaching Kast's ears. He jerked violently against his restraints, control of his body ceased, driven to find relief from the forces outside of the walls. What was happening? His mind splintered under the weight of the pressures he felt. Pain seared white as his body thrashed against his restraints. *What?* It stopped. He heaved desperately, despite the restriction around his chest. He didn't care. Whatever had happened had stolen his breath, the experience was fire, and his thoughts struggled to reclaim clarity.

Then he saw it as if he were there. He was outside, floating above what looked like the city, just beyond a great battle.

A battle between the two greatest enemies he had ever known.

He let out a scream, but no sound came out. His mind failed to adjust to the new reality within which he existed.

He looked up at the two creatures fighting. Black scales of the deepest color a dragon could possess. *Insanity.* Kast had heard whispers and rumors, but how long ago was that? The beast was as ferocious as depicted, if not more so. Scars coated the dragon's hide, telling the story of thousands of battles. *Thousands of victories.* Vasiss stood taller than Kast. Even as large as Kast was, he was still only two thirds the size of the King of Insane.

If Kast knew where his heart existed right now, he was sure it would have stopped while watching Vasiss pour his being into demolishing the opponent before him.

His opponent—a man!

Not just any man though. It was The Cloak. The man who had thwarted Kast completely and ruined any pursuit of his purpose. The human who had cast the spell that had transformed Kast into a man. Kast remembered the fear that coursed through his body when he saw what he was flying into. Pure terror.

The one odd thing now was that The Cloak didn't have his cloak. The Cloak must have discarded it. What would Kast call him now? *Whatever.*

The man that stood, or floated, or whatever, was thin, but well-defined muscle laced through his limbs. Mottled grey hair fell to his shoulders. Kast shuddered. The Cloak's face was old, and the signs of age dwelled strongly. There was no hair except thin and wispy grey eyebrows that sat above the man's eyes. Two pure black eyes filled with the deepest evil. His mouth curved upwards in ecstasy. *The battle thrilled him!* Kast could tell from the twisted demeanor that The Cloak displayed, this man had no greater purpose than be in the thick of slaughtering dragons. Or rather, fighting them. Or fighting something. Kast wondered if there were an opponent that could challenge The Cloak. *Maybe The Cloak was right where he wanted to be, then?*

Kast realized something. Ever since his transformation, his eyes were the meager eyes of a human, but here in this . . . realm, his eyes were the eyes of a *dragon*. He could see every detail clearly.

Kast watched the fight rage. The Cloak and Vasiss seemed to be equal. Then The Cloak clapped his hands and some kind of purple shroud misted around his frame, solidifying into something that looked like a make-shift cloak. *A magic cloak.* Such tenacity!

The Cloak gained a burst of speed and moved faster than the King of Insane now. He found holes in the beast's defense and exploited them. In a split second The Cloak landed multiple attacks, throwing Vasiss back through the air gracelessly. The Cloak summoned magic in his palms, throwing blast after blast at the Insane King. Only the first few connected before the dragon adapted to the new fighting situation.

Vasiss's head went reeling backward. *The Cloak has him!* Pounding with a ferocity unseen before, The Cloak pummeled the King of Insane. The black beast fell behind in power. Kast couldn't help but hope that Vasiss fell in battle. Kast knew more about Vasiss than he knew about The Cloak and was, therefore, more apprehensive of him. But now, The Cloak looked to be the strongest champion.

The Cloak began to drift downwards. Somehow Kast managed to maintain distance, drifting downwards with him. Vasiss swam through the air, darting in, testing the merit of The Cloak, and flying back out. A neutral ground had been made between the two, but it wouldn't last. Only until The Cloak completely fell to the earth below would the battle rage.

Then the tides of battle changed.

A dragon who lay waiting under the rubble of burnt and broken buildings rocketed upwards, straight at The Cloak.

The man paid the beast as little mind as he could, dispatching the dragon quickly.

But Vasiss was quicker.

Almost faster than Kast could follow, Vasiss lurched towards The Cloak, rolling forward using his tail as a whip. Kast knew what happened, but he couldn't see it.

The Cloak took the full force of the tail. The force threw the man far out across the forest. Kast shuddered again. The Cloak was gone. Even if the man were alive, as unlikely as that would be, it would take hours, if not an entire day, for him to return to the city.

Laughter chortled out near him. Insane laughter.

Kast turned and found Vasiss staring directly into his unseen eyes.

"I'm coming for you, too, nest rat!" More laughter as the insane dragon's chest welled up.

Kast knew what was coming next. He tried to cower as a torrent of flames coated him. It was terrible. He screamed beneath the fire before the pain took him and he blacked out.

Kast woke up immediately, an ache splitting his skull. He was back in the cell. His chest heaved. What had just happened? Was it real? How did Vasiss know where he was? Kast breathed, slowly regaining control. It didn't hurt to breathe anymore for some reason. His head dropped to his shackle around his chest.

The metal was *torn* slightly, ripping away from his chest. He stared wide-eyed at the metal. Something was wrong. He looked around the cell, everything seemed normal. Except for a new pile of dirt and dust on the floor. Kast pulled his hand against the shackle. It wasn't free but it felt looser than before. What had happened?

He was distracted in his thoughts, processing the strange vision when he heard a scream. A girl's scream and frantic running. More than one person was coming.

The first footsteps sounded lighter and less clunky. He could also hear beyond the first set of footsteps metal rhythmically clashing against itself. *Armor.* Of a kind. It was sort of muted. Who was coming?

A blur sprinted across his vision. *It was the girl.* Her head turned to see him strapped to the wall. Kast watched her grab the bars of his cell, snapping to an immediate stop.

"Help! This man is going to get us killed!" Her voice was somewhere between trying to be convincing and desperate. She looked different—clean, and with new clothes. Her hair was different. *Whatever.* If she was so prepared to take care of herself, why should he help her? She was better off without him after all. Look where he had ended up, by her conniving hand, nonetheless. *No, I deserve this.* He sighed; the pain now gone from the trivial motion. At least the world afforded him some relief, in its own weird way.

"Go away, girl." His voice was distant and uninvolved. *Disgusting.* He was reduced to this? He preferred the death that he was somehow certain was lurking outside. A roar and the sounds of battle resounded through the walls as if to confirm his thought.

"No!" She threw herself against the bars. A noise from where she came stole her attention. She became more frantic. "Please! I need your help. I'm sorry for betraying you."

"Shut your mouth, filth." Strange, why was he angry? It didn't matter, did it? Of course not, the canyons she cleft through his being meant nothing. Nothing. She meant nothing. *I deserved it.*

A disturbance erupted outside of his vision. Outside his cell. Kast watched the girl's eyes widen. She backed up, one hand on the bars, the other distraught and flailing in the air. A soldier came into vision, the man had a terrible limp and moved slower than seemed normal. Kast took one look at the girl and a smirk broke his lips.

"You made him mad." Whether he meant to taunt her, Kast had no idea. He didn't know why he did anything anymore. He was so sick and tired of the pointless antics and antagonizing that he found pleasurable. He hated himself. He hated squandering every ounce of energy on this dung-filled life. Why couldn't he go back to having his thoughts swirl uncertainly? The clarity brimming in his mind only amplified the pain he witnessed.

Why?

What kind of question was that? What did he care if he ever figured out this trash existence?

The girl screamed out again, bringing Kast back to the charade before him. The damsel was in distress again. The worthless, cry a lot girl. She was pathetic, with no strength to actually make change happen. Kast spit on the floor. *Disgusting creatures.* He scolded himself again.

The man limped towards the girl. She didn't even realize he was exaggerating his pain. In a flash, the man had lunged forward and gripped the girl's arm. She wasn't getting away.

"Now yer mine!" The man's voice slurred. Kast could see the wild, crazed look in his eyes. In another setting, this man may have been one of the most level-headed of soldiers. Now he clenched his hand, digging his grip into the girl's arm. This man was crazed.

"Help! Help!" Her voice broke octaves Kast hadn't heard from her before. Her hand clung tightly to the bars of his cell.

What did Kast care?

The man moved his other hand and grabbed the girl's hair, controlling her head. Now his dominance was complete. Kast hung in his chains, still and watching, expressionless. *Did they have to do this right in front of him? Couldn't they let him die in peace?* The girl swung her free elbow and nearly caught the man in the gut. His hold on her gave him the better position, however.

"You little tramp!" He screamed, inches away from her face. Using his hold, he slammed her face into the cell bars. A quiet grunt escaped her lips, her eyes were dazed from the impact. A trickle of blood ran down her brow, down the corner of her eye mixing with her silent tears and down her cheek.

Right in front of Kast.

His fingers twitched. *Why?* What did he care?

I don't.

The man pulled her back and socked her in her gut. Air wheezed the rest of its way out of her lungs.

I don't.

The man raised his metal-clad fist.

Why?

He ripped the girl's hair back. She flinched as the man lined her head to take the most perfect of punches. There was no way she would be able to respond now. Her body was operating off reflexes, and she was helpless. Broken. *Weak.*

So what? Why should I care?

Kast watched the man's fist move forward.

It connected, ripping a scream from the girl's lips. The metal on the glove connected with her pretty face. A face contorted horribly in excruciating agony.

Why?

The fist wound up again. Strike. Scream.

Strike.

Scream.

I don't care.

Strike.

No more screaming.

Why?

Wind up.

Time had slowed. He watched the man's fist move slowly through the air. It was a great punch. Something told him the punch was even better than the others. The girl would either die or be permanently scarred. Her face was already mutilated by the man's attacks. Maybe she was already dead? Kast's hands gripped the loosened chains holding him. The punch almost connected, but why did he care? Why!

Why?

Bright light from out of nowhere fell across his face. His heart illuminated.

I am a dragon.

Kast blinked.

And then he was holding a completely shocked soldier in his hands, his fingers clenching the throat of his prey. He might not be able to spew flames in this form, but his eyes worked well to drench his opponents in his hot fury.

Let's see how you like it.

Kast decided on his plan of attack. Winding up the arm that held the man's throat, Kast slammed him into an opposing cell's bars, shoving the pathetic heap through and into the cage. Kast stared. The metal had given slightly, but he still had no idea how the man-made it through. If he was still alive, it wouldn't be for long.

Kast turned to find the girl. She had been thrown in a miserable pile onto the ground. Her blood pooled on the floor. Kast looked at his cell. Whatever happened had shattered not only the metal bars but also some of the stone surrounding it. The chains on the wall lay in pieces on the floor. The anchors were ripped completely free from the stone. It was a mess. Kast looked at his arms. Only one wrist still held a shackle from before, and a single chain link dangled freely. *Whatever.*

He moved towards the girl and lifted her up. She was soft. Her head rolled lifelessly, losing blood by the buckets.

This.

This was all his fault.

Kast with open eyes saw the girl through a new sight.

There was no turning back now.

He looked her over again. Was she dead? He didn't know how bad she was. He looked, and grief flooded over his face.

Recover.

His only thought, his desire. He was a dragon. Somewhere inside, truth was a fire. And it had begun to be kindled. The tiny flame, a dragon's flame, would grow. He knew it! Somehow. So much more than the torrents he could breathe. It was life in his chest. A tear dropped from his eye. The tiny flame gave so much light in his darkness.

Why? Another tear fell.

Recover!

Kast felt another tear fall. If his eyes weren't being clenched shut trying to hold those tears back, he would have seen his hands begin to glow, softly at first, then stronger and stronger. He was holding her, supporting her shoulders.

He wasn't strong enough to hold the tears back. They began to fall.

Kast. . . .

That voice. That voice that always showed up at the wrong time.

Kast. You would turn your back on me? You would betray me?

Kast's face clenched further at the hate for whatever inside of himself tried to interfere.

Yes, voice, whatever you are. I would trade everything to make this right. How can you not see? How could you have been so blind? How could I have been so blind?

Kast opened his eyes to look at the girl. This was all his own fault. *Why?* His jaw slackened as he noticed his hand gleaming. It was beautiful. A testament of the kindling inside.

What if the world saw his light? Kast wondered as he stared at the gleam.

Let them.

Let them all know the might of a dragon untainted of the touch of insanity.

Was he? Was he free? Was that enough to atone for his wrongs? *Why do I care suddenly about this?* He couldn't help but doubt the change in his thoughts. Could he truly be free from his selfish insanity?

He was interrupted when the girl stirred, and her now-restored face began to twitch. He laid her down. She wouldn't take his presence well. He backed away a few feet and sat on his knees watching her. Blood coated her face. Somehow, he knew it didn't matter, that she had been healed by his . . . *power?* He gave her space, regardless. How could he have been so cruel? How could he have completely missed everything?

She sat up and rubbed her head. He didn't know if she would have a headache or not. She looked around, confused and taking in her situation.

She doesn't know a thing. Kast tried to console himself that she hadn't seen his actions. He didn't like the idea of being exposed. A great and mighty—no. Not a dragon. A man. Just a man.

"What happened?" she muttered the words, struggling to form the sentences. It might take her a minute to recover her thoughts.

"Enough to put us here." Kast still wasn't sure, but somehow it wasn't unusual.

She must not have realized who she was asking. When she recognized Kast nearby, she flinched, shoving herself to her feet. She wobbled, regaining her balance. Kast stood and stared.

"We need to leave." His voice wavered slightly, and anxiety pelted against his resolve. The force of terror still lurked outside. The force he could feel so much clearer than before.

"What . . . what do you want?" She still stuttered her words out.

"Well, pending disaster, to take you home. Same as before." Or mostly. He didn't know about the *after they made it home part*, but he wasn't going to take any indulgences. He would disappear and hopefully find some way to make amends with this life if they didn't demand it from him.

A look of distrust streamed across her face.

"Whatever." Spite and contempt congealed in one simple word from the girl's lips. He couldn't blame her.

"We need to go." He turned, hesitating for a second. She wouldn't have taken his hand if he offered it. He waited for a second for her to rise and then moved quickly back the way the girl had come.

The end of the prison room exited out into a little corridor with stairs at the end. Only lamps lit their way. Kast moved forward. He couldn't figure out the balance of moving too fast and not fast enough. He grimaced at the strange change in his behavior. She's always kept up before. He set the pace they needed, hoping it wouldn't be too much for the girl. He passed a landing in the middle of the stairs as they continued by cutting back and going upwards. They weren't too far below the ground level of the keep. They could make it out of the place fairly quickly. He stopped at the top of the stairs, trying to gather which direction they should go.

"This way." The girl passed by him, heading hopefully towards the outside. Her voice was curt, not expressing anything unnecessary.

Kast followed closely. She moved well. She must be feeling somewhat better. A few turns through some ornate rooms, and they stood before a door to the outside.

"This is a side door away from where I saw most of the fighting earlier." The girl cut the conversation off, as she really wasn't interested in talking beyond the necessary.

Kast had so many questions, but he knew now if ever, wouldn't be the time. He pushed the wooden portal open and peered outside. *Clear.* He moved, the girl following closely behind him. He took a second to look, the fighting seemed to be on the other side of the keep. The girl was right. They could make it to one of the city walls. Maybe they would be lucky to find something to help on their journey. He ran, the girl hard on his heels. They didn't have time to go slow with the foes that they faced. He somehow felt the presence of the dragons. *Twenty-four.* His mind kept telling him every time he thought about the dragons as if answering his question. Sometimes the number dropped. It never increased.

The streets whizzed by at their pace. The looming buildings lining each street hung overhead, shadowing the streets. Kast and the girl made it halfway to the city's wall when the buildings around them erupted in splinters and debris.

Kast halted immediately, jumping back to shield the girl from some of the flying rocks and chunks of wood. Thud after thud resounded through the city around them. Kast's mind was screaming. Screaming numbers. *Eight, nine, ten, eleven.* He stopped counting at fourteen. They were surrounded. It wasn't a good situation.

But his flame.

"Girl, I'm going to make an opening." He prepared himself for what had to be done. His desire for the girl was so steadfast that he found he had no need to question the direness of the situation. "Use the opportunity to . . . ."

Before he could finish, an eager dragon plunged at the two. Kast saw his movements. It wasn't an attack meant to kill. These dragons were attacking without intending to kill for some reason.

Wrong decision.

Power surged through Kast's veins. He found his body flying with the mere twitch of thought. His fist flew forward fast, faster than he had ever moved—as a dragon or man.

His fist connected with the beast's massive chest. Kast watched with seeing eyes. If it weren't for the overwhelming clarity, he would be confounded on the actions occurring. The dragon's chest caved under the pressure of his fist, and the monster hurtled backward through the air, tearing through buildings and everything else in the way. His feet found the street again, the force of his punch throwing him back.

"Go!" Kast roared, shredding his throat with the screech billowing out of his chest.

Another dragon lurched straight at the two, only to be met by Kast's unrivaled fury. From the corner of his eye, he watched the girl sprint down the nearest alleyway. He dispatched the dragon with only a few punches and leaped off the dragon towards the girl to help cover her escape. A dragon landed right in the way, on top of one of the buildings. Kast stared intently. *Not good.* The dragon welled up, inhaling as much air as it could. Kast covered himself with his arms as best as possible, preparing for the inevitable.

The dragon released its flames, drowning Kast in a sea of fire. The monster held the breath for a few seconds before exhaling. The look of surprise that coated the beast's face was nearly as strong as Kast's. Winding back, Kast jumped and threw another punch, catching the monster across the face, crushing its huge skull. It fell to the ground dead.

Somehow, he had made it through the flames unscathed. He looked at himself, shocked the essence of fire didn't even linger. Staring forward, he began to realize the scope of his ability. He would make sure the girl got home. This wasn't the end of the story. He would make amends.

Everything would work out.

Kast jumped viciously at the next dragon in his way to the girl. Catching the beast's gaping mouth, he ripped down on the jaw and tore the mandible free from the rest of its skull. The dragon flailed in pain, a bitter scream tearing from its exposed throat.

Kast dropped, catching the failing roof of a building. It had just enough support left for him to jump forward. He was almost to the girl. No dragon would touch her, and she would be fine. He had the power to save her.

Kast flew through the air, landing in a vacant area in one of many squares in this city. He looked behind him. The girl was just entering the same square from a side street. A look of shock began to form at his appearing ahead of her. She just shook her head, running all the harder. They could make it. The dragons had pulled back and kept their distance from such a dangerous enemy.

The girl turned away from the center of the square towards the side that led a short distance to the castle wall. Kast ran, catching up and falling alongside her. She made no comment.

They were only a short distance away from the street opening leading to the gate out when Kast grabbed the girl and threw them both to the side. The girl was completely stunned, flying through the air. A look of disgust struggled across her face before they landed. Their quick landing on the ground was echoed by a much larger and louder explosion. Kast had felt it coming. The heavy presence, the burden. A scream tore through the air, and the girl cowered under the weight of the noise. Kast stood, amazed such a force had so little an effect on him. The biggest force around.

The King of Insane.

"Well, you finally came out to play, didn't you? That was quite nice of you, I should say. Though it was a little mean what you did to my dragons, not to mention my brother and my name. In fact, I don't think I want to play, after all! It's time for you to die, you little rats!" The words were instantly followed by a mighty roar and a douse of flames.

Vasiss, the King of Insane—*the Insane King*.

Kast tried to remember all that he had known about the terror, but nothing more than the black beast's incredible insanity came to mind. It was as if his mind had said it was unnecessary to know much more than what it did.

Vasiss would be a fierce opponent indeed.

But his flame.

Kast walked between the dragon and the girl. Yes, he would protect her. *He would win.*

"Girl." Kast tried to get the girl's attention without removing his own from his opponent.

"Ah! The puny maggot dragon has been turned a man!" The black dragon wheezed his laughter. "And he even has play powers now!" Vasiss chortled more at that last sentiment.

What did he mean by powers? *What did Vasiss know about any of this?* Kast had no words for something so wretched. He had only a fist to crush the Insane King.

Where did that come from?

He stood his ground, relishing in his newfound confidence. His fire would never be quenched.

"Girl, run." He hoped she had heard.

"Play!" Vasiss screamed his insanity for the world to hear. "Play! Pla . . . ."

Kast threw his knuckles forward and, in a blink, he flew forward into the Insane King's snout, sending his head caroming. This wasn't that hard.

"No, you don't, you blighter!" Vasiss roared, responding with his own claw flying forward.

Kast caught the dragon's strike and threw himself forward using Vasiss's claw. His foot caught the black beast unawares. *Two for tw . . . .*

Kast's thoughts were interrupted by the dragon spinning, using his tail as a whip. Somehow Kast withstood the attack, but he flew across the square. His feet caught the ground as he tried to maintain his balance on landing, and the cloak that he still wore flared in the wind trailing past him.

Vasiss launched himself through the air, his insane mirth gone, replaced with pure anger. Kast ran, his sprint fueled by his unknown power. At the last second, he dropped to his back, carried forward underneath the beast by his momentum. He barely missed Vasiss's claws.

Kast immediately rolled over as he slid underneath the dragon and shoved off the ground, battering his back into the beast's belly. The monster's flight was thrown off along with whatever pain such a move had caused. The monster roared. The King of Insane was well past angry by this point. Kast knew he wasn't supposed to have even got one hit off on the monster, let alone *three*.

Kast landed he was on the side of the square where he had started. The girl was gone. *Good.*

"Good for you, you second-rate nest rat!" Vasiss screamed at Kast. "But that was the last time you'll ever defy me!"

A dull tingling nested in Kast's ears. Apparently, the black beast was louder than he had thought. *Or Kast was leaking strength.* Whatever this was. He had to end it here and now.

Kast dropped onto his hands. One foot stretched out behind him and rested on its toes. The other coiled underneath his stomach, tensed with energy and ready to launch with great force. His amber eyes stared forward, straight into the onyx pits of the Insane King. Kast thought deeply, his mind fell to the flame, the gentle spark that had begun to grow—so brightly. He relished in its heat, its power, and light. He glanced at his arms. A shroud of white had encompassed him.

Power.

Vasiss threw himself forward, tearing up the world with his steps of rage. A colossal battle roar tore from his maw.

Kast answered with a cry of his own, uncoiling his pent-up power and throwing himself towards his enemy. The world was torn to shreds in his wake.

The two closed the distance between them fast, their roars never ceasing.

One second.

Raging.

Two seconds.

Collision.

Kast launched from the ground, pouring every ounce of his power into his charge. His eyes watched every detail so clearly. He flew straight and true for the beast's heart. He was so close.

Then the monster threw its clawed fist forward, connecting with Kast.

Kast flew backward at an impossible speed.

An impossibly loud crash blew up around him.

What was happening?

Then another crash happened, and another.

Kast lost count after twenty. Every crash seemed to hurt more. His eyes turned inward. *The flame!* The kindling of a great fire flickered. Every hit on Kast was like a gust, beating down on the struggling passion. Soon his body screamed for relief. The world had already turned black. Even if his eyes hadn't quit in the first place, the speed which it all happened would have overwhelmed his eyes.

Kast began to slip and fade away, the pain slowly rising to a loud cacophony. The light faded so fast, and the fire was enfeebled.

Then the largest explosion filled Kast's ears. The most painful yet happened.

In a sudden gale, Kast's flame was smothered to oblivion.

He plunged into the eternal void.

CHAPTER THIRTY-ONE

The throne froze under her reign. Probably chilled by her icy heart.

Elizabeth leaned back against the glorified chair. Her fingers laced together as she held her hands to her mouth. It had been nearly three weeks since that hog's rot had stolen what was most valuable to her. *Misbegotten street scum.* She cursed that filth nonstop since the incident. Her fingers clenched, crushing themselves. She would gut the cretin herself. First the eyes, a knife in her hand to put tiny slices across both. She reveled in the imaginary screams ripping through her head. A shiver of the deepest pleasure crawled up her spine. She watched herself impale each eye multiple times, over and over again. Oh, the glory! The ecstasy. She found her back arching, the thoughts of revenge gripping her. Her hands had moved to grip the armrests. She hated that refuse.

"My Queen!" The doors to the throne room blew open. A man strode in hurriedly.

"What?" Elizabeth shrieked, startled from her thoughts. Her eyes narrowed at the man, her eyes in a tight glare. It was Maximillian, the commander of her forces. *The idiot.*

"Your Maje . . ."

"Just get it out already, you incompetent man! Before I have your position handed to some other second-rate waste of breath!" Why couldn't these inferior footmen actually be of use?

Why couldn't more of them be like that cloaked mercenary? Her heart shuddered at the thought of that man. The power brimming from his being. The capability billowing around him. Her heart twisted, swooning over the power that man held. The power to uphold justice. The power to crush insolent knaves. A shuddered ripped from her core. She would have justice, the wrong—all of them! — would *suffer.*

"We have received a message from Harrington yesterday. They have made claims that your handmaiden was recently recovered from the oppression of the drag—"

Elizabeth jumped to her feet from the icy throne.

There was a chance Aurah was still alive?

She had agreed to hire those mercenaries, but she had thrown away all hope that her sister could have ever survived the dragon's clutches. She had just wanted *justice.*

That beast deserved to die, and she would make sure it writhed in agonizing *justice.*

"If the blasted message arrived yesterday, why am I only now hearing about this?" Her voice had become shrill. *Didn't these morons understand the severity of the situation?* Her rage swirled again, stirred by her servant's stupidity.

"My Queen, we were merely testing the validity . . . ."

"Did I give you permission to speak, you inferior . . . ." Elizabeth's eyes roved around for half a second as if no word could possibly fully describe this man's incompetence. ". . . you inferior knave?" She was screaming again. "Why did you all commit this treason and hide this from your Queen?" Maybe, impossibly, this man still could be redeemed, as stupid as he was.

"My Queen, Harrington has fallen under the attack of a mighty thrall of dragons, the likes of which has not been seen, even on the day of the Capital's attack."

Elizabeth stared. Silent. Completely silent.

Aurah.

"Leave." A cold and monotonous tone left her lips.

The soldier turned crisply and exited the throne room. She was alone again. She fell back against her seat. She had ordered every servant and guard to leave her alone. They probably found relief away from her. She could only imagine how they whispered about her current condition, but she was Queen. She would not be opposed. She would rule with the iron fist her kingdom needed. Rage welled up in her soul.

"Mother! Father!" Her voice threw the scream to the abyss. "If only you hadn't incompetently allowed the world to rape your kingdom!" She screamed her anger. Her frustration. "You've allowed the trash to molest the righteous! You offered your necks to the sick and twisted!" Tears fell from her eyes, and sobs ripped through the Queen's body, emanating from her soul. "If only you weren't stupid and had the nerve to stand up to the world's waste, Aurah would never have had to suffer! None of this would ever have happened! Why did you let this happen?" Elizabeth screamed her voice hoarse. It was her parents' fault, the last King and Queen, for dying so stupidly, for showing mercy when they should not have. That very act forfeited the lives of so many who were near to the monarchy, so many who had put their utmost trust in Elizabeth's family's hands.

Including Aurah's parents.

Elizabeth was just like her weak, *caring,* parents. How could she face her own failure in protecting the innocent?

In protecting Aurah?

Why had that stupid handmaiden disobeyed and taken Elizabeth's place, jumping into the dragon's clutches?

Elizabeth collapsed to the ground, weeping.

A dam of feelings broke and surged past her reserves. She hated the filthy mongrels lurking in the streets and in the hidden corners of her glorious hovel of a kingdom. She hated the illegitimate cads pilfering the innocent. She hated the virgin purity of every man, woman, and child, the virgin purity of life being assaulted by the hate of others. She *hated* them all.

Elizabeth hated life.

Her teeth clenched together. Her face formed a scowl again. Clenching her fist tightly, Elizabeth dashed her knuckles into the cursed throne.

The icy void that stole the life from so many.

Elizabeth hated it all.

Strike after strike abused the stone seat.

Screams rang out.

Blood fell in a red rain. Elizabeth heaved shallow gasps from the rush of pain. Tears of liberation poured down her face from the experience. Her unharmed hand clutched the arm of the chair as she held her bloodied hand out. The pain warred against her inexpressible ire. The battle in her soul rocked her being, creating insurmountable climaxes between the tensions. *Relief!*

She could handle this. This was something she was able to do. Her thoughts cleared. The clouds of haze dissipated under the storms of pain.

She would have her vengeance.

She would murder whoever defied her justice.

She sat down on her blood and leaned back in her chair, lulled to sleep by the rhythmic heaving in her chest and the regular throbs in her hand.

She could handle this.

CHAPTER THIRTY-TWO

Charlie and the rest of Lizard Guts huddled around a fire, slightly away from the city, in the forest.

No one said anything.

No one needed to say anything.

There was no way to put anything into words, anyway.

It was silent save the occasional crackle of the fire.

And the horrid scream from that monster.

He had made his way back to the city far more quickly than any thought possible. *What was he?* Charlie didn't even have the capacity to process that. His mind filtered through the men he had lost in the battle. Not once in the history of Lizard Guts had they ever walked away from a battle without knowing they had been victorious.

Now...

They sat wondering if they were capable of challenging the black dragon, called Vasiss, and his army of dragons.

Most sat wondering how they ever fully missed the existence of the monster.

Charlie sat wondering how anything could be terrible enough to best their boss in battle.

A scream tore through the forest nearby again.

Something was terribly wrong.

Something was happening to him.

And Charlie had no idea if it meant that he would suddenly turn on them all and murder them or not.

Lizard Guts sat around the fire, silently. Every man was most certainly thinking the same thing— the value of their life and how little the sum of their existences amounted to in light of the forces they faced.

Charlie hunkered lower, trying to savor the warmth of the fire, wishing for a drink strong enough to make him forget everything he ever knew.

CHAPTER THIRTY-THREE

Darkness.
Solitary.
Dark... Cold.
A void. Nothing.
So alone. Empty drifting.
A pressure pulling him to the end.
His meager life, a fleeting moment, ebbed silently away.
And then light. Could he see? There were no eyes here.
There was nothing. Nothing but . . . .
But the warmth flowing in.
A flame, *something*.
Warm, life.
Together.
Freedom.

Kast blinked, and a haze welled over his eyes. Flashes of... *green* overwhelmed his vision. Words. *Then darkness.*

A scream ripped the air. Who was screaming? Kast's eyes fluttered open. *Green again.* Then there was no more green. It was black now. His lungs hurt. His throat was shredded. *Darkness.*

Pain again. A sudden sharp bite on his . . . *back? Darkness.*

How long did these visions last? How long must they continue?

Something new. A . . . smell. Yes, that was the word. *Warmth.* He *moved.* Drums beat somewhere. *Everywhere.* His neck. His skull. *His chest.* Fast and faster the throbbing hammered. A discomforting feeling seized control. *Panic.* He moved . . . *up?* His eyes flashed opened.

The light screamed, tearing into his eyes. He screamed back. Sheer terror. The beat thundered in his ears.

Warmth found his shoulder.

A girl.

Girl . . . .

Her . . . .

Then darkness.

How long did the void have a hold on his soul? How long did he remain a slave to the darkness? How long did he remain empty and ignorant? How long did his life teeter between the *sense* of warmth and the clutches of despair—*of death?*

Then something happened.

A spark.

Only one.

A single spark; the color of gold and purple mixed together.

One was enough.

A spark of hope.

Something clutched to that spark. Something *starved.* The spark was swallowed whole.

Then a miracle.

Another spark fell.

And more!

Hope did not disappoint.

Hope... in what?

The sparks rained down. Purple mixed within the gold.

Down on the frozen ashes of kindling smothered.

Fire.

Fire!

Sparks poured upon the ashes of his life and flames erupted. Light blossomed all around! The void illuminated, and life welled up!

How long since this place had been this bright? How long? The bristling light shined on the empty holes of his being. And then he saw what the light revealed.

What glory.

What... significance.

Potential.

Pure and unbridled potential.

The flame was in mere kindling, reignited by the sparks of gold and purple.

But if left to burn, hope would find the potential inside of him. It would find the world of potential supporting that flame. Supporting the kindling.

If left to burn, it would find the fuel that would ignite brighter than any star in any sky.

Kast stared at himself.

If only the flame would continue to burn. *Then it would reach his heart.*

Then it would never be quenched.

It would never falter.

It would never fail.

It would never extinguish.

But the darkness seized, constricting the light and the void fell about the struggling flame again.

Such a force could never awaken.

Such a fire would never alight.

It was impossible.

His darkness was too deep.

His sins so wrong.

Such fire didn't belong to the monster that he was. It just couldn't.

Kast's eyes fluttered open. Light streamed into an unknown room. Stone encompassed a window. Light streamed in, illuminating the dust in the air. His head lay on an unknown pillow on an unknown bed. His knowledge of human things had grown over time, but it was still mostly minuscule. As he looked around, he could recognize things of human value.

Shelves lined the walls. Books rested on their support. Jars of various substances, some dry, some wet, were standing alongside the books. It was a small . . . *cottage was the word.* Or Hut. He wasn't sure. He tried to move his arms, but he realized his body had sturdy pieces of wood, in pairs, wrapped tightly around his limbs. He vaguely remembered something about these things and their purpose. Something to do with human medicine.

His mind struggled to know his position. He wondered if that was why he resorted to identifying what he did know, which was so little. He didn't realize it, but he had been holding his breath. Maybe he was anticipating something disastrous. He worked, forcing himself to breathe correctly. His chest screamed in pain. *Oh.* That was why he had been holding his breath. His chest was wrapped with a white cloth. *Tightly.*

In fact, the more he began to think about his body, the more his mind became overwhelmed with the sense of pain. It began to become uncomfortable. His body ached. Was there even an inch that didn't think it was necessary to inform him—*that something was wrong?* His labored breathing continued, regardless. He would need air. He hated the feeling of his lungs constricting.

What had happened?

Yes, that was the question of all questions brimming in his mind. How did he end up... *here?* Where was here? Who had the skill or resources to tend to him this way? What were those visions he had earlier? His memory was patchy. Did he even see those things? He didn't like this. He began to struggle to make himself move.

Pain.

He tried to speak but he had completely missed the fabric wrapped tightly around his jaw.

Panic.

He didn't care about the pain. He had to move. *Move!* he screamed at himself.

Then a bell chimed. Kast stopped his thrashing, looking for the source of the noise. *A bell.* A string—*twine.* His thoughts identified it quickly as if compensating for his immobility. A string attached to his leg ran to a bell hand above from the… *rafters.—Stop it!* He was sick of his mind filling in the blanks like that. He wanted to be free of this new prison and the pain.

"Quickly, girl!" An unfamiliar voice cried out.

An older man hobbled into the room. He was balding, and what hair he did have was greying and long, sticking outwards in untidy tufts. He wore leather trousers and a leather vest over a stained tunic. It was sturdy clothing, though of humbler means than Kast had seen so far. Perhaps the most unique feature of the man was his crutch and that he only had one leg to move on. Kast had no idea what to make of him.

But his heart seized in his throat when he saw the girl who followed behind. His self-proclaimed ward, created by his own destructive desires. He hated himself. The growing flame inside was condemning, standing as a testament against all that he should have been. *What was that even?*

"We need some more of the numbing powder." The old man pointed to a jar with a green-tinted substance inside.

Kast watched the girl grab the jar and move towards the old man, who was preparing Kast's bandages for something.

Kast grunted loudly. Trying desperately to get their attention before they applied whatever that powder was. If the man said the powder numbed, it would probably make cognitive thought difficult, if not impossible. He doubled his grunts, trying to distinguish them from grunts of pain.

The old man may have ignored Kast's first grunting, but Kast's second bought caught his attention. Somehow the man had missed Kast's eyes—or maybe decided it was natural for someone in this predicament to have their eyes open.

"My stars, girl!" A look of incredulity rested on the man's face. "You were right! He did heal amazingly quickly!" The old man shifted his position and leaned over Kast's head. Kast grunted, confused. He had so many questions.

"Shh, shh!" The man hushed Kast. "It's a miracle you are alive right now, young man. The injuries that you sustained are beyond anything I have ever tended. If it weren't for this young miss convincing me you would heal, I would have never taken you." The old man turned to point at the girl as if there were some other young girl present.

Her face stared blankly at Kast. She set the powder jar down and turned, leaving the room.

"Oh, dear. I suppose the frustration I felt from her was towards you after all. No matter. At the rate you're healing, you'll just need one last good sleep."

"Mmm. Mmmm—" Kast grunted, trying to fight the bandages, but his mouth refused to work. His body failed, and his mind screamed out for answers.

"Shh, shh!" The old man hushed Kast again. "You're in safe hands. I am just a mere hermit of the woods. I was in the midst of escaping from that disaster at the city . . . ."

Kast shuddered tremendously at the mention of that nightmare. He had so many questions. His mouth began to try and form words again, interrupting the old man.

"Stop it now! If you move too much it will take even more time to heal. My name is Dale. I found the girl escaping the city. You . . . well, you showed up and we hauled you here to my home in my cart. You need one last good rest, young man. Please, trust me." Dale pleaded with Kast.

Kast didn't know why, but the words got to him. He released any tension in his body and relinquished the desire to talk at the moment. He found the pain subsided slightly. *Good.*

"Here is a powder made from some herbs and other elements. I usually can only rub the powder on the body where the blood flows most. If you think you could force yourself to swallow something, the powder's effectiveness will be greatly increased, you'll be able to recover much quicker. I should say there is a good chance you will feel like you're drowning."

Decisions. Already he was being asked to make decisions. He looked at the strange man and nodded. Whatever it took to get better faster. Even if from the hand of a stranger.

The man moved away to a side table. The noise of fumbling arose from something Kast couldn't see. He turned back holding a... *cup.*

"Here we go. A little at a time. Are you ready?"

The question made Kast realize just how unsure he was. He nodded hesitantly. The man smiled at him.

"That's a good lad. Here we go."

Dale removed the bandages around Kast's mouth, to his great pain, and put the cup to his lips and poured the lukewarm liquid. Just a little was hard to swallow—Kast couldn't control the muscles in his throat just yet. Dale was right, this did feel terrible; was this what drowning as a human felt like?

"There we go." Dale's words encouraged Kast.

He poured some more into Kast's mouth and waited patiently until Kast had consumed the medicine. Kast noticed his mouth had begun to feel numb. It must be an effect of that area directly coming into contact with the mixture. It was good, though. He found it had begun to become easier to swallow.

Soon the cup was empty, and Kast felt sleepy again. The pain had begun to evaporate, though in a few certain places a muted prod continued to poke him. He looked up into Dale's eyes; the man merely smiled at Kast as he fell back to sleep.

Would he get better?

Whatever.

CHAPTER THIRTY-FOUR

Kast's eyes fluttered open, this time with more vigor. Even without testing, he knew he had healed well enough. His eyes flowed down his body. The pieces of wood were still attached. Bandages wrapped firmly around his midsection held his undoubtedly shattered ribs together as they healed. The man had been surprised at the rate at which Kast had healed. Was that because humans healed much slower? Or because the severity of his wounds transgressed the boundaries of the normal human threshold? He looked at his restricted limbs again—would it be fine to free himself? *Only one way to find out. But first...* Kast moved his arms, little to no traces of pain existed. His hands had remained mobile despite the braces on his arms. Reaching up, he found his face. The bandages around his head had been reapplied. How could he ever thank the old man? *Dale.* In one swift movement, Kast ripped the cloth off his head, reflexively stretching his jaw. He winced gingerly as his muscles seized and cramped from the sudden stress. He would have to be somewhat gentle on himself. How much of his body had just rebuilt itself?

He worked to relieve his arms next. The instruments to help his body heal came off easily, then the bandages. Kast was about to swing his feet off the bed when a thought occurred to him. Leaning forward, he stretched out his back. Sweet and tender agony rippled through his muscles. He held to the motion for a second before carrying on. He needed his body to limber up. Even now the girl and he must keep moving. There was no opportunity for relaxing.

Kast searched for a second before he found what he was looking for—a string attached to his left foot. Gently, he worked at the knot until he figured out how to undo it and let the string fall away. Now he didn't have to worry about someone keeping him in bed. He wouldn't lose that battle if he was already away from his rest. He flashed a smirk to himself over his cleverness.

Now that he was free of any alarms, he swung his feet over the side of the bed. His feet hit the floor. For some reason, it felt like it had been forever since his flesh had contacted the world. He stretched his toes and some cracked as he clenched them. Despite the unsettling nature of being a human, he was fascinated with the experience. They weren't as filthy as he had once thought, and the capability they displayed was worlds beyond anything dragons had accredited them for. He began loosening the bandages on his legs—there weren't even any scars! His gaze raked across his body. He hadn't had a second to truly take in being a human. It was strange but elating. It was new but ultimately comfortable.

He sighed. He wasn't out of the fire just yet.

He had no idea how things would resolve, but he surprisingly didn't find that as depressing as he once did. He just knew that the recent events had changed his heart to see things to the end and make right his wrong. *Speaking of which...* Kast winced from his body's tenderness, preparing mentally to make his body continue.

With a push, he stood, shaky at first, but his body regained its balance and strength with only a few steps. He raised his arms above his head and stretched. There was a weird feeling in his muscles that felt like it would go away with stretching, but no matter how much he did stretch, it never left. He lowered his hands and looked around; clothes rested on a nearby table. *Clothes.* Yes, those were necessary in the human world. He looked down. The cloak he had wrested from that bandit was gone. That seemed so long ago. He stood with only bandages covering parts of his body and a simple cloth wrapped around his waist for modesty. He must find a way to thank the old man. He moved to the clothes and began the struggle to dress. It was one of the strangest tasks he had ever set out to do. The cloak had been much easier to figure out how to wear. Each piece of this clothing was a fight to the end, though eventually, he managed to find a satisfactory result. *It will have to do.* His mind took a matter-of-fact tone.

He moved to the door, not sure what to expect. Were the clothes even laid out for him? They fit well. Or as well as he thought clothes should fit a human. His shoulders slouched as his hand moved to his forehead as if to wipe away the angst. *Just keep moving forward.* He breathed the words to himself as he undid the latch on the door. The world on the other side revealed itself.

It was the dusk of evening. In one mere moment, Kast realized how out of place he was, and unprepared for what lay ahead of him. *Oh, well.* He looked around, his head moving in all directions. Where were the other two? He took a few steps forward when he smelled something.

A delicious aroma wafted on the air, calling out to Kast. His stomach growled fiercely. He didn't know humans could make such a loud noise.

"Ah, I see our sleeping prince is finally awake!" The old man's voice called out through the air. Kast had no idea where the sound was coming from. "Though while you may have been clever enough to remove the string for the bell, you overlooked the condition of human hunger!" The voice called out mirthfully.

The old man appeared, with the girl close behind, and a look of joy coated his face. Kast was wary of the old man's jolly spirit. He had known older dragons once who held the same demeanor and had tricked Kast into their wit and mischief when he was young. Dale looked suspiciously similar as if Kast was about to be the subject of some joke.

Dale laughed suddenly. An odd mixture between shaking uncontrollably, and yet trying to maintain his balance with only one leg. The girl merely looked to the ground and turned back to where they had come from.

"Oh! I didn't really believe you, girl! He is terrible at dressing himself!" Cries of laughter rang out, piercing Kast's ears. Kast watched as the old man's laughter won out over his stability and he fell to the ground, rolling with joy.

Kast blushed, clenching his teeth. He was embarrassed for some reason. It was...*irrational,* his response to the man. He looked, down at himself again. He hadn't thought he had done that bad of a job, considering he had seen other humans wearing the same kind of attire and matched them. *Mostly.* He began to criticize and determine what could have been done better.

"Never mind that for now. We'll sort you out later. Come, grab some stew, and help me up!" Dale threw his hand out towards the dragon turned human. His voice carried loud energy from his recent bought of humor. It seemed misplaced to Kast.

Kast grabbed the outstretched hand and hauled the man to his feet. *Foot.* He began to smile at his own correction. There was something infectious about this man's attitude. Better proceed with caution. Dale stood while Kast bent to grab his walking crutch. He winced standing back up.

"You're a downright miracle, boy . . . ." Dale began talking again. "But you still need a little more rest before you can think about exerting too much force on yourself. Come fetch yourself a bowl of stew." He turned from Kast and hobbled back from where he came and where the girl had returned.

Kast followed. The smell of food and burning wood filled the air. The air itself was crisp this time of night, and the chill nibbled at his nose. He saw the girl sitting off to the side, staring intently at the fire. What looked like one of those so-called *bowls of stew* rested in her hands, as well, though she wasn't eating it. A large pot hung over the flames and inside bubbled a thick liquid. Chunks of . . . *stuff* floated in it. Kast really wasn't sure what stew was. He hadn't eaten much more than bread and water as a human. There was that dried meat once. His stomach growled again. *When had he last eaten?*

He was looking forward to the experience of stew. He found his mouth had begun secreting a liquid of its own. Was this in response to the smell filling his nostrils? The old man handed him a bowl and a wooden object that looked like a smaller, shallower bowl with a handle on it. The girl had one of the smaller bowls with a handle and another bowl that sat next to Dale had one resting in the bowl of stew, too.

Kast sat and held the bowl out near the pot. Dale grabbed a large metal handle with a larger bowl on the end of it that was left hanging above the whole mixture.

"Here you go, lad." Dale began scooping the food into Kast's bowl while recounting strange details of his cuisine. He was in the middle of an extremely detailed explanation of his prized herbs when a twig snapped overhead and a large black something landed into the mixture. "Ah!" Dale cried out excitedly. "A Womer nut! Those are the best in stews!" Giddily, he drowned the nut, shoving it with the ladle to the bottom of the stew. "That will add a lot of flavor!"

Kast stared curiously at the man. He had no clue about anything concerning human cuisine, but he was captivated by the apparent intricacies that went into cooking. That and the opportunities of sheer luck Dale regularly boasted of. From the corner of his eye, Kast watched the girl set aside her bowl completely. *Must not be hungry!*

Kast eagerly withdrew his now-filled bowl of *stew*. His stomach growled, shouting its approval. He looked oddly at the small bowl sitting in the stew in his bigger bowl. Dale stared and laughed again. "You use the spoon to put the stew in your mouth." Kast stared for a second before he gracelessly, and greedily shoveled the food into his waiting mouth. What was the word?

Delicious. With a hint of . . . *disgusting* somewhere in the mix.

He didn't care. He devoured one bowl and held out the container for seconds. It wasn't until he asked for a sixth bowl that he realized it might be rude to eat all of someone's food.

"I'm sorry." He changed his request to an apology immediately, a look of horror developing across his face.

Then confusion as Dale bellowed out laughter, louder than before. The man shook furiously as glee consumed him.

"Son, I haven't had anyone enjoy my cooking this much since . . . ." The man paused as his mind traveled backward through the years. "Well, no one has ever really enjoyed my cooking! Especially with one of those nasty Womer nuts ruining the mix!" The man resumed his laughter.

Nasty? Kast was confused again. What was human cuisine? What was this meal? He looked at the instruments of dining as if they were deadly poison. Kast still wasn't sure if he was willing to trust this man. Suddenly, he wished the bowl of stew and the spoon wasn't in his hands anymore. He looked back towards the pot and could see the Womer nut floating in the stew.

Dale caught the look on his face and fell off his seat with laughter again. Somehow, Kast didn't think the man's lack of a leg correlated with how often he was found rolling on the ground in laughter. Kast also wasn't sure either if he wanted to help up the old goon again. He remembered what the girl had done with her bowl of stew earlier, and thought she had the right idea. He set his to the side on the ground also, unfinished. He had had enough to eat anyway. He felt eyes on him and looked over at the girl, who averted her gaze. Kast dropped his head and stared at the fire. She would never forgive him, and he couldn't ever expect her too. He shouldn't want or expect forgiveness.

He wondered about the situation on hand—the group of them around a campfire. Laughter, food, warmth. *Peace.* Under other circumstances, is this what life would be like? An ache developed in the core of his being, his heart. For so long he knew that there was something, something intangible, looming on the fringes of his desire. A hole, stealing every ounce of joy. Something was missing, and now he finally understood what it was. Or at least—he had a much better idea of what he was missing. His shoulders rolled backward, stretching out. The ache in his heart seemed to translate to his body. The tiredness he felt in his bones, the angst of tendons. No wonder he had started sighing so much. He was missing peace.

But would peace last forever? *Maybe.* Most certainly not the way things were now. He still needed to find a way to make peace, before he tried to hang onto it.

Kast's thoughts reeled themselves back in. He was healed—mostly. He was clothed—mostly on that front, as well. He was fed and his mind was clearer than ever. *Probably.* He found his mind sidetracking while he worked to understand his situation. He sat still for a second, eyes closed and facing the ground with the heat of the fire working its way into his skin. The old man's laughter subsided and was exchanged for audible eating noises.

Kast's mind rattled in a million different directions, trying desperately to seize that next step in his thought process. The relaxing atmosphere was working against his thoughts though. They were crushed from the pressure of so many enemies.

That's it.

Kast sat at attention. Why had he forgotten everything? What had happened back in the city...? *In Harrington?*

What had occurred that had caused all of the injuries he had? Where was Vasiss, the Majesty of that dragon thrall, *The Insane King?* Kast felt a shudder ripple down his back.

That monster was impossible. He seemed to thrive in the very thing that dragons loathed and went to great lengths to cure—insanity.

Where was The Cloak?

Who was The Cloak?

Why hadn't Kast and the girl been found yet?

For that matter, why had they somehow managed to seize the improbable? How did they avoid being found, wandering the world, before they made it to Harrington?

Why had Vasiss and The Cloak arrived at approximately the same time at Harrington?

Why did they fight each other with such *passion?*

Why could Kast suddenly view the battle up close as he did? Was that even real or did he pass out and imagine things?

Why did the girl come for him in his cell, or rather, trust him enough to take her to safety?

Who was that soldier that hurt the girl and what had Kast done to him?

Why?

His thoughts raced from the enigmatic healing of the girl to the power surging through him and the ability to fight on par with a dragon in a human body, to his fight with the Insane King.

His fight with the Insane King?

How was that possible?

What had happened afterward? To bring him here?

Kast found his eyes drawn to the girl. Maybe most distressing of all the questions was *why is she still here?*

She was sitting on a fallen log and had leaned back against a tree. Her form receded into the shadows of the night. The flickers of the fire broke occasionally over her hidden figure. Kast found his voice.

"What happened?" So quiet. His thoughts were so laden down with his struggles that his words came out stiff and hushed.

Dale had already set his spoon and bowl to the side and was in deep thought. Both of the old man's hands clenched in front of his face. A serious look seemed to replace the humor that had thrived moments earlier. The girl shifted in her seat. Tension filled the air. Kast could feel it.

"Lad, you are absolutely one of the most clueless people I have ever met." Kast saw through the man's statement. The jovial demeanor, the mirth. It was a disguise.

Something terrified this man.

"I don't really know. I don't know what I saw. I don't know why this girl implored me to haul your apparent carcass away with the hopes of it healing—and yes, I said carcass." The emphasis the man put on the word unnerved Kast. "You were dead, lad. Your body was mangled in a way no human should ever be mangled. I don't know what happened, but you came surging through that city wall like it was made of straw. Not to mention all of the buildings before that—my stars! And you didn't stop traveling after you came through that stone and brick either! You flew through the air, tearing through trees until you hit the ground and started rolling!"

For some reason, the old man had become upset, his speech became excited and uncomfortable. "I would have left yer body for the Savages if it weren't for this girl! I tried to hold her back, but she got away from me, running towards you!" Now emotion began to well up in Dale's voice.

Kast clenched his fists. He didn't understand humans. Why was Dale upset over the destruction of another? Someone he had never met before.

"I . . . ." Dale floundered in his speech. In a rage, the old man kicked his bowl and spoon, spilling the contents everywhere. His head turned away towards the night. Kast could see a tear shimmer as it fell down the man's face.

"Who are ya, son? Who . . . what . . . are you? I ain't never seen anything like it before. The wall destroyed by a man's body as if it were some kid's plaything made of twigs! I promise you if it were a normal man who came booming through that stone . . . well, you wouldn't have." Dale gulped, and his breathing became ragged. "Your bones and innards would merely have been plastered across the other side. I've worked on humans before. I would know!" The man was nearly shouting, his finger jerked towards himself, emphasizing his knowledge of such facts. "That's not all!" His lip quivered in remembrance, the ghostly visions haunting the man. "Son." More quivering and struggle. "I just, I just don't know what I seen. I know there were dragons, and my heart nearly stopped at the sight of those wretches." He was beginning to ramble now, and he sounded like he had an equal amount of questions as Kast, if not more.

Kast felt inconsequential. This man had been so kind, and for some reason, his existence made Dale uncomfortable. Kast gripped his hands together and waited silently for Dale to collect his emotions and thoughts. Why did he feel accountable to Dale? The man's reactions to the desolation of Harrington cut Kast deeply. Was this what people really felt at the sight of a dragon? Much less an attack from one?

What about all the cities he had attacked? All in a selfish pursuit of his own ambition? It all seemed folly now.

"Son, I want to believe the best, but after all of that, I just can't. I don't know why this girl insisted on reviving you, or even knew that you could be revived in the first place. I don't know how the dead can come back to life. I don't know what to believe right now." The man's voice became sturdier as his emotions were brought back under control. "Is there anything you could say that would help me understand?" Dale looked Kast in the eyes now.

Kast felt uncomfortable underneath the man's stare.

"I don't know if there is much that can be said to ease your confusion, your awe, or your distrust." Kast began, not sure himself of what he would say. He could only think of being honest and going from there. "I'm confident that there is too much you wouldn't be able to understand, nor should you be required to. I can tell you we were the target of that attack and that we have been on the run from both dragons and bandits—the men caught up in fighting the dragons. They were the ones responsible for the bolts of light that killed the dragons." He breathed in relief. It felt good confessing the truth. "My goal is to return this girl home to the Capital . . . ." His voice wandered at the end, for the ambiguity of the situation still confounded him.

Dale clenched his fists and stood up. He nodded his head at Kast.

"It isn't the most satisfying explanation, but maybe I don't need more. It certainly felt like the truth." His words radiated confidence. "If you're heading to the Capital and you need to get there faster than these enemies of yours, I may have a suggestion, but I will save it for the morning. Until then, let's get some sleep. It sounds like there is a long day ahead of you tomorrow, and I doubt even you, lad, are completely free from your injuries." The man made to move to his house.

"Wait." Kast found his lips moving again. "What happened to the cloaked man who was fighting the dragons? What happened to the big, nasty dragon? The Kin . . . the big nasty one." Kast trailed off into a mutter. He suddenly decided it would be best not to reveal more information than necessary to Dale. He looked at the old man. Kast was filled with questions. Would they be safe? What kind of time constraints did they have? He settled on the one that would help them the most. "How long ago was all of this?"

Dale looked back towards Kast. "You have been sleeping for roughly two days. As for the two you questioned about specifically, that man returned somehow and began fighting that *big nasty* dragon in the sky, though not for long." Dale grimaced at the unknown. "We took the opportunity to leave. I tried to leave you because I didn't know how much time we would have to escape safely." He paused, his thoughts were a flurry across his face again. "Come now, it's time to sleep." Dale turned and went inside. The door closed behind him.

Kast made to move for it as well when something brushed past him. *The girl.* She stopped right in front of him, her back a reticent wall.

"Dragon." Her voice was sharp. Her body clenched after that one word.

Kast waited for the girl to say something. He watched as she shook her head to herself and went inside.

She would never forgive him, and he could never expect her to.

It was time to sleep again. Between his full belly and exhausted body, there was much rejoicing at the thought of rest.

CHAPTER THIRTY-FIVE

The sun poured down through a break in the trees onto Aurah's chilled skin. The light contrasted the gloomy situation festering all around her and the dragon with whom she still wandered the world. They threaded their path through the scattered rocks that littered the riverside. The bubbling of the water brushing against the shore lulled her thoughts away from reality and towards her companion's demeanor.

All of this—this pain, this destruction, this death, and hate. Everything seemed to originate from this very monster beside her. He had attacked the human cities and shattered the fragile peace the Kingdom had established. *And for what? All of this? For a girl?*

For her?

No.

Aurah reminded herself of how she had somehow managed to convince the beast into bringing her home. Her thoughts chastised the creature and his wanton selfishness. She didn't understand most of his actions. She couldn't make sense of anything that was happening—then or now. It was all so surreal. She had given up trying to grip reality and instead let it flow in cascades around herself. Like oil on water, the truth never seemed to establish itself clearly to her. Would he kill her for her betrayal? He certainly wouldn't tolerate that from her, would he? He was such a monster.

So why did he put himself in the way of harm for her? Because she was something *special* to him? Aurah couldn't see that being the truth since she wasn't even the one he wanted in the first place. And where was the beast's frivolous pride in all of this? When would it surface, only to berate her again? She cowered at the thought of his anger but sneered at the thought of his *kindness.* There was no other way to put it. Aurah hated attributing anything good to his character. And could anyone truly blame her? What was she to do? Could she really begin to justify forgiving the brute? Could she be expected by anyone to do so?

She stopped walking at that thought, her hands clenched. It was revolting. She looked down and jumped off a boulder. Her feet struck the rocky ground. The river moved quickly beside her. Running, always running. Did a river realize it was pointless to take water somewhere else? It was in vain, constantly flowing. *All for what?*

Why was she herself moving forward? Why did she decide to press on to the next point? Just to find out if they would survive or not? Her enemy blurred itself behind the veil of virtuous deeds, and her allies were as weak as she was. Nothing made any sense anymore—not her actions, not her feelings, not who was at fault—if she even could consider herself to be at any sort of fault.

She didn't ask for any of this! She didn't seek to be captured and stolen away. She didn't seek the torture of the past few weeks. She didn't want the salvations the monster that had stolen her away brought time and again. Yet, here she was. She was broken and moving forward, as pointlessly as the flow of the river they walked alongside. The villain beside her, the monster confined to a human form—was always so silent and contemplative. He didn't seem interested in broaching the distance between the two of them. He didn't seem interested in her at all. He was pure evil and was a liar. She couldn't trust the monster.

Aurah clenched her fists. This much was clear: if she couldn't trust him, she wouldn't trust him. With anything. Her words, thoughts, and especially with her forgiveness. Maybe that was what she needed to think—that he would never be forgiven or find grace from her. She was filled with much approval and joy at the thought.

But not every part of her.

There was something inside that still fought her resolutions, her decisions to condemn this creature as unworthy. *Why?*

The sun again broke through a slight parting in the trees past the rocky shore. Its warmth brought her slight comfort. She had watched it as it traveled from its rise in the morning to its position now. It was roughly just before noon. They had been walking for quite a few hours. By her guess, they were about halfway done with the current step of the larger, meaningless trip.

Dale, the old man, had given them some food and set them off on their journey after they awoke. After walking them a short distance from his cottage, the hermit had set them to follow the river towards the south. Apparently, there was a small logging settlement nestled on this river where his recommendation would find them help and direction forward. The settlement belonged to a family whose business had grown favorable over many years to the Kingdom. If Aurah remembered correctly, she had heard of the settlement as being a valuable resource for the Lower Lands, especially in recent times when timber was necessary for rebuilding what the beast beside her had destroyed.

The most pertinent and interesting fact, though, about the settlement they were coming upon was that it was located right on the edge of the massive cliff that separated the Upper Lands from the Lower Lands. Often referred to as The Face.

They were that close. That close to the colossal cliff that sheared the Kingdom in half.

Being near the cliff made Aurah feel odd. It was comforting in its own strange way. In the past, at the Capital, she could always see The Face in the far, far distance, even if it were somewhat small. It was something that had always been there. She found a glimmer of relief in its presence. It was odd.

She set her herself forward. She had no idea what was coming next. She didn't even know where to go from here, but she found a certain relief welling up in herself, a spark of hope that seemed to shine from The Face. Knowing something for certain finally seemed to break the impressive wall of her trials. One giant mountain impacting another. Maybe there was hope? Maybe she could believe things would work out? Maybe she could believe she would make it despite all her questions and fears. Maybe she would make it.

She looked to the light shining down from the sun, all her questions rising to the cloudless sky.

Maybe.

The world passed Kast by one minute at a time. A muted throb echoed through his mind. Ever second slithered by uncomfortably. Ever since he woke, his mind had been on one thing—the girl. Maybe he had been fortunate enough to be distracted from his thoughts by the presence of a kind person for once, but now that Dale was gone, Kast had to face the reality. He licked his lips. They were dry and he was thirsty, but he didn't want to get wet trying to take a drink from the river.

He ran his fingers through his hair, a habit he had begun to develop quickly since becoming a human. He had to face the reality that for some reason this girl defied the obvious and sure action someone in her position should take—abandon the wicked and exact revenge.

But no, she had saved him. He turned his head to the side, glancing at her walking along the river. *She saved me.* Those words echoed repeatedly throughout his thoughts. Was it a mere reaction? Was it real? He had no idea, but he did know they were moving forward again and for at least a few more hours they would go together.

Kast pushed his arm to the side and twisted, stretching the sore limb. His body recovered well with both the food, despite its unpleasant characteristics, and the sleep. A muscle in his back twitched as if moaning sorely. His body still informed him regularly about the severity of his recent injuries. His head slumped, and he exhaled roughly as he began to massage his eyes. He couldn't even express with words the situation they were in.

Every time his mind moved close to decipher the tangled thoughts in his head, the vaguer those thoughts became. Dale was kind, but he didn't do much to help Kast know how to work through the issues facing him. If anything, the old man made things worse. Before they had taken off, Dale grabbed Kast's arm to his surprise and told him words that made the dragon's soul crawl.

"Everyone is redeemable. There isn't a thing done that can't be forgiven, though some may take more time than others."

Such a short statement, but Kast scowled at every word. What did that old man know? Did he know the heartache Kast felt? Did he know the sins the dragon turned human carried on his shoulders? Could some kind hermit really know the depravity that faced Kast's existence? *Could he really?*

Kast shook the thoughts off and picked up his pace, spurred on by a mixture of desire to create as much distance between himself, the enemies that pursued them, and the old man that sent them onward to their next destination. And what would happen when they got there? To this settlement, as Dale said.

Kast was familiar with all of the times that he had flown over the edge of the large cliff face, but as a human, he hadn't the slightest idea how to scale the large formation.

One step at a time, he guessed. There were obviously much bigger things to figure out first. Kast looked over at the girl again for a moment before dragging his head back quickly. It would be awkward to be caught staring, but his thoughts drove his eyes to see the object of their energy.

How long could this not knowing anything go on? He didn't know what the girl wanted. She had barely accepted his plea to take her back home. And now, Kast knew that she wasn't beyond turning him in and finding some other means to make it home. There certainly would have to be a defining of directions, and from the way it looked, it would be soon. He would accept her desire to travel home without him. After what happened in the last city, there was no way he would force her again. No way could he align himself with those who hurt her any longer.

Kast turned his eyes forward to the bends and crooks in the flowing river. It wouldn't be long before they arrived at their next destination. It wouldn't be long before he engaged in one of the worst confrontations of his life.

CHAPTER THIRTY-SIX

The air swirled in torrents around his wings. Their descent placed stress on Snide's body that demonstrated just how exhausted they were. Among a mass of thuds, Snide landed on the rocky ground before the cavern the reign of Vasiss occupied. *Home sweet home.*

Vasiss landed in front, practiced grace filling his steps. He hadn't been himself after the last battle. His usual senseless discipline was gone. Snide saw that in the King of Insane as he sat on his haunches, staring at the stone beneath his feet and the sloppy landing of the remaining dragons. Snide swiveled his long neck and head towards the remains of the thrall. Grief gripped his soul.

Nine dragons. Only nine dragons left, including Vasiss and himself.

What would be the consequence?

What would be the consequence of the humans defying them so?

His head drifted forward again. *Vasiss.* Snide could only ponder the possible thoughts roaming through the Majesty's mind, though he doubted the desire to truly know what was inside the King of Insane's head.

Vasiss sat completely on his hindquarters, his entire frame slouched. Snide couldn't remember his little brother ever being affected this way. What was in his mind? Snide's stomach clenched as he watched his ruler.

Then slowly, ever so slowly, he noticed Vasiss was trembling.

Slight at first, but it grew. Laughter began to cry out from the monster, a deep muffled sound resonating from the black dragon's belly, crawling forth from that terrible maw. Snide was glad it had been a while since he had last eaten, as it was so unbecoming for a dragon to retch their food. His thoughts were interrupted by the sudden cut off in laughter.

"Snide." The voice of evil slithered from the black dragon's throat, frying along every inch of the words spoken.

"Yes, Majesty!" Snide locked his form in place, staring forward. *Something was off.*

"Snide."

"Yes, Majesty!" Snide's voice wavered in fear. Off wasn't a strong enough word; something was terribly *wrong*.

"Do you doubt the command of your *king*?"

"No, Majesty!" Snide was so grateful for the discipline that carried him to respond and not cower. His heart slammed in his mighty chest. His willpower teetered dangerously. Maybe Vasiss could hear his heart beating? Snide shuddered at the thought.

"Good." Vasiss let the word ring out darkly, fading to a momentary silence. "How long will it take to gather the Court?"

The Court.

"The Court? Which Court?"

"The *entire* Court, *Snide*."

The entire Court!

"Majesty, it would surely take at least a week to…"

"You have three days… *Snide*…" The voice of evil had spoken. Vasiss began to rock with laughter again.

Then the laughter stopped.

"Oh, and *Snide*?" The voice had faded slowly every time after saying his name.

"Yes, Majesty?" It was all Snide could do to maintain his voice. *The entire Court.* His brother was insane, but even for Vasiss, this was very out of character. The defeat at the hands of the humans. *That cloaked monster.* This did not bode well. Snide was very, *very,* unsettled.

Vasiss's tail struck lightning-fast, catching Snide by surprise, grazing him across the cheek and ending across the face of the dragon next to him. The dragon fell over dead, its head dropped, and blood poured from its face.

Vasiss brought his neck around, turning his head to stare into Snide's frozen gaze. It was like a tendril of darkness had shoved its way into Snide's eye socket and drove straight down into his heart, just to hold it still for a single moment. A look of laughter did curl the King of Insane's maw, though the deadliest evil emanated from his eyes.

Now there were only eight of the dragons left.

"Don't think I didn't see the lack of discipline. You had better not fail me now, *Snide.*"

Snide stared forward, blood pouring down from the new gash. He would not fail again, that was very certain. His brother would never give Snide the chance to fail again. *The entire Court!*

"Yes, Majesty!"

CHAPTER THIRTY-SEVEN

Evening was falling and Kast felt a soreness in his limbs. It was only a mild journey, but given the circumstances, the cry for rest was understandable. Being a human was still a new experience that he wasn't used to yet.

Ahead they could see the end of their trip coming close. Kast could see that the river bent and flowed out of sight between two rows of erected timber. Dale had said they would know they arrived when they came across the first section of—what was the word? — *palisades.* There were a few guards standing by the river entrance. Dale had told them a little bit about the Logger's Outpost, how it being built on the river offered a means of transportation that made providing the timber a very profitable endeavor. The settlement would send different crews throughout the Upper Lands to harvest a load of trees near some branch of the river. Then, once they had their load, they would travel with the wood back to the settlement.

Dale had told them it was dangerous work. With all the bandits roaming the area, the logging crews had to be large, and every man doubled as a soldier. They were, however, very proficient at their work and very skilled fighters, so they were rarely challenged. For this reason, many of the cities in the Upper Lands also hired the Logger's Outpost. While the river was the primary means for serving the Lower Lands, after dropping the logs off the side of The Face, that is, their ability to efficiently harvest timber and defend themselves made them an invaluable resource to the wilder Upper Lands. There were quite a few other reasons Dale had given that described the beneficial position that the Logger's Outpost was in, but Kast, while interested, didn't care to dwell on trivial things.

His head turned towards the girl. His chest clutched at the conundrum facing both of them. For a while now, Kast felt his body tense as they approached the settlement. After the approach to Harrington, he had realized how little his companion truly needed him. After whatever happened in Harrington, Kast realized he would not force himself into the girl's life. If she wanted him to take her home, he would gladly do so. If she wanted peace and relief from his presence, he would gladly do so.

But as much as Kast hated the thought of putting her into a confrontation, she would have to decide what she wanted.

Would she reject his help and turn him in again?

He looked back at the guards. It wouldn't matter, either way. Kast would get the due punishment he deserved. If he had learned anything, it was to be resolved towards what was right—and paying for the evil he had caused was right. And not causing any more pain was most certainly right, too. He had no fear of what was to come; he was committed. Committed for the better this time.

A husky voice with a thick accent yelled out at the dragon and his companion. "Stop! What business have you coming by the river way?" Direct and to the point. A good guard, just as Dale had told them would be the case.

Kast felt the girl's gaze fall on him. Time to step up.

"An old hermit by the name of Dale sends us along this way. He told us to mention his name when we arrived at the Logger's Outpost." Kast had placed hope in the instructions that Dale had given them, but now he began to question and wonder if it were a clever idea, after all. If it would work out.

"Ay! Doesn't Boss 'ave a brother or sumthin' like that?" The thick accent of another guard threw the question out for the others to hear.

"Ay, 'e does, and since you were the one to bring 'em up, you can go tell 'im 'e has a visitor."

A short groan graced the air as the guard who must have mentioned their boss turned and ran into the settlement. Kast fidgeted nervously. He had no idea what was happening as they waited a short distance away. This could be the worst decision yet. Maybe they should run away. They still had time, *right?*

"Ay! Are you twos the ones who called me 'ere with me little brother's name?"

Nope, no time to run after all.

"I guess we are. We're a little unsure of Dale's intention by sending us this direction, we don't mean to be a threat or anything . . . ," Kast called out hesitantly, doubting their ability to actually gain entrance to the Logger's Outpost.

"Dale's a good man. Doesn't give out 'is name that often. You're welcome 'ere, so come on in. Ma name's Dane."

Kast walked forward towards the man who apparently was Dale's older brother. It was starting to darken outside, but there was enough light to tell the details of his figure. In many regards, this man was like Dale, though he seemed more . . . *stout,* and he had both legs. Kast wondered what the story behind that loss was. Dane didn't wait for them long. He turned and followed the path past the palisades into the settlement. The only certainty that Kast had was that they were in the right place. He had no idea of what more was to come. He glanced to the side to see the girl following. Her shoulders slumped, but her head was moving around warily, searching for any signs of danger. She seemed to huddle close to Kast, and she hadn't turned him in just yet. Strangely enough, that didn't relieve much of the pressure Kast felt.

Before long, they followed Dane down another path. The settlement contained an array of log houses hugging both sides of the river. Spots throughout the small village seemed designated for fires where women and men gathered in clumps, mostly with groups of their own gender, but in this place mingling between the two seemed natural and not out of place. Smoke wafted from the tops of the little log homes as groups of kids scuttled back and forth throughout the streets the houses outlined. The frequent loud outburst of laughter was also no strange thing here. The settlement was very jovial. Kast looked around at the surge of human dens. They were all built in a way that seemed to indicate a deferment towards a centralized point.

Dane set a steady pace, waving and nodding very often. Children parted, making way for the man, his presence stirring their already energized nature. The centralized point that Kast had guessed about came into view. It was a larger building, similar to the other buildings in the settlement except that it was bigger and demonstrated a little more grandiose. The building was one of the few around to have an expanse of open ground in the front of it. There was a growth of wildflowers scattered all through the small field. It was like the house was built in the middle of a tiny meadow.

On the side, slightly set apart, was another building. A well-worn path cut through the meadow, eventually splitting to lead to either the main house or the side house. Kast wasn't exactly sure what purpose the slightly smaller building possessed, but a wealth of delicious aromas was dispersing freely from the building.

Food.

And tasty food at that, by the smell entering the dragon's human snout.

Kast found his mouth beginning to make more of that liquid again because of the delicious smells. They had eaten the little bit of bread Dale had given them, but that had been a while ago, and now Kast was hungry. His stomach echoed his thoughts, grumbling loudly.

"Sounds like 'unger is among yer companions tonight," Dane noted as they approached the complex of buildings.

Kast rubbed his head awkwardly, not sure how to respond.

"Ah! I understand. Sorry for using the local dialect for so long. I rarely speak to outsiders so I often forget it might be a little difficult for them to understand," Dane apologized, his accent gone in a second.

"You changed the way you speak?" Kast was puzzled. He knew of only one way to speak. As a dragon, there was only one way necessary.

"As a part of the family in charge of this place, I need to be able to communicate with the culture around here and out there." The man held up a finger as he walked forward and swirled it around his head.

Kast nodded, though the idea of needing to speak in more than one way was beyond his comprehension.

"If you come with me, we'll get you well-fed and then you can tell me your story and how you came to know Dale."

Kast's ears perked at the upcoming activity. As a human, he found eating to be a much more . . . *pleasurable* experience than before. He had begun to look forward to it more than he did as a dragon. Maybe humans weren't bad in every way.

Dane led them to the side building and opened a door at the end of the path for Kast and the girl to enter through. The faint smells from before had gained strength, welling up, and in torrents raced out of the building to berate the three. Kast fell against the doorway overwhelmed by the amazing amount of perception the human nose could manage. He lost track of time as he separated the unique smells. He couldn't wait to eat. Maybe it would be stew again?

"Well, you are a strange one ar'nt ya?"

Kast looked and saw a smile had crested on the man's face. Dane had resorted back to the accent again. *Was that a significant detail?* Kast smiled back weakly, making Dane belt out with laughter.

"Come on, dreamer. It tastes better than it smells." Dane slapped Kast on the shoulder, ushering him deeper into the aroma's sanctuary. The girl followed behind quietly.

They walked into a decorated yet humble cavern. Large fires burned in their stone surroundings merrily at either end of the rooms. A large and long wooden table sat in the middle of the room between two rows of tall logs and ran down the length of the room. The pillars looked to Kast to be supporting the ceiling. Four other smaller, but still fairly large, tables filled the rest of the room surrounding the pillars. Besides an assortment of furniture gathered around the various fires around the edges of the room, there wasn't much space for anything besides dining. A room where the piles of food and the glorious smells seemed to originate was located at the far end of the cavern. Those who looked to be servants were scuttling about, applying the final preparations for that night's meal—particularly carrying said food.

"This is the Mighty Mess." Dane's hands waved around again. "The Logger's Outpost's famed dining hall. Everyone you see here is either a guest or resident on this humble estate. You wouldn't have seen it from out front, but behind the main house are dormitories for the guests lodging with us." He turned his head to look at the two besides himself. "Everyone pitches in and helps prepare the meal with whatever needs to be done. There are no such things as servants in this settlement, so have at it, and we will talk after the meal." Dane shrugged his shoulders and turned to see to some task that needed to be done.

Kast stared, wide-eyed. *Help? Prepare?* His head rocked back towards the commotion in the room. The thought of helping out overwhelmed him. Maybe he could find something else to do. He turned to ask Dane, but when Kast looked, he had already left. Kast felt his heart fail. *Help?* The confusion mixed with the delicious smells created a distressing situation for the dragon. What would he do now? If he didn't help, he certainly couldn't expect to take part in that night's meal.

"Dragon." A cold, dead, voice cut through the warm and cheery air.

He turned to see the girl looking elsewhere, her hand pointing towards a group of men hauling in armfuls of wood.

"There. Go ask them if you can help." The side of her face tensed up and lines creased her brow. She turned away without another word and left, finding some chore for herself.

Kast felt alone, but that had to have been one of the nicest things she had ever done for him. Aside from convincing a man to save his life. *A good sign?* Kast dare not trade the promise of a wonderful experience with food for the confusion the girl had brought him.

Kast turned and walked the short distance, approaching one of the men carrying wood. The man noticed him instantly.

"Well, if it isn't a new arrival!" The man spoke without an accent. He must not have been a part of the culture around here either. Multiple ways of speaking. *Strange.*

"Yes. We . . . I . . . we just arrived." Kast stumbled as he tried to decide whether it was proper to specify the girl's presence as well. He had no idea how humans talked.

"Well, good! You look young and strapping. It's a pleasant enough place, but for some of us older folks it's nice to have young blood help with the more physically demanding chores."

Kast thought the man didn't look terribly old, but perhaps he just wasn't accustomed to human ages yet? "Certainly! I would love to help. What are we doing?" Kast gave the best smile he could. The man hesitantly returned the smile.

"Chopping wood. There is an extra ax outside and a pile of logs. If you show up the other men will get you going."

Chopping wood. Kast had never chopped wood before. He took a moment on that thought—of course he hadn't chopped wood before! He nodded to the man and moved out the door. The world had darkened significantly since the river, and the only light that shone was what emanated from a large fire a short distance away from the building. Three men stood swinging axes, splitting wood. Those swinging the axes would replace the log while another worker would grab the freshly cut pieces and haul them away to a nearby pile. It was strange, the logs could sit flat because of a flat cut. Kast wasn't sure, but axes didn't seem like they would create that kind of separating cut in the wood. Kast stood awkwardly for a second before he managed to catch a man's eye.

"Oh good! Now we have some serious help!" This man was definitely a foreigner as well, his accent—or lack of one— had given him away. How many foreigners inhabited this place?

The vibrant mood was becoming infectious, Kast found himself smiling more. He even forgot the hardships on hand. The hardships on hand. *The girl.* His thoughts shifted quickly, reminding him again of the issues yet to be faced, and the joy of the moment faded away slightly.

"Grab an ax and set yourself up on a log. We could chop forever, and this place still wouldn't have enough firewood!" The man exclaimed that sentiment loudly. Apparently, joy seemed to make people louder. *At least these people.* Kast looked around and found the ax the man had mentioned. As for the log, he was clueless.

"I'm sorry, but I haven't chopped wood before, I'm not sure what to do." He felt slightly out of place confessing his inadequacy.

"Never chopped wood before? Neither have I!" The man laughed heartily. "I'm a passing merchant. I've always had hired help to take care of such things, but I like this place. It gives one the feeling of personal contribution. It fills the soul with so much good. I feel like I could live here happily forever." The man was holding his ax as he talked, he turned to face Kast and smiled largely.

Infectious was definitely the right word for the atmosphere in this place. The trials weighing on the dragon's human shoulders seemed to fade away one at a time, each relieved by the stranger's smile alone. What was this place? What were humans? What was life? Kast couldn't help but compare the despair and isolation he felt as a dragon against the peace and unity of this one meager settlement.

How did he even begin to process that?

"If you need help with the motion of swinging, I'll be more than glad to walk you through it," the man offered kindly.

"Yeah." Kast had to think for a moment about what the man's offer meant. "I would appreciate the information very much."

"Well, the theory is to get the most powerful swing so you can split the wood. At first, your ax will need more support, so separate your hands and put one farther up on the handle." The man grabbed the ax as he had been before starting to split the wood. "Then you swing it and give it more power. The momentum will keep it going. You just need to hang on and keep the blade straight and aimed correctly as it drives through the wood. Here, watch." The man finished showing Kast the motions slowly, then proceeded to split a log. It didn't look difficult, but the consequences could be severe. *Right?*

Kast picked up his own ax and held it the way the man had shown him. It felt good and natural. His head turned to watch the man a few more times. He observed the stance and motion in a manner more thorough than had been explained. The concept was still the same though. Kast raised the ax like the man and swung.

Miss.

What did he do wrong the dragon wondered? He picked the ax up and swung again, this time it chipped a chunk of wood off, but the ax twisted in his hands.

"That will happen if you don't keep the blade straight. With all of that force coming down between the edge of the blade and the log, if you aren't straight, it will deflect the ax away. Try it again but hold the ax steadier.

Kast nodded. He was grateful for the man. He raised the ax again and swung.

Miss.

"Well, no one is good at first." The man laughed heartily. "Keep trying. There's no shame in struggling."

Kast raised the ax repeatedly. Each time, he either missed or the ax hit but twisted. He doubted anyone was this bad at first. Now the dragon was frustrated. The goal was so apparent before him. He raised the ax, angry, and swung. He completely missed the piece of wood but instead found a nearby rock in the ground. Both the rock and the blade shattered to pieces. Kast's chest heaved, infuriated. *Great, now the ax is broken!* He hated not knowing how to be human. He was just so irritated he could . . . . He threw the handle down and shot forward to grab the log in front of him. With his fingertips, Kast found a hold and ripped the log in half with his hands, sending the pieces flying to the sides. He heard his voice crying out his displeasure over his failure. He stood over top of the mess for what seemed like an eternity.

"Are you alright, son?" the helpful man's voice asked him. The tone had transformed utterly.

Kast was jolted from his stupor. He noticed instantly the sounds of busyness and chopping had ceased around him. Only the fire dared speak up with its consumption of the wood on top. Kast looked towards the man who had helped him. Everyone involved with chopping peered through the darkness. There was enough light to see what Kast had just done. They stared, their mouths gaping open. He felt embarrassed again. *Irrational!* He hoped they couldn't see his blush in the darkness.

"Maybe you had better try again another time. It was probably just . . . just the light." The man spoke again, and a few other voices mumbled their agreement alongside him. The atmosphere shifted from infectious to strangely uncomfortable.

Kast nodded slowly, completely unsure of what to do with himself. He looked at the ax—what was left of the ax. Not only had the metal fractured into many pieces, but the wood itself had splintered where his hand had held it. He could just make out grooves from where his fingers crushed the wood. *Not good, definitely not good.* Kast held his hand aloof as if the handle had been poisoned. What did one do in this situation?

Kast jumped as a loud voice rang out from inside the dining hall.

"Good enough all! Time to eat!" The voice declared the chores were over.

Kast turned to look at the other woodcutters, but they had already filed away quickly. He stood alone over the disaster. Why did he feel . . . *frustrated?* Why did their rejection hurt? Why did his failure hurt? Why did he want them to accept him so badly? He was confused at the new wave of emotions that swelled in his heart. He stared at his fist, watching the muscles on the back of his hand bulge larger with every squeeze of his fingers. It felt like his whole body was doing that. Tensing up and pulsating. Squeezing then releasing. He felt like his breath was stolen, that a gaping chasm ripped his chest wide open. He released the pressure, and a whoosh of air rushed past his lips. He had been sighing so much lately.

He shook his head. *No.* This wasn't about him anymore. He caught his breathing and steadied it again. The truth of his situation and direction calmed him, reminding him of his bigger purpose. He had to be prepared for this to be difficult. He had to be resolved to face that difficulty. There was nowhere he could run away from his responsibility. There was nowhere to escape the consequences of his actions.

I must pay for what I've done.

Kast turned and walked through the door, leaving the mess behind him. That was all he could do—leave the mess behind himself and try to make things right. He had done enough in pursuit of himself. He stopped before moving through the door. He had found inner resolve and strength. It was odd, the difference it made and the stances it took—condemning even his selfish behavior from before. There was much hope in the thought of paying for his wrongs.

Yes, I must pay for what I've done.

The smells of the food wafted into his thoughts and began to pull him away from the depths of his heart. Someday he would make things right, but maybe ignoring life now wouldn't exactly fulfill that end? Maybe there was a way to make things right, and live well? The smells enticed him from his gloom and brought new hope into his heart. He would give everything he had to live well, and at the moment, the aromas made Kast believe that wouldn't be the most distressing thing.

He noticed the group of men from outside, huddled together on the far side of the room with their backs to the door Kast had just entered. It had been dark out there, and they would rationalize what they saw the dragon turned man do. They would be fine. They would forget what they had seen.

Kast hoped.

He moved forward as many of the people finished their chores and found their seats. It looked like a small crowd. Food and drink lined the tables. Only part of one of the smaller tables was prepared to be used, leaving the three other tables and the biggest table untouched. He didn't know where to sit. He hoped he wouldn't fail at eating correctly. It seemed easy enough at Dale's the previous night.

"There you are!" Dane grabbed his arm from out of nowhere. Kast saw the girl in tow under his other arm. "Tonight, you both will sit with me. It's rare that Dale would send travelers my way, so you are my special guests."

Kast felt Dane leading him with one hand on his arm. Kast looked over and saw a blank stare coated the girl's face, as usual. She averted her eyes away from both of the men and moved after Dane's leading silently.

"After dinner, we will share our stories, but that is after dinner. For now, it is dinner!" Dane declared obvious facts, but the atmosphere justified his enthusiasm and speech. The incident with the ax already seemed a distant memory to Kast.

Slowly the crowd of people found their seats and waited patiently, most staring up to where Dane was leading Kast and the girl. He motioned to where Kast and the girl were to take their seats and then turned to face the diners.

"Tonight, we reflect on the truth of perseverance and a resolve of undying commitment," Dane called out to those listening, pausing for a moment to let the opening statement settle in the minds of his listeners. "Once, there was a group of travelers roaming across hills and lands, mountains and seas. Their goal was firmly set in sight. They always persevered onwards of one accord, driven forward. That is until one unfortunate happening left the peoples blocked by a mighty boulder, with no way to progress, but rather, only to regress. The arguments and debates among the people raged long and hard. Some of the travelers left—seeking another goal, forsaking their original pursuit. Others gave up any kind of searching entirely. Yet, some stayed. Patiently waiting for the answer. Not long after arriving at the boulder one among the travelers offered a solution. In their palm, they held a seed, very tiny. Incredibly small. As best as they could, the peoples managed to plant the seed as far under the boulder as they could while still allowing the needs of the seed to be met."

"For years, the people waited with resolve, committed. They watched the sprout raise from the soil and slowly grow into a sapling. The travelers settled, passing on the vision to the next generation, then the next after that and so on. Others came along to join the patient waiting while others left, like many of those before them. Despite the more sensible and immediate reasons to quit, there were always the few who were resolved to stand fast, waiting to move on towards the bigger goal to which their hearts were committed—those who persevered through the trials of living and of fear."

"One day, under the colossal sway of the magnificent tree, the mighty boulder was as a pebble and cast aside. The travelers reveled and rejoiced at their hope fulfilled. Now they would progress and move on. In droves, the travelers who had waited on the tree, now merely those under the charge and promise from the past, moved forward only to realize immediately that there was nothing beyond the boulder. The people sat despairing, all of their hope gone, and time wasted. Then, one filled with much wisdom came and explained what they saw."

"The goal was never arriving where they thought the destination was; the goal was always moving forward. The goal itself was perseverance and resolve. It was commitment. In an unraveling and opening of the wisdom granted to them, the peoples rejoiced again. Their hope had been fulfilled. They had been given the precious wisdom of perseverance and resolve and lived so forevermore." Dane finished the story shortly, standing before the silent guests as they pondered the message to his words.

Kast sat with his hands limp in his lap. His mind wrestled with the meaning in the words. Hope. Perseverance. Resolve. *Commitment.* What were these to him? The diners erupted in applause at the short story, interrupting his thoughts, and immediately began to dish out the steaming food that lay before them. Kast would have to take time to process Dane's words. He smiled; something in the story had encouraged him. He felt stronger in some obscure meaning of the word. He looked down as his stomach gurgled again. It was time to eat, though. He watched for a moment, then copied Dane, dishing out in the same amounts of the same types of food that he did. Kast looked at his...*plate.* Maybe humans should make bigger plates?

Dinner went fast for Kast. The food was *amazing.* He had never experienced something as wonderful as delicious food.

He cleared the first plate quickly and filled the second one up even more. Humans definitely should make bigger plates. He was shocked to try what Dane had called dessert. It was sweet but good. Kast liked sweet, but his attention was stolen mostly by the other dishes, not dessert. By the end of his feast, Kast had filled up and emptied plate after plate of food. Dane laughed heartily at his guest's appetite and encouraged him in his exploits, helping by dishing food ceaselessly onto the dragon turned human's plate.

The dining hall emptied slowly as the occupants left, probably to retire for the night. Dane stood, turning away from the tables and the few who had remained in the hall. Kast stared at his empty plate and the leftover food lining the table. His belly was full but what was to be done with all the rest of it now?

Dane answered the unspoken question. "Don't worry about it. The food is left out and the doors unlocked so that the struggling and poor may fill up. They respect the privacy of the space, but they will filter in throughout the night." A smile beamed from the kind man towards Kast.

Kast stood up, satisfied. Dane turned and was heading to a chair by a nearby fire. The girl had already taken a seat. She left the meal before either of them had finished.

"So, you both owe me story as to why my brother is sending two strangers to my doorstep. Especially after the catastrophic destruction of Harrington." Dane had changed his tone slightly. He wasn't angry, but he was stern and expecting. Apparently having a reference from Dale only got one so far.

"Dale saved us from the destruction of Harrington," Kast spoke as he moved forward and took a seat around the fire. The girl merely stared into the hearth. "Well, mostly just saved me. I was injured. The girl pleaded with him to carry me along despite his efforts to leave me behind." Kast motioned to the girl and paused for a second. He needed to be careful about what he told the man. "We are simply heading to the Capital."

"Oh! You have a bit of a journey left to go then. It will take near three days north to get through the canyon pass to the Lower Lands and then a few more days to make it the rest of the way there. Good news is that bandits aren't so rampant on the Lower Lands—the Capital makes sure of that. You'll have to be careful of any packs of Savages though, unfortunately. With all of the recent loss of cities by the attacking dragons, the grip of man has declined significantly." Dane let his words trail off.

Kast didn't know whether to continue or not. He wasn't sure how to handle being interrupted, though he guessed he wasn't going to say much more. Dane answered Kast's question by continuing his own thoughts.

Dane's tone was businesslike. He came across as a strong leader to Kast. "You know, I can tell you two aren't natural traveling companions. I'm sure Dale saw it, too. We see a lot, him and me. I see that you're not lying, but you're not telling me everything either, so I'll keep this to the point. You're welcome for the night, but you are to leave first thing tomorrow morning. We will give you provisions enough for a week, but the rest is on you. I don't like not knowing whether my people and I are going to be destroyed. I'm sure you have come to appreciate it, as well, but we have a great peace here. I will not let that be tarnished—even for the sake of two needy travelers with the word of my brother. To tell you the truth, most of the guests here have been here for a little while. No one new has been let into this settlement for fear of the path of destruction that rumors seem to indicate is following the same path as you two. However, that old goat, Dale, has wizened in his age and I trust him completely not to have sent the wrong people here." Dane was finished.

Kast sat, watching the tongues of fire licking the darkness above. One after the other. *Fire.* His thoughts moved to a time when fire was at his command. Now he was some wet and scale-less human. What was life now? From killing humans, *murdering,* to relying on their help. How the chasms in his soul had shifted. How life had changed. There was something that caught his attention, though.

"You mentioned that Dale has wizened in his old age. Was he foolish when he was younger? Is that what accounts for the loss of his leg?" Kast in his innocence pried open a personal topic. He listened to Dane laugh at the question.

"No shame! That I do like about you, young man." Dane's hand moved out and patted him twice on the shoulder. Roughly.

"I'm sorry?" Kast was confused again. Learning normal human actions was difficult.

"No, don't be! I admire honesty." Dane leaned back into his chair, for a moment Kast nearly saw a spitting image of Dale—only not missing a leg. "I like to tell the story. I like stories in general if you hadn't noticed." Dane smiled. Kast smiled back politely. "Anyway! A long time ago Dale and I weren't on such good terms. He was rather foolhardy and lazy. Despite all of the time together since then, I still don't fully understand what was going through his mind and why he acted the way he did. I suppose it doesn't really matter, because he did what he did, and in my heart, I feel that he has more than made up for his actions." Dane sighed, running a hand through his thinning hair. He stared into the fire for a second.

"Dale was ultimately responsible for the death of our family and many of our people. He had a penchant for adventure and action. His mind resided in the clouds, and it wasn't uncommon for him as a boy to hurt himself when working with the timber." Dane clenched up; his hands were held out in front of himself as if something were held tightly between them. "Dale often argued and fought with the family. Things weren't so . . . peaceful back then, like they are now. We needed to commit a larger amount of our workers to guard the settlement, which meant less to spare on the actual production of timber for the Kingdom. He dutifully signed up to guard the settlement, which was good! Except when he also eventually told the family he wanted to leave on some rag-tag adventure." Dane released the tension in his shoulders. The light of the fire danced across his face. "I don't know. Maybe it would have been okay to give him a moment to enjoy his own life instead of being condemned to the life of a lumberman. Whatever the answer to that thought is, he left one day. No goodbyes. We didn't know when or if he would be coming back."

"Years went by before we ever heard from him again. He looked…fine, but his time out in the world had changed him. His spirit didn't seem so free. He seemed greatly weighed down by burdens only he knew of. He stayed with us for a brief time before he up and left again." Dane smashed his fist into the arm of the chair. His pleasant smile was replaced with a fierce scowl. "That heap of dung, as we found out later, had gotten himself involved with some gang of marauders, and his mission was to help them take the logger's settlement."

Kast sat staring. He never would have guessed the kind old man in Dale was ever capable of committing such a crime.

"He had a conscience, though. Filled with guilt, too, I imagine. The night before that scum gang of thieves arrived, Dale had taken off, splitting away from them. The gang, as I found out later, was waiting for the dead of night before attacking, but Dale slipped away, sprinting to warn of us of impending doom. We hardly believed him, but when we saw that trash gang slipping through the shadows of the woods, we knew our lives were forfeit. You see, it wasn't just one group of bandits. That filth had actually joined together to take the settlement. Who knows? Maybe they would have moved on from here to bigger things like the Kingdom? It was a grueling battle; we were caught off guard. Most of our men were ready, but it was too late. Dale fought like a beast, slaughtering the men he had once aligned himself with. Our family was killed. The men in the battle, the women in their beds alongside the screaming children." Dane's emotions shone in his eyes. "I don't care how hard he fought, that little misbegotten knave could have burned in the belly of a dragon for all of eternity as much as I cared. He carried the weight of what happened on his own shoulders." A tear dropped from Dane's eye.

Kast sat back in his seat, completely taken by the story. Dale was responsible for something so . . . *so horrible?* How did Dale even live with himself?

"What happened next, even I'm not so sure. Out of the black of the night came this . . . *man*. Wrapped up in a cloak and those inexplicable purple lights—and I know those lights to be purple because they were such a rare color for us to have seen. He fought with great fury. The way he moved, though, was just unnatural. He didn't use any weapons, just his bare fists. It was incredible, I don't even know if what I saw was real or not. He joined the fray and the horde of scum quickly fell. I was completely unaware, the fool that I was, enraptured with the glorious battle that cloaked man did, but a crazed man came out of the night, seeking my own head as his trophy. That bandit berserker was fierce-looking, maybe the only real warrior the enemy proffered. Dale shoved me out of the way just in time and somehow the swing of the man's blade was enough to cut most of the way through Dale's leg. Dale fell before the man and was about to be ended when the cloaked figure returned and slaughtered the assailant. The cloaked man turned quickly to Dale and . . . ." Dane's voice trailed off for a second. A ghost haunted his eyes. "The cloaked man *healed* Dale's leg. The leg was nearly severed so he finished removing it. Then what was left was somehow closed over with flesh. A flash of purple light appeared and then seemed to be swallowed by my brother's injury. Only Dale and I know of what had happened, and even he was mostly faded from the incident. My heart nearly stopped when the cloaked man finished with him and looked at me. He didn't do anything except turn and leave. He just left like that. I don't know what it was." Dane shook his head.

Kast had sat up at the mention of magic healings, the purple lights, and a cloaked man. Kast couldn't be sure, but it was too similar to be a coincidence. From the corner of his eye, he could see the girl fidgeting nervously, too. Dane continued his story.

"Through the following years, we rebuilt. Dale poured himself into the work this time, even though he only had one leg. After a while, we rebuilt a relationship and a confidence. He did so much for the settlement. He was the one who devised the idea of a saw, instead of chopping everything with an ax, for instance."

Kast cringed at that word. The memory of earlier raced through his mind again. He felt his cheeks warm with the flow of blood.

"Our productive capabilities more than tripled with saws, and a whole slew of new jobs were created. Eventually, everything was rebuilt, and many people have come to find that the life here offers much to be desired, despite the lessened security. Although there hasn't been a single attack since that bandit raid so long ago. Dale eventually left, probably to seek solace in the life of a hermit. I think he sees too many reminders of his past around here, though I know he deeply enjoys the merry that thrives in the lives of every soul within this community." Dane stood up suddenly. "Well, that's the story between Dale and me. It took some time, but I learned something from him. Always remember the story of a scar, but never forsake the actions of the present." He quieted down and look around for a second before speaking again. "There is a room set aside in the dormitory, I'm afraid you'll have to share though. If you follow me, I'll show you where your beds . . . ."

Kast interrupted Dane. "If you don't mind, I'd like to stay here for the night. I like the fire and the chair will be sufficient for me."

"Suit yourself. It might get a little noisy with some of the others coming in and out." Dane smiled at him.

Kast couldn't help but smile back. The man was pleasant, despite having a terrible story. Dane motioned for the girl to follow and he led her out of the room to the dormitory. He sat back in the chair. He knew that it would be important to get as much sleep as possible but there was just so much that sat and burned in his mind. The Cloak appearing in a story, and from quite a while ago, no less. The unexpected side to Dale, and even Dane, and the message of the story before dinner. Maybe the two were playing him somehow? It was crazy, everything that lined up. At the end of every line of thought, his mind landed on one thing. *The girl.* What had she thought about everything? Was there a chance of forgiveness? What was Kast supposed to do? Should he ask for forgiveness? Should he try to take her down that road of confrontation, or should he allow her the barrier to block the pain of his presence? Should he just accept the coming punishment at the Capital? Was there any hope? Was he so certain on the means to make amends for his actions?

He slumped into the soft cushions of the furniture, his thoughts singing a song that lulled him to sleep.

CHAPTER THIRTY-EIGHT

Kast stared at the dying embers of the once crackling fire. He had decided to just sit in the chair for a moment since waking a brief time ago. It must be morning, judging by how low the fire was—and his back. Despite the initial comfort of the furniture, it had turned out to not be the best place for one to sleep. His arms stretched high into the air as he tried loosening the muscles. With a last glance towards the fire, he stood. They were to leave and continue their journey very soon. Rest seemed to bring a certain relief to his mind's meanderings, but it did little more than settle them for a moment. With Dane's conclusion the night before, it seemed obvious that the girl would travel with Kast as they made their way back to the Capital. But this journey just couldn't happen together unless both he and the girl were with the same understanding. Kast needed to know what she wanted. It was time to confront her.

He gritted his teeth. The anticipation made him pessimistic. He would deserve every and any word the girl decided would be necessary to throw at him. Yet, he must figure things out with her, at least a little.

Kast glanced around the room. Dane was right, the food was mostly taken care of by the morning, finished by those who needed it. Kast admired that kindness. *Maybe that's why there is so much peace around here? Even the lowest are taken care of.* His mind was in such a state that even the insignificant things he saw caught his attention and caused him a moment of pondering.

He turned for the door when he realized that he didn't know where the girl had slept, or how to find and confront her before they were to leave. In fact, he had no idea what to do with himself until Dane found him. It was slightly awkward, waiting for what was promised and not knowing when or where it would be fulfilled. *I'll just go and wait outside, surely, I will be noticeable in the open.* He made to move again for the door when it opened from the outside and someone walked in.

It was the girl.

Uh-oh. She must have come to find him. Maybe this dining hall was where they were to wait after all? She saw Kast standing and staring. She dropped her head towards the floor and began to move towards him. Kast's skin crawled and his stomach churned. *Already? This is happening already?* He didn't feel prepared enough for this conversation. Somehow his resolve seemed tested. He wasn't so sure a confrontation was good anymore. He didn't know anything anymore.

The girl stopped at a nearby seat at a table and sat. Her gaze stared off into the distance. What did an evil and cruel dragon turned man say to the victim of his selfish ambitions? How did he convey repentance and a desire to make amends? He stuttered through those thoughts. The idea of so much clarity in his situation was, ironically, confusing in itself. His heart began racing in his chest at the thought of even one word.

He moved closer, wrenching himself away from his position of safety some odd distance away from the girl. He could do this. He would beg her—no, he would respect her more than that. He would merely offer his help. *Then his head?*

He clenched his fist. *Be committed. Your fear is unnecessary.*

He released the tension coursing through his sinews and flesh. He breathed slowly.

"Girl . . . ." His voice scraped out of his mouth. Despite his efforts, it sounded weak and unsure. *Pathetic.* "We . . . I . . . I need to talk . . . ."

The doors to the dining room slammed open violently and Dane stormed in, a look of urgency on his face. "There you two are!" Behind him . . . .

"Dale?" Kast found the tension of his confrontation with the girl gone. He watched her out of the corner of his eye stand up and face the two newcomers. Confusion was on her face, just as much as it felt on his own.

Why was Dale here? How was Dale here?

"Quickly, come close!" Dale ushered the two into a conversation. Despite the closing space between the four of them, the girl managed somehow to maintain a respectable distance between herself and Kast. "You need to leave, immediately. Danger is right on the doorstep of this place." Dale's eyes were stricken with terror. "It wasn't until the noon hour after you both had left my cottage that I saw from a distance that man who fought on par with the dragons back in Harrington, followed by a gang of bandits or what have you. I raced as best as I could back to my cottage and readied my horse to warn you both. I've been riding all night to get here before they did, and I can certainly promise you that they aren't more than an hour behind me."

Dale was slightly unsettled by the whole happening. His chest breathed a little heavier than normal and his eyes seemed widened, both by the lack of sleep and the abundance of fear.

The girl spoke. "Why are you helping us, then? We've caused enough lives to be harmed and ended." Her eyes flickered towards Kast's direction. The emotion was mixed, not pure, but there was hate. Most definitely hate.

"Because I received a second chance, young miss, and I'll be cursed if I don't repay the graces that I received myself to those that need it, too," Dale answered her firmly. Even Dane seemed to behold his brother with a little respect. "I'm sorry, brother, if I endangered the settlement again, though, this was more than . . . ."

"Stop there, Dale." Dane interrupted his brother. "I learned the same things you did, albeit differently. That is the truth that this place is built upon, and it would be shattered the moment I refused it. You know yourself that most of the workers here were once members of the various bandit gangs that roamed these lands. Everyone deserves another go at things." He turned to the two. "Your packs have already been prepared, and you must leave quickly. Every second cou..."

"Actually, Dane, I have been thinking about something." It was Dale's turn to interrupt his brother. Dane turned suspiciously towards Dale. "Do you remember that ridiculous tale from the earliest recounting of our family history at this place?" Dale nearly had a smirk on his face. Dane's eyes widened at the suggestion of something that went beyond Kast's understanding.

"Dale, you know there was no way to counter the drop. We tried so many times."

Dale pointed straight at Kast. "Not with him we haven't!" A wicked smile had plastered itself onto his face. Dane looked back and forth between the two.

"What's so different about him?"

"Because I *know* he is capable of sticking it through to the end. Besides, you know the truth yourself. They'll never make it through the pass before being caught, let alone if they would make it to the pass in the first place. This is their best chance, and he can make it work!" Dale smiled at his brother, slamming his finger in the air straight at Kast. Dane in return had begun to smile back.

"You crazy old lunatic! This is on you!" Dane clapped his hands forcefully together, a look of glee on his face. "Come, there's no time to waste!" His voice was raised.

Excitement?

Kast ventured a look at the girl. Her face mirrored how he felt *perfectly.*

Dane and Dale turned quickly towards the door that they just came through.

"Hobble faster, you old coot!" Dane turned back towards his brother laughing.

"I only need one leg to kick your rump, you sorry excuse for a cow!" Dale had begun laughing as well.

Kast remained in place, jaw slack and eyes wide at the spectacle before him. They were more than likely in the very clutches of a most horrendous enemy and these two old men were laughing like little kids. Something in Kast's mind screamed at him to run. He saw the girl was clenching her fists as well. When she caught Kast looking at her, her face dampened, and she sprinted forward after the two men. *So be it.*

Kast ran, too, catching the door before it closed. It didn't take long to catch up with Dane and Dale. Especially Dale.

"Hey, young girl, carry an old man, would you?" Dale asked the girl as she passed by him to catch up with Dane. *She is probably making as much space as possible between her and I.* Kast assumed the worst.

"I don't like warts!" The girl dropped the insult to Dale and carried on to Dane, who was half running and half laughing at the girl's jibe. Kast was bemused at her rare words. Her face still, though, seemed determined and set.

"Here!" Dale yelled out excitedly and latched himself onto Kast's shoulders. Kast stumbled and nearly fell but caught himself. He helped the man up and held his crutch for him as his arms wrapped around the dragon turned man's shoulders and chest.

When he was settled, Kast ran and quickly caught up with Dane and the girl. Dane was laughing hysterically. *Why?* Dale was echoing the same right into Kast's ear.

"Looks like you have a big nasty wart now, young man!" Dane struggled in his running as most of his air was being used to laugh. Kast saw the girl's cheeks blush slightly at Dane's comment. Kast couldn't help but smile at the ridiculousness of the situation. He hadn't even been awake for half an hour. Everything was moving fast. *I guess that's the way it happens sometimes.* He let the merry these men had wash over him before he nearly gasped at an astounding realization.

This is fun!

It had been so long since Kast had truly felt these kinds of feelings.

Dane took a sharp left suddenly.

"Left, fool! Left!" Dale screamed in his ear like a little child.

This is crazy! Kast corrected his course immediately, almost throwing the old man off.

"Watch it now, you have to treat your elders like fine teaware!" Kast smiled at the man's chiding and shook his head.

They ran through the streets of the settlement. Very few people were out this early. Those that were laughed at the scene the four of them were making. Many waved to Dane and even Dale on Kast's back. There was certainly some history in this place. History that Kast would have loved to dive into if it were a different situation or time.

Dane reached a building that sat on the edge of the riverside and fumbled a moment with a key to get the door open. It wasn't long before a large padlock fell to the ground, flying to the side after Dane kicked it out of the way. What was in this building that could answer all of their problems? What were these two brothers thinking that could possibly help them?

Kast reached the dim interior of the building and looked at what Dane and the girl were gathered around. His eyes adjusted to the dark better as he caught part of Dane's words. "We made it out of a couple of barrels that have proven to float the most effectively."

A barrel. What in all of the heavens?

"Put me down, boy!" Dale cackled wickedly into his ear. Kast stopped and helped the old man regain his balance as he dropped off his back. Dale hurriedly hobbled his way over to the object of interest. "We don't have much time, Dane!"

"I know, I know!" Dane practically yelled back. He grabbed something in the gloom and yanked a large dusty old woven cloth away.

Kast had no idea what he was looking at.

He looked and saw the girl's face. Her mouth hung open slightly, her brow furrowed down. She kept looking across the thing. Kast felt better, he wasn't the only one confused now.

"Is all, all right, sir?" a voice called out from the door. Kast turned to see a group of men file into the building. A look of wonder on their faces.

"Yes, yes! It's better than it's ever been, McKay!" Dane called out excitedly. "Do you by chance think you could rustle up a knapsack full of some food for these two? I've forgotten to grab what has already been—"

The man, McKay, threw a filled knapsack onto the ground. "Already done, sir! As soon as I saw ye' were heading here with Dale and yer companions, I thought *just maybe,* so I collected what I could! Are we really trying again after so long? Are we really doing it for real this time?" The man named McKay bristled with enthusiasm, his thick accent slurring from the excitement.

Kast didn't like any of it one bit.

He had no idea what was going on or what to expect. He looked at the girl again and realized she seemed to resonate with the same thoughts. *Common ground at last!* Though he wasn't sure if it was for good or bad, they would find out, he guessed.

"Open the door, McKay, and have your crew help prepare the float! You'll get an extra week of holiday for this!" Dane didn't even care to speak with his accent. Probably from being so excited himself.

A roar of applause and approval belted from the man named McKay and his men as they moved to the side of the building by the . . . *float?*

In a burst of light, the side of the building opened. Someone had slid a large door open, revealing a special dock on the other side of the wall. The river gurgled by, unaware of the events occurring just above it.

"Wait!" the girl cried out. Her mouth hung open complete, her head hung forward as her hands floated unsure in the air in front of herself, as if trying to grasp something to hold. Kast felt horror crawl up his spine. She was terrified, so he should be, too. *Right?*

"No time, girl!" Dale responded quickly, his smile never diminishing.

"No, no, no! This can't happen! Are you guys *insane?*" She had begun to shriek. Every person in the room stopped and turned their heads toward the girl. Then an absolute outburst of laughter. Kast was really nervous now. She hadn't been this vocal in quite some time, and now they were the humor in some really *strange* joke. Something big, and probably really bad, was happening.

"Absolutely, girl, but with the situation on hand, you need a little insane to get ahead," Dane responded abruptly.

The girl stared, the same look of shock never leaving her face. She faded back for a second as the men picked the float up and gently set it into the river. Kast watched one go to tie a rope to the dock.

"No time!" Dane called out. "You two, it's now or never. Your pack there will most certainly feed the both of you for a week, so grab it and get in!" Kast watched the girl tremble and started to do so himself. He really wished he could fly again. He would fly so far away from this place and never, ever, come back. *Ever.*

"Now!" Dale roared at them.

Kast jerked forward and scooped up the pack. He turned to face the girl, staring into her petrified eyes. She returned the gaze for a second before jumping forward herself.

So be it.

The float that sat on the river was what looked to be a large open *barrel* that was taller than it was long, and it was surrounded by four other smaller barrels. They were all covered in a thick black substance on the outside, but Kast could see that these *barrels* were made of wood. Metal rods, other pieces, and a bit of rope had been used to attach the contraption together to make a fairly sturdy, floating, vehicle on the water.

"This will keep you level on the river, no matter the rapids," Dane spoke quickly, instructing Kast and the girl on what it would do. Kast was lost. He didn't know some of the terms Dane used in his instruction. "Understood? Good!" Dane finished his explanation, not giving a moment for questions. Instead, he shoved them both onto the dock towards the center barrel.

Kast hesitated but seeing the girl do the same he jumped in. He turned to look at her. Her expression was unpleasant. *Right, she has to be closer than she would like to be.* He tried to give her as much room as possible. She gingerly lowered herself beside him.

This was *insane.* And Kast had no idea what *this* was.

"Good deal, you two! Have a great trip. We love hearing about the experience afterward and how to better improve everything!" Dale called out merrily to the two as a man pushed them away from the dock.

The river took them quickly, clipping along at a steady pace. The settlement breezed by quickly, faster than Kast had ever traveled as a human—except maybe when he had fought the bandits attacking the caravan or Vasiss in Harington. *Was he even human then?*

Kast's thoughts could hardly wander due to the command of the racing water that the river held. Of those who were awake in the Logger's Outpost, most stopped what they were doing and gathered around the river to watch, covering the shores and the various bridges built over the river. Looks of incredulity and disbelief littered their faces, but most had nothing but awe and respect displayed.

Kast didn't like this one bit. Especially the part where they weren't given any sort of means to control the float. They were trapped in its confines, controlled by the river. *What on earth or the sky above had let them believe this would be an okay idea?*

What even *was* this idea in the first place? No one had thought to tell either him or the girl the answer to that question.

They reached the far wall of the palisades and the guards saluted to them as Kast and the girl raced past, shock and awe on their faces. Kast tried to ignore their looks and the uncomfortable feeling in his gut.

Kast wasn't sure, but they seemed to be picking up speed. The air whipped by more quickly. It was very cool from the autumn morning. The water, when it splashed against their vessel, was *freezing*. He looked around and noticed that the bank slanted slightly downwards, and the river with it. The water surged violently, the top white and foamy. Kast could see that a wealth of fallen trees and boulders displaced the rivers flow, causing the churning waters, which in turn had caused the occupants of the float to be thrown about viciously. Kast became dizzy from how often the thing spun in the water.

"Dragon!" The girl cried out, her voice rising above the rage of the river, eyes fixed forward.

Kast turned to see what the problem was. He noticed the trees had thinned out considerably and the ground had become heavily populated with craggy rock formations. He could see a gigantic mountain range in the far distance to the north, just peeking through the trees on the riverbank. A large, long, line trailed from the distant mountain and eventually cut across, in front of them.

Oh!

That was what the girl had screamed about.

That stretched line was the edge of the Upper Land. They were right on the edge of The Face now.

They were right on the edge of The Face in a floating barrel charging right for the edge of that colossal cliff.

The fear. Everything suddenly made sense now.

The dragon screamed as waves of terror rolled up his stomach. "What were those *idiots* thinking?"

The girl didn't respond, but rather gripped the edges of the barrel. Her knuckles turned white and her face was pale. They ran into a wave, causing the Float to lurch for a second. Water blasted them, and they became drenched immediately. It was even colder than just being sprinkled by the specks from before.

This was not good. Kast had never measured The Face specifically, but from all of the times he did fly over it, the gargantuan cliff had to be some thousands of feet, and they were headed straight for it.

True terror.

The water roared loudly, interrupting his thoughts. The Float churned, threatening to throw one or both of them out.

This. Was. Insanity.

The trees gave way completely. Kast stared, wide-eyed.

It was *beautiful.*

Clear blue skies stretched from one expanse to the other. He could hardly take it in. This hadn't been anything new to him before, yet it felt like he was witnessing it for the first time ever. He noticed that the girl shivered nearby, from cold or fear he didn't know. The top of the cliff was broken terrain, and the very few patches of rock of any significant size were bare and smooth. Kast turned to look forward.

The edge was closing in fast.

He gripped the sides of the Float.
The clifftop flew by.
Then they were on the edge of the world.

CHAPTER THIRTY-NINE

Charlie sat on his horse. The Logger's Settlement lay before him. He held the reins of his horse tenderly. The events of the past week weighed on him heavily at the moment. His mind wandered restlessly from thought to thought. The horse snorted and stamped impatiently.

He had been driving them hard.

The men were conditioned for this kind of wear, but it was seriously taxing fighting dragons and getting little rest. On top of that, the shock of learning about that monster's existence was quite draining to the men. Particularly since his screaming episode the other day, after the fight at Harrington.

Harrington. It was one mad scramble in a fight that size. As much as he hated that *monster* controlling Lizard Guts, Charlie was appreciative of the specific battle training He had conveyed to them, saving more lives than Charlie thought possible. Honestly, he thought they were all dead the moment he saw what they were up against. And now, that monster kept shoving them face-first into that fire. That *death.* To lose even more men.

Charlie shut his eyes in the memory of those that he had lost. The visions of their gruesome deaths haunted his memory. He opened his eyes at the sound of one of his men behind him speaking to him.

"What are we doing here, boss?" The voice was worn and uncertain. They were conditioned well, but any man would need a break after what these men had been through.

"His orders. He says they're here. We will confirm soon enough. Hold for now and rest while you can, I don't know how much longer this nightmare of a chase will go on for." Charlie was emotionless. Maybe the nerves were singed for good. He felt routine in his motions. He only felt tired and hungry—if that.

Charlie's ears caught the sound of a joyful conversation. *What is joy anymore?* He couldn't help but question what came across as a forlorn and worthless emotion.

"I still don't understand why it will be any different this time around, Dale. You know what happens when the land runs out. Nothing but straight drop."

"I already told you it will all be fine, Dane! Oh, here we are."

Two older men, one missing a leg, appeared at the entrance to the settlement. The one with both his legs did the talking.

"Greetings, foreign travelers! How might we be of service this fine autumn day?" The voice was cheerful. It bugged Charlie for some reason.

"We're looking for two travelers on account of the Queen. A young man and woman." Charlie voiced the words as if they were rehearsed—nothing more, nothing less. "If you have seen them, or are housing them, the Kingdom requires their presence immediately. The man has committed great crimes, and the woman is a hostage of his despicable nature."

"We get lots of travelers, young man . . . ."

Charlie felt his grip tighten on the reigns. Maybe just his irritation was working. He didn't like to be called a *young* man.

"But since the recent tales of attacks on the nearby Harrington, we have shut our gates and walls for the time being to strangers. We have no knowledge of any travelers for near a week now." The man answered resolutely.

Lies.

Charlie clenched his reigns much tighter. His fear still functioned. Maybe that was why he was still alive?

The monster nudged the thought into Charlie's mind, shoving his will into the forefront of Charlie's thoughts. Would there be no peace for anyone? Was this truly the fall of humanity in this land?

Mine.

Charlie's thoughts were interrupted by a forceful impact between him and the old men. The monster appeared out of nowhere and stood amid a small crater, staring into the man, Dane's, eyes. Charlie tried to pry himself away from the horror that was to occur. The unquestionable deaths to ensue. Charlie was frozen in place and his heart raced. It always raced around that monster.

The monster took a step forward and raised a glowing hand. Poised to kill. Charlie could see an aura of purple dancing in front of his eyes.

Then the monster's blackness in Charlie's mind stopped unexpectedly. The unstoppable fiend was completely halted.

Charlie watched from the side. His head turned towards the one-legged man—Dale. The monster's hand dropped and the glowing faded. How long did he stand there, staring? How long before he would slaughter the innocent again?

The presence in his mind turned away. Sharply. Charlie felt a tug on his mind in the same direction. His mouth hung open completely. It was *impossible.*

It was impossible.

How?

The monster walked away. The farther he moved, the more powerful the tug became on Charlie's mind until he couldn't ignore the force anymore.

Regaining control of his hands, he spurred the horse forward.

He looked at the two men, both stood petrified. They should look thankful—Charlie was.

Such a short, strange encounter.

They were the only men Charlie had ever seen live after being confronted by that monster like that.

Something was so wrong, and Charlie didn't understand any bit of it.

How he wished, as he so often did nowadays, that he had a strong drink to burn away his conscience.

To burn away the fact that the monster suddenly began screaming out again. A horrid noise of shattering filled Charlie's ears while the breaking of darkness and confusion and madness filled his mind. Something about those two men had contributed to the further deteriorating of the monster that he was.

With a fleeting thought, the monster left Charlie with a destination to make for and suddenly he disappeared. From mind and reality. Charlie was stunned. *What had happened?*

Charlie could hardly contain the desire to wail unceasingly as Lizard Guts followed his lead.

As he followed that monster's enigmatic direction.

CHAPTER FORTY

A urah stared.
Aurah did nothing but stare.
She couldn't breathe and she couldn't think.

The world before her was absolutely stunning. In the far distance to her left, the mountain peaks seemed more level than ever before. The sky stretched and the blue glowed brilliantly. The sun radiated passionately.

The ground hurled itself away from the dragon and her, carrying the river to the base of the mountains and forever in the other directions.

The ground.

The ground.

She screamed. She couldn't hold in the reaction any longer. The river had thrown them off the side of the cliff, and they hung in the air for a second before the float crashed back on The Face.

She never realized it before, looking at the cliff from a distance, but the edge of The Face had rounded slightly and angled sharply downwards some distance before it really did become the drop she thought they had just gone over. Unlike the stone before, this stone was smooth. Particularly where the river ran wild.

They were now riding the slant, picking up speed with every moment that they traveled. The water had cut into the rock, hollowing out its path, but most of the river gushed over the rounded edge and tumbled chaotically straight for a doom it would never fear.

The float scraped violently against the rock and caught a rough edge where the river cut into the rock.

The float bucked, kicking her out of her seat.

A strong hand grabbed her arm and pulled her back down. She looked at the dragon. A look of terror fell across his face. His chest was pumping uncontrollably. *The beast was terrified of falling!*

How ironic.

Aurah gripped the edge of the barrel and held on. She didn't care anymore how close to the beast she had become. They were going to *die.* What in the world were those crazy old men thinking? Who even thought of doing something like this?

Her face turned back towards the fast approaching ground and the end of the rounded edge. Her hair broke free of its tie and was whipping all around.

The ground!

How would they ever make it out of this?

We won't. Those crazy old men saved themselves and disposed of the trash. No one would ask any questions, and no one would know any different.

Her thoughts barely registered. There was only the rising scream that reached a crescendo in her mind.

Her gut twisted in agony at the sight before them, squelching at the sight of the treetops farther below than she could even comprehend.

Then she saw her deepest terror.

The edge of The Face, the sheer drop, only a short distance ahead of them.

The water fanned out more as the cut in the rock shrank in size, propelling Aurah and the dragon faster still down the incline to their deaths.

This was how she was going to die.

Never mind revenge towards or forgiveness for the monster beside her. Never mind how she would make it home or what to do when she got there. Forget Elizabeth completely. Forget everything.

Elizabeth.

Her thoughts seized at the thought of the young monarch. What kind of trial did she go through at the loss of her most faithful and loving servant? Her sister? Aurah's imagination went wild with the state Elizabeth would be found in when she heard that Aurah's body had been found. *If anything would be left.*

The float lurched viciously again.

This time Aurah was ready and seized the side of the barrel in response holding herself with all the strength she had. She turned her head to see what had happened.

Her mouth fell open.

The dragon had jumped out of the barrel and was fighting their impending deaths. With one hand gripping the float, the other trying to maintain balance and a foot that stomped into the rock to try and slow them down.

The dragon's foot never did more than shatter the surface of the rock. *Nothing more?* Maybe the beast really could shatter the rock and hold them to safety?

The dragon's foot caught a rock and he was ripped away from the barrel in an instant.

Aurah watched with horrified eyes at her only hope falling farther and farther behind the float.

Never mind . . . there was never a chance, anyway.

She slowly turned forward, staring her death in the face. Why hadn't she just given up long ago? There was no point in trying to defy impossible odds. What could she do? She couldn't even exact revenge—or justice, as Elizabeth would probably call it. Aurah couldn't defend herself. She couldn't do anything. She was helpless and dependent. She couldn't even decide if that was bad anymore. After all the stories and talks from Dane and Dale filled with their moralistic nonsense. This is what you get for trusting. *Trusting anything.*

She crouched down, huddling into the faux safety of the float.

Let death come. Let it all end.

Before she could recognize it, the float stopped grinding against The Face. The pit of her stomach dropped as she fell into free fall.

She was in the air now. Every drop of hope was completely gone.

Then an arm wrenched her from the float, clinging to her tightly.

Arms—strong. Safety? What?

She turned her head and saw a magnificent look in the dragon's blazing eyes.

Those once amber gems were white with some unknown fury. The dragon held her in one arm as they plummeted mercilessly to the ground. The wind whipped through his brown hair.

He had ripped her from the float before she had flown too far away from him, and now they *barreled* downwards.

Aurah laughed at her joke. It would have made more sense if they were still in the float and the barrel that was their death sentence. It would have been funnier if they weren't about to die.

The ground looked closer than before—but only slightly. She couldn't tell at this distance. She couldn't tell anything. They fell, tumbling through the air and twisting about. Aurah clutched the dragon's arm, trying to focus only on him and stop the dizziness.

The dragon roared next to her ear. It was loud, but it didn't hurt. It comforted her.

She watched him. Held in his iron grip, she saw the tenacity swirling inside his shining eyes.

Why was he fighting so hard? What could he possibly get from all of this?

Aurah had no power to change anything, so as soon as she felt the fall, she resigned from the struggle because giving up and accepting death would be the simplest answer to all of her problems. So, why did he fight? Why didn't he just give up, too? Why did he have to be stubborn and defy death's decree?

Her heart seized in her chest.

She couldn't understand it.

He was always there. He was fighting so hard. The only reward could possibly be the knowledge of knowing that he returned her, right before his death by her hand.

Why?

"Why?" she screamed. Her pent-up frustrations and her confusions whirled away, caught by the gusts of wind encompassing them. She screamed for so long. Their fall just continued. The beast's efforts seemed menial. Her voice adding to the anxiety of their doom.

Then he spoke.

"We only have a minute or two left, girl!" His teeth gritted tightly together, yet he managed to scream out the words. It was all a meaningless struggle.

"How do you know?" she screamed back. Her throat ached from all the screaming.

"Because I'm a dragon! I know heights! I have a plan, but you better be prepared for death because my plan is hardly anything!" The gusts of wind stole some of his words. She could barely make out what he said. Aurah's heart fluttered in terror as the adrenaline coursed through her veins.

"Of course, I'm ready to die! Are you too stupid to realize where we're at?" Aurah screamed, but she was certain her fading voice collapsed under the pressure of the racing air.

"Dragon!" She called out to him, hoping he would hear. She didn't know what she would say, but she felt like talking in her last moments. And he was the only one around.

She waited a second. He didn't seem to hear.

"Drag..."

He cut her off, yelling over her words. "Thirty seconds!" The water fell in cascades all around them, down The Face.

His reminder of the fall made her notice the world more vividly.

She could begin to make out the treetops. First the tallest ones, then more of the shorter ones. The waterfall collected in a small body of water at the bottom of The Face before running away through the forest in the Lower Kingdom.

The dragon yelled right into her ear. "Hang on to me, girl! I need both of my arms!" She didn't need a second instruction. Instinctively, she clutched her arms around the dragon, burying her face into his neck. She couldn't watch any more. They would hit the water with a violent force, and they would both die. Her thoughts drove her deeper into the dragon.

The falling water thrashed around her as the dragon jerked violently.

She looked up and watched him as he leveled them both out in the air. Now they weren't swirling around in their descent as much, though they still jerked about, despite the dragon's efforts.

"Come on! Work!" He was screaming. The white light in his eyes had dimmed since he had collected her from the float. What was he trying to accomplish?

Then she remembered the strange shroud of light that surrounded him when he faced the dragons in Harrington.

Is he trying to do that thing again?

The dragon threw a punch into the wall as they sped by, to no avail. They bounced off and away from the rock. The ground was racing to meet them, and the beast's screams were growing louder and louder. He leveled out again and dived for the wall, throwing another punch. It was all Aurah could do to hang on through the frantic wrestling.

Nothing.

"Dragon, stop!" She screamed into his ear. "We're done. It's over!" She yelled the resolution. She couldn't believe that it came from her own mouth. Somehow, she had hoped it would end differently, but no more.

The dragon stopped and turned his head. His eyes, now amber, were inches away from her own, and the heat of his breath panted on her face.

She had never been this close to a man before now that she thought about it. *Dragon.* She corrected herself. Why was she thinking about this? She didn't know, she just looked, feeling his warmth for the first time. Why was it comforting?

The monster smiled back at her. A beautiful white smile. Whiter than she was used to seeing in anyone. How had she never noticed? She guessed she really didn't pay attention to the beast. *Why should she have?*

He smiled, then reached up, grabbing her arms.

He was doing something, but she just stared into his eyes. The amber gems were a beacon of solace. *Why?*

He kicked off the wall.

He was powerful. They flew out over the looming water, breaking the descent only slightly.

He twisted her around through the air and made sure she sat above him. The smile never left. He even had a tear in his amber eye. *Why?*

She didn't understand again, but this time for a different reason.

Facing her, his body began to glow the brilliant white that it had back in Harrington. He had summoned that strange power after all.

Dragon. What is he doing?

The white surrounded them.

Then they hit.

363

CHAPTER FORTY-ONE

The water below raged in a maelstrom from the water falling from far above.

Aurah plowed through the surface. Her body writhed in pain.

It was torture, compacting and crushing her.

It was impossible to describe the sensations coursing through every nerve in her body. Her ears screamed at the pain as water flooded her mouth.

The dragon had been ripped away as soon as they hit; the light surrounding her followed him. The throbbing crested its fury through her bones the longer the beast was away.

It was freezing— maybe that was death?

Aurah swirled violently through the dark waters. The momentum blasted her through reality. It seemed as if she moved faster than reality. Somehow, she had disconnected, and the black had slowly seeped inwards towards her heart.

Her lungs seemed to fill up. She didn't have the strength to swim or save herself. She hadn't hit the water well.

Of course, she hadn't hit the water well! Who would, after that fall?

Swim! Her mind screamed. *Futility.*

Which way was up?

Swim! Her thoughts never stopped screaming, but there was no answer to them. She let them rage as the darkness of the world and her hopelessness surrounded her. They were an odd comfort.

More deeply she drifted. Soon, the ice of the water faded away from sensation. She floated.

This was the end.

Dark.

Frigid.

Empty.

Alone.

She would die the way life had desired her to die.

Alone, freezing, angry, hurt—broken with a warmth invading herself.

Wait, warmth?

A warmth encased her frail form, interrupting her thoughts.

Life coursed through her veins again. Her world twisted wildly. She was spinning endlessly through the churning water, but something solid began to steady it. In a rush she saw a light above her, racing with the vigor of life. Was it what came after death? What was it?

The water broke, bellowing out its ire at the soul stolen from its clutches.

Chilled air pelted against her soaked face. An arm surrounded her while another flailed without coordination.

It was the dragon.

How?

She hung limp in his arm. Dragged through the water gracelessly, she could offer nothing to help. *Sorry . . . I guess.*

She watched the dragon as warmth permeated her mind, restoring her thought bit by bit. She recognized the beast's struggle.

He had never swum before.

It must have been a miracle he pulled her above the surface before she, or even he, had drowned.

What was she thinking? She questioned herself forcefully.

Can I even think? She couldn't feel her body. She could hardly feel his warmth. The air filled her mouth, but it wouldn't go any farther. She wasn't breathing. Like sharp needles and pinpricks, the warmth that was restored fought against the frigid bite of death. The depths of the water still clung to her, fighting to claim her life.

But the dragon waged war against the water, beating out a brilliant battle march.

Why? What could he do?

She hit something solid and with a lot of force. The dragon had thrown her onto land and fought to follow behind closely.

She heaved, coughing frantically. The shore was littered with large rocks, but she couldn't see any more than that. Her chest screamed in agony as her body convulsed, forcing the liquid death out. The dragon climbed ashore near her. *How is it possible? He hit harder than me!*

He started laughing.

Laughing.

He was laughing!

She couldn't hold it in either.

This is ridiculous!

They just plummeted what was probably thousands of feet.

And they had survived.

Survived.

She laughed with him, their voices rising in a beautiful chorus, creating a soulful harmony. The voices drove the sword of hope through the heart of death.

Her laughter broke at times as she coughed. More water expelled from her lungs.

Laughter.

She sat up on the rugged ground, leaning against a larger rock. She looked at the dragon. He had already turned to sit the same way on another rock, facing her.

Laughter.

They both shook with the insanity of it all, laughing horrendously. She didn't comprehend any of it and doubted he did, either. They sat there gasping for breath and spewed it back out just as fast.

Laughter.

Her gaze drifted and met his.

Laughter.

She stared into the deep amber.

Laughter.

Then brokenness.

The beast's laughter caught and turned to desperate inhaling.

Struggle.

Aurah's chest clutched. Death was gone, but terror jumped in and dug its claws deep to rip out her heart.

Panic.

Her breath caught as she watched the incredulous look dissipate from the dragon's face. The color drained from his countenance and his mouth struggled to rest. His eyes widened, gripped by whatever horror they beheld.

Weeping.

Aurah covered her mouth and tried to move backward, still breathing heavily. Panic shattered her.

The dragon fell forward and held his head in his hands. His body rocked as sobs released and filled the air.

Wailing.

Aurah stumbled, shoving herself away with her clumsy feet, from the beast and the terror pouring forth from him. What would he do? Her hands covered her trembling mouth.

A tear fell across her cheek, and her throat knotted up; her emotion berated by the dragon's broken agony.

Why am I crying? I don't care about this wretch! This is all his own fault! I hate him! Why did I ever save his sorry hide? I don't need him! I would rather die than need him! This blasted beast ruined everything! I hate him! I hate... Him?

Right?

Aurah clung to a rock, gripped by the mass of hate and confusion. But her resistance was weakening. *How dare she feel for the beast?* The pain of the deepest sorrow swam freely in her broken heart as she faced the darkest night ever—darker than any would ever understand. She hated him! Why did he always have to save her? Why did he end up here, weeping before her? Tears had begun to fall freely from her eyes.

The old world was coming to a desperate end. Every ounce of normalcy was shattered, and a new creation was rising from its grave.

What was this newness?

The dragon fell prostrate before her, lying awkwardly on the broken ground of stone and chunks of wood. "I . . . I . . . I'm sorry!" The beast dove into humility.

Humiliation?

His voice raised to the heavens above, piercing the still sky into a thousand pieces. His screams resounded with his sorrows and woes.

"I, I can't be sorry, though! I can't apologize for the crimes I have committed. I can't be right! I can't! I can't!" Aurah was broken by his brokenness. She was shattered as he was shattered.

Why!

More than a question, the word voiced her every angst and heartache. The giants she faced couldn't be understood. There could be no reconciliation. Yet, why did she *feel* for the mongrel? Why couldn't she just condemn him? He had no part in her world.

Right?

There had been chance and opportunity, one right after another, to separate from the beast. Why, then, was she still here? Why couldn't she just end it?

"I, I know the weight of my actions." The dragon struggled fiercely to speak as he looked up from the ground. Tears soaked

his face even more than the water did. Aurah sat, dismayed at
the turbulence flowing from him. It was more than she could
bear, yet she couldn't move, petrified by the scene before her.
"The weight of my actions shouldn't be forgiven, nor . . . n, n,
nor would I ask you to!" A new bout of weeping interrupted
his talk. He lay with his head down again, speaking to the
rocks and the world below. "I, I can't make sense of what I'm
supposed to do! I don't know why I am still alive. I don't know
why I'm like this. I don't understand! But, but I want to make
this . . . this good again. I want to pay for my crimes. Girl!
I'm broken in innumerable pieces. The only way out is death,
and I can't even do that!"

He was finished, interrupted by tears that poured stronger than the falls nearby. Aurah was appalled at the display
before her. The weeping and the water falling off the edge of
the world rang out.

Her stomach caught in her throat. She couldn't make sense,
either. It was like the only option available for either of them
was the option that neither of them could accept. There was
nothing else but their hate and confusion and misery.

Aurah could never restore her world to the way it was
before if this beast existed within it—but she could never
restore her world at all if this beast didn't exist within it.

Hers was nothing but a life now doomed to this existence.

But . . . .

What if?

It was insanity.

It made no sense.

It made her cringe. She choked on the very thought of it.

What if the only way out would never make sense? *Then
how in all of existence are we supposed to escape from the lunacy
life has handed us?*

Her thoughts raged. Her teeth gritted in frustration. It
wasn't fair! It was like being tied with chains and locked in
place, yet still being expected to win some twisted race.

No.

What if... What if I just did it? What if it happened just because? Maybe I'll never understand? What else do I have. . . .?

What else did she have?

What else?

"Dragon." Her voice choked and caught. *Was she sure?* Her throat and voice tightened and were unrelenting. It was hard to breathe and not because of the water still in her body. "Drag . . . ." She wept, her precious tears falling in waves. Her hair fell uncouth. Now she was wailing.

Blasted beast—I hate you!

"I . . . I can't do this without you!"

There.

She said it.

Those words held such a mighty weight.

She gave in, forfeiting resistance.

The power crushed her spirit to the ground. "I need your help! I need you! I'm sorry! I'm sorry! Sobs stole her speech for a moment "I'm . . . I'm sorry!"

What was she sorry for? She didn't understand. She didn't understand anything, though she did know one thing—the more she admitted her dire position, the more she felt the tension roll off her and the more she felt its power weakening.

She kept rambling. Words fell like the water from far, far above. Her heart released its horde of grief and ache with every mutter.

She let go.

She let it all go.

What was this?

Why was this the thing that helped?

She didn't know. She didn't care. Maybe she would understand someday the reality of letting this . . . *hatred* go, but now . . . .

She hated herself more than anything now, caught between the disgusting tension of overlooking the dragon's actions or hating him forever for it.

Would she ever be alright?

She had begun to hope so. For once, the situation had changed. Letting go of every ounce of hate—even if for a second—allowed her to breathe again.

A hand touched her hand.

She reeled backward, the sobbing shearing off, leaving only the noise of their gasping and the splattering of water to fill the silence. Aurah gaped at the beast's hand that had touched hers. His tears had quelled their flow, but the emotion still reigned in his face.

He reached out again—more slowly. It was revolting. It was all she could do to hold still enough. His hand came closer and she pulled back. The weeks, the days, the hours, the minutes, *the seconds,* of harm this monster caused her welled back up.

She almost grabbed one of the many rocks and repeated that wonderful action from so long ago.

No.

No, that wasn't good. Maybe it was right, but somehow good and right didn't work together this time around.

But she did decide to not be some prey, some helpless person in all of this.

If she didn't have the strength to fix things and put them back the way they had been, then she would offer forgiveness.

If the beast was desiring to right his wrongs—truly—she couldn't deny the belief that he truly did, then she would offer forgiveness.

If she was understanding that hating this monster forever would only hurt herself, then she would offer her forgiveness without it being pursued.

Aurah had no idea what to make of her emotions, her feelings, or her actions. She didn't know if she would ever understand or believe the conclusions that seemed to dawn on her mind.

But she did hold out her hand as the monster gently took it into his.

Her soft, puffy eyes stared in his.

"Girl, I'm so sorry. I'm so sorry in ways I don't even realize yet and can't express. My heart's grief is genuine . . . but I'll let you be the judge of that. I'm sorry you're in the worst place of your life because of me. I'm sorry for the pain and the misery and the fears and the darkness that you have had to face because of me. I don't deserve forgiveness, and maybe that isn't what I'm asking for, but I would like to make things . . . *right*—and not for myself or to switch or whatever stupid nonsense poured from my wicked mouth before."

"I want to make things right because things *need* to be right. Because you need help to be restored to what is right. I'm sorry I ripped you away. Please let me return you as best as I can—at the cost of my own life even." His eyes darted around, barely able to bear the weight of her gaze, but he did manage to look her in the eyes.

He did stand accountable.

She squeezed his hand gently; somehow, that wasn't as unpleasant an action as she thought it would be. She fought the knot in her throat, never taking her eyes, nor her hand from his.

"I hate you, dragon. I want to kill you. I don't know how you'll ever make things right, but I'm willing to try. I haven't had a moment's peace while holding that blasted anger in, and I'm tired. I'm so worn, dragon. I don't understand my own actions or my own way, but I'll trust you enough to return me." Aurah laughed, her eyes rolling before she looked up at The Face and the waterfall they just rode down. "That may just be the only way you'll die, anyway."

He laughed with her. "After every close call already, I doubt it." His face cracked a grin and smiled at her—something she found herself returning. It had been so *long* since she last smiled. It felt like a bridge for tension to leave her encumbered shoulders. "I think we have earned ourselves a short break. How you managed to hang onto that bag, I'll never know, but I'm glad you did. Let's see what food we have."

Aurah started, shocked by the bag on her back. She hadn't realized its existence. She was glad to have been some sort of help.

"Come, girl, let's go try and make a fire and hope we don't attract any Savages just yet."

She laughed. "Just yet, dragon?"

"Or ever again, I hate those blighters more than you could imagine." They shared a short laugh together. *It felt so good to laugh.*

"Dragon?" Her voice called out softly.

"Girl?"

"My name is Aurah."

The last piece to her puzzle. The one thing she had left.

The one thing she had once decided never to give away to this beast.

He smiled brightly at her, his white teeth crowning his beaming face.

"Thank you." The words fell kindly from his tongue. "Um, my name is Kast."

Aurah couldn't help but return the beast's smile.

She tried to stand but found that her body struggled. Kast rose quickly, their hands still together for the moment, and he helped her to her feet.

Kast supported her weight as they walked the short distance to the forest edge to make camp for the night.

Leaving behind the greatest challenge either of them had ever faced.

CHAPTER FORTY-TWO

Aurah walked in silence beside Kast. The road lay stretched out before them.

They always piqued her thoughts—these long stretches. It was almost like a game that she would play to pass the time. Without disruptions in the road, Aurah could compare her stride to dragon's better, count how many steps it took for her to match his one, and see if there was any regularity or recurring pattern. Or, she often found herself trying to count how many tunes she could hum before the next bend.

But the road, more often than not, was not straight. It curved up and down and side to side through the hilly forest, dodging obstacles and the occasional piles of stone. Her feet crunched on leaves and other dead matter from the forest.

Aurah guessed that travel had become a scarce commodity with all the dragon attacks happening on top of the already present threat of roving bandits. Her thoughts stopped for a moment, pulling her back to reality. Turning her head, she looked at her companion.

He was the dragon that had caused all of this.

All the death and brokenness. The Kingdom was alright at dealing with bandits, but dragons—that was another story. Kast walked slightly ahead of her—the result of his longer stride and the extra steps Aurah had counted that it took to keep up with him. His head faced forward. He was extremely determined. In retrospect, she could see that facet in all his actions from before. This time, though, he was proving his determination to return her home. It was still early morning. They had left their camp about an hour earlier, neither one of them certain which direction they were headed, although they both knew to head away from The Face.

They had spent the previous evening mostly resting. It was a bit rough at first with wet supplies and wet food, but they soon were huddled around a warm fire. The food was much appreciated, even though it wasn't very appetizing.

They were slow to make conversation. The emotion and adrenaline of the fall had begun to wear off, and though her decision to work with Kast was still solid, she found herself reeling from the opening in communication. What did one say in her position? He did most of the talking, anyway. Kast seemed to especially like the conversation and had the most to say. She didn't mind at all. It was good to talk with some-one, and a dragon turned human had provided a wide range of interesting topics.

His voice called through the air and interrupted her thoughts.

"Do you mind if I ask what you are thinking about?" Kast had turned his head and was looking right at her. He had caught her staring off into space. He smiled as the realization crawled across her face. Aurah turned her head with a slight blush. She stared forward at the gradual hill they were climbing.

"I was just thinking about how extreme and odd all of this is." She let her hands trail out the sides to accent her statement. "It isn't usual that one has a conversation with a dragon, you know." Her breathing became slightly heavier from walking up the hill.

"You seem to be handling it well for a human, though."

"Well, I think I had some time to get used to it. I do remember a certain time when I introduced your face to a rock." Aurah's wit was still sharp, finally unsheathed after so long. Kast grimaced in remembrance.

"Yeah. Welcome to being a weak and frail human! It's going to be great!" His voice raised in volume. "Smash!" His hand balled into a fist and hit the open palm of his other. "So great." His voice faded out. Aurah looked over, and his eyes seemed distant.

"What do you really think since . . . ." She struggled to describe his change. "Since the transformation?" His dark eyebrows perked up—they were so filled with life and energy. Whether he knew it or not, he said a lot through his expressions. Especially expressions using his brows. He turned his head to face her.

"I think..." He muttered to himself for a second. "I think it's hard to put it in the right words. I think I was lost and despairing, and..." His gaze grew distant again. "I don't know. I just can't seem to be satisfied with what has happened—even though I know that there has been good in it. If it hadn't happened, I would be . . . ." His voice cut off more sharply than before. She had some idea what he was going to say. Though they were hard thoughts to think—she swallowed roughly.

"Why did you do it?"

Her voice seemed hollow, trespassing on forbidden ground, imposing into the deepest secrets of the creature beside her. She wanted to know, and if she was honest with herself, she felt almost entitled to know.

"What do you know about dragons, Aurah?" His voice had become factual. His body tensed, and he walked much more rigidly than before.

"Not a lot. I once did a little research with what resources we had—which wasn't much. It described that dragons were brown and vary in size. The rest, however, didn't seem much more realistic than fairy tales."

"Like what?"

"Like it said that some dragons are peaceful, and others are the most destructive forces known to exist. It did mention incorrectly that all dragons are brown, and from what I have seen, that isn't true. Multiple shades of course, but that black dragon—that monster—he didn't fit. The book I read really only held ideas and vague uncertainties more than anything." She trailed off. How much of it all could she really have trusted?

"Would you like me to explain the reality behind our existence, Aurah?" Kast's question sounded forlorn and heavy, but curiosity drove her to knowledge.

"Please." She asked quickly but remember her manners. "That is—if you want. I don't want to push you into misery." She looked thoughtful. "At least right now." A smile broke out on Kast's face.

"I would love to tell the tale of dragons, but it isn't much of a story. It's really simple and only gets complicated based on which dragon is involved." His brow furrowed serious again. "The first, and main thing, you need to know about every dragon is that they—we—are each born with a unique purpose for our lives. There are rumors and myths in the dragon realm, just like with humans, but generally, there are some popular beliefs that seem to be true. The first is that a dragon's size is based on his purpose. The larger the purpose, the larger the dragon."

Aurah stared forward, memories flooding her mind. The dragons. The big and little one that interrupted Kast's attack on the Capital. The varying sizes of all the dragons she had seen. She shuddered violently at the thought of the black beast. *That monster's purpose must be something incredible!* She stopped walking suddenly. She turned her head towards the dragon beside her.

He was only a little smaller than that black beast!

Her mouth gaped open as she stared at him. *What is his purpose?*

"I see your memory is somewhat good." Kast stopped with her and smiled. His beaming shattered the gloom. "My purpose had a lot of importance behind it, though I never really understood it."

Aurah stared for a second before walking again.

"What do you mean you didn't understand it? You didn't understand why your purpose was so important or . . . ." She stopped walking again. Shock coursed through her body as she turned to see Kast looking in her eyes. Dread haunted those amber gems. "You don't know what your purpose is!" The statement seemed incredibly spurious. He had to have had a reason for ending the lives of so many people. It couldn't have been for nothing at all. She watched his posture slunk down, forcing out a sigh, as his hand rubbed his face. "How could you?" Every wrong she was overlooking, it seemed so much worse if it all was senseless. Without a reason. Everything she was forgiving—could she forgive something like this? *Like him?*

"The dragon who is bigger than me, the one you referred to as black—he isn't black. He is one of the deepest shades of brow—."

"I don't care what color that monster is!" she screamed. Why did emotion well up like this? She couldn't wrap her mind around what he just said, that he didn't understand his purpose. *What does color have to do with how vile you are? It's because he really is a monster. A monster that wanted to trick her!*

"He's that color because he's insane!" Kast yelled over her words.

Aurah shut her mouth at the force of his voice. She stepped backward, afraid of him. She watched him shake with anger. Danger lurked in the amber of his eyes as he stared wildly at her.

"All dragons *are* brown, but their shade is determined by their sanity or lack thereof! If you remember so well, you'll remember just how dark I was! How deep the brown ran through my scales!" Kast closed his eyes and turned away. He seemed unsure what to do with himself but ended up leaning on a nearby tree and covered his face with his hand.

What does he mean by insanity?

He was gripped by insanity. *Isn't that the same as everyone else, though?*

She looked at him. He was grieving over something that was *fresh.*

He was broken, too.

She really couldn't handle the yelling, but maybe he needed to yell. Aurah knew she had a few things she wanted to yell about herself. Reaching out her hand, she felt the strange urge to go and comfort the wretch. She withdrew her hand and stood to look at him. Kast looked away from the tree towards her, his face stained with his tears.

"I'm sorry, Aurah. I didn't mean to shout. It was such a dark place to be, I can't even imagine it the way I am right now. I can't remember the folly of my thoughts or the depression of my mind, but I know it was bad. Sometimes…things— things were clearer than others. When I was consumed with the folly of my mind, with the insanity, I was apathetic. When whatever clarity did come, I hated myself; though maybe not enough, because I always gave back into the urges of my darkness. I. . . . I can't come to grips with my thoughts or actions. I can't see clearly about that time, but I know now that it wasn't good. I'm sorry." He turned back away, wiping his eyes vigorously.

"Why do dragons seem to go insane like that, Kast?" The words fell out from her mouth tenderly. She didn't like how fragile this whole companionship thing was, but she figured she could try to work through some things. *Maybe.*

Kast walked back towards her as he finished wiping the tears off his face.

"When a dragon doesn't fulfill their purpose, they slowly drift into insanity. Most dragons take their own life if they don't foresee their purpose being answered before their insanity consumes them. Pride, I guess." He scoffed. "It's worse for the bigger dragons, too. The bigger one's purpose is, the faster insanity seems to take them." Kast clenched his jaw. "I held out for so long, longer than I should have. I was so close to my own death. The darkness of mind held me captive and I couldn't think straight. I reacted in my insanity because it was all I knew."

Aurah stared at him, her face empty. The answers seemed to flow freely now. His words seemed true, and that truth was that he was weak and tossed about by the forces of his own mind and desires. It all started to make sense, though it didn't make things any more tolerable. She still held him accountable for his actions. *But maybe this will help?* Her conscience offered her a line of hope.

"What is your purpose, Kast? How does a dragon *know* his purpose?" He had answered many questions, but he created many, too.

"A dragon always has a general idea of their purpose. It's the thing that fills their thoughts the most. As they mature, they begin having dreams that symbolize more deeply their purpose. A dragon must meditate and work out their purpose and then pursue it. A dragon who is fulfilling his purpose witnesses the unhindered clarity of dragons." He stopped, pausing mid-thought, his face creased for a moment before releasing. "A dragon who doesn't fulfill their purpose witnesses the misery and darkening of their mind. I always had trouble deciphering my dreams and thoughts, but I knew it involved a *maiden* somehow." He paused between words, laboring to bring his thoughts forth. "I was to protect, or horde, or possess, or serve one in some fashion, but beyond that, I have no idea. I didn't even know what maiden! There is so much agony in this for me—in not knowing. It crushes me and leaves me in pieces that I can't put back together."

He sighed deeply again. He seemed burdened. His body slouched and breathed deeply quite a few times. Aurah watched him closely for a little while more.

"I'm sorry for your pain, drag—Kast. I don't mean to be careless at your hurt, but I don't know how to process it for myself right now. I . . . I decided that I wouldn't hold your past against you, at least for now. Please, I may not fully understand, but I am trying to believe." She felt confident in her words, though she wasn't confident in the slightest about what was to come.

Kast faced the road again started walking forward, Aurah turned and followed. He tilted his head in her direction.

"It feels good to share that. I don't know enough about myself at the moment, but I'm glad you're aware. I really do want to return you home. For some unknown reason, that much is clear, and I'm sure that's what needs to happen. That is if you're still willing to bear with me." A small and tender smile cracked the placid stone of his face.

"Thank you." She couldn't fathom what else to say. Maybe she didn't need to say anything else? Maybe things would work out just by sharing?

Maybe.

CHAPTER FORTY-THREE

Time passed by rather quickly for Kast and Aurah. They spent a few periods in silence, but the questions about each other's past lives were endless, and they filled their moments walking on the road with conversation. It had been two days since their fall down The Face. Kast shuddered at the thought of it. He found himself trying desperately to stretch out his wings every time he thought of the memory. Humans had a much different response to heights than dragons. He couldn't help but be afraid as a mere man, but as a dragon, he could precisely calculate the distance to the ground and how much time he had until he would hit. His thoughts carried him away in his remembrance of flying. He would always miss the feeling of the air supporting his mighty wings.

"Here." The girl handed him something.

Moldy bread for breakfast again. They had tried to dry it out as much as possible, but the result was that their food decayed rapidly.

"I really miss the meal we had at the Logger's Outpost!" He whined loudly—a habit that he had soon developed as a farce. The girl's demeanor was lighthearted, and it bled over into Kast.

"That's the last of our food, so be thankful for now—and hope that we can find some more soon. I'm not sure what in nature will kill us and what won't when we eat it." She turned her head and started fumbling with the bag.

"Oh! So, you're not all-knowing, after all?" Kast jested with her. He found out quickly that her wit was not to be underestimated. She had once attributed it to a certain man named Morris Baker. *A man I certainly have displaced from normalcy . . . .* Kast shook his head and wrestled against the surmounting accusations against himself. He blamed himself a lot now. It was hard to accept responsibility for something so heavy and still move forward.

"I know more than you, dragon." She didn't look up from the bag, almost finished taking care of what little supplies they did have. *But no food.* Kast grimaced. He didn't like not knowing where his next meal was. As a dragon, he could just go and hunt whenever he was hungry, but now . . . .

"Do have any guesses about where we are or how much longer we have to go, Aurah?" He looked down the path they were traveling. The trip had gone much better than both expected. *No bandits. No Savages... Yet. Best it stays like that.* He looked at his hands. He didn't understand the power that had surged through him before. He hadn't ever heard of something like that in a dragon. It was just another question he wouldn't ever have answered.

"No, sorry. I know what a rough map of the Lower Land looks like, but I'm not sure exactly where we are. Judging from the general direction the sun has been moving, we have been heading southeast by some margin. The Capital is more east then south, though, so I don't know what road this is or where it's going." She scrunched up her face.

He had no idea either. The world made much more sense from the sky. Kast felt an overwhelming fear from the uncertainty, and he looked at the girl again, his face set with understanding and determination.

"Well, let's keep going, and maybe things will work out. The world is bigger as a human, but it still isn't so big that we won't find something before long." He wasn't sure of his words, but he had to have some hope. *She needs some hope.* He was amazed at how much his thoughts began to focus on her. This whole journey was for her. Maybe it was his way of paying for his wrong? *No, I'm certain that's what I want to think, but it's not as simple as that.* His choice wasn't just a means of accounting for his actions. He genuinely wanted the best for her. Aurah looked at him and nodded. Her gaze seemed to drift through him. He wasn't sure, but it looked as though she appreciated his consoling her. Her mouth held the hints of joy in their corners, and her eyes grew less dull, being filled with life with every second.

How could I ever have done what I did? How was I able to hurt such a precious creature?

Kast's thoughts contradicted every one of the selfish actions in his insanity. It didn't take much, but the more he saw who this girl was, the more appalled he became at himself. It was more of a burden for which he had no idea how to atone.

Stand strong, Kast.

He smiled back at her, strengthened by some voice inside. Some voice calling him away from where he had been. Calling him to the Capital.

From the west to the east.

To her.

He turned, breaking sight. They did need to keep moving. Aside from the constant threat of bandits and Savages and whatever else lurked in the world, he needed to get her ahead of the cloaked man. Kast still had no idea how or why The Cloak had tracked them all this way.

The hair on Kast's arms and neck stood on end.

And that monster. He tried his best not to think of the Insane King. The girl closed in near his side and interrupted his fears.

"So, what is a dragon family like, Kast? How were you born and raised?" Her voice was simple but curious. There was a lot to talk about. He wanted to know about humans, and she wanted to know about dragons. He smiled in relief.

The girl's question was the start of a conversation spanning a few hours. It was impressive the amount they could talk.

It was impressive how much they both were willing to talk. Despite all that had happened, Kast guessed both of them were the same kind of lost and confused, and instead of blaming and hating each other, they helped each other out of the same pit.

He was still certain, though, that didn't mean either of them was completely comfortable around the other. Even if a hole seemed filled, it couldn't just be patched, like that. It was waiting to swallow either one of them into its depths and break their spirit once again. Waiting to break their tender trust.

They finally ended talking after some time, content just to walk. She handed him what she called a flask. It was full of water. That was something both humans and dragons had in common. They needed water. They had found a fresh stream along the way, thankfully, and filled up the container. He told her then he didn't think he would ever need to drink water again after the trip over the falls. She told him it was because he stunk, not because he needed to drink it. He proceeded to dunk her in the stream and said the smell was gone now.

He realized his mistake fairly quickly and made a mental note that pranks leading to an ongoing discomfort s were less ideal than others. She stayed quiet immediately after, and he fretted desperately. That is, until she tripped him into the water. They both laughed and spent the next hour or so sopping wet.

This really had to be best for both of them at the moment. So much darkness had consumed them for weeks on end, and it was time to shatter that barrier of grief and move on.

"So, I think I understood what you had said before, about breathing fire, but . . . ." The girl struggled to straighten her thoughts. "...but how does water make fire again?" She took back the flask.

Yes, humans weren't exactly situated well to control the elements of nature just yet. They didn't understand a lot of things. "Water is made of *something* that when also mixed with the air from my lungs makes another *something* that burns very powerfully." He did his best to simplify the terms. He had tried once to broach the topic of a dragon's anatomy with her and explained what part of a dragon separated the various gases of water to make a compound for burning. It took a little while before the girl's mind stopped reeling. He refrained from introducing too many new concepts to her at once.

"Huh. That's strange. I always thought of water as just water." This time around, her thoughts were less strict and more nonchalant. That would probably be the best approach for a human to take to understand some of the more advanced concepts of the elements.

Dragons were by no means the most knowledgeable of creatures, but they were wise and intelligent. Many had spent time studying veiled concepts and understanding the more detailed points of nature.

"Everything around us in the world is one or more of the basic elements alone or joined together. There are some who believe that fire, earth, air, and water are the only foundational elements that comprise everything around us, but from what I have heard, I disagree. I believe that there are a lot of unique and specific elements out there that somehow interact with each other, and that's what makes up everything around us."

Aurah's face twisted in contemplation. The idea of seeing the unseen was always a difficult one to master—for both dragons and humans. "I think the more you talk about it, the more I begin to understand, though it still challenges everything I assume about life, knowing there are so many unknown and undiscovered details out there."

Kast nodded. There being unknown parts to life was bound to be certain. *Always.* He looked around, taking in all of life. The sky was slightly overcast today, but the sun still broke through the clouds. Light filtered through the trees which were steadily become scarcer.

"Wait!" His sudden cry jolted the girl beside him. Aurah stood tensed and ready for danger. Fear rested on her face.

"What is it?" She cried back. She was still on edge, the condition of the past few weeks leaving deep scars and habits.

"The trees, Aurah! The trees! Come on, let's go!" He jumped forward, running towards what he had hoped was nearby. The girl took a second longer than him to start moving, but she soon caught up and matched his pace.

"Kast, what is it?" she cried out, panting.

"The trees are thinning! The forest is ending!" His feet carried him more quickly.

Soon the solid wall of trees began to glow, the darkness grew lighter and lighter. The front was breaking. Empty existed beyond. The road curved slightly, but for the most part, it began to straighten out. Soon it aimed straight at the brightness to come. The distance between trees grew so that the normal became an open ground. With the lack of trees, the ground harbored more ferns and other sun dependent foliage.

The girl overtook Kast, letting loose and sprinting with all she had. Kast laughed. The promise of newness to their situation didn't necessarily mean answers, but it did mean new, and new brought hope. He began to sprint, as well, and overtook the girl. They raced the short distance to the edge of the forest.

Plains.

And these plains weren't small either. They were the same plains that the Capital would be located on, however far away.

"Kast, look!" Aurah pointed to a shape in the distance. It was a city. "There is hope! This is hope!" She looked at him, her smile reaching into her eyes.

"There is, isn't there?" He laughed. "Well let's go and see if they can help." He made to move forward, but her hand gripped his arm. It was a startling motion, contrasting with mere seconds before. "Aurah?" The girl's mouth opened, but then closed immediately before opening again. She inhaled and released her breath slowly.

"What happens when we get there? We are close enough to the Capital that I'm sure a guard could easily escort me home. What about you?"

"I . . . ." Kast stopped as realization filled him. "Hmm, I hadn't thought this far ahead yet." A moment of silence fell between the two. Kast stared, scowling at the ground. So many thoughts raged, taking his mind every direction at once. Reaching up, Kast rubbed his brow and sighed as he often did. "My decision remains the same, Aurah. I promised to take you home. Maybe if I can make sure you are handed off to someone who is able to get you there, then I will. Let's get to this city first, though, and see what happens." He smiled at her, but she looked down and turned away from him towards the city—her hand sliding slowly off his arm.

She looked back at him and nodded with slight hesitance. "Thank you."

An hour passed quickly in silence. The walls of the city loomed larger as they traversed the plains.

Anticipation grew in Kast at what was to happen at the city, but something was wrong.

Kast couldn't place it. But the feeling swelled the closer to the walls they had gotten. He threw his hand out to block Aurah from taking another step as if another step would put them in the worst of perils.

The hair on the back of his neck stood on end. Kast did not like what he was feeling.

Something was desperately wrong.

And familiar?

Aurah gasped.

"Kast . . . this place, this city . . . ."

Please, don't say it. Pangs of regret surged through him. Nothing was left untouched. *Please no.*

"It's, it's been destroyed. It's Avante." Her voice had grown muted and quiet.

There was no denying reality. They both knew what had happened to the city.

He squeezed his eyes shut and covered his face with his hands.

No. I'm sorry, I'm so sorry. I didn't mean . . . .

"No. No. No. No!" He heard a voice cry out. *It was his own.* It was the worst feeling he could ever feel. Was he truly prepared to face the consequences of his actions? He couldn't breathe. His lungs, they stopped and gave out on him. Short gasping heaves rocked his frame.

But an arm wrapped around his waist.

Why was there such kindness to a monstrosity like him? How could anyone forgive the crimes he had committed?

The arm pulled him forward towards the gates.

"No!" He resisted.

"You need to." No emotion, just a pragmatic and rational tone flew from her lips.

He was a fiend. He was sick and cruel. He was a monster that deserved the worst death possible. There was no way he could ever be right. There was no way to atone.

"Come on." The voice lulled him forward the short distance to the gates, beyond the stone walls.

So much stone and most of it was probably hauled here through many painstaking years of labor.

And I destroyed it.

Visions and recollections flashed across his sights.

Burning.

Crying.

Dread and agony.

The unspeakable truth of the end sinking deeper and deeper into his victims by the moment.

The helpless thrashing and struggling toward life that now completely eluded them.

The screams of maidens

The wails of the young.

He had enjoyed every second of it.

"Stop!" He shrieked, gripping the sides of his head. "Stop! Stop it! I'm so sorry!" He dropped to his knees, clenching his face. "Please, stop!" His weeping filled the dead silence of the world around them.

Avante once again was filled with a mighty dragon's roar.

Every ounce of pain, and heartbreak, of fear and terror—

—all of it flooded his existence, turning to tears and pouring from his eyes.

How long did the dragon weep?

No longer.

Kast raised his fist and hit the ground.

"Stop!" Kast screamed out his pathetic plea as if his voice could ward away the welling guilt. He clutched at the earth as if trying to anchor himself and keep from floating away.

The world hated him.

He hated himself.

There was no place for him anymore.

How could he answer for this? For feeding the earth at first with torrents of blood and then trying to wash it clean with rivulets of tears.

A tender arm draped over his shoulders.

Why?

His mind screamed at the searing touch.

"I am convinced of your repentance, beast." The voice trembled. *As it should tremble. Look at the monster before it!* "But . . . but I learned something recently."

Kast's sobbing spluttered. *How could he?* What had he stolen from the world? What atrocity he had committed! Could he even grasp it truly? His weeping intensified.

"Kast, I learned to remember the story of a scar always, but never to forsake the actions of the present. Please, understand that much. Please…"

Kast poured out his emotion. He had never understood a thing. He had never counted the cost of his actions. His heart was shattered, even more than he could have ever imagined possible. The countless lives that were quelled by his wretched grip.

"Kast." The voice was firmer this time. "You were a monster, and if you wish to remain one, then I encourage you to wallow in your despair and die." Aurah stood, wiping tears from her own eyes. "But if you want to do whatever you can to move forward, then I encourage you to stand and bear the weight of your actions. Because . . . ." Her voice quaked. What emotion was she feeling? He could only see the black of the ground that his face wept into. "Because I know you're a mighty dragon! And I know you can endure what is set before you, even if it is impossible and so terribly wrong. Even if you do deserve to die the worst way possible! I know you will still fulfill your purpose, and I know you will stand taller than any dragon ever could have stood." Her voice rose to a gentle yell, spurring him forward. She covered her mouth with the back of her hand. Her eyes widened in response to her words.

He was shocked too.

What is wrong with this girl?

Enduring the wrath and hate, and depravity of his broken mind, then forgiving him and now encouraging him.

Life coursed through him, though.

He hated it, but he thrived from it.

Power filled his bones.

He could stand again.

The weight inside intensified at his resistance, but he stood, nevertheless. Understanding the way was meaningless.

He must stand.

He would stand.

"Thanks, girl." He wiped his tears with the back of his arm. "I don't know how to proccss any of this, but I'm going

to get you home, and then I'll fret over how to make amends."
He sighed and scrubbed his face with his hands.

"Yeah, sure." Her voice sounded uncertain, as well. The
weight of his actions had to rest on her, too. Did she really
think so much of him now? She should change her mind
about her forgiveness and make him stand accountable for
his actions. That's what he really deserved. Aurah walked
forward towards the middle of the destroyed city. "What are
the chances of a storehouse or other food source still being
intact?" An honest question, but it still hurt. He was at least
glad for a change in topic.

For forward motion.

"What's a storehouse?" Kast asked innocently.

"A place where a merchant or someone else kept food and
other supplies," Aurah explained quietly.

"It would be worth looking for. I . . . ." He stood then
seized from talking about his actions in the past. "I wasn't very
thorough in my insa . . . back then . . . ." His voice trailed
off. He couldn't just blame everything on his insanity. This
was his fault. He needed to bear the weight of his wrongs.

"Kast, I don't know enough about any of this to try and
tell you about it myself, but you need to be able to accept
the reality of what happened before you can even begin to
forgive yourself. When you're not the crazed monster striving
after himself, then you're . . . you're *good*." She fumbled for a
second, muttering to herself. "You're..." She stopped. "Never
mind. Let's see if we can find something worth eating."

Kast wasn't sure what to think. But there was no way this
girl would truly forgive him. He would just return her home.
Maybe his way would make itself clear by then.

Or not.

CHAPTER FORTY-FOUR

"No! Careful! You're going to . . . ."

"Blast it! Curse the skies!"

Kast tried wiping the pain in his hand away. It didn't work.

"I told you to be careful!" Aurah grabbed their fresh supply of water and poured it over the dragon's newly burnt hand.

"I was being careful, girl!" Kast gritted his teeth. The pan had tipped and without thinking he grabbed the metal handle and seared the flesh on his palm. The cool water seemed to work wonders. For a second.

Cooking was hard, and now he had begun to regret the interest that he displayed in the menial task. He wished he could just hunt and eat his food raw like he did when he was a dragon. He wanted none of this human cooking nonsense.

"Well, not careful enough! You of all people should know flames are hot!" Her chiding including a strong dosage of poking. Kast wasn't sure if he liked it. His pessimism probably just stemmed from the pain in his right hand.

He watched the girl hold the cooking device called a pan with a coarse piece of leather they had found in the storehouse earlier. They had also found a wealth of foods, including salted and smoked meat. It was nothing short of spectacular—except the part where Kast burnt his hand trying to save the pan of pig meat called bacon. He looked at his hand. It had turned red and some parts of the skin bubbled and turned white. It began to throb quite painfully.

"Yeah, that will last a little while." He looked up to see the girl had repositioned the pan on the fire and was now staring at his scorched hand. She began to laugh. "The mighty dragon scorned by fire! How ironic."

"Bah!" Kast wasn't sure if he was open to laughter right now. For now, his hand dominated his thoughts. He didn't like to be burned, but the more he thought about it the bigger the smirk on his face got. It was ironic and funny. The girl caught his look and smiled back at him. He liked her smile. It belonged on her.

"Well, the good news is that the food is all done now, and we can actually eat something that tastes good!" Her smile widened. Kast responded in kind at the good news. He could use a warm delicious meal. The smell had been teasing him for the last hour or so since they had found the storehouse. A lot of the buildings around had been burnt to the ground. Wooden timbers not fully burnt lay in heaps where homes and shops had collapsed.

Kast was thankful that, for whatever reason, the corpses were gone. Aurah had mentioned hearing the Kingdom had discussed dealing with the remains. Maybe the Kingdom had responded after all? Or maybe Kast had burned them and destroyed them all when he attacked?

Maybe even something else more gruesome.

Kast felt a ripple travel through his spine, leaving goosebumps. He didn't like that last thought and fought to control his imagination.

They had set up camp next to the storehouse. Aurah said from the looks of it, it belonged to a wealthy merchant. It was blocked with some large stones that had fallen in the way, but it wasn't too hard to shove them aside—particularly with Kast's inhuman strength. The sight inside was glorious enough to sing tales about. The door and the stairs down below had still been intact, thankfully, too. Aurah had told him that if the storehouse hadn't been sealed, then the food inside would have rotted. She was still somewhat skeptical about whether the food would be rotten. How delighted they were to see the treasure trove inside, miraculously untouched. Kast had wanted to cook something wonderful. He was also infatuated with the idea of controlling fire to create instead of destroying and had asked to help make dinner.

Aurah broke into his thoughts and handed him a plate of food. Kast would never grow tired of the sensation of holding one of these miracle devices loaded with piles of edible goodness. He smiled widely at the variety of food in front of himself. There was bacon, what the girl called eggs, and a slab of . . . *cheese*. Bacon grease ran around on his plate, wonderfully drenching all of the other foods in its foretold glory. Aurah had said it made things taste better, so she cooked the eggs in it. Kast tucked into his meal. She wasn't lying. It was delicious. They enjoyed the meal together with no noise except the crackling of the fire and the scraping of the wooden plates. It was very pleasant.

They had cooked quite a bit of food, but Kast kept devouring plate after plate. Soon he was full and leaned back against the storehouse, content. He took a sip of water to wash it all down. He couldn't remember being this content before. It was such a beacon of light in the midst of a desolate life.

"Well, as always, you ate more than your fair share, dragon." Aurah smiled at him warmly and leaned against one of the stones moved from the opening of the storehouse.

Kast smiled back, staring gently at the girl. He had never really taken the time to observe her appearance, or just how beautiful she appeared to him. She had found some objects of personal interest in the storehouse, namely a few odd pieces of leather. She had taken one and was now just tying back her hair.

Aurah turned her head and stared off into the distance while absently playing with her braid of hair. There was something about being around her. It was pleasant after one got past all of the pain.

Kast smiled.

He couldn't remember a time when he felt so fulfilled.

He opened his mouth to ask a question when something terrible pierced through the air.

A high-pitched shriek cried out through the world.

And another.

And another.

And another.

More filled the air.

More than any he had ever heard before.

His eyes locked onto the girl's petrified face.

There was no way this could be happening.

A shriek called out.

It was right next to them.

Kast jumped to his feet while the girl dived into the storehouse. *What was she up to?* Maybe he should hide, too?

Before his thoughts could finish, she emerged carrying two sticks with cloth on the end. They smelled strange. She shoved one into his hand and plunged the other's clothed end into the flames.

"Don't just stand there, you stone head!" she yelled at him as she pulled her stick out, now ignited.

Fire!

It wasn't much, especially compared to the number of Savages that screamed around them and what the monsters were, but it was at least something. It was more than he thought of. He copied her and plunged his stick into the fire and ignited the cloth.

"Dragon! She screamed. Immediately he heard a cry pitch out from behind.

He spun, the stick trailing behind. He didn't realize how close he was to being mauled until the stick contacted the Savage's face causing the filth to lurch away. In a second he saw more dark shapes then he could count racing through the rubble of the city.

Kast turned to run after the girl.

Not good.

He caught up with the girl, the flame on the stick trailing in the wind. For some reason, it didn't fade quickly. Maybe the odd smell?

"Dragon, what are we..."

"Down!" Kast cut her off by shoving her to the ground and swinging the club, catching another Savage across its head. The stick cracked slightly. They had no chance of survival. Not like this. Thoughts flashed through his mind of the power that helped him defeat the dragons back at Harrington, but now—he didn't know how to invoke that power and save them. Or even if he could invoke that power anymore.

"Kast!" Aurah sprung to her feet and ran forward.

"I know!" He didn't know if he really knew; the stress of the situation clouded his judgment. He searched frantically, hard on the girl's heels. *Something . . . please, something.* His thoughts begged for some sort of bastion of security. Some sort of hope.

Wait!

He slowed for a second. A literal bastion appeared in his sights. It looked more militaristic than the other parts of the city and at least a large chunk of the stonework remained intact.

It will have to do!

"Aurah! There!" He cried out. Her head turned just enough to catch the direction his hand pointed. She nodded vigorously, the pressure of the situation exaggerating every movement. Kast ran, leaving the girl ahead of himself slightly. All he could think about was protecting her. Somehow this formation seemed to make the most sense.

A snarl ripped out from behind himself and pain ripped across his back.

Kast screamed out and hit the ground hard, rolling. The savage was on top of him faster than he could ever have imagined.

The beast screamed, baring its teeth inches away from his eyes. The foul breath and slime from its mouth coated his face.

Then it stopped with a scream.

Aurah darted in and slammed the flaming end of her club into the surprised creature's eye. It screeched, lashing out in its pain. Aurah turned and grabbed Kast's arm, yanking him forward towards the stronghold.

Please.

Kast found himself pleading.

If he died here, if he let the girl die here, he would never make things right. He couldn't stand the pain of that thought.

He ran hard, his pace fueled by the fury that the thought of failure invoked in his heart.

The cries rang out louder and louder behind them.

Kast had no idea if they would make it.

But they did.

The broken stone wall lay in pieces at the foot of the small tower. One side had completely collapsed exposing the interior.

No time for second thoughts! He screamed at himself.

They raced over the wall and crashed through a wooden door on the inside of the building, slamming it shut behind them. The girl searched frantically for a second before throwing a wooden beam across some metal bars surrounding the doorway. Their torches brought light to the dim room. There weren't any windows. *Were they trapped?*

The door bulged dangerously as a Savage slammed into it and stressed the wood and iron. It wouldn't hold for long.

"Kast! What do we do?" The girl's eyes filled with fear. He didn't need that much light to see the truth in her eyes.

I need to be strong.

"Look for some way out of here. If we're trapped, we're trapped, but if we can move to a better position, then we need to!" He shouted louder than he meant to, but the adrenaline raged through every fiber of his being. The girl didn't seem to care. She ran the length of the room searching for some semblance of hope.

Thuds and savage snarls boomed continuously from the door. Soon the sound of splintering wood rent the air. Light had begun to stream in through cracks in the door.

Not good.

"Kast!" The girl's voice yelled across the room. He looked. She was standing next to a strange wooden apparatus. "This ladder goes to the next floor!" He peered up at the ceiling. He could barely make out what looked to be a square door in the ceiling.

"Let's go!" He ran forward the meet the girl, who was already at the door in the ceiling. Her torch lay on the floor so she could climb. Kast stopped nearby while she fumbled to open the thing. The vicious cries grew louder behind them.

In the light of the fire, he saw something shiny to his side.

It was a sword. *A sword.* That would be nice to have right about now.

"Kast!" The girl's voice yelled. Light poured into the room from above. She had opened the door. He handed her his torch, and a look of confusion crossed her face until she saw him wrench the sword free of its resting place on the wall.

"Move!" Kast roared. The girl didn't hesitate to obey his command. The sound of the door breaking grew louder. Kast leaped up the ladder with the sword in tow. He had no idea how to use the thing, but it was more suited for killing than a flaming stick.

He arrived on the second landing of the bastion. Another door led further away into the building, while the walls facing outwards, towards the city, lay in shambles, exposing the bitter remains of the world. There were Savages everywhere down below.

"Go further in!" he yelled.

Howling, followed by a lot of crashing, erupted from the room.

The barrier had been broken.

It wouldn't be long now.

He turned to follow when he was thrown to the side by a massive force. He hit the wall and tried to regain his breath.

A Savage.

The girl stopped her flight and turned to face it.

"Run!" Kast yelled with what air he had.

He jumped at the beast with the sword. The creature side-stepped the attack, surprising Kast, and snapped its teeth at him.

"Not fast enough! Kast bellowed at the beast.

Swinging the sword faster than the Savage could move, his strength with the edge of the blade lopped off the monster's front leg. It screamed at its prey, falling under the pain.

Kast lifted the sword up high with the point down and plunged the blade deep into the beast's chest. The cries and thrashing lasted for a second before the Savage slid off of the blade, dead.

Kast didn't waste a moment on his victory. He turned and ran after the girl, deeper into the stronghold.

It was getting dark outside, but the moon was out and poured light down on the world and through the windows scattered around the place. Rooms passed by on his right while the wall on his left was the only thing standing between himself and the outside world. The passage raced by. Holes littered the walls. Stones lay in piles where destruction had decimated the building.

Kast had no idea where the girl had run. He jumped through the door at the end of the corridor and slammed it shut behind himself before mimicking what the girl had done below, throwing a wooden bar across it to hold it shut.

He clenched his teeth together. *Where did she go?* Kast jolted forward, picking one direction and hoping for the best.

The windows to the outside world disappeared and now, door after door passed by on either side of him. How big was this building? It seemed to span a larger distance then he initially thought. *Curse humans and their perception!*

The girl's scream pierced the air, echoing off the walls.

Kast ran even harder.

He couldn't fail.

Not here.

He had to make up for his mistakes; he couldn't live if he didn't.

He couldn't.

A bright light poured into the building from a door that hung open. High pitched screams shrieked, one after another.

Please! Kast's thoughts roared violently. *Please make it in time!*

Kast aimed for the blinding light.

The door came and went.

The world slowed down.

Was it adrenaline? Or was it more? This room's exterior wall was destroyed, as well. Light flooded in all around. A Savage hung in mid-air flying slowly towards the cowering girl. Teeth bared and claws outstretched. Eyes consumed with their bloodlust. Another Savage nearby gripped Aurah's stick in its clenched jaw, shaking it to shreds.

Time only plodded along.

Kast was too late. His body moved so slowly. *Too slowly.* The monster nearly had the girl between its teeth and was closing the distance faster than Kast could move. It was all over. *Everything was over.*

Everything.

Everything.

No.

Kast saw clearly.

His movements stopped altogether as he came to a standstill.

The monsters continued their madness, raging forward, ready to end their prey.

But Kast stared, understanding so much at that moment. "Absolutely not."

Kast stated the words simply.

Move.

His thoughts were meager.

Kast blinked.

When his eyes opened, both Savages hung skewered on the end of his sword.

The girl took a second to understand what had happened, then she gaped at Kast, staring incredulously. Her look shattered as her arm flung out, pointing behind him.

It all happened so slowly.

Kast saw everything.

He turned.

Time could move slowly.

He would move how he pleased.

Kast watched a Savage fly through the air, lunging straight at what had been the dragon's exposed back.

He swung the sword and the beast's head went flying away.

There was nothing short of an army of these curs.

Kast would finish them all.

Time resumed.

Kast flung himself off of the landing towards the ground, luring the teeming beasts to him. The horde immediately pounced upon the exposed man. Sword flying deftly, Kast fought. The blade swished through the air, catching every creature unawares.

Gore littered the world around the dragon.

Kast dodged tooth and claw, ignoring the wild screams from the monsters.

There had to be at least fifty of the beasts in the pack.

Now there were no more than thirty.

The monsters dived, driven by the smell of their comrades' blood.

Kast danced between their ranks, swinging a weapon he had never held before. Bodies fell in pieces as the sword sheared through bone and sinew with little effort. Kast's eyes glazed over at the sight of the wretches falling in torrents. The rancid smell of their filthy bodies and blood littered the air.

Kast dispatched another Savage when a shrill cry came from above.

The girl!

He blinked.

He was in the air, his muscles reinforced with power.

He launched himself immediately towards the upper level and the stench of the Savage.

There was no cry from the girl.

Aurah.

Kast blasted into the next room.

The girl lay, eyes bulging. Her arm was matted in blood.

Her blood.

Her blood.

Frenzy.

Kast threw the sword down and caught the beast with his hands. He threw the beast into the room's far wall—away from the girl. He would keep her clean from the mess to come.

Kast blinked.

The beast was in his hands. With barely a flex of his might, he ripped the beast's leg off.

Kast didn't stop.

The other leg came off just as easy.

And then with both hands tore the monster's mandible clean from its skull.

Die in the worst way possible!

Kast cursed the beast and spit on its carcass.

The girl.

He arrived at her side as fast as he could complete the thought.

She gasped unevenly. Kast had no idea if she even registered reality. He cradled her mangled arm. The beast had completely shredded it. He didn't have much time if he was competing with blood loss.

Heal.

A light filled the room. Kast, for the first time, recognized that his body had begun to glow, and now it glowed even brighter as the light moved through his hands and surrounded the girl.

Her wide eyes looked up into Kast's.

I'm sorry, Aurah. I'm so sorry.

Kast watched the arm rebuild. Tendons reformed and stitched themselves back together. Soon the new skin covered her arm, and color returned to her cheeks. Her breathing leveled out. She never took her eyes from Kast's, and he could only stare back into hers. Before long tears began to fall down her face. Kast wasn't sure why until he realized tears had already fallen from his.

He was weeping over her.

His heart ached to make all things right. He felt so powerless and enfeebled. Incompetent. There was no way to cross that barrier, even with the magnificent powers that coursed through him.

The glow subsided gently and left the man and woman in the dim light of the room. The stench of Savages rose up in the air. Kast didn't care. He was closer than ever. His heart yearned for the opportunity.

"Thanks, dragon." The girl's voice came out weak. Kast imagined that the healing did wonders, but rest would certainly be needed now. There were no more words to be said. Kast helped the girl up when he collapsed to his knees. Apparently, there was a price to his power, or maybe he was unexperienced using it yet. The girl helped him up in return.

"Thanks, girl." Kast flashed a smile at her. She blushed. They carried each other out of the room and stared out at the city below. Savages lay in pieces scattered everywhere. Some whole, some cut in half. Some battered beyond recognition.

"Are there any left?" *A simple question.* One that made the girl whimper as she asked it. Kast answered proudly.

"I got them all. If I remember right—and it's kind of fuzzy—the remaining few fell suddenly when I heard your scream." He breathed heavily. Aurah smiled at him, helping to hold his weight. They made their way out of the building together, heading back towards the campsite. The earth had been torn to shreds by the Savage's hard pursuit. Kast wondered if there was anything left of the storehouse or if the monsters wrecked it all.

They arrived at the scattered and dying embers of the fire from earlier. He didn't care to take account of much more. They were both exhausted.

Kast grabbed the girl's waist and moved her into the storehouse. It looked untainted. *Good.* He closed the door behind him, enclosing the space into darkness, and stumbled slightly down the steps. He collapsed to the floor, the girl following closely to steady him as she fell herself.

They sat on the floor and leaned their backs against each other as their breathing filled the air, calming slowly over time.

"Kast?" The weak voice rasped behind himself, quietly.

"Aurah?" He breathed back.

"My arm?"

A question.

"It's good."

Silence.

"Kast?" More rasping.

"Aurah?"

"You?"

Concern?

Concern.

"Good." He was breathing slower now.

Silence.

"Kast?"

The poor girl.

"Aurah?"

Quiet.

"Thanks."

Tears welled in his eyes and washed a trail through the grime that coated his face. Kast reached behind him and found the girl's hand. He squeezed it with every drop of tenderness he possessed.

The hand pressed back gently.

Their exhaustion overcame them, and their breathing lulled the man and woman to inevitable sleep—leaning against the safety of one another.

Sharing the warmth of hands.

CHAPTER FORTY-FIVE

Kast woke slowly. His body was sore. That strange power had taken a massive toll on him. He looked to his right. The girl had shifted and leaned against him more than before, her head laying against the back of his shoulder. Her hair filled his face. Her mouth hung open slightly, letting the quiet breathing escape.

He inhaled deeply. The smell of her hair was filled with the wear of much travel, but there was still a beauty to it. A grimace rolled across his face.

He didn't deserve this.

Something so good.

He moved forward and caught her shoulders, tenderly laying her on the floor. She didn't seem phased in the slightest. He stared into her peaceful face. She seemed so...*secure.*

Kast's hand clenched.

He didn't deserve any good from this girl. He couldn't enjoy it.

There's no way.

He stood, his body stiff and sore. His breath caught in his chest before the pressure released and caught again a second later. He moved up the steps towards the door. He almost pulled it open without thinking.

What if I missed one of those monsters last night? Or something else is waiting? He froze in place for a second before deciding. *No use in worrying. It's just best to get it over with.*

The latch on the door released easily and Kast opened it as quietly as he could. The hinges creaked gently. He opened it just enough and he slipped outside, closing the door behind himself. He had made the girl's life hard enough as is. He didn't even want to think about growing attached to her—if that nonsense was even possible.

Something inside nagged at him, though. The peace they both seemed to find in each other's presence. *No, I don't deserve that good, and she doesn't deserve the atrocity of caring for a monster like me.* There was no other answer. It was the only thing that made sense.

He had to take care of her and protect her.

Even from himself.

The morning had frosted the world over. The chill was unexpected. It had been fairly warm for autumn, but now, Kast felt the bite of the cold, morning air. He set himself to make a fire. It didn't take long before he had gathered enough wood and tinder to get the flames going. He even found the spark maker—whatever the girl had called it. The fire soon began rising and offered warmth to fight the morning air. He huddled around the tongues of fire, seizing every ounce of heat they offered up. His mind wandered back to the girl and the ridiculousness of his thoughts. What would happen if he did stick around? He would certainly be found out. Too many things could go wrong. *Right?*

Was that it?

Or was he just afraid of being vulnerable with the girl? *No.*

What was he even thinking? The girl showed him kindness, not interest. *Interest?* Where were these thoughts coming from? It was almost like he was insane again. It was ludicrous.

"It's impressive that this storehouse was never recovered."

Kast nearly jumped out of his skin. The girl sat next to him wearing a heavy coat. He stared with wide eyes, and his heart hammered in his chest. She was so quiet and had startled him, ripping him away from his thoughts once again.

"And why would that be Aurah?" His heart leveled out quickly, the fear alleviating, though the tension still remained in his voice. "Maybe you could make a little noise sometimes, just to let me know you're there?" Aurah smiled at him.

"The goods in this place are quite expensive and valuable." She threw another coat at him. "That will keep you warm, I knew you wouldn't have thought of the cold." Kast grabbed the coat and greedily donned it. She laughed, watching him. He smiled back. The cold really was distasteful.

They sat and stared at the fire.

She started to speak and thought hard. "You know, Kast . . . I'm certain I can convince Elizabeth to pardon you."

Kast froze. Not even the coat could hold the chill of her words at bay. He stared wide-eyed at the fire, completely unresponsive. *What did this mean?*

"It's just an idea, nothing crazy." The girl retracted her suggestion on seeing his still response. Aurah ended up staring at the fire, too.

Great, now things are awkward. Kast didn't like this. This girl needed to hate him and struggle to allow him any sort of good grace. Her willingness to be kind and look out for him just didn't make any sense. The silence welled up between them.

"How's your hand?" Now she was trying to shift topics. He looked down, trying to change the conversation, too.

"My hand!" He stared at it for a second longer before showing the girl. The burn was completely gone.

"Huh, I guess I shouldn't be surprised. Only a dragon in a human's body would have the luck to heal that quickly." She turned her head to the fire while Kast stared at his hand for a second longer.

She had mentioned that he was a dragon in a human's body. Yes, maybe that was the way he should think of things. He wasn't human. He was a beast. His place was elsewhere—if anywhere.

He continued to stare at his hand when a thundering arose in the distance.

Both Aurah and he moved to their feet, poised and ready for whatever was coming.

Whatever it was, it was loud and moving quickly. A slight cloud of dust and ash rose in the near distance. *What was it?*

They looked at each other, still worn and exhausted from the previous evening's escapade. They stood when the sounds of horses and the clink of armor became distinguishable. They stared as a small unit of soldiers rounded a street corner and came into view.

Kast counted quickly.

Twenty men—all mounted.

Kast stood apprehensive, though Aurah had become much less so. She seemed to find familiarity in the group. He clenched his teeth. This was an unpleasant encounter. He wasn't ready for confronting the humans just yet.

"Ho, strangers!" A man stepped forward from the soldiers and addressed them. Kast stared when Aurah spoke up.

"Ho, Capital scouts! What brings you here?" The man turned to face Aurah. Kast had to quickly seize control of his reaction to step in front of her. *What was that?* He scorned his instincts. He didn't know himself anymore. The man didn't seem to notice Kast's reaction.

"My response depends on who is asking. If I might say, you two fit quite a few details of some travelers that the Capital has been searching for recently, and under current circumstances, it is quite odd for anyone to be traveling." The man sounded distrustful and wary.

"I am the woman the Capital has been searching for," Aurah stated bluntly. Kast was shocked by her open proclamation.

The man on the horse seemed to examine her more thoroughly. "This man has joined to help me make it safely back home. We took shelter at this city last night when we're attacked by a pack of Savages. If it wasn't for his skill with a sword, we wouldn't have made it through the night, sir."

Kast just stared at Aurah. *Why did she lie?* Well, it was more like a half-truth, but why didn't she just turn him in? Why did she try to offer him the chance to live? Why didn't she demand his life? He couldn't come to grips.

"Well, you may just as well be who the Capital has been searching for, but that isn't for us to decide here." The man had challenged them. Kast felt the beads of sweat run down his neck when another voice rang out.

"Captain! It's incredible! There must be at least forty or fifty Savages a short distance away. All killed and chopped to pieces!" A soldier on a horse rode up from behind. Kast really didn't like being surrounded. He tensed and was ready to spring.

Aurah looked at him, a certain pleading filled her eyes.

The man who spoke must have been the captain. He looked at Kast and Aurah. Doubt filled his eyes.

"You two will come under our escort to the Capital. Then, and only then, will it be decided who you are and what is to be done with you." The captain turned. "Bring up two of the spare horses!" He rode away, leaving Kast and Aurah to stand by themselves and under the authority of another.

The soldiers were not ones to wait on others. At Aurah's request for food, they handed them a meager breakfast of some cheese and dried meat, then told them to eat while they rode. Aurah was slightly caught off guard by the urgency the soldiers conveyed, and she could see Kast was the same, though neither of them dared disobey in the slightest.

Aurah felt more comfortable around the soldiers then Kast seemed to be. Her peace happened to grow sturdier as she rode beside Kast, a strong warrior in his own right, while they were also surrounded by an ensemble of soldiers. The hours passed by as they headed northeast, according to the sun. The forest which loomed on the horizon came quickly, and they soon were surrounded by an endless stretch of trees again. This time they followed the new road away from Avante, presumably towards the Capital.

Aurah had a lot on her mind, probably a result of reality inserting itself into her life again.

She couldn't believe her response to Kast. It seemed impossible in light of all he had done to her, but there really was something so genuine in his actions.

She stopped her thoughts again. They continually made their circuit, following the same circular path. There was one thought in particular that she hadn't confronted.

Aurah had no doubt anymore whether Kast was sincere about protecting her and making sure he righted his wrong. It seemed silly. The dragon turned man exercised his amazing power and protected her, a damsel in distress. Her heart in those moments was strongly convincing itself to trust him. She had no idea why, but she felt so at ease around him. Perhaps it was the genuineness?

Or maybe it was because despite the company she kept previously, she had never met someone so determined, so committed and genuine. Or rather, maybe he fits alongside the company of those whose resolve shined on Aurah daily. She gripped the saddle's horn. The reigns were tied to the horse in front of her.

That was just it. This was where her thoughts broke and circled around. The next bit of thinking her mind almost did was *dangerous.*

Aurah thought of Elizabeth. Elizabeth was always of such a strong resolve to justice. How did that compare with the dragon turned man beside her? He seemed just as resolved, but was it to a different end?

And what about Dorian?

Aurah's breathing stuttered as she looked at the beast sitting on a horse beside her. She couldn't avoid it forever.

How had she ever forgiven the monster?

Aurah's stomach clenched. She had *loved* Dorian. Or at least, what felt like a growing attachment—a seed planted and ready to begin its growth, destined to blossom.

Kast had stolen that from her.

She glared at him from the corner of her eye.

Stop.

What was she doing?

Aurah's breathing felt ragged. Dorian was an open wound in her heart. He was one of the bravest, stalwart, and committed men she had ever met. Somewhere in her heart, there was still hope.

Hope that somehow, in her vain attempts to restore the world to exactly the way it was, she might be able to restore that loss as well.

But Aurah knew she could not.

Kast and Dorian were similar—Aurah blanched at the thought, and a fire burned in her gut as she tried to extinguish it. The journey back to the Capital sparked all sorts of thoughts and dug up all kinds of hurts. Things Aurah had hidden away from her consciousness, things that made her hope for death more than their confrontation.

Her mind wandered, thinking about Kast. She blushed at her audacity earlier, around the fire. Inviting him to find pardon and favor. *For what?* She still didn't know. There was something about his perseverance and always being the one to help her—to save her. She felt safe around him. Maybe she wanted that to continue? Aurah grimaced as her thoughts only led to more confusion. More questions and no answers.

Forgiveness wasn't as simple as falling thousands of feet off of a cliff to spark the change necessary.

Leaves crunched under the horses' feet. It was the time of year when leaves began to fall, making way for the winter. The soldiers all around wore heavier uniforms to keep them warmer in the cool air. She became acutely aware of how warm the coat she had found in the storehouse made her. It was a good find. She looked at Kast, riding beside her. He was grabbing the horn of the saddle—his reigns were held by the soldier in front of him, too.

A strange look had occupied his face. Aurah couldn't determine what he was thinking. She hoped he wasn't afraid. It was so sudden, being taken into custody, but Elizabeth would most certainly see the genuine repentance that Kast held and would offer her grace to him. Especially at Aurah's request—she had no doubt about that. She wouldn't be able to talk to him openly now, though, not with all these soldiers around. She needed to wait for Elizabeth's pardon before revealing who he was, or they might react accordingly. Her head faced forward.

At the very least, she would make sure that Kast was pardoned. She had to.

They would be fine.

CHAPTER FORTY-SIX

The night was much colder than the day. It was clear and cloudless, and only the light of the campfire thwarted the presence of the gleaming stars in the sky. Aurah huddled close to the fire, not caring about the stars now—the cold reigned victor. Even with the heavy coat that she had found, the air still seeped into her core. How she craved the comfort of a soft and warm bed. Yet she was here, camping for the night in the forest, a day's ride away from the Capital. *So be it.*

She could last one more night.

One more night. She could hardly believe the journey had gone on for so long. She was even more awed that she had managed somehow to survive the whole ordeal. Every bit was thanks to Kast. The leaving home and suffering part, but also the living and surviving part, too. She smirked into the fire, rubbing her bare hands together near the flame. It was a crazy adventure. She doubted even Elizabeth would believe every detail. How they escaped harrowing battles and vicious enemies. She shook her head, the fact of her survival was impossible. *Well nearly.* She smiled again as she thought of Kast. She had spent the rest of the trip processing the hurts and pains. Kast a time or two looked at her worried, but she smiled and tried her hardest to indicate that she was okay.

Which she was. She had at the very least come to grips with the fact that she would struggle with the last three weeks for the rest of her life, but one thing she had slowly cemented on was that Kast was sincere about making amends for his wrongs. *All of them.*

She looked up suddenly. *Where was Kast?* She hadn't seen him in a little while. She stood up, head swiveling to find him. *He's probably alright, but I should find him anyway.*

Aurah left the heat of the fire and went looking for the dragon. She didn't want to raise attention to her worry, so she decided to not inquire of the soldiers if they had seen him. *They probably would respond gruffly, anyway.* She scowled at the thought. They didn't have as much kindness out here. After walking most of the perimeter, she decided to search towards the middle of the camp. She felt the watchful eyes of multiple guards while she searched. *Let them.* After they found out who she was, they would be like they always were before.

She stopped her search.

No dragon here.

She was about to turn back to the fire when she overheard a voice.

"I don't know what's possessed the Queen like this. This is the sixth patrol in two weeks! She has us constantly roaming these lands for nothing. Now we have to drag two lone travelers back with us, which is, without doubt, going to end up miserable for them. There's no chance that poor girl survived the dragon's wrath."

"I agree. It's been hectic since the dragon's attack on the Capital, and I'm not sure what has gotten in her Majesty. But then again, with all of these scouting patrols, it's better to be preemptive with anyone who might be an enemy, you know? You heard the tales about the cloaked man who fought off the dragons and how the Queen hired him, right? The Capital is extremely vulnerable, and we can't risk anything for anyone."

A second voice responded.

"I doubt the Queen's actions are for the Kingdom's sake. Even with all of the possible forms the enemy may have. Haven't you heard of those who have already been interrogated by the Queen? They are still behind bars. This is madness, and we are the Queen's arm to commit it. I can only imagine just what she'll do when she finds that dragon who stole her servant."

"If we find it."

"Yes, if . . . ."

The voices fell silent for a second.

"I hope we don't," the second voice blurted.

"Me, too. The Queen, though. She can't wait to murder the beast. She keeps rambling on about justice, but I think it's brutal, the way she talks about the beast. It's not like it doesn't deser . . . ."

"Aurah!" A voice whispered from behind her, in her ear. She jumped, nearly screaming. She held her mouth just in time. She hadn't realized how quiet she had become, listening to the voices talk. She turned quickly to find Kast smiling at her. Payback from that morning.

She didn't smile.

Her heart was torn asunder.

There was no way it could be true.

Could it?

Her mind roamed wildly and then a memory. It seemed so long ago. When everything was good. The day she had gone searching for the gift and . . . Aurah gulped. The memory was difficult, but she had been getting better at accepting reality.

The day she had gone searching for the gift and Dorian had pointed out that Elizabeth was very *committed* to right and would need someone close to help guide her through the torrents of her own justice.

Where was Aurah when Elizabeth had needed her the most?

"Aurah, is everything alright?" Kast's look of worry returned. What could she say?

What were they to do?

Her heart broke from the sad tales she heard about Elizabeth, and the unavoidable future for Kast. She wanted to weep.

No.

She knew what she had to do. She wasn't sure why, but she would do it. She wasn't sure why the dragon turned man, right next to her, had affected her this way. She only knew it wasn't right to condemn him to death—not after all that he had done. No matter the hurt. He wasn't that monster anymore. He had fought it and he had changed.

"Aurah?" Kast's voice was strained. They were still on such unsteady ground. She looked him in the eye.

"I'll tell you tomorrow. For now, let's get some sleep." Kast stared at her for a second, then nodded. She wasn't sure what he took from all of that, but she knew what she had to do.

The soldiers had erected simple tents for the night. Many probably slept in their armor or with it nearby. They had even spared two tents for their travelers. Aurah looked at them as a dying courtesy. A last kindness for the certain misery that the soldiers were bringing them into. They all knew what was happening to the foreigners caught outside the city. Those who were brought in for interrogation.

Aurah disdained herself for putting so much trust in Elizabeth. Then in an instant, she grieved for the terrible sorrow Elizabeth must have borne. Aurah, herself, was torn by the situation.

They accepted the already erected tents, where she and Kast said goodnight and turned into their own. Aurah heard the sounds of sleep soon rise all around.

But she didn't join.

What seemed like hours had passed before she peeked her head out to take a good look. She could only see two guards, but most of them had gone to sleep. *Probably worn out from all the patrols recently.* Slipping out of the tent, she sneaked her way towards Kast.

Sound asleep. He must really trust her and what she said about having him pardoned.

Her face set.

She couldn't betray that trust. Not after everything he had done. Despite the horror he had committed, she owed him a lot.

She reached out her hand to touch his face when he spoke quietly.

"Girl."

She jumped. That was twice now. *Who was keeping score?*

"I hope you have a good plan." He must have read her well enough to know something was going on. She sighed her relief. They were in this together once again.

"The best I can muster at least. Are you ready to go?"

"Be careful, they have a guard especially for us, hidden in the shadows. He seems to be drifting into sleep for now, so let's move quietly." Kast climbed out of his tent and grabbed her hand—leading them stealthily away from the low light of the dying fires. Aurah was conflicted. *This was my rescue!* Inside, though, she was secretly glad he had helped take charge of things. "So, what's the plan? Kast asked when they were hidden in the shadows—away from any listening ears.

"We steal a horse and release the rest of them so the soldiers can't follow."

Kast stared at her.

"That's it?" He seemed incredulous.

"Unless you can sprout your wings again and fly us out of here, that's all I have." Her response was quite tart. He smiled.

"I could just use my glowing power to fight them all?" A smug suggestion.

"I doubt it. Do you remember what happened after the last time you used your strength, at Harrington? Kast, you didn't recover it, even after nearly a week. It barely even came out for us as we fell down The Face, but your body just didn't recover." He stared at her, dumbfounded. She stared back. Surely, he had figured that much out? "Dragon, you have been thinking about your powers, right?" He looked at her again, blushing with a small smile.

"Well, kind of, but I'm not certain the need for it to recharge is the only reason it doesn't always work. Other than that—no." He smiled again. Aurah's shoulders fell and she covered her face with a hand.

"It's not a big deal, but you think you would try to figure out something that powerful as quickly as possible. From what I could gather, your body does need time before you can use it again. Maybe I'm wrong, but right now, I'm guessing that since you used it so recently, you won't be able to use it for a while." She glanced around as she whispered quickly. They were wasting time. "Therefore, we need to find another way out of here. Horses are the best option as long as our pursuers don't have them, too. Thus, we take for us and beat the rest away."

"Okay, then let's do it." Kast turned towards where the horses were kept and headed that way. Aurah ducked behind him and followed. *I guess we'll figure it as we go then.*

The horses were all gathered in one place, tied to the trees where they had left the road to camp. There were two soldiers standing guard. They didn't look as tired as the others. *Probably because of what they were guarding.* Aurah reasoned there would be stricter punishments for the guards of the horses if anything happened to them. Good for the soldiers, bad for them.

They were about to move forward when an armored hand seized Aurah from behind.

"Got you!" The captain yelled. In a flash, a fist flew into his face knocking the man onto the ground. He remained completely still.

"That will keep him down for a moment, but we need to move quickly now. The guards will be coming!" Kast spoke quickly, urgency rolling off of his voice. They moved towards the horses when Aurah realized something.

"They've been unsaddled!" She breathed.

"Can you saddle them?" Kast turned to look at her.

"I've only seen it done. I don't think I can." This was getting worse and worse.

"Can we ride them without saddles?" Kast's jaw clenched. They needed to get moving.

"Yes, I think so. You just have to keep a better balance if I remember right."

"Then let's do it." Kast interrupted her suddenly. He turned to the first horse and untied the rope, fast now that he had some practice. The horse's head perked up at the unexpected motion.

"Help me up, Kast!" Aurah stood beside the horse. No saddle meant nothing to step on.

Kast grabbed her waist and lifted, tossing her onto the horse. *That works.*

"Soldiers rise up! We're under attack!" Aurah's head spun to the sound of the voice. It came from where they had dispatched the captain. *Not good.* She watched as Kast quickly untied the horse and handed her the rope.

"Hold this." His voice raised in volume. It didn't matter much anymore. Aurah watched as shadows raised from the tents, heading quickly to the loud voice.

"Over there! They're on the horses! Get them!" The voices screamed and in an instant, they rushed towards Aurah. Kast ran from horse to horse, ripping their ties from the trees and slapped their rumps, scaring them away. He was yelling now.

Aurah's horse jerked violently underneath her, racing away. She lurched forward and clung to the horse underneath her. Kast quickly vanished behind her as the horse navigated the trees, trying to get away from the commotion.

The horse soon found the road and began to run along it. Aurah was thankful that the forest was flat and simple, the horse could have charged into something in the dark. It was dangerous to ride at night. She worried about Kast too, but she knew he would be fine for the moment. She held on to the rope and worked on maintaining her balance for now.

Soon, as if inspired by the thought, Kast showed up alongside her. *Running. On foot.* Aurah looked over and made eye contact. He waved his hand at her, she nodded back understanding what he meant with the motion. She turned back to the horse and worked to calm the horse down, pulling slightly on the rope. She hoped it would stop soon.

They ran that way for a few more minutes before the horse calmed down enough to slow to a trot.

"Whew, I was afraid this thing would never slow," Kast spoke with half a smile like he didn't just escape from an entourage of soldiers.

"I think you fail to see how lucky we are to have gotten out of there so easily, dragon." Aurah's voice was simple and to the point.

"Not easily. I ended up having to smash a few soldiers to get aw . . . I mean, I made sure not to use all of my power on them." He corrected himself when he saw her face. She wasn't worried about him. He would be able to fight his way out, but she was worried about those men committed to fulfilling what had to be Elizabeth's insane ambitions.

Elizabeth. Aurah's thoughts soured again, gripped by the reality of what her sister had to be going through.

"Kast, are we free from the soldiers?" She was still slightly shaken from the whole escape. She pulled the horse to a complete stop. It complied, calmed enough to just stand.

"Well, I only fought the ones I needed to, and left them alive, and I didn't manage to free all of the horses so I'm certain they could catch us if they wanted." He smiled at her. "I'm not sure they want to, though. I think they realize how fruitless it would be to pursue us."

Her body slumped on top of the horse. It stamped its foot impatiently as if wanting to run or be left to sleep again. She ran her hand over her hair for a minute.

"What should we do?" She couldn't take account of the situation well enough to make a decent conclusion. Kast scratched his cheek, thinking.

"Let's get you home. Let's stick to the original plan. I'm sure Elizabeth would not hold it against you for coming back." Kast spoke, but he wasn't completely certain. He didn't know Aurah's home like Aurah knew it.

"I think you're right. Hop on and let's keep moving."

Kast moved towards the horse and mounted with minimal help. Even without a saddle. The horse didn't seem to mind at all, except for the desire to get moving again. She was about to spur the horse forward when she realized how close Kast was.

Sitting behind her.

His hands rested on the horse's back, surrounding her.

She gripped the rope in her hand.

The reality of it all playing out before her again.

Elizabeth.

"Kast." Aurah tried to find the words.

"We'll talk later, girl." The breath of his words found the back of her neck. Goosebumps rose along her arms.

She turned as best as she could to see him and nodded. He smiled ever so gently back at her.

She turned forward, nudging the horse into a trot.

Tears were already falling from her eyes.

CHAPTER FORTY-SEVEN

Kast jumped down from the horse and walked alongside it. He stretched his legs vigorously as he went along, trying to remove the effects from the trip. They were on the fringes of the forest again. A different side of it this time, though. The Capital sat out on the plains similar to those of Avante.

He looked at the girl still on the horse. She had covered her sorrow well on the trip, but the stains on her face told him what he had known to be true while riding.

Kast would remember the trip fondly.

Their last moments together. Aurah really was a rare creature. He would leave, having gained so much from his time with her.

His throat caught as he thought of how she was the one to counter his impossible insanity, though he didn't know how she managed it. Pursuing her gave him direction and hope. *Strength.*

Aurah held out her hand and he took it, helping her down. Even after her feet hit the ground, their hands didn't part.

It wasn't that long since they had hated each other with every beat of their hearts, but through some of the most impossible situations they had grown to depend on one another, and kindness had blossomed between the two of them. Kast still didn't know how any of it was even imaginable, nor why, suddenly, it took every ounce of his incredible power to hold back the emotion welling up in himself now.

"Dragon." Her voice shook slightly. He gripped her hand tighter and looked into her eyes. The last act of kindness, no— of *love* that he could give was to help her move forward.

"Girl, I don't think you need to say it for me to know the truth. I'm sorry things didn't work out as you had hoped, and I don't know what the future looks like for either of us." He paused, really taking the time to consider his words. "I said I would offer myself to get you home safely and since there still is a slight distance between here and there, I am more than happy to go . . . ."

"Stop!" She ripped her hand away and backed up. The horse stamped its foot slightly from the noise. Aurah clutched her arms to her chest trying to avoid his gaze.

"Girl . . . ." He took a step closer.

"Stop!" She turned away, raising her shoulders. She shook.

"Aurah . . . ." He took another step.

She began to rock harder, and the sound of tears grew louder.

"Hey…" He made to move to her but was interrupted when she turned and threw herself into his embrace. Kast was startled by the action at first but soon returned it. He combed his hand across the back of her head, soothing the sobbing which now poured forth freely from the girl.

Kast gulped hard.

He didn't deserve to be cared for like this. All he had done was what was right, but he still had mountains to atone for. Did forgiveness really cause this between people? Did resolving to be better for someone really heal that much? A new tear fell from his eye, followed by another. His tears were silent, but vigorous, echoing noiselessly alongside the girl's. He clutched her close.

This was goodbye. He would never be able to appreciate the wealth of a person this girl was. He would never again experience the goodness this girl offered. She would never let him waste his life by taking her that last stretch home, and risk confronting whatever lay there, waiting for him.

Maybe he had saved her a few times through the past few weeks, but never as much as she had saved him by the lessons she had imparted to him. He was so thankful.

He lost track of the time holding her.

Things had grown exponentially since falling down The Face. All he could think about was the little time he had spent with her, and how he wanted more.

"Girl . . . we need to leave soon." He hated to admit it.

"Kast . . . ." Her tone intrigued him.

"I know you were the one who treacherously murdered countless numbers of people . . . ."

He tightened, as she had called direct attention to probably one of the most unforgivable actions of any creature. Actions for which he was responsible.

"I know you were the one who destroyed my life, who threw me into countless horrors—and all for your own pleasure." He gaped, exposed. He hated himself, he still hadn't found a way to move past it all, and now that she was calling attention to his wrongs, he felt disgusting. He would never be free. You were the one I hated most, so much so that I tried to kill you without hesitation."

Kast was starting to feel hurt from the recounting. *Yes.* Yes, he knew the depth of his transgressions and betrayal.

"But . . . ."

But?.

"You always showed up when I needed help the most." He stared at her hidden face, not knowing where she was going. "In a world that should have killed me—or worse— you were there. Even if it was for the wrong reasons." His jaw fell slack. "Despite the bitterness in my heart, which I still justify at times, you grew away from the creature that did all of those wrongs. You raised your head and always charged to my side. You saved me countless times!" Her voice was a little louder now.

Her eyes still stared at the ground. "You even changed before I did! You put up with my hate and when our lives truly were on the line, shattered by a common struggle." She breathed deeply. "You helped *my* insanity. You cleared the fog and haze from my head. You made me see what was right by your actions. I know now that it's because of your selfless determination for me that my walls broke. Like the dragon you are, you conquered my hate in an incredible way! I can't feel that way towards you anymore. I can't think badly about you, even though I know you feel like I should. I am so thankful."

She stopped suddenly and looked up into his eyes, tears coating her cheeks—cheeks raised in a smile. Her eyes beamed at him. She stepped close to him, wrapping her arms around his chest. Electricity charged through the wall of his confusion and shock.

She leaned in and kissed his cheek delicately.

She held her lips to his face for what seemed like an eternity. Then she backed away.

"If anyone hates you, it isn't me—the one who probably should hate you the most." She was staring away again, a blush across her cheeks.

They stood like that for a second. Kast staring at her, Aurah staring away from him at the world around them.

"Help me onto the horse," she muttered, hardly finishing the sentence.

Kast grabbed her waist, the last feel of her that he would ever savor and lifted her onto the animal. He was thankful it had decided to stay when neither of them had thought to hold its rope. He backed away as the girl situated herself. He grabbed the rope and handed it to her. The animal would last a lot better with the lessened load.

"The Capital is only an hour or so away by the looks of it." He tried to find anything to say, as he stared at the forest. "Will you be alright?" She faced forward and nodded.

"You?" The words barely crawled away from the girl.

Kast clenched.

I don't deserve this good.

"Yes…" His voice shook. It took all the control he had to hold himself together.

"Goodbye." Aurah kicked the horse into a run and left Kast. That was a good thing because he couldn't hold back the tears anymore.

Falling to his knees, he held his face, releasing his soul.

The world shook.

Rent in half.

The heavens thundered.

The stars erupted.

All of existence stopped.

Kast grappled the earth.

The treasures of his healing soul were stolen by the tragedy of his actions.

It was over.

He hated it all, reality rending his hope in a cataclysmic shattering.

His mouth opened, but no screams erupted forth.

He hated reality.

He hated the potential for love.

He hated righteousness.

He hated how right could be so good and so bad at the same time.

Kast lay on the ground, weeping, his heart torn in pieces. For once he found something precious, but the good that he pursued demanded his separation from what he had grown to love.

A dark shadow encompassed Kast, slowly.

At first, it was light. then it grew darker.

A wild gale blasted over top of Kast, hurtling towards the Capital.

What?

Kast's sorrow was interrupted.

What?

He stood suddenly.

The shadow belonged to a shadow.

Black to black.

Shade to . . . .

Dragon.

Kast lurched forward, consumed.

No!

He ran. He flew. His feet blurred beneath him. The world rushed by. He wouldn't make it time!

The trees broke and the sight before him was like a knife, stabbing his heart as many times over as there were trees in the forest, drops were in the river, stars were in the night sky.

Vasiss dived at the girl, toying with her. His chest inflated and he released waves of fire scorching the plains with abandon. Aurah leaned into the horse, riding hard to avoid the flames.

This wasn't happening! Why here? Why now? What was going on?

Kast sprinted through the plain, grasping for every opportunity to intervene. He was so far away.

Vasiss dropped suddenly, looming over top of Aurah. A claw lashed out, colliding with the girl, blasting her away from the horse.

"No!" Kast screamed, throwing himself towards the monster.

The monster seized the animal, tearing it into pieces.

No way.

No.

"No."

Kast blinked.

The world shook, rent in half.

The heavens thundered.

The stars erupted.

All of existence stopped as Kast plowed into the side of the black beast, the King of Insane.

Vasiss screeched from the sudden impact, rolling along his side. He repositioned himself in the air, trying to recover his bearings from the unexpected attack.

No.

Kast blazed.

Somehow the air solidified beneath his feet.

He launched himself again at the beast.

Kast blinked.

Vasiss screamed as he connected with the ground, creating an impossible crater.

But the King was far from finished.

On his feet faster than Kast thought possible, the monster began to emit a glow, the color of his scales. Black seeped outwards slowly, a thin layer coating every inch of the insane wretch.

Kast was slammed with an insurmountable force—barely above the ground. He caught the force but blasted away. He had to stop before he went too far. He had to survive.

She needs me.

Kast stared at the ground and focused on it. In a mere second, he found himself landing. The power surrounding him decimated the terrain.

He looked up.

The monster stared back into his eyes.

They were in this position once before.

Kast's teeth clenched.

His eyes darkened utterly.

The bastard would pay.

His mind, so clear, turned inside.

The flame.

Not just a flame.

A raging fire.

Ignited and blazing.

Kast watched as it reached the very potential he had seen after Harrington.

His heart.

His eyes found the Insane King.

Kast started this time.

Vasiss responded the same.

The distance shortened between the two in an instant, their roars never ceasing.

Three seconds.

Two seconds.

Collision.

Kast connected and Vasiss went blasting backward. The world shredded under the dragon turned man's fury exerting itself on the black beast. Kast landed, watching the monster crawl to his feet. He stumbled before he found his wings.

Vasiss limped through the air back over the forest.

Defeated.

Kast watched for a second, then ran to the girl. It didn't take long to find her.

Kast heaved when he saw her. She seemed to be in one piece. There was some bruising, but what was wrong?

He would heal her!

He dropped and gingerly touched her to impart the life he carried.

He looked deep inside and the fire roared. This would work.

Then the fire extinguished. The world swirled around Kast. Dizziness and exhaustion seized him.

Heal.

Nothing.

Heal!

Still nothing.

He was empty. He had nothing.

He wailed. He was empty. He had nothing anymore. He was burned out. His body was recovering as the girl had said. Because he was weak, Aurah was going to die, if she wasn't already dead. Kast couldn't stop it from happening. He was powerless. His tears fell over her.

A rustling caught his attention.

An eerie and foreboding rustling made Kast take his attention away from the girl. He looked around.

Then Kast heard the worst noise possible.

A shrill high-pitched screech.

And then another.

And another.

A whole chorus of the curs sang.

Why had creation allowed those wretches to live? And so many!

"No!" Kast screamed.

In the short distance, he could see the emerging monsters rise from the grass on the plains. The wind caught their stench and blew it across his nose.

Kast grabbed Aurah, lifting her as gently as he could. Tears poured. This was the end. Fate had given them something so good, then ripped it away in the worst way possible. There was no good. There was no reward.

Kast moved as quickly as his worn body would let him back towards the forest. It was a meaningless effort, but he couldn't just give up, could he?

He didn't know anymore.

The trees came. The monsters screamed again. Much closer. He made it to the path. The clearest way was the best option for moving. Unfortunately, it was the same for the Savages, as well. He looked for anything that would help him fight against the cretins.

Then he saw something and felt his gut twist. What was fate doing? Why did this happen? What were these confrontations? Would there be no solace?

Sheer reaction.

In a mere moment, he knew the decision that faced him. And in even less time, he made his choice.

Running, he approached as fast as he could. The Cloak stood in front of his troop, shocked at the sudden appearance of Kast holding the girl.

Shocked.

Kast didn't care about the consequences. He dropped to his knees at The Cloak's feet. The man's strands of grey hair tumbled across his strained and wrinkled face. A look of confusion etched into the deep lines trailing through his features.

"Please." Kast tried to speak. "Please! Save her! Save her! Save her!" He bowed his head to the monster. "Take me! Kill me! Just save her! Save her!" Kast wept openly before the man. The sounds of the Savages raged nearby.

The Cloak just stared.

And stared.

And screamed.

Kast gawked at The Cloak as he gripped his hair, and his whole body shook violently.

He screamed loudly before Kast. The old man's lungs roared into Kast's face.

"Hey, what did you do?" A bald-headed man raced forward, yelling at Kast.

What did I do?

"What do we do? What now?" This time the bald man yelled his question at The Cloak, hoping to be heard over the screaming.

The Cloak tore locks of hair from his head and raked his nails across his face. Rivulets of blood trailed down.

Screeching some pain, some gruesome horror that haunted him.

A purple ball formed in The Cloak's hand in a second, and in the next it blasted through a nearby tree, felling it. Dropping to his knees, his hands fell open onto the ground as some unseen weight crushed the man. His eyes blaring open, he stared forward.

Screaming. Blood dripped from his face.

The Savages cried, close by.

The blood drained from the bald man's face as he stared at The Cloak.

What would happen now? Would the girl be alright? What happened to The Cloak?

Kast didn't know. He stayed on his knees for eternity, holding the dying girl.

The girl who had annihilated his insanity.

He held her as she faded from life, and he couldn't do anything more to stop it.

The Savages screamed again. They were nearly on top of them.

The bald man wasted no time.

"Lizard Guts! Fall back! Gale, carry the girl!"

The band called Lizard Guts reacted quickly. A man took Aurah from Kast's arms. Kast nearly killed the man.

"Stop!" the bald man yelled at Kast. Why he obeyed, he didn't know. The bald man grabbed his arm, pulling him away from the closing Savages and The Cloak.

Kast turned against the man's pull and watched The Cloak. Something was blaring in Kast's mind. It was coming from The Cloak, something . . . *evil.*

A purple sphere began to glow around The Cloak. This time, black laced its way through the purple aura. The sphere grew slowly. Kast and the bald man next to him gaped at the Cloak.

The sphere devoured and killed everything it touched, turning everything to ash. The life of the forest blackened immediately. Colored leaves greyed and faded away. Nearby trees shriveled under the touch.

The Savages plowed forward, intent on their prey.

But they were wrong.

They were the prey.

The sphere grew larger, growing outward through the plants and everything living. The Savages that ran into the aura first let out their screams, a mix of whining and shrieking until they stopped altogether. Kast watched the creatures fade to ash.

"Move!" The bald man wrenched on his arm, dragging him away from The Cloak.

What? Move?

The orb of decay raced faster, heading straight for them.

Kast sprinted through the woods. The whole troop of men had already disappeared in their escape. The bald man ran with a fervor, barely matching pace with Kast.

Then the air stopped, just like so long ago when Kast fought The Cloak at the Capital. The air surged past the men, threatening to drag them into The Cloak's demise. Kast and the man grabbed trees and held on as the air raged. They looked up. The aura had ceased its expansion, but the rushing air dragged so much into its field. The Savages were all gone, their whine quelled. Kast looked for The Cloak in the midst of it, but the aura had grown so dense that it was a solid wall. Kast held the tree, hoping the phenomenon would end soon. He lost track of time, focusing only on his grip on the tree.

In an exploding roar, The Cloak's strange magic ended, leaving a crater in the earth that matched the sphere's shape perfectly.

And no Cloak.

Kast released the tree reluctantly and stumbled backward. He gasped, trying to recover the air that was stolen away. He rested for a moment, when something encased his wrists, clenching tightly.

"I'm sorry, but you have to come with us now," the bald man panted. He had wasted no time.

"I don't care! Just get the girl to someone who can heal her!" Kast looked at the man as desperately as he could. He just wanted Aurah to live. The man nodded at him.

"The locks stay on. I need to find my men and then we head straight to the Capital where I'm certain they will have healers ready and waiting," tried to reassure Kast. *Why?* Kast nodded again. The bald man turned and began to move towards where the troop had headed.

Would the girl be alright? He tried not to think of the damage she had taken. He was trying to stay positive. He wouldn't be able to handle the truth that he ended her life. *All because of my purpose.*

His arms were restrained with some odd-looking device.

Would everything be alright?

He walked after the man, carrying only the smallest amount of hope.

CHAPTER FORTY-EIGHT

Kast tripped into the cell, propelled by the arms of the soldiers behind him. They had left the locks on his wrist. The cell was the only one in the room. On the wall opposite Kast's cell, an archway led into a corridor heading to the rest of the world.

He had heard the bald man, whom he had learned was named Charlie, tell the Capital that he was the dragon and that they had turned him into a man to pursue him better. Kast was shocked to see the horrifying character who was hailed as the Queen. She not only scorned Charlie and his band named Lizard Guts for being unreliable, but she also beat Kast with her fists. She had stopped after a couple of swings. After all that he had gone through, the punches didn't seem like much but compared to what he was expecting, it was more than he wished to receive again.

What was he thinking? This is what he deserved. Forget the good graces of Aurah. She was so kind and compassionate, but compassion couldn't atone for his mistakes. This was what was right and good. Dying to make amends.

Though he would sorely miss her company.

Charlie had informed the soldiers that the locks on his wrists were enhanced to counter the dragon's power. He wasn't going anywhere, even if he wanted to. He did hear the healers examine Aurah and make a quick synopsis—she was severely wounded and needed immediate medical attention. They rushed her away.

Tears fell from his eyes. There was no bed in this cell. Nothing but cold stone and iron bars. He didn't care. He sat on the floor, against the wall and held his face weeping for his lost friend. He tried so hard, and the moment he agreed to try to save himself, she nearly died. Maybe she was dead. He wept more, remembering the best goodbye he could muster as they carted her away. It had all happened so fast. He wept for her. He wept for the destruction.

He wept until his body throbbed in an uneasy sleep.

He awoke in a hazy and a fading place. There was no definition apart from himself. He looked at his hands. *No locks.*

Where was this? What was going on?

He felt a gentle tug pull his mind in a direction. He didn't know how to control his body, but as he thought about the urge, he moved. It was a dark place filled with green. He couldn't make out the world. The tug was faint, but it had grown stronger the closer he got to it. He found the source.

A dying ember.

A light suffocated and ensnared by the surrounding darkness.

Dying.

His attention was drawn away.

Something was screaming.

The gravity wrenched on him. *So many.*

As he thought, he moved. He wished he hadn't

Teeth gnashing. Violence. Swarms of snakes gathered, slithering around each other, but they weren't the worst part.

In the middle of the swarm was a mighty serpent, black as ink. It was still while the fumes of hatred billowed from its existence.

It turned its beady eyes, so distinct in a world of the undeterminable.

It released a torrent of flames straight at Kast.

He shot to his feet in a stupor. The guards outside of his cell startled, held their *spears* at the ready.

"Sorry, bad dream."

"I didn't know monsters like you could dream, but I'm certain they're all bad since you can." The guard was unpleasant.

Kast didn't begrudge him that. He looked out a nearby window. It was evening. He had slept for a few hours. *How is Aurah?*

"Hey, how is the girl who was brought back?" Kast turned towards the guards.

"Shut your mouth, trash." The guard turned away from him.

"Shut it for me. How is the girl?" Kast had no care what these guards thought. If there was any chance to convince one to tell him about the girl, then he would do whatever he could to take that chance.

"Scum! We're—"

"That's enough, guard." A dangerous voice cut off the man's retort. The Queen emerged from the corridor. She looked beautiful, but the kind of beauty that was meant to lure one to peace. There was a monster living beneath the surface.

Kast stared. Everything he wanted to say contradicted his resolve to die as payment. He didn't like the woman standing before him. If that wasn't evil radiating from her, then it was something near to evil. She leveled a cool gaze on him. Her eyes were empty quarries, and all he could see in them was a pit of stone. Heartless. *Vengeful.*

She leaned close to the bars and hissed her bile towards his face. "That's really nice of you, monster, to be asking about the person you herded to the slaughter like some swine, but you're nothing but a heap of dung, and you'll feel every ounce of torment you levied out on her and the rest of the world!" She turned away quickly, whipping what bit of the dress would flow freely. She walked toward the opposing wall, then stopped. "The girl will make a recovery, though she will bear many scars from your filthy involvement. I doubt anyone else could have

made it through a journey with a creature as revolting as you."
Elizabeth turned her head slightly. He could see nothing more
than her profile in the fading light. "I just came to tell you that
tomorrow, the gallows are waiting for your neck. You'll find
out when it's time to die, though. I won't make this easy for
you in any sense of the word." She faced forward and walked
towards the opening of the corridor, then stopped. "Oh, and
dragon? I hope your last night is miserable." She left quickly.

Kast fell to his knees, gripping the iron bars. He wept
even more tears.

He stayed that way, emotion flooded from his inner being.
She will be alright!
All was well.
He felt the pull of exhaustion again.
Pass the time. Let it be tomorrow.
He could sleep well now.
He could die well.

CHAPTER FORTY-NINE

The world was cold. *For once.*
The sun was warm. *For once.*
His arms felt. *It's been so long.*
Pain. *It's been too long.*
Dirt.
Air.
The leaves on the trees. *Beautiful. It's been too long.*
Where was he? He could hardly remember anything. Such a haze had occupied his vision. *But now he saw with clarity.*

He remembered his unforgivable transgressions

He remembered his...*task.*

He remembered the pursuit.

He remembered . . . *the dragon.* And the girl.

He choked back the memories. *For now.* There was much to pay for, but later.

He thought about the dragon. *A beacon of light. How?* The chasms that dragon had torn in his soul. *Why?*

He lay on the ground, staring at the sky.

He could feel more, smell more, hear more. *See more.*

He remembered something astonishing, the blade that cleaved the darkness away. *How?*

He began to remember so much of his past. So much he had always known—*but now it made sense again.*

He cringed, feeling the hurts of so long ago.

The failures. *The betrayals.*

He remembered so much.

Then his mind broke the barrier and he remembered.

"My name . . . ." A weak voice sprouted into the air. *Slowly.* The pain of using something long-dormant stressed him. "My name . . . ." He tried again. He had almost forgotten how to make the sounds. "My name is . . . ." *Almost there.* "My name is . . . ." He gasped.

"Fill."

He rocked up and sat on the forest floor. He stared around wide-eyed. At first, things came slowly, like a lesser gravity well. But with time the gravity strengthened, and his lost memories berated the wall of his psyche. The pain in his legs would subside. *It always did before . . . .* He was drained of energy. He had just gone through a transformation. *More like a shattering.* His body had responded from the impossible stress and relieved every ounce of energy in the attempts to purge itself of the lingering evil. *It worked.*

He stood on his feet. He wasn't where his recent transformation had happened. That part of the world would be scarred. *So, where was he?* He inhaled. He slowed and listened. *My magic helped to purge my body from the darkness blinding me. It also saved me from the purging itself. And after so long . . . . I have finally accomplished my life's goal. Well, almost accomplished. There is still work to be done.* Fill was exhausted, but he wasn't finished. He understood what he must do. He had finally found what he had been looking for. He had spent so long looking, too, but now, the chance was real. Maybe things would work this time.

The world went dark, interrupting his reunion with lucidity.

His eyes glassed over.

How did I miss this?

He clung to a nearby tree, watching as courts of dragons flew by overhead. *It's an entire army!* They must have belonged to that black knave *Vasiss.* That monster was more trouble

than Fill could handle. He had fought well, but now . . .
. *Now we only have one hope.* It was about time the wretch
was dealt with, though. Eventually, Vasiss would come to
dominate everything, *only to find domination was different
from ruling.* Everyone from old knew the mighty dragon's
grand purpose. Everyone supported him. *Until he embraced
his insanity freely.* The monster was evil by nature on top of
the consuming insanity.

The dragons overhead ended their incredible procession.
They would wait until the right moment to strike.

Fill only had until then. Turning, he sprinted towards the
kind presence radiating from the Capital. He would be there
soon enough.

Hold on, Kast.

CHAPTER FIFTY

A large rumble woke Kast. He looked up from the wall he had leaned against. There was a window high up with more metal bars. It let the frigid air seep into his cell freely. If he thought about it, the stone beneath him was terribly chilled and stole the heat from his body. He hardly felt it. Life was surreal in light of the death that was inevitable. Well, maybe inevitable. He slumped back to the wall. *No fighting.* This was good, paying for the crime and the hurt he had caused Aurah was his only duty now. Releasing her from the pangs of attachment was his due. He smiled as the stone ripped the warmth from him.

The rumbling from outside the window steadily grew louder. He stood to try and look out and see what the commotion was.

"That's the sound of your death, trash. The whole city gathers to see you dead." A guard behind him plunged the words into Kast like a stinging dagger. Kast smirked to himself. They didn't know how thankful he was for the opportunity to pay for his wrong. They were doing a service, not wounding him.

Kast sat beneath the window for some time, thinking about every moment with Aurah. The guards barely moved at their posts, but he could tell that they both kept sneaking glances in his direction. *Terrified of the big bad dragon.* He smiled again and looked at his hands. Thoughts of how much pride had consumed him before he accepted his new paradigm. He was glad Aurah would be alright, and he kept thinking about how much better off she would be without him. There was still one thing that bothered him, though. He couldn't place it. He was trying to process everything from the beginning, but every time he confronted this catch in his mind, it became elusive. It slipped away as soon as it was about to be discovered. He had received so much clarity already, yet his thoughts were arrested again, stuck on an unknowable detail.

Footsteps from the hall pulled him back to reality. It wasn't long before the bald man, Charlie, and some other men appeared. Kast counted six of them in total.

"Stop!" The guards took an immediate defensive position, leveling their spears with Charlie and the other men.

"Hold up!" Charlie shouted back at the guards. "Here's a written order from Her Majesty. We're to escort the beast to the hanging." He held out the paper. The guards shot a quick look at each other before one lowered their weapons and took the paper. Charlie rolled his eyes when the paper was finally taken from his hand.

"Looks real. We're to escort the dragon with these men, then we report to the captain." The guard told the other. They nodded at each other and stood out of the way.

"About time," Charlie muttered to himself. Kast could hear him despite the whisper though. The man named Charlie turned to Kast in the cell and noticed him staring. He stared back for a second before turning to the guards. "Unlock the cell." A simple command. "Harvey." One of the men began to move. Kast couldn't tell what he was doing. Maybe it was some measure of safety against the beast? He wouldn't resist, anyway.

Kast watched the guard move to the door and produced a key to unlock it. With a creak, the iron swung open. Kast lurched to his feet. He laughed as all the men jumped from the unexpected motion. All except Charlie. The guards had their spears pointing at Kast in a mere moment. Lizard Guts toyed anxiously with their weapons—whatever it was that they wielded.

"Cute, dragon. I'd ask that you not do that again. Not unless you want Harvey to fill your gut with holes." Charlie's face remained placid and unaltered. Everyone else seemed to relax at his words. Kast gave him a small smile. Playing around at a time like this, where did that come from? It must have been from his time with Aurah. He probably learned a thing or two about acting humorous at inappropriate times from her. He smiled bigger at the thought. Everything on his mind from earlier had been replaced by the men before him and the thoughts of the girl.

"Right. I'd rather we kill me in front of the world anyway. I have a sincere apology to give them." Kast held out his hands in front of himself, his wrists still shackled with the locks. It seemed so long ago when the restraints were suddenly thrown on. He moved forward slowly to appease the tension that welled up in the room. Charlie merely watched him, probably trusting the man named Harvey to be a quick and efficient shot.

The men and the guards surrounded him and led him away down the hall and outside of the jail. The morning was chilly. The sky was clouded, it was gloomy outside. No rays of sun broke the grey. *How fitting.* Kast seemed to relish the appropriateness of his coming death. He continued walking down a path littered with stones and other debris. He had noticed when he was brought into the city before that much of the city still lay in shambles from his attack. The city hadn't done much in the way of recovery.

Kast noticed it again as he was led outside of the small jailer's compound and through the city streets. Children and adults alike stared at him. Openly and from the shadows of alleyways. Many were covered in dirt, some looked diseased and sick. Others shivered at the cold. Everyone seemed hungry and underfed. They all stared at the entourage as it passed by.

The streets gave way to a large square at the foot of the Capital's palace. The large building loomed overhead ominously. Except for the few stragglers they had passed, it looked like the whole city was gathered in the square. The moment they entered the square an army surrounded them.

"We'll take it from here." Charlie turned at looked at the two guards. They nodded and walked off, probably to find their captain. He moved to the front of his men as they surrounded Kast completely. Kast counted twenty-three of them, not including Charlie. Charlie began to march forward, and Lizard Guts followed hard on his trail. The people in the square melted away, creating a spacious path for them to walk through. Beyond the parting masses lay Kast's doom. The gallows sat erected directly in front of the palace, raised above for all to see. On its side sat an erected balcony where the Queen stood, guarded by a few soldiers.

This is it. Kast found his heartbeat racing. He wasn't scared, it was just nerve-wracking. He laughed at himself. *Am I worried how I'm going to look hanging while the life is wrenched from this body?* He shook his head; he was trying not to laugh at the thought. It was strange, so strange. Lizard Guts split and surrounded the stairs, walling off the rest of the world, only leaving available the way forward to death. Charlie walked up the stairs, stopping midway to look back at the dragon. Kast looked into his eyes. He began to walk up the stairs unquestionably. There was something about the man named Charlie, something that made him not want to resist. There was certainly a level of distaste in the man's eyes, but whatever was there went beyond a meager hate of the dragon. It was as if every connection of their gazes conveyed a simple plea—*no more trouble, please.* Kast wasn't usually the most perceptive, but when it came to the man named Charlie, it was clear to see a deep desire for peace.

Kast stood at the top of the gallows and looked out at the world before him. How many eyes? How many souls lay their gaze on him right then? How many wrongs would be satisfied with his death? How many people would be satisfied with the payment for his actions?

At Charlie's beckoning, Kast moved to the center of the platform and the executioner wasted no time placing the rope around his neck. The rope shortened, pulling Kast to the tips of his toes. He was barely standing as he tried to keep his balance.

"People of the Capital!" The Queen's voice rang out to the city before her. Only the sound of a gentle breeze would challenge the Queen's voice. "We have felt and witnessed the consuming wrath of the mighty dragon who has declared itself an enemy to humankind! Who has lured even greater enemies to our doorstep, and who has stolen the precious peace we once thrived in! We grew bountifully as a nation, standing strong together. Yet by the heinous fiend's malevolent power, we were cut down and stamped out. We witness death in inconceivable numbers, our progress is thwarted, and our value is undermined!" She had begun to scream at all the wrongs he had done. "Now, with sheer determination and power, men have finally grasped the threads of the life of this monstrous villain. I ask, therefore! What shall be done to it?" Her voice rang out, echoing off the buildings consumed by the people before her.

"Kill him!" A single voice yelled out. Kast could see the man crying out, raising a fist. His voice resounded outwards, repeating the phrase. Then in a sudden explosion, the rest joined in the mantra.

"Kill him! Kill him! Kill him!" Over and over again, the voices cried out for justice. He aimed his head at the woman monarch who stared back at him. They stayed like that for a time. The Queen reveled in her glorious revenge.

Kast watched her turn and make eye contact with the executioner. She raised her fist.

And threw it down.

CHAPTER FIFTY-ONE

Aurah woke, gasping. Pain and soreness throughout her body screamed at her, yet again. An incredible noise reverberated through the walls. She was in a small room. An older man stood at her awakening, walking towards her. She began to wrestle herself out of bed, fighting against the pain. What was going on? Where was she? She was on the horse when that black dragon came out of nowhere and had started attacking. The next thing she remembered was being beaten off the back of the horse. *The horse.* She had seen that much before fading. She still felt weak. Actually, she felt like heaving. Her stomach churned horribly.

"Hold, hold, Aurah!" The man laid a hand gently on her shoulder, pressing her back into the bed. "Don't move. You'll hurt yourself." He tried to quiet her, but she was unsettled by the loud yell outside.

"Kast! Kas . . . ." She tried talking, but every part of her screamed in pain.

"Don't worry about that monster. He'll be dead soon, and then we can all move past this." Aurah sat up, ignoring the pain. "I'm serious, Aurah!" The man tried to push her back down. "Those men who brought you may have healed you with some strange magic, but they said you still needed time to recover!" He was pushing against her, and when he backed away, he turned to a shelf. "Stubborn girl. Some Baneswurt will quiet you. Why the beast matters to you I don't know."

Aurah's thoughts cleared. The man stood rummaging through a cluttered pile of glass containers, all filled with strange substances. He had mentioned that she had been healed. Though her body ached, she seemed to be whole. She was getting tired of being hurt badly then healed by some strange power. She must have been injured badly because she still felt terrible despite being healed. She sat up, moving her legs off to the side, to rest on the cold floor. *Baneswurt.* That name sounded familiar. She looked up and a memory replayed itself from the time she was helping Dale tend to Kast's wounds in his hut. He had eccentrically rubbed some of the powder on Kast's body over his heart and under his arms. Kast had remained completely still for quite some time after. Dale had told her he much preferred to allow others to ingest the substance, but Kast wasn't able to drink it. She looked at the healer before her. He was mixing the powder into a cup of water. She was ready. She stood quietly, denying the pain in her limbs.

The man turned around, holding the cup, only to be shocked by the girl. Aurah seized the Baneswurt from the man and shoved the cup into his mouth, drenching him in the mixture. His eyes went wide. Aurah smiled as the man began to wobble weakly.

"Why, Aurah?" He dropped to his knees. "How?" His eyes closed and he fell forward. She tried to catch him but was too weak to move quickly. She didn't worry long. He hadn't hit too hard.

The door to the room was left open and she poked her head out, gripping the doorway. Sometimes her body was strong and tolerant, but in a moment, it would give out, and she would nearly collapse. The hall was clear. She knew where she was. It was the healer's ward, attached to the palace. The cries outside continued. She didn't need to see to envision the scene. She moved as quickly as she could in her enfeebled state. It was funny. She spent so long dreaming of being back home, and now she wasn't satisfied with it. What—*who*— she wanted was about to die.

The door out came after many limps and groans from Aurah's lips. Thankfully, she wasn't so far gone and could still open them. She passed the threshold, heading out towards the balcony that was for conducting public gatherings. No one was around. Everyone was in the square, letting their voice raise to the heavens. She could make out the chant. *Kill him. Kill him.* A tear fell from her eye. They didn't see the change. How could they? He—and probably all dragons—would always be hated. The yelling grew louder and louder until the noise almost hurt to hear. She would never make it in time. There was no way.

The path towards the balcony was straightforward, cutting across the grounds to the wall that surrounded the Palace. Aurah would occasionally weaken and lean on a statue or some other feature before she could move forward again.

Then she stood at the small steps. The cacophony of noise rose over the walls. How long had she wasted with her weakness? She planted a foot on a step, then another. Pain coursed through her legs as she climbed the stairs. *Kast.* Saying his name filled her with determination. The kind of determination that put her on the top step of the balcony to look out across the peoples of the city. Everyone was cheering and shouting. Then she saw Elizabeth.

Elizabeth was staring at the executioner with her arm raised.

No! Aurah shot forward, denying pain. Her arms flailed in front of her, hoping to stop the motion. Maybe that would be all she needed to do? It was all she could do.

She collided with Elizabeth, gripping the surprised woman's arm, keeping it mid-way up in the air. Aurah looked over at

Kast frantically. He still stood on the gallows. He was staring, his eyes wide as he realized what had happened.

Her emotions fluttered at the sight of him. She couldn't help but stare, consuming every second feverishly.

"Aurah, what are doing? What are you doing here?" Elizabeth stared at her in shock, yelling at her. The city took a second before they realized what had happened. They all quieted down, stunned at the interruption. Aurah breathed much easier, though the fear of all eyes being on her weighed heavily. She looked at Elizabeth. She gulped hard.

"Elizabeth, stop!" She didn't mean to yell, in fact, it hurt to yell, but the emotions and the adrenaline all pumped through her veins. Elizabeth took a step back. Confusion settled across her face. Aurah had her attention, and unwittingly—the rest of the city's. "Killing him isn't right! I can't explain, but there is so much about the dragon that has changed, so much that will change our hate of him!" *Please, Elizabeth,* Aurah pleaded in her mind, hoping her words would be convincing. Elizabeth stared, still trying to understand what was happening.

"Aurah? Why are you here? You need to be resting! What do you mean this monster doesn't deserve this?"

"Stop it, Elizabeth! All you're concerned with is the idea of revenge paraded around as justice. This dragon is accountable for the wrong he has done, but through our time together, he has more than paid for his wrongs and demonstrated a change. You can't kill him."

"Listen to yourself! You must have your head too hard, Aurah. Defending him like that. There's no way *it* could ever have paid for the wrongs it served you." Elizabeth was angry and yelling.

This was not going the way Aurah had intended or even hoped. *Elizabeth . . . .*

"Aurah, I think you need to go back and lay down before you let loose with any more of your nonsense. Even if the beast had atoned for its atrocities against you, it will *never* pay for its crimes against humanity! It must be slaughtered!" Elizabeth screamed at Aurah.

Aurah stared, her mouth hung open. Elizabeth was gone, consumed with this broken idea of justice. *Why?*

"Guard! Take this petty girl away!" Elizabeth shouted, a crazed look coating her eyes. Aurah saw her truly now. Elizabeth was in so much pain. She was unkempt. It wasn't visible far away, but now that Aurah was up close, she could see it clearly. Elizabeth's hands had been wrapped. You could see dried blood staining her knuckles. Aurah had never seen Elizabeth like this.

Strong arms gripped Aurah from behind. Elizabeth smiled and turned back to the dragon on the gallows.

"No! Elizabeth! Please!" Aurah thrashed against whoever held her, trying against all hope to save Kast.

It was too late.

She would never make it in time.

Elizabeth had just dropped her arm when a streak fell from the sky, snatching up the executioner.

A large, black streak.

As fast as the streak fell, a spurt of crimson erupted from it, and a building erupted behind the gallows, blasting rocks and debris into the crowd. Aurah stopped fighting the arms that held her and stared in sheer horror.

Vasiss was here.

"Filthy humans!" The Insane King began to speak. He threw something at the crowd. *The executioner's corpse.* "I've had just about enough of your trash, so consider these words informing you of your impending death to be the last respect you'll ever get!" He roared at the masses. The people screamed and began to trample each other, trying to run away.

A swift movement near the dragon caught the corner of Aurah's eye. *Lizard Guts!* The man pulled out a weapon of some sort, and aiming at Vasiss, he fired quickly. The bright bolt flew fast at the monster but a pitch-black shroud erupted from his body, swallowing the bolt. Vasiss's neck pitched towards the man, his jaws snapped together and receded. Even from this distance, Aurah saw what was left of the attacker fall over.

A leer crested the beast's face. Facing the crowds of people, his lungs welled up and he released a torrent of flames. The heat seared Aurah, even as far away as she was. She and the guard that had seized her turned to shield themselves from the inferno.

She turned back when the heat subsided, free of restraint. Her throat caught at the sight of so many people murdered, charred and burning. Her mouth gaped, hanging open. There wasn't even a moment to scream.

"Aurah, what's going on?" Elizabeth grabbed her from the side. Fear lined every feature. That's right, she had never seen *that* terror of a dragon.

She had never met Vasiss before.

"Kast isn't the bad guy, Elizabeth." She looked to the soldier who had seized her only moments before. "You! Your Queen is in danger. Take her to the palace and protect her!" Aurah was giving the orders now, and as if she needed a reminder, her body convulsed from pain. She gripped the rail on the balcony. The soldier needed no further prompting; his Queen was in danger. Grabbing Elizabeth's arm near the shoulder, he began to pull her away towards safety. Aurah turned and headed towards the gallows.

"No! Aurah! What are you doing? You're insane!" Elizabeth screamed at her. Aurah turned to look her straight in the eye. She saw what she had always seen, but this time she understood what it was. *Fear.* Maybe she couldn't be hard on her. That fear was the fear of loss. Elizabeth couldn't cope with loss, not after what she went through as a child. Aurah stared back.

"Elizabeth, more wrong decisions will never bring back either of our parents. It won't fix their mistakes, nor even keep us safe." Aurah kept her gaze leveled at the Queen. "It's time you grew up and stopped justifying a life consumed with your own pain. There are bigger things than our hurts, no matter how deep they run or how much they hinder us. There is no room for petty revenge in this world." What was she saying? Where did that come from? She turned back towards the gallows and knew in an instant.

Thank you, Kast.

Vasiss had engaged in a rampage, destroying the parts of the city that were whole. *I can't worry about him right now.* Focusing again, she looked for a way down. There should be stairs that would let her head to the square. It didn't take much more searching before she found them. She let go of the rail to move forward, only to collapse immediately. Her body refused to move, but she had to get Kast free. An arm wrapped around her waist, and she turned her head in surprise. *Elizabeth.*

"Elizabe . . . ."

"Shut up, Aurah, I'm helping you with whatever stupid plan you have. If you have the nerve to speak to me like that, then what you're doing must be important. Just know I don't like it—or you—one bit for doing it." Elizabeth glared at her. Aurah felt so many mixed emotions.

"Thanks, then. Let's go. Kast is the only one here who has even the slightest chance of challenging that black monster." She turned, supported by Elizabeth and made for the stairs.

"Your Majesty!" The soldier called out from behind.

"If you want to do any good then tag along, otherwise keep your mouth shut!" Elizabeth yelled at the man. She kept her arm around Aurah's waist, and they eventually made it to the stairs. Before they took the first step, the soldier came along the other side of Aurah and helped her down the stairs. The world looked much more menacing at the bottom of the square. Aurah shook her head; she couldn't become distracted. The gallows were only a short distance away. They made their way around some debris when a rush of wind hit, blasting the three of them to the ground. *So much pain!* Aurah cringed as her body absorbed the fall completely. She looked up. Vasiss had swept by them and landed in an uproar.

"Well, look at that! It's the little girl and the nest rat!" Vasiss screamed the words. The black shroud from earlier had begun to pour from his scales. Aurah had no idea what it was, but it wasn't good if it was associated with that monster. Vasiss aimed his head toward Kast who was still wrestling to stay on his toes. Aurah grimaced. "Looks like you've got your hands full! It wouldn't be good if . . . ."

Vasiss lashed his tail out, knocking out some of the supports for the gallows. It tipped dangerously, but worse—Kast was now completely hanging by the rope as the floor under him angled away from his already struggling feet.

"No!" Aurah screamed, jumping to her feet and moving forward. Something plowed into her side, pitching her to the side. She barely caught a glimpse of the soldier who had restrained her earlier, now in her place. Then he was gone in a red burst as Vasiss's tail whipped out, catching the man. Aurah withdrew to her mind. She couldn't handle this. People dying, impossible odds, her body quaked, her fists clenched on the ground as she gasped, each breath a battle to achieve.

Then a mighty roar.

Missiles of light burst from every direction, peppering the black serpent. Vasiss launched to the sky. Lizard Guts kept the Insane King away. *For who knows how long.*

Aurah gasped, wrestling her emotions back under control. She clenched again and looked up. Kast flailed on that rope. He needed her, she needed him. She forced herself to her feet, her head turned back to Elizabeth. Her sister lay hunched on the ground, completely gripped by the magnitude of the situation. She was out now. Aurah turned. She had already wasted too much time. She stumbled, her body fighting against her stubbornness. She had to save Kast. One step fell after the other, then her body screamed, tearing itself apart in agony— then more steps. She fell at the bottom of the stairs, gripped with pain, her mind split white at the force of the torment. She kept going. She couldn't walk anymore, so she crawled. The stairs moved behind her, one after the other. They rocked back and forth, nearly dislodged by Vasiss's attack earlier. She hoped they would stay intact as she slowly crawled up their expanse. By some unknown stroke of luck, she found herself embracing the top step. She had to save Kast. She tilted her head up to see his eyes, bloodshot now due to the circulation being cut off. His eyes were trying their hardest to look at something. The flailing and swinging on the rope interrupted his gaze regularly, but then she saw where he was looking.

Their eyes met. His eyes were matted with tears. His mouth opened, choking out ghastly noises.

"Ruuuuu! Ruuu! Mmuumm!" He screamed as loud as what was left in his lungs would let him. Tears poured down his face as he kept up his efforts. Then his eyes widened.

"Isn't this wonderful!" Vasiss landed violently next to the gallows. He lowered his head to level with the two of them. "A nice little reunion where I finally murder you trash once and for all!" The dragon's screams finished Aurah. Her mind splintered under the pain of the noise and her body. She tried to look at Kast but couldn't even do that.

At least we die together.

Her vision cleared again for a moment. Maybe fate wasn't so kind after all? She stared at the black beast as his chest welled up—inhaling air. *Any second now . . . .* She watched the monster finish his intake, then she watched as his head wound up to burn them, the bright light of flames welled up from its terrible throat. She could begin to see the first tongues of fire.

She felt the beginnings of death's release surround them.

CHAPTER FIFTY-TWO

Kast fought as hard as he could to breathe, but there was nothing holding him anymore except the rope around his neck. His nose snorted hard, trying to force inwards, but nothing would stop the inevitable. He was already out of air. The world was turning white, and he knew blackness would come soon after. Aurah lay at his feet, he didn't know if she were dead or alive. He didn't even know how she had managed to recover.

He looked at Vasiss in front of him, then stopped struggling. His body ached for the end. He wished he could have sorted out the last little quirk before dying. He wished that the girl wasn't involved, but maybe this was for best? All that was ahead was pain and suffering. He accepted their fate. Maybe there was an afterlife where he could meet her?

He watched as the Insane King's flames welled up, crawling forth from his throat. *This is the end.*

Then, it stopped.

Faster than he could follow. That wasn't saying much in his current disposition though.

A purple ball blasted the beast in its great maw. The black shroud tried to protect him, but it was too slow. The Majesty's head caromed away, releasing its torrent to the sky. Before Kast could even grasp what had happened, a man in a cloak flew up at them and deftly severed the noose holding Kast in the air. The cloaked man caught Kast, and purple began to encompass them both as he tore the rest of the rope from Kast's neck.

"Her! Aurah!" Kast pointed desperately at her. The cloaked man jumped to her side and purple surrounded them the three of them. What was it?

Life.

Kast watched as her body breathed more quickly, then it leveled out. The girl lifted her head to see the purple around her, then she looked at Kast. He longed to protect her. Why did he want to protect her so much? Then she looked at the stranger. Kast followed her gaze, staring at the unknown man—no, not a stranger.

It was The Cloak.

"Quick! Kast, Aurah, stand and get off this blasted contraption!" The Cloak spoke. He seemed so different. *Why?*

Kast moved quickly to the girl and jumped off the death device. He landed near Elizabeth.

"Aurah, you need to take the Queen somewhere else!" Kast turned to look at her. She seemed slightly taken aback by the sudden shift in things, but he watched as the cloud in her eyes dissipated. She dived deep into his chest and clung tightly.

"Filthy swine, why don't you die?" Vasiss had regained his bearings and was screaming.

"Long time no see, little pup!" The Cloak had stood next to Kast and Aurah and was confronting the Insane King.

"So, it was you, after all! Lost in your darkness, were you?"

A purple orb seemingly materialized out of nowhere and slammed into Vasiss's chest, knocking him backward. Bits of black shroud faded away, interrupting the impact. The Insane King screamed at The Cloak's audacity.

"You filth! It's time for you to die!" The monster threw his head back towards the sky and released the shrillest roar Kast had ever heard from a dragon. Kast watched Aurah and

Elizabeth cover their ears in pain. It was strange. They were the only ones . . . .

"Lizard Guts! Charlie! Be prepared! Our worst nightmare descends!" Kast reeled at the sudden thoughts in his head. Aurah seemed to be doing the same thing. They looked at each other in awe. "My name is Fill! I'm sorry for any difficulty at my hand before, but now is not the time to discuss that. The greatest threat to all life stands before us, and I need your help in combatting it." The Cloak—no, *Fill*— spoke quickly. Kast had no idea what to expect.

Then the sky cleared.

Clouds swirled from violent torrents in the air.

A bright light shone as an impossible number of dragons fell from the sky, diving to fulfill mankind's destruction.

Kast stared. He had never seen so many dragons. This was unthinkable. There was no way they would ever survive. He looked at Aurah. She was already staring at him.

"Kast, I'm sorry. I'm sorry for your insanity and your mistakes. I'm sorry life wasn't better for you. I really wish things were different." She spoke quickly. He stared at her as the words poured from her lips. When the last syllable fell, he straightened up.

Resolved.

The bolts of light began again, picking up where their last barrage ended. Dragons rained from the sky, destroying the world beneath. Kast watched in awe.

A dragon landed behind them suddenly. *They were falling from the whole sky!* Kast had only stared at one point in the sky. Dragons were diving *everywhere*. Darkness covered the land.

Fill ended the dragon with a fast orb.

"Kast! This is no time for games!" Fill threw another orb and engaged in more combat. Something was strange. Kast looked at Aurah. Everything had begun to turn hazy and obscure. He looked at his hands. The light of the world dimmed.

Then the world went black.

Kast looked around. Darkness. So . . . *familiar.*

Why am I here?

It was so real this time. He looked at his hands. He could see them against the stark backdrop of the blackness.

The darkness.

Consuming him. He felt the emptiness.

He felt the void leeching the life out of himself.

"You're finally here," the voice echoed through his mind. He turned and looked around. Memories of every time he had looked inside of himself flashed back. He walked through the shadows as memories appeared before him. Step after step echoed on the shadow beneath his feet. The memories from so long ago, when he was consumed with his insanity.

"Yes, Kast. Insanity . . . ." The voice rang out.

He remembered this darkness. How pleasant it was to fall to its embrace.

But then he remembered something greater. Hidden in the darkness.

He remembered finding his light, how a little ray illuminated the depths of his mind.

The beautiful potential.

A tear fell from his eye.

"Yes . . . you remember." The shadows swirled in front of Kast. Out of the churning, a form stepped forth. It was . . . *him.*

"You have cost me much, serpent scum. Your sanity is my feast." The form began to walk forward, the shadows stirring under his feet. Kast felt nothing in this place. *This is emotion. This is thought. This is the war I must fight—the greatest enemy.* Even Vasiss himself paled in comparison to the creature before Kast. He stared at the approaching mass. The insanity within himself begged to be given the forefront of his mind.

Kast had never understood fully before.

"Kast." The shadow was close.

Kast had never truly relinquished his fear.

"Kast!" Closer.

Was he really committed?

The darkness in the image of a man splintered and welled up before Kast. He stared watching as it transformed.

"What will you do now, scum?" It screamed its fury as it turned into something Kast hadn't seen in some time.

A dragon.

Himself.

"This is true power! Let your insanity rage! Give up your foolish purpose and this nonsense that has kept you so far away from me! Drink of my ire and let me feast on your mind!"

Kast felt the pull, deep and tantalizing. He remembered the blood that pooled on his tongue and the feeling of unrivaled power. He remembered the destruction and carnage, the fear—oh, the smell. Kast inhaled.

He fell to his knees. Darkness loomed around ready to strike and consume him. He felt the warmth inside already dissipating. He was drained. He tried to scream as darkness began to scour his new clarity from his mind, filling it with his anger and hate. *He loved every pulse of power the darkness carried to him.* His body arched violently on his hands and knees as he tasted the wealth of his insanity.

Then he felt a tight grip around his middle.

It was warm and life flowed into his being.

He remembered so much.

He looked forward and saw what he had been pursuing all along.

He looked forward and he saw the answer to his pursuit.

His purpose.

Not Elizabeth, as he had first presumed.

Aurah.

Tears streamed down his eyes as he saw her light fading. The grip around his middle loosening fast.

No! No! I can't, I can't do it! I can't fight!

Kast screamed soundless words as his purpose faded before him. He could never save her. He could never fulfill his purpose. He could never...

"No, Kast." A hand gripped his shoulder and pulled him to his feet. He looked at who had helped him.

Fill.

"*Light-bringer!*" The insanity in Kast's heart roared at the appearing of the cloaked man.

"What do you choose, Kast?" Fill looked him straight in the eye, but it felt like the man's eyes pierced his heart. The darkness dived down on them, but a sphere of gold and purple deflected the relentless monster. Kast stared at the form of the girl, nearly gone. He looked at the old man, staring back at him.

"Why?" All he could manage to ask. It didn't matter what was happening here, in this place. *Who was this man and why was he here?* The only questions that mattered. Fill smiled. Strange, yet fitting.

"Mine is to help another with theirs," Fill said, unable to stop smiling, his enigmatic words glazing over Kast.

Kast stared at the man, and every ounce of his energy pounded through his mind. The beast of darkness, in a harmony, hammered against the gold and purple shield.

Then a thought.

His purpose.

He knew in an instant. He looked at the shadow, at who he was.

Then he stared at the last rays of the girl—gone.

He stared back at the mysterious man.

"I know my purpose. I know myself." Kast's face set boldly against the monstrous darkness.

"I am resolved." Though he merely spoke the words, their weight cried out through the sanctum of his mind.

His hands ignited, enflamed with a white fire.

"Then be resolved." The vision of Fill faded away.

The girl! His mind screamed.

Be resolved. The voice echoed through his mind.

Resolve.

The gold and purple sphere had dissipated, but now a white one replaced it. The darkness screamed at the touch of the light. Hurt and dying.

"No! Lizard slime! You . . . ."

Resolve.

The fires on Kast's hands exploded and grew, devouring the shrieking darkness.

The world around him illuminated, and he saw so clearly. The form of the girl returned, life flowing from his light.

Then he saw it again.

His immense potential.

His heart.

Waiting for the first lick of flames to be lit and blaze forever.

It would burn brightly because he was resolved to burn brightly.

The flames on his hands seemed to sense the waiting potential, and without hesitating another second, the fire spurted from his hands.

And ignited Kast.

Kast opened his eyes. Dragons surrounded them on all fronts. Fill danced between their massive forms, and purple magic flared in all directions killing dragon after dragon. Flashes of the bolts shot out, picking off the monsters, but for every dragon killed, ten more took its place. Vasiss laced his way through the throngs of his army, diving down at Fill—then dashing away. It was only a matter of time before they were all overwhelmed and consumed.

Except for Kast.

He looked down. He had fallen to his knees. The ground and debris around him were destroyed from some kind of force.

Aurah clung to him, burying her face into his chest. *The poor girl.* He stroked her hair as she looked up at him, tears lacing her eyes. Gusts of wind blasted all around from the dragons. He set her aside.

I will stand for you. I will be your might.

Rising, a shroud of light began to encompass him. Every dragon seemed to notice immediately. Another dragon cry shrieked through the air. The dragons pulled away to the sky above them and formed into a single attack. Kast watched them all focus their attention on him.

"Kast!" Fill cried out, tangled between a few dragons who remained to distract him. His voice reached Kast somehow.

Let them come. Kast stood defiantly.

Kast felt an immediate shift in the air, a pull as the air rushed by. He looked towards Fill. The strange man looked too preoccupied to have used his strange trick to control the air. Kast looked back at the horde of dragons now driving at them. In a moment, he knew what they were doing and why the air had shifted.

Kast stepped forward, past Aurah, and planted his feet.

I will shield you.

The dragons fell faster, and then the rushing air stopped. Every one of the beasts coiled up and released.

A storm of fire rained down, searing the tops of buildings and scorching the air. Kast felt the immense heat.

I will not falter.

He stood and spread out his hands. Light grew in each palm, encompassing the area around himself. He was completely enshrouded in light and the heat from the dragons vanished.

In a flash, Kast threw the light into the oncoming flame, swallowing the blaze whole. The light blasted through the waves of dragons, disintegrating them into ash.

The blistering winds from the army of beating wings caught the ash and threw it around.

So many dragons, dead. Kast watched the skies. The flames were gone, and the remaining dragons pulled back for another attack.

It seemed that what he had thought was a mass of the lizards attacking them, was really only a small portion of their entirety.

The howling of the dragon's cries filled the air again. They plunged from the sky, landing and attacking in a fluid motion. Kast moved to meet them but collapsed onto his knees.

It still is too much for me. He reflected on the drain he felt. He watched as a dragon lashed its head out at him but fell dead to a bolt of light that pierced its skull. Fill was there soon after to fend off another attack. Kast felt the light restoring what the attack had strained in himself. Light streamed into his hands gradually, though weaker and less than before. The restriction he felt from the attack finally seemed to let loose.

Kast moved fast to the nearest dragon. He remembered holding the sword back in Avante and the light formed similarly as he swung and severed the beast's head from its body. A fountain of blood erupted, pouring out into the maimed square. Kast flung himself quickly to the next dragon chopping with all his might, felling the beast. Dragons dropped quickly, lashing out at him. Kast danced like Fill in response and cut the beasts in whatever way he could manage. Blood pooled all around piles of dragon limbs and corpses. Eruptions and screaming filled the air as dragons landed one after the other, then died painfully.

"Kast!" Aurah screamed. A dragon dived at her. Kast launched himself toward her and severed the snout of the beast from its face. Fill had appeared in an instant to defend her from another with his magic. Kast noticed his magic had grown significantly smaller. *Even he had a limit.* Another dragon dived down, snapping at Kast. He sliced hard, but his sword of light vanished. Kast continued the swinging motion forward, turning it into a punch. The beast went sprawling, knocking others out of the way.

He looked around desperately. Even the flashes of light had grown infrequent. They were spent and all alone.

He felt despair begin to creep into his heart. Maybe he needed more something more? His light wasn't bright enough.

"Kast, Aurah, get down!" Fill cried out violently. Kast dived down on Aurah who had already been kneeling. They lay among the rubble and debris as Fill slammed a pair of purple orbs together in his hands. Beams of light erupted in every direction, flying through the width of the square and piercing through dragons and buildings. Dragon carcasses dropped as the monsters jumped to the air to avoid the deadly attack. Only some were lucky enough to live.

Fill turned and jumped, landing beside Kast and Aurah. He put his hands together and light began to pour out. Another orb of magic, laced with gold surrounded his hands, this was different than the rest. *A final attack.* Kast could only surmise. It was *pink.*

"Fill . . . ."

"Kast, there's only one way out of this now!" Fill yelled, cutting him off. He turned his head, a grave look rested in his eyes. "I'm sorry Kast. I'm completely drained, but you're not!"

Wait. Kast felt confusion furrow his brow. Fill was wrong about him not being spent. He had used all his power stopping the flames, then killing the dragons. He had no power, whatever it was, left.

"Fill, I'm drained too!" he screamed back. Dragons began to pick up their attack again. Fill's attack shocked them to a halt, but only for a moment.

"Kast, you still have an impossible amount of your dragon spirit left. You're not drained. It's your human body that is failing to channel that power!" Fill began to look desperate at the dragons swarming closer.

Why was he so committed? And what did he mean by human body failing to channel power? Kast stared shocked as he realized the gravity of what Fill offered him. He looked at the magic in the man's hands. It was *that* magic. The same pink magic orb. The same magic that had changed *everything.*

"Kast, I'm sorry this is the only option I can offer. You need to know beforehand that the entirety of your being can't handle the stress of the transformation more than twice. After that, the threads of your existence begin to unravel, and you will fade into death."

Kast stared.

Fill was offering to turn him back into a dragon. He was implying that his human body was holding back his power, it was a suitable conduit. *Great. But . . . .*

His eyes found Aurah, who was staring at him with a look of horror. She had heard. She knew what it meant, too. A dragon dived, spurting flames at them as it passed. They all ducked as the fire skirted around their group.

"Kast!" Fill screamed again.

Kast was at a loss to think when Aurah moved to her feet and threw herself into his embrace. He held her tight. It was so impossibly wrong, how he had scarred her. He deserved to die, but something inside said that although death was justice, sometimes justice didn't make things right. You needed something bigger.

He needed love.

In an instant, he understood the effects of his journey and the change this girl had on him. He understood why his insanity had disappeared, even though she had proven not to be what he was looking for. He understood why he was shattered, then rebuilt.

It was love.

Love for her.

He had found himself serving her accidentally—maybe love was the answer to all of their insanity? Their darkness.

Maybe he wasn't supposed to just fulfill his own purpose, but instead to express love? The acts of service at his own expense? His lack of insanity seemed to resonate with that truth. He looked at her. *To love a maiden, to cherish. It's so clear now.*

He remembered the grip of insanity—the thought bristled at the back of his mind. But while he remembered that, he looked forward to the light that this strange idea of loving another was his fulfillment.

His face set in an instant.

I will not fail—

His hand moved up and brushed across her cheek. She had healed because of the impossible strength and power of love—the same love that shattered him. It didn't seem so forlorn anymore. It didn't seem wrong. Wishing to die to make amends—that was selfish. He knew how to make things right.

"Aurah." She looked up into his eyes as her tears fell freely. *This is right.* The wind blustered harder and harder as dragons surrounded them in larger numbers again. "Girl." Her brown eyes stared deeply into his. "I love you." He leaned and kissed her forehead.

—I will save you.

In a split second, he threw himself into the magic surrounding Fill's hands, and his momentum carried him forward past the old man. This would fix everything. He was confident. He smiled a fierce smile.

A trembling filled Kast as he ran.

They would all know true terror.

The magic stretched itself over his body, then sank below his skin. Kast felt strange, but he kept running.

He noticed instantly his body began to change. His skin became more translucent, then the skin split and peeled away, slowly revealing the scaly hide beneath. His limbs became disfigured, growing in blobs of flesh. He fell forward, running awkwardly until the transformation straightened out his gait enough. He was already at least five times bigger than he was before. He was growing fast. *No wonder the body can't take much of this.* He reveled at the magic. Maybe there would be a way to strengthen himself to transform again?

He moved forward as he realized tears had been falling freely from his eyes.

Kill them first.

Save her.

Love.

He leapt into the air. His wings had returned and were just big enough to maintain flight. He felt so different. Even more than when he was a dragon before. Now he had conquered his insanity. There was a great power in his love.

He swung his claws forward, gracelessly he massacred a group of dragons who were shocked at the new enemy.

His body finally began to stabilize to its normal form. No, he was bigger than before. This time . . . .

I am the monster.

His lungs swelled up and he released a burst of flame. Dragons dropped, charred. He looked down. *Perfect vision.* Aurah's face held a look of sheer terror.

Good. Let her remember who I am.

Kast swung his body, his claws catching the throat of a dragon that tried to snap his leg. The body dropped.

Kast threw back his wings and blasted forward, knocking into dragons, and throwing off their flight. He rolled over his shoulder through the air, inhaling the air then releasing it to catch the unsteady beasts in his inferno. His wings beat again, throwing him just above his previous position, dodging another mass of dragons who all dived to kill. Kast dropped, raking his claws through one of their eyes, and crushing another's head with his jaw. He jumped off a body into another pile of dragons teeming above him.

Back and forth the mighty dragon raged across the swarming ranks, dropping any dragon stupid enough to try and take advantage of his vulnerability.

He would kill them all.

A massive dragon plowed into his side, rolling Kast over. The dragon looked familiar. The beast dodged Kast's counter expertly as his tail whipped, catching Kast across the belly. The dragon tried to run but jerked to a stop suddenly. Kast wrapped his tail around the mongrel's leg and twisted in the air. The dragon whipped through the air before being launched into the ground. The beast hit. He lay still.

Kast didn't waste long in victory. He released another torrent of flames, dropping more dragons. Their numbers seemed endless. He watched below as Fill helped Aurah and the Queen try and escape from the hail of dragons. Thankfully, they had gone unnoticed so far.

"Nest rat!" The black beast took advantage of his lapse in attention and clawed Kast, drawing blood. Kast roared. He spun, swimming through the air and swung his claws, too.

Hit.

Scales and drops of blood flew off of Vasiss's hide as they locked in the air spinning wildly. Their distance to the ground lessened, hindered only by the occasional beat of their wings. Their feet clawed at each other, struggling to connect. Their maws snapped, lusting to quench their thirst for blood.

"It's time for you to die, nest rat! You've defied the impossible, and I'll spread your entrails across the world for every blasphemy you've committed!" Vasiss screamed into his ear. Kast had no words for the misbegotten wretch. Dragons departed from the fight. They left their commander alone in the battle, not daring to interfere.

Suddenly, Vasiss inhaled and moved his claws to Kast's throat, catching him unaware. Vasiss released a violent torrent of flame, coating Kast in the deadly blaze. He fell still as the flames rolled over his body, boiling him alive.

Then the flames died down—

—and Kast was surrounded in light. Traveling down his body from where the flames burned him, white began to cover his body. Cracks ran across his scaled hide pouring forth the white light.

Fear welled up in the Insane King's eyes.

"No! You're nothing but a waste of scales!" Vasiss screamed at Kast, who merely stared back at the beast. Kast rolled back and kicked his claw into the dragon's gut, knocking the air out of him and shoving him away. Vasiss screamed violently as the black shroud again poured outwards and coated his body from the unexpected damage.

Kast smirked. There was no holding back now. How poetic it was that his enemy wore the darkest black, while he wore the brightest white.

How cruel this beast had been, while Kast's heart had beat love through his veins.

Light erupted from his body completely. He felt its power. *His power.* With a mere thought, he looked at the Insane King in front of himself.

Then he was barreling through the beast, and the black cloud around Vasiss dissipated in the light surrounding Kast. Vasiss screamed as his body flailed backward.

I'm not finished. Kast let out a roar and whipped his tail, slamming it into Vasiss again and sending him plummeting into the ground.

I'm not finished. Kast dived straight at the Insane King. His chest swelled up again and the fire followed suit.

But something happened.

A plume of shadow rose violently from the dragon's body and devoured the fire. In a moment, Vasiss was locked with Kast again. The dragon screamed in Kast's face.

Kast looked pitiless. Insanity gripped many dragons, but his opponent chose to embrace it. Kast focused his spirit and he grew brighter, swallowing the darkness.

This time Kast heard no scream. He only felt pain.

Vasiss's tail whipped around, clutching one of Kast's wings, wrenching on it to tear it free. No words and no noise came

from the beast latched onto him—just darkness. Kast struggled to free himself, but the agony from the monster's grip
inhibited him.

Then he saw what was happening. Fear gripped his heart.

Fill, Elizabeth and Aurah were directly below, surrounded.
Dragons darted back and forth, routing the group below.
Vasiss seized the opportunity, and now they were plummeting
directly for the three below.

To crush them to oblivion.

Kast closed his eyes and was in the white of his mind—all
darkness had been staved off. He saw Aurah clearly, standing
before him. His purpose. But then to his surprise, more people
began to appear next to her, Fill, Elizabeth, Dale, and Dane,
others who he didn't know the names of; so many people
stood in his mind.

The last piece of the puzzle fit into place.

The elusive uncertainty.

Resolve. Love. What he was aiming for. It's what every
dragon aimed for in some manner.

The crowd before him in his mind.

This was why he was a dragon.

This was why he was resolved.

This was why he loved.

These were who he loved.

Kast opened his eyes. He could see through the monster's
tactic, but there was only one way out. Only one way to serve
and love everyone.

As a proper dragon should.

To truly fulfill his purpose.

Kast let go of Vasiss, opening himself up to the monster.

Vasiss dived for the opening immediately, but Kast threw
him to the side, dragging his claws through the Insane King's
throat. The Insane King's face contorted in a scream, but no
sound came out. His eyes were incredulous.

Kast smiled.

Air escaped his own neck, too.
It was torn to shreds.
The price he knew he had to pay.
He looked down.
He was successful.
He had been resolved.
Now, he would forever live in his resolution.
Now, they were free of the danger.
It was all he could do.
But he was glad he could do it.
Kast closed his eyes.
A mighty eruption billowed from the city.
Kast hit the ground, dead.

CHAPTER FIFTY-THREE

Fill stood solemnly, gripped by the magnitude of the situation before them.

He stared at the rubble as the dust cleared.

He stared at the monster that had saved their lives.

He stared at the body of a valiant warrior named Kast.

The girl beside himself was deathly silent. Looking on in horror. Her hands covered her mouth and she desperately hoped the thing she feared most wasn't true.

Fill felt the emotion welling from the girl. Minds weren't his to read. Minds were to be felt, and if one deemed necessary, to be spoken to.

This girl was wrestling with the reality of the sacrifice before her. Back and forth the thoughts in her mind raged. He tried to hide from the girl's thoughts, but his heart was already shattered, witnessing the things she did.

"Aurah . . . ."

"Yeah. No! Let's go! Kast is waiting for us. You said your name was Fill? Le, let's, let's see Kast." She hid her face, stifling sobs. "Let's go to see him. We need to celebrate his, his victory." Tears poured down her cheeks.

Fill started to move towards the dragon, when something took him by surprise.

A tear fell from his eye.

Traveling through the folds and creases in his leathered skin.

The poor girl.

He reached down and held out his hand.

"Let's go, Aurah. We need to thank him." The girl fought so hard to hold back her sorrow. She nodded hesitantly and took his hand. Fill helped her to her feet and supported her as they began walking towards Kast. Fill looked around. The dragons had all landed; none were dashing through the air now. Quite a few, especially a large dragon Kast had fought, surrounded the other body that had impacted the ground.

They walked the short distance before standing on the edge of the crater. The dust had cleared and settled.

Kast lay before them, asleep in his eternal rest.

The girl dropped and wept. Never had Fill heard a bitterer cry of agony. He stared at the fallen warrior for some time, appreciating how stalwart he was.

A rumbling occurred, growing louder from behind. He turned sharply. The girl was unaware, lost in her grief. It was the large dragon. The beast stopped a safe distance away and bowed his head towards Fill, who felt the intention of the beast's mind. *Respect.*

"I am sorry, Light-Bringer." A rumble filled the air as the dragon lifted his head and turned towards Kast. "I am sorry, Dark-Slayer." He lifted his head again. "We will give peace to the human lands, though there are still free dragons who may rampage in insanity. We wish to encourage humans in their existence. Survive."

"Thank you, Strong-One. All humans will accept your peace. Will you consider giving humans the favor of a dragon by clearing what dead you may?" The dragon looked at Fill, then nodded his head again. He turned and let out a roar. The dragons lifted to the sky, then when the beast roared again, they swooped down upon their dead and began to carry the corpses away with them. Fill watched the King of Insane's body fly away between two dragons.

Weeping brought Fill back to reality. He turned and stared at the lizard sleeping peacefully. Completely cured of his insanity for once. Fill smiled. It was a sweet scene.

Thank you for all eternity, Kast.

CHAPTER FIFTY-FOUR

"What else can we know about dragons, Fill?" Elizabeth's voice asked to sum up the research session. The woman wore an amulet that pleasantly surprised him. It was a talisman of the old order of dragons, a symbol from a time when dragons lived vibrantly—as the dragon Kast had just done. It was an enjoyable time, filled with peace. Fill remembered it fondly.

"That is all there is to know, young monarch. With this knowledge, your people should be able to grow heartily and deal with any future threats from dragons." It was three days after the battle ending in the Insane King's death. *And Kast's.*

Out of the city's remaining survivors, a few scribes had been assembled from the masses and set to rebuild the Capital—now finally named Kastoria. Fill remembered much of the world before the last dragon insurgence. How it had thrived vibrantly. In one fell swoop, dragons had fallen to their own darkness and tried to seize absolute control, ending in the mass destruction of both humans and dragons alike. It was really something that humans had rebuilt as they had.

He smiled to himself. It was a dragon that stopped the newest insurgence, quenching the darkness that gripped the majestic creatures. Insanity begins to grip the beasts the moment they stop living for the betterment of the world and when they start seeking to fulfill themselves. Through miraculous circumstances, Kast had come to overthrow the reign of insanity in his own life.

He lived wonderfully.

Fill sighed. The weight of sorrow was a sharp pinpoint on his mind.

Aurah.

The poor girl's grief consumed her. It was a strange phenomenon. As Kast began to shatter the façade in his own life, the light that broke him began to break those around him, drawing them in deeply. *Aurah.* There was a persuasive sway that a dragon possessed. Beyond definable reason, one could grow attached to a dragon.

Fill had an answer, though.

"Elizabeth, the pyre must be lit tomorrow. The funeral must happen then." The woman looked at him, then nodded. "You have everything you need. I must tell you now, this will be the last time I will be available to you for help. Carry the world into an era of unprecedented peace and prosperity." He smiled at her then turned away. He had one thing to do before preparing for the day tomorrow.

Fill passed through the halls. He wasn't sure where his goal was but followed the feeling of pain until he arrived.

They were outside on the balcony staring down into the square.

At Kast.

"Aurah, we need to talk." The girl sat on the balcony, staring through a large, broken, section of the banister surrounding the structure. She didn't look at him. Fill ran his hand through his mangy hair. "Aurah, you need to know what Kast did to . . . ."

"Shut up."

Sorrow.

Fill dropped his hand. These emotions weren't easy. He moved to the rail and leaned against it, staring at the source of their peace.

"His death means more to me than you'll ever understand. No, his life means more to me than you'll understand. He helped break the death grip that held me under its grim sway." He stopped speaking when his words didn't register on the girl's face.

She stared desperately. It wasn't merely sorrow. It was something worse—the result of witnessing the life of a dragon so closely and then having that joy torn away.

"I can reunite you with Kast." He stared at the body of the dragon. A tear fell from his eye again as the sheer emotion he felt from the girl overwhelmed him.

"What in the world are you talking about?" Her voice was shrill. She stood suddenly.

Anger.

"You think you can say what you want about him? You never knew him, you were just some villain yourself, consumed with his destruction or whatever it is you wanted. You don't have the right to stand there and say impossible things just to get—"

"Aurah, I can't bring him back, but there's something you don't know about dragons that would serve you as an option." Fill stared at her. Compassion flooded his heart. There was no way he could let her carry on through this torment. Not without a choice, at least.

"What are, what do you mean?"

Confusion. Then hope. Despair.

"I can reunite you with him, but if you don't do it tomorrow, your chance will have lapsed forever."

Nothing.

The girl stared at him. No disbelief. No incredulity. No nothing. Just staring.

He stared back.

Hurt.

"Why do I want him this badly? After all that he did? Why, Fill?" Tears fell from her eyes.

"That's just what happens when dragons pour themselves out for someone, Aurah. It always happens. I'm sorry."

Grief.

The girl fell forward into his arms and wept.

"What do I need to do, Fill?" She looked into his eyes.

Resolve.

He smiled. Kast taught all a thing or two about being resolved.

Fill headed down the halls of the human palace. It was such a hard place to be but ending things was necessary. It was the best he could do for all the trouble he had caused.

Charlie leaned against a wall, turning his head from looking out of the window. His body tensed as soon as he saw who had approached.

The steps in the hallway were deafening as Fill approached to look out the same window. They were looking down at the remnants of the gang of men named Lizard Guts, resting together on a dilapidated terrace.

Charlie pushed off the wall, glaring. "I lost a lot of men because of you."

Distrust.

"I can't make the wrongs I did right, Charlie."

Discomfort. The man squirmed, hearing his voice.

"But I can leave you in a better place."

Anger.

"What do you think you're doing?" The man roared. "You're nothing but a monster that slaughters for the sake of it. You might have everyone fooled, but you'll never fool me! I won't believe for a second that you're good."

Fill stood silently, staring and recognizing for the first time the man before himself. Charlie's wild emotions pummeled his mind. Here was a man who had lost everything and sacrificed, even more, to make sure that others wouldn't lose the same. He wasn't just a commander, a man in charge; he loved and cared for his men.

Charlie collapsed to his knees suddenly and bowed his head low to the ground sobbing in tremendous sorrow.

For the second time in forever, Fill felt a tear run down his face. He felt the weight that the man weeping before him felt.

"I'll make this quick, then. Charlie, I've never seen a better leader of men than you. Looking back, I was evil, but you were the good that kept my evil at bay, even at great cost to yourself. Therefore, I talked with the Queen. She agrees heartily that Lizard Guts would make an excellent specialist guard and you would make a great commander."

The sobbing broke and slowed.

"You know, I lost my wife and son to those blasted beasts. I joined you eagerly for their blood. You know what I learned?" Charlie stood, the anger never leaving his features. "I learned you were just as bad as those flying monsters. I kept as many people as I could safe from your wretched grip, and now you're telling me that you have finally started giving me good things?" Charlie spit on the ground.

He is right in his anger.

"It's yours for the taking. I can't change what has happened, so you decide what you want. The men have always been yours to lead. Keep all of the weapons and tools, you will need them for what is to come. I have also given the Kingdom the designs to make them."

Charlie was quivering. The emotion flashed by so fast, Fill couldn't understand which the man felt the most.

"Goodbye, and good luck Charlie."

Fill turned to move back down the hallway.

"What's your name?" The question felt like it trapped Fill's legs, locking them together. The emotion from the man was suddenly clear and focused.

"My name is Fill, and ironically many have also called me Light-Bringer."

Charlie scoffed at the last part. Silence filled the air between the two of them. Uncertainty ran rampant through the man's emotions.

"I will never forgive or accept you, you bastard. But. . . . Thanks." Fill turned to see Charlie out of the corner of his eye. He was back at the window, staring at the men below.

I've never seen a better man, Charlie.

Elizabeth stood close, watching the procession as they honored the dragon that saved them all. She had mixed feelings. There were pangs in her heart that desired his blood, but there was a louder cry for this forgiveness Aurah seemed to embody. Elizabeth had wrestled with the thoughts for a while before committing them as lifelong lessons to learn. She stood beside Charlie, the man that had led the gang of men repeatedly to the Kingdom's salvation. The few men left from that gang stood behind him. Their discipline had been instilled very well.

Before them, a large multitude of logs and oil had surrounded the body of the dragon. Many of the citizens gathered to watch the body of their savior dragon be honored in the service. Most didn't know the true identity of the dragon. It would be a while before she thought it would be good to reveal that detail to the public. She reflected on the decisions to honor Kast, naming the Capital after him—*Kastoria*—and giving him a proper farewell. Even if she hadn't learned everything about forgiveness, there was a lot that she did see. Most of it came from the beast's actions in defending Aurah.

Aurah.

She turned her head to look at the matured women. She was much different than before, this time about a month ago.

Her tears had finally dried yesterday. Elizabeth smiled. The thought that Aurah was moving forward made her glad.

"We are here to represent the dragon named Kast!" A man above, on the balcony, held a scroll and cried out for the crowd to hear.

Elizabeth blushed. It wouldn't be long before someone figured out that the man on the gallows that they all were eager to hang was the same as the dragon they honored in death.

"Valiant in life. Immortal in death!" Elizabeth watched Aurah fidget. "We gather in honor of the great sacrifice the honorable dragon made to defend humanity and send them forward to a new age, an age where lawlessness will cease, and peace will reign supreme. Where dragon and man may co-exist together. We light the pyre as a beacon of the love the mighty Kast shed, and as a sign of the new times to come!" The man finished his speech.

Elizabeth watched Aurah staring at the beast. She had no idea the emotion her sister felt, but she did have something to offer.

"Would you like to do the honors, Aurah?" Elizabeth found her voice shaken. She didn't know why she felt emotion. Maybe Aurah had a way to convey the gravity of the loss on them all? Aurah tightened, her fists clenched. Then she looked up at Elizabeth.

"I'm sorry. Elizabeth. This is goodbye for us, too." Her voice cracked.

Goodbye? What does she mean?

"That's silly, Aurah. I need you by my side to help raise the Kingdom to an age of prosperity. There is no goodbye!" As the words left her lips, she knew how fruitless the argument was. How final Aurah's words were. "What do you mean, goodbye?" Elizabeth broke into tears, crying out from what was said. She hid her face into her arm, tears soaking her dress. She looked at her scars—scars she had inflicted as a means of coping. Somehow, they did that, somehow, they distracted her from the pain, but Aurah, and Kast, helped her face that pain. Now she could really begin to build the Kingdom. She looked up at Aurah. Tears fell down her face, as well, but she wiped them away and smiled.

"You'll always be my big sister, but you and I have different paths to take now. Things couldn't be the same anymore, either. Not after the things both of us have gone through. Please don't take this as a mere rejection, Elizabeth. I love you, but . . . ."

"Is this about Kast, Aurah?" The words drifted off her tongue. She watched Aurah furrow her brow in response—it was. "H . . . how?"

Aurah stood upright. "There are things about dragons, and the world they go to after this one. Fill can send me there at the expense of another dragon's spirit." Her words were a simple statement.

"Aurah?" The girl looked Elizabeth in the eyes, and a look of mourning fell across her features.

Elizabeth couldn't hold back anymore. She moved to her sister and wrapped her up, crushing her tightly against her chest.

"I'll miss you so much, you have no idea... I . . . . I love you, Aurah. You—." Elizabeth choked, tears falling freely from her own eyes. "I give you my blessing to go through with this, Aurah."

Weeping.

The women wept together, holding each other.

"Aurah, it's time." Fill's voice interrupted the farewell. Aurah pulled back and nodded. Elizabeth wiped the girl's eyes with her sleeves.

"The best for you, Aurah." She took a step back, then a thought occurred to her. "Aurah, where is Fill getting a live dragon soul?" Aurah looked shocked for a second—she hadn't thought about that. They both turned to Fill, who was staring at them. He smiled. Laying his hand on Aurah's arm he spoke.

"Come this way, Aurah, and all will be made known." He smiled slightly again.

Elizabeth watched the man lead her sister before the body of the dragon, and then he began to conjure whatever magic he possessed. A white orb floated on the man's hands. Then it drifted between the three of them—Aurah, Fill, and Kast. The orb split and drifted in between them all.

Suddenly the scene began to change.

The small greying old man began to grow.

Fast.

His skin fell away and scales replaced every inch.

Before long, a full-sized dragon stood before them all.

Elizabeth watched with her mouth hanging open. The crowds of people shifted nervously. Talking erupted, and fear rose.

"Peace humans! It is merely I, Fill. The spell requires the natural form to complete." The beast smiled at them all. His scales were an exceptionally light brown, almost changed into a muted grey. "I was lost in my insanity, but the dragon, Kast, unexpectedly and unintentionally led me to the cure of my darkness and to the fulfillment of my purpose, to help another fulfill their purpose. I am Light-Bringer, a guide and a sage of dragons from a time long past. And now the exchange—a human soul for a dragon's soul. It is complete!" Fill roared and at that moment a large white form erupted from the dragon as the body fell over lifeless. The spirit of the thing stared down at them all, smiling. Then it turned to a human and faded to eternity.

Elizabeth turned quickly in fear and covered her mouth. Aurah lay on the ground, still and lifeless. Elizabeth dropped to her knees weeping. *Aurah!* She sobbed until a warmth covered her shoulder. She turned quickly and her eyes widened in disbelief.

Aurah, white as the dragon's spirit, had one hand on Elizabeth's shoulder and the other—

—in the man Kast's hand.

They both smiled gleefully at her, then looked at each other. Joy beamed from their eyes as they turned and began to walk away into nothing.

They stopped. Kast leaned into Aurah's ear and whispered something. Aurah looked surprised and excited. She turned back towards Elizabeth, then back to Kast, finally back to the eternity. She ran with Kast hard on her heels—

—both of them replaced by the forms of two dragons galloping into eternity.

The End.

487

ABOUT THE AUTHOR

Sedrick Bowser is a blue-collar worker by day and author by night. *A Dragon's Purpose* is his first novel. He is passionate about writing stories filled with epic truths. He lives in Sturgis, Michigan with his wife, Tonya, and family. He loves to connect with people on Facebook (@sedrickbowserauthor).

CPSIA information can be obtained
at www.ICGtesting.com
Printed in the USA
FSHW011439150320